REVENGE

VI
DESTINY SERIES

CJ COOKE

Revenge
Destiny Series: Book 6
By
CJ Cooke
Version 1.0: January 2024
Published by Cate J Cooke
Copyright © 2024 by Cate J Cooke

Discover other titles by Cate J Cooke at www.catejcooke.com

All rights reserved, including the right of production in whole or in part in any form without prior permission of the author, except in cases of a reviewer quoting brief passages in review.

This book is a work of fiction. Names, characters, places and incidents either are products of the author's imagination or are used fictitiously. Any resemblance to actual events or locales or persons, either living or dead, is entirely coincidental.

Formatting : ©2024 Incognito Scribe Productions LLC

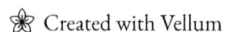

❀ Created with Vellum

Also by CJ Cooke

Refer to my website for all book updates: www.catejcooke.com

Destiny Series

Destiny Awakened

Destiny Rising

Destiny Realised

Revelations

Retaliation

Revenge

Stoneridge Pack Series

Wolf Hunts

Shadow Wars

Blood Feud

Hidden Moon

Stoneridge Shadows

Cursed in Shadows

Freedom in Darkness

The Arcane

The Arcane: Part One

The Arcane: Part Two

Chapter 1

Britt

The smoke clawed at my lungs as I screamed my grief into the silence. It wasn't smart. I had no idea if any of our enemies lingered in the area, but I couldn't keep the pain inside of me.

Kneeling in the blood-soaked sand, I clung to Geta's body as my mind flashed back to the day I'd died. The desperate fight for survival as the demons plagued the academy. The day I lost so much more than anyone had realised.

I knew exactly what my friends had been through as they fought for survival against the angel army. The difference between them and me was that there was no way into Valhalla for them now they'd died here. Even if there had been, it would take a Valkyrie to pull them through, and they were all gone.

Aria.

It was too late for her to save the people here, but if the angels were intent on wiping out the Valkyrie, would that mean they'd gone to the packhouse too?

I wanted to curl up on the floor and let the grief take me away.

But I couldn't give up. Geta had given me my final mission, and I owed it to her to do as she'd asked.

I looked down at the woman in my arms. Next to Aria, she'd been the fiercest warrior I'd ever met. She'd shown me what this second chance at life could be if I wanted it enough. That the gaping hole inside of me didn't mean it was the end.

I could still stand.

I could still fight.

I could still live.

Looking around at the desolation, I let myself sink into the sorrow for just a moment more. The long mess hall building was a smoking ruin, and the training sands were stained with the blood of my fallen friends.

This whole place was tainted now.

Valhalla was gone. Everything that this place stood for had been torn away.

By Odin.

"I don't know if I'm enough to do what you need me to," I confessed to Geta.

She couldn't hear me now. I didn't even know what happened to the Valkyrie when they died. Did she just slip away into nothingness? After everything they did, it seemed so unfair. There should have been a place for them to rest, not that any of them would want to. I had a feeling that if there was a final resting place, they'd all be doing whatever they could to find their way back here.

Maybe that was all we could hope for? That the Valkyrie weren't gone. They'd find a way to return.

But even as I thought it, I knew it was a lie.

And the grief returned for me again.

But with it came the faint echo of rage burning around the edges of my sorrow.

These men and women had sacrificed so much, and for

what? So Odin could cut them down just because someone dared to disagree with him?

What did he do for anyone? He was just one more in a long line of men that took what he wanted and fucked over anyone who dared to stand in his path. He wasn't a god. He was a pitiful excuse for a man who needed to be shown his end in a brutally satisfying way.

My eyes scanned my surroundings again. Geta had told me to find the ravens, and I had no idea how.

But it was more than that.

How could I leave them all like this?

I was only one person, and I couldn't give them all the burial they deserved.

Laying Geta down in the sand was one of the hardest things I'd ever done. Smoothing her hair down, I gently wiped the blood from her face. She looked so peaceful. It didn't suit the fierce woman she'd been in life.

"What am I supposed to do now?" I asked her.

She didn't answer me, of course, she didn't, but I heard her anyway. I heard every time she'd told me I already had everything I needed. To dig deep and find a way. *Any* way. Because I was all that was left now.

Sitting back on my heels, I closed my eyes and took a moment. I brought to the front of my mind all the faces of the people I'd lost and the hopes and dreams I'd never see come true. Then I thought about the person who was responsible. The person who had torn everything I loved away from me.

And I felt it.

I wrapped it around my heart, and I felt my soul catch fire. I embraced the pain, the darkness. Because there was only one thing left to live for now.

Revenge.

It felt so wrong to be rooting around in Geta's house. I'd never been here when she was alive, and now she was gone, I was invading the last bit of privacy she had left.

The angels had done a number on Valhalla. All the buildings were in ruins, and while the fire had touched the cottage, it didn't seem to have taken hold too badly. Most of the roof was gone, and char led down the walls, but the interior was mostly as I imagined it would have been.

My eyes brushed over the window as I turned around, trying to decide where to look, and I quickly turned away. I couldn't think about everyone outside. I couldn't linger on the fact that I would have to leave them on the ground where they'd been slaughtered.

Over by the fireplace was a single chair now stained with smoke. A small table sat beside it, holding a book. For some reason, this jumped out as so strange to me. I couldn't put the image of the woman I'd known sitting beside a fire and reading. I nearly snorted when I picked it up and flicked through, only to find it was a book on war strategies and battle techniques. Of course, this would be Geta's type of book. I was pretty sure this was her version of relaxing.

Moving out of the small living room, I found a bedroom. A shudder passed down my spine as I stepped over the threshold. This was so wrong, but I knew it had to be done.

Geta had to have something in here that told me how to get out of Valhalla. She'd told me to find the eagles to escape this place. I knew they lived at the top of the world tree, but I had no idea how to get out the gates. Aria might have opened them before the battle with the Gjallarhorn, but they'd firmly slammed shut once we returned.

We should have known then that Odin would be coming for us. He'd closed off our only means of escape and sent the angels to do his dirty work.

Looking around the bedroom, there were only two things

that kept pulling my eye, the first was the bed and the weirdness that elicited in me, and the second was a leather breastplate hanging on the wall.

It struck me as such a strange object to hang. It was clearly Valkyrie-made armour, but Geta hadn't worn it when we'd gone into battle. In fact, I'd never seen her wear it. Not even when Aria turned up, and all the Valkyrie had pulled out their best leathers and sharpened their favourite swords.

Moving over to the breastplate, I carefully removed it from the wall. As I did, something dislodged from the back and fell to the ground with a thud. Cringing at the thought of having broken one of Geta's prized possessions, I was surprised when I looked down and found a slim wooden box.

Before I thought about how strange it was, I sat on the bed's edge while examining it. The box seemed at first to be a solid piece of wood, there was no latch or any hinges that I could see on the outside, and I had no idea what had made me think it was a box in the first place. Then I remembered, and shaking it, I heard the rattle of something inside.

My shoulders slumped as I realised what I had to do. It shouldn't make me feel as terrible as it did. Everything here was destroyed, and everyone else was dead. Why did the thought of breaking open one box feel so wrong?

Because enough had been torn apart, and I didn't need to add to the loss here. But what choice did I have?

Before I could change my mind, I dropped the box back to the floor and pulled my sword. Placing the tip against the edge, I slammed my palm down on the hilt and winced as the crack resonated around the room.

Hopefully, wherever Geta was, she'd forgive me.

Picking up the box, I turned it over in my hands. It had cracked straight down the side, and with a little effort, I pried it open. Inside I found a letter and a golden amulet shaped like an eagle set inside a golden circle. I had no doubt this was what

I was looking for. Geta had told me I needed to go to the eagles, and now I was holding one in my hand. This had to be some kind of key.

Placing the amulet back in the box, I set it beside me, staring at the folded piece of paper in my hand. I knew I needed to read it. The fact that Geta had known to leave this behind was blowing my mind, but I was scared to look inside for some reason. Opening this letter meant not only was it all real, but she'd known this would happen. I didn't know if I was ready to destroy the pedestal I'd placed Geta on. How was I supposed to reconcile the image of the woman who'd trained me every day with one who'd stood by and let all our friends be slaughtered?

My hand shook as I opened the paper, and I realised my eyes were squeezed closed.

Get it together, Britt! You can do this. Strap on your lady balls and get this shit done.

I kind of wanted the voice in my head to be Aria's and was strangely disappointed when it was just me ranting to myself. My head had been a lonely place since I'd wound up here; there was something so weird about only having your own thoughts and feelings in there.

Taking a deep breath as if it would make everything better, I looked down and hoped that whatever I was about to read wasn't about to pulverise my already broken heart.

Britt,

I know how hard it is for you to read this letter. Just know that writing it is the second hardest thing I've ever done in my life. I'm sure by now you already know what the first was. I only hope that once you reach the end of this note, you'll understand enough to be able to forgive me.

Decades ago, I was visited by a young kitsune. She told me a tale that had my blood running cold; it seemed too impos-

sible to be true. But I could see the celestial part of her, and I saw the sheer desperation on her face at having the impossible task of trying to prevent what would be the end of us all.

She told me of a world where the magic was completely gone and the end of everything. Every being, every realm, nothing left but emptiness. But she'd seen a way to prevent what would happen. One single line of events that would save us all. To keep the world walking the correct path would require great sacrifices of so many. So many lives would be lost and destroyed along the way. And with every tear she shed as she told me of her burden, I knew she was telling me the truth.

There was simply no other way.

One wrong step and everything would be lost.

I gave her the Star of the Valkyrie, knowing that when the gates were sealed, we could not leave this place without it. And I agreed to do what needed to be done. That the Valkyrie would bear the cost of a deal they never knew of.

We had no choice but to tread the path she'd foreseen.

I can't tell you how many times I've been tempted to spill my secret over the following years. To stop what will inevitably come. Perhaps losing my life in this quest is the penance I must pay for staying quiet. For not standing up and saving the rest. I have made arrangements for the Valkyrie to pass on to another place, but I have not included myself in their numbers. I don't deserve the same salvation as they will find. It's the only way I can make amends for the things I have let happen.

I know you must be breaking right now. Seeing what you have, the weight of the task I've laid on your shoulders. But please know that you can do this, Britt. I know you can. I've seen the woman you are and the warrior you've become.

This final task won't be easy, but I know you have the skills and the fortitude to see it through.

There lies a well at the base of Yggdrasil; at this well, you will find the seers who can tell you where to find the ravens. They were once Odin's most trusted advisors. When the madness first took hold, they tried to stop him, and he cast them out. The seers will be able to guide you to them. The ravens hold the key to stopping Odin. They know the location of the Raven's Claw. It is the only weapon that can put Odin down for good. It's said that only a reigning raven can wield the claw to slay a god, and Odin knew this when he had them imprisoned. Traversing the tree will be difficult, which is why I'm sending you to meet with the eagles. If fate is on your side though, you will find an easier path to the base of the tree. If not, travel to the top of the tree, and you will find the eagles there. They will help you without question.

I can't tell you anything else. I can't risk diverting you from the path you need to follow. Just know that the journey is so close to ending. I know you can do this. You can save them all, and in doing so, you will gain so much along the way.

Trust in yourself, and trust in those who will join your journey.

I'm truly sorry that I could not be there with you.

With this note, you must have found the amulet and the breastplate. Follow the map I gave you for the hunt; this will take you to the edge of Valhalla. When you reach the river, hold the amulet up to the light, and it will show the path. Trust your instincts from there, but the breastplate will keep you safe. It will guide your spirit when you need it the most. Do not part with it; you will need it in the coming days.

Be safe, Britt. Pull on that fierceness I know you possess and show Odin the wrath of the Valkyrie.

Geta

And there it was. She'd known all along. She'd lived her life beside the people here, trained with them, fought with them, all the while knowing they'd be slaughtered.

It was then that I realised how cruel it had been to let her carry that burden. How alone Geta must have felt bearing the guilt of the task laid at her feet. The only thing I couldn't forgive her for was allowing herself to pass into nothing as some kind of penance for a task she'd had no choice in. For not realising that we'd have loved her anyway. Our only reaction at discovered the truth would have been sadness that we hadn't been able to help her shoulder the weight.

Chapter 2

Britt

The breastplate fitted like it had been made for me. Although, I supposed it had been. As I tied the last strap, I tried to think back to every interaction I'd ever had with Geta. It was driving me crazy knowing that she'd been told about all of this before it even happened.

I could remember the day I stepped into Valhalla after Aria had pulled my soul from the flames. I'd been so confused but happy that I was back in my body again. That was before I realised how much I'd lost in crossing over.

Geta was the first person I saw. She was waiting for me at the gate. Looking back, I supposed that was strange. The gates had been closed for so long, and no souls had been sent to Valhalla. I didn't even think twice about it at the time, though.

She'd been so happy to see me. If there had been a part of her that was sad, it hadn't shown at all. And there had to have been. Hadn't there? How could she have stood there with that smile on her face and actually meant it when I was the signal that everything was about to come to an end?

I shoved the morbid thoughts aside and grabbed the pack I'd already filled. I'd managed to scavenge some supplies from the wreckage, enough to get me through about a week if I was careful. After that, it was anybody's guess if I'd need more. I was about to go up against a God; what chance did I have of walking away from that?

But there had to be a chance. That was the whole point of what had happened up until now, to give us a chance to survive. Because this fight wasn't just about the need for revenge that burned through my soul. It was about saving all the realms and everyone in them, regardless of whether they deserved it.

Shouldering the pack, I turned to look around Geta's tiny living room. Part of me wanted to curl up in a little ball and stay here. Find a way to bury all the bodies I was trying to ignore outside. But that wasn't my purpose in life now. I had to look past the things I wanted and do what needed to be done instead.

Every step I'd taken up until now had been to bring me to this place. To give me the skills to get through this and do what needed to be done. To kill a God.

I would do it. I'd make Geta proud, and I'd show Odin that there were consequences for his actions. He wasn't above us all. His word wasn't the final one. If he struck out at us, we'd strike back, and I'd have my revenge for the lives of every friend I'd lost in this place.

The leather straps of the pack creaked in my hands as my grip tightened around them. The sense of purpose and resolve that filled me was nearly enough to fill that empty, gaping hole I had inside. The neverending sense of loneliness I'd had since I'd gotten here.

But as my hand reached for the door handle, I heard something I hadn't expected to ever hear again in this place.

I heard voices.

My hand tightened on the handle as my heart soared. I

wasn't alone! But then, the harsh reality of my situation pushed it aside. Because I *should* be alone.

Instead of opening the door, I dropped low to the floor, moving to the now gaping hole that had once been a window. The glass was long gone, but it would still let me see who was outside.

Pressing myself close to the wall, I peered out, keeping myself hidden.

The first thing I noticed was the wings, and that treacherous heart of mine skipped a beat until I saw who they belonged to.

Angels.

Moving through the fallen Valkyrie, three angels searched the bodies. Kicking the corpses over to check their faces as they bickered amongst themselves.

"I'm just saying, what did you do to piss off the archangel to get us stuck with this job?" one of them snapped, reaching out and tugging one of the Valkyrie's wings out of his way.

I heard the snap of bone as he wrenched it to the side and let it drop limply to the ground. He didn't care that these were people. He had no fucking respect.

"I didn't do anything," the other one spat, kicking out at a body as he had a tantrum. "Just keep looking. The quicker we get through this, the better."

"But it's fucking impossible. You realise that, right? This is one of those jobs that there's no way we can fucking complete it. How exactly are we supposed to know if one of these swords is some magical god-killer?"

"I don't know. I guess it's some kind of you-know-it-when-you-see-it type of situation."

The third angel had moved away from the bickering pair, he seemed to be taking a bit more care with the fallen, but the disgust on his face made his feelings clear. This wasn't a job he wanted to do either.

But what they were saying was interesting. Were they looking for the Raven Claw as well? Why did they think it was here? There was a lot more going on than I knew about, and I had no idea if I should hang around and try to find out more.

"Wait, why is the cross empty?" one muttered suspiciously.

That was when I realised my mistake.

I'd cut Geta down. I'd laid her peacefully on the ground with her hands crossed on her chest and her sword in her grasp. As soon as they saw her, it would be obvious that someone had been there. That someone had survived.

My eyes scanned the room as I thought through my options. I couldn't take on all three of them. And letting them find me here wouldn't exactly go well for me. I could try and fight my way out, but I didn't want them close on my tail when I had no fucking clue where I was going.

No, as much as I hated it, the only option here was to slip away before they could find me and see where I was heading.

I didn't have one of these little cottages myself, but I'd been in Aria's when she came to Valhalla, and she'd had a small yard at the back you could access through the kitchen. The back of Geta's cottage was a wreck, but I was fairly confident I could squeeze through.

If I could make it to the yard, it would just be a case of jumping the wall and slipping away into the forest. I'd have to circle around to head back out in the direction I was supposed to go, but hopefully, if I could find somewhere to lay low, I could wait it out.

Once they gave up the hunt for me, I was betting they'd head back to wherever they'd come from to make a report. They were right, and there was no way they'd find one sword amongst all those bodies. Whoever was in charge would want to know they had a survivor to deal with anyway.

Having an entire horde of angels after me wouldn't exactly

work in my favour, but if I could get enough of a head start, I'd hopefully be out of Valhalla before they had any idea where I was.

I'd always known getting through this would be hard, but turning it into a race against the clock made it feel impossible.

Quickly slipping off the pack, I shoved it through a hole in the wreckage heading in the direction I was certain the kitchen would be. It was just a section of roof that had collapsed, so it wasn't too difficult. The hardest part was making sure not to dislodge anything and alert the angels to my presence here.

With some wiggling and mental cursing, I squeezed my ass through the tightest spot, only suffering one deep scratch down my back in the process. I could feel the trickle of blood running down my skin as I moved toward the hole in the wall, which had once been a door.

Checking the floor to ensure I wasn't leaving a trail of blood behind me, I quietly listened at the wall. I could still hear the angels bickering as one of them tried to organise the others into a search. It worked in my favour that none of them particularly liked one another. They seemed more occupied with hating each other than looking for me at the minute.

Their voices sounded further away, so I slipped out of the house and slung the pack back on my shoulders.

I winced as it brushed over the wound on my back, but then sucked it up and jumped the wall, pulling myself over the top and dropping silently to my feet on the other side.

I listened again in the shadows at the back of the camp, trying to gauge where the angels were. They sounded closer, which wasn't good, and I knew my time was running short.

About ten metres of open ground had to be between me and the forest edge. Without any cover, my only option was to make a break for it and hope they didn't move to this side of the buildings. Either way, standing here wasn't doing me any favours, and I needed to get my ass in gear.

Before I could second guess myself, I pushed off the wall and took off at a sprint. I was pretty sure I held my breath the entire way. Thankfully it was only a short distance because passing out now wouldn't be good for my health or life span.

I didn't stop when I hit the treeline, sprinting as quietly as I could into the trees; I kept running until I could put some distance between myself and the angels now searching the camp. I was running in entirely the wrong direction, but this wasn't about getting to my destination right now; it was about not being found.

After about ten minutes, I took a running jump at the biggest tree I could see and hooked my hands onto one of the lower branches, letting my momentum carry my legs; I swung forward, hooking my legs onto a higher branch and then pulled myself up.

Balancing carefully on the sturdy branch, I checked the ground below. There was no sign that I'd been followed, but that didn't mean I wouldn't be. I'd been as careful as possible as I'd dashed through the trees, but I knew I'd left enough of a trail that a talented enough tracker could follow.

At least to this point, anyway.

I took a moment to catch my breath as my eyes took in the layout of this section of the forest. Thankfully the trees were dense enough that I was fairly certain I could pull off the crazy plan I had forming in my mind.

Cinching the straps on my pack tighter, I wiped my palms on my trousers. Part of me felt like I needed to work up the courage to do this, but then I heard Geta's voice in the back of my mind. *Waiting for the right time is waiting to die. There is no time like the present. See your move and take it.*

So I leapt.

My arms stretched out in front of me; I caught the lower branch of the tree next to me and gained enough height in my swing that I grabbed a branch for the next tree before pulling myself up. The boughs on this one crossed over a neighbouring tree, and on light feet, I ran across the branches, not stopping until I hit the trunk and held on for dear life.

My heart was pounding. Was it wrong to say that it was a rush? Running for my life while my friends lay dead behind me wasn't really the time to start enjoying myself. But as I made my way along the next branch, I took a deep breath to prepare myself and then leapt. This was freedom. This was casting aside everything holding me down and just taking the leap.

My mind cleared as I slowly made my way through the trees. I had a general destination, more of a direction than anything else. Still, at least my pounding heart and aching limbs proved I was alive. No matter how much I questioned if I deserved to be.

I didn't know how long I'd been moving, but after a while, I clung to the tree, settled in, and listened. All I could hear were the sounds of the forest. There was no indication I was being followed. It would seem that the angels hadn't caught my trail, and for now, I was on my own.

Always alone, always the one left behind. I couldn't even catch a break in death.

Chapter 3

Aria

The packhouse was eerily quiet as we checked our bags one last time. Kyle had sent the pack to the new fae lands to seek shelter while we were gone, and the Elites had gone to make sure they were safe on their journey. Echo and her mates had left with them after Frannie's funeral. I hadn't thought we'd embed another jewel in the Elite's memorial rock so soon. But it seemed appropriate for Frannie. She'd been fighting for us from the shadows all this time; the least we could do was acknowledge that.

Beneath Aeryn's glittering diamond, there was now an electric blue gemstone that glowed in the moonlight.

"Are you ready to move out, sweetheart?" Liam asked as he helped adjust the straps of my bag.

The nod of my head didn't convince me, let alone him.

I knew this was something we needed to do. Confronting the person responsible for all this was something *I needed to do*. We couldn't keep living like this, constantly looking over our shoulders for the next sword to fall. We'd lost so many, so many lives taken unnecessarily because of the machinations of one man.

And I wanted to do this. The need for vengeance burned inside me like a living flame. I couldn't go on like this. One of us needed to die, and I had no intention of letting it be me or anyone else I loved.

But I was scared. I was absolutely terrified about walking out the front door and going on this journey. Because I didn't know who I'd be by the end of it.

My life before might not have been completely honest, but I had two rules, and I gladly lived my life by them—don't take a life, and never hurt women and children.

To say I'd broken those rules now was a massive understatement. I was practically dripping in blood at this stage. And now we were setting off to do it again. I was losing myself; I knew I was. Every night I closed my eyes and I heard their screams. The worst part was that I never heard them the first time around. I was so lost to the blood lust, to the need to fight, that I didn't even notice them dying at my feet. It became all about the need, and that feeling clawed at my insides even now.

How was I any better than the people we were fighting against? How would I walk back into a normal life when I was practically drowning in all the blood I'd spilt?

I didn't realise my body was swaying until strong hands grasped my shoulders to steady me. When my eyes came into focus, it was Braedon's calm face in front of me, his soft smile settling some of the raging fear inside.

"I see you, Aria. I see you to your very soul, and you shine with such a pure light that you could never be anything other than a force for good. I know you're worried about what this fight will turn you into, but just know I see you. And I won't let anything happen to that light inside you. I will guard it with my very life, and whenever you need reminding of the true colour of your soul, I will always be here to tell you again and again, as many times as you need me to."

His lips met mine in the softest of kisses, and I sagged against him. It was like a weight had been lifted from my shoulders, and when my eyelids fluttered closed as I returned that kiss with more need than I'd felt in a long time, I could have sworn I saw the soft glow of light he was talking about.

When we finally pulled apart, my head came to rest on his chest, and I took a moment to soak in the safety of feeling Braedon's arms around me. A pang of guilt struck me then. This would be his first time returning to Asgard after we fought through Odin's army at the Bifrost. I wouldn't be the only one feeling the apprehension of returning.

"Are you ready to return to Asgard?" I asked him, looking around at the rest of my mates as they watched us with nothing but love shining in their eyes.

There had never been any jealousy between us, and the guys had never had trouble seeing me in the arms of one of the others. If I was honest, I didn't know how they did it.

"Not really." I felt his shrug, but I also felt a slight tremor in his body at the mention of the place.

Asgard didn't hold any fond memories for Braedon; he'd been forced into doing terrible things and still had the nightmares to show for it. That was probably why he could understand the turmoil inside me right now. He knew what it was like to have a past filled with regrets and a stain on your soul that you had to learn to live with, no matter how impossible it might feel.

Kyle's soft smile quickly turned into a frown at Braedon's admission, and I saw how his eyes moved across us both. The alpha inside of him didn't like this.

"We can delay," he offered. "There's no reason to set out today. If you need more time..."

"There's no more time to be had," I interrupted, pulling as many of my fractured pieces together as I did. "We have to go back to the world tree and Valhalla. I need to see with my own eyes what he's done. There could be survivors."

It was the one thought that had plagued me as soon as the call of the Gjallarhorn had gone unanswered. When the battle was over, we dealt with the bodies and put more of our loved ones to rest, but then the frenzied activity began. It had taken us three days to reach the point where the pack was moved, and we were packing everything we'd need to set out at first light. We weren't strangers to long journeys, and filling those packs was almost therapeutic in a way. But through it all, one thought had slammed against the edges of my mind, pushing and pushing, screaming to be heard. What if someone had survived?

I had friends back in Valhalla. More people than just Britt. But, fuck! I'd lost her once, and I wasn't ready to accept that I'd lost her again. That I'd failed her again. This was supposed to be her second chance, and just like her first life, she'd never even had a chance to live it.

So I clung to the hope that there were survivors, and with it came a desperate need to help them. Because I couldn't take any more. I couldn't take the death, the pain, the guilt. I was losing myself to it and fast losing the energy to fight it.

Chapter 4

Britt

I woke suddenly as I tipped to the side, grabbing the branch beside me, trying to keep my balance. Falling asleep in a tree was definitely not something I'd be recommending if I ever made it out of this. Maybe it would have been easier if I had some rope, but I'd hightailed it out of Valhalla with just the barest of provisions. I might not have rope, but at least I wouldn't starve any time soon.

Now that I was awake, there was no point lingering in this place. I quickly dropped to the ground, straightening my clothes as I surveyed my surroundings. The angels hadn't followed me out of Valhalla; if they did, they hadn't been able to track me so far.

But I couldn't get complacent now. Staying in one place for too long was foolish. Anyway, I had a task to do, and I wasn't exactly going to accomplish this by sitting in a tree all day. I had to get to the river, and if I moved fast enough, I could make it there before nightfall. I'd taken this journey once already when Geta sent me out on the hunt, so I at least knew the way. I was just going to be doing it on foot this time.

That ache of emptiness rose inside of me as it always did

when I was in a situation where my wolf would have been able to help me. I'd thought it was one of the reasons why Geta had sent me out on the hunt in the first place. That it was her way of showing me that I could survive without my wolf.

My fingers clawed at the breastplate, almost like I'd be able to carve a way inside my chest and find a way to recover her. Waking up in Valhalla had been both a second life and a second death all rolled into one. Because I might have woken up as Britt, the woman, but the wolf, the part of me that had kept me sane in a world that wanted to crush me... was gone. I was born with two souls, and only one had been saved.

I'd never told Aria. Perhaps I should have been honest with her when I saw her last. But I could already see the weight on her shoulders, and I knew that if she didn't believe she had saved me, she'd break. I was the one light that she could look to through the darkness of what needed to be done. How could I take that away from her? When she'd given so much to save everyone else around her, it was about time someone stepped up and did something to save her from herself.

Aria was the best of us; she was my friend, my comrade, my general. Hell, I might have had a bit of a lady crush on the girl if I swung that way.

Lingering over the past wasn't going to do me any favours, though; right now, I had a hell of a lot of ground to cover, so pointing myself in the right direction, I set out. Pushing down those old sorrows on top of the new ones I'd gathered, I prayed the hole I kept them in wouldn't overflow. Now wasn't the time to look at everything I'd lost; now was the time to crush that doubt and grief and forge it into a rage to fuel my wrath in the coming days.

After a few hours, I found a bush with enough berries to quell the ache in my stomach. It would help stretch the limited supplies I had with me further. There was no saying how long this would take and I didn't have time to scavenge much from the ruins.

The river wasn't an unachievable goal. Camping there for the night might even be a viable option. I could fill my belly with fish and at least not have to break into the food in my pack unless it was an emergency. That would mean not leaving Valhalla until the morning, though, and I had no idea if I was being pursued.

Wow, this was definitely not the sort of plan you wanted to hang the hopes of the world on.

Could you even consider it a plan? In fact, now that I thought about it, was me against a crazy god and an entire army somewhat more of a death wish than a plan?

It was as I stumbled along through the undergrowth, considering my impending demise, that I felt like I'd walked into a cloud of static. A shiver ran down my spine, and I quickly dropped to a crouch as I carefully surveyed my surroundings.

Something wasn't right about this place.

I'd walked through this area two days ago and hadn't felt it then.

I was cursing the loss of my wolf when a soft sound reached my stupid inadequate human ears. I'd never felt this sensation before. It coated my skin and seemed to slither around me. Something like this would never have been able to sneak up on me before.

Fuck! I needed to be more careful and get used to these dulled senses if I wanted any chance of even making it to my destination.

As slowly as I could, I drew the katana from my back. It had been given to me by Aria, and it was my most prized possession. It had seen me through the Blood Moon battle, and I had faith it would do the same now.

Because there was no doubt in my mind. Something else was out here. And whatever it was, it was looking for prey.

The soft scuff sounded again; this time, I could get a general direction because I was waiting for it.

I moved slowly through the underbrush, placing my feet carefully just as the Valkyrie had taught me. I fell back on every lesson I'd ever had as I moved downwind of where I was certain my target was. This wasn't a time to get complacent. This was a time to draw on every skill I'd ever learnt and survive.

I saw them then as I approached a small clearing, but even as I crouched watching the scene before me, I couldn't understand what the hell I was looking at.

Two men stood before me; one appeared injured like he'd been through some shit recently and definitely wasn't recovered enough for what he seemed to be doing. He was hunched to the ground, a sword in one hand held at an awkward angle. Another man stood before him, shielding him from whatever they faced. He was braced for an attack, a blade in each hand, and both crackled with the soft red glow of magic.

But there was no one in front of them, not a single soul. Yet both men seemed braced to fight an army.

"Are you sure the watch said now?" the one standing asked, risking a glance over his shoulder at his wounded and exhausted friend.

It was a mistake he wouldn't make twice. You never take your eyes off a target. Hopefully he'd get a chance to learn from this. He just had to survive this first.

As soon as I peered into his eyes, I felt something click into place deep inside me, in that place that had once held my wolf. The resurgence of a bond I'd never been able to experience before surged to life inside me, and I instantly knew this man.

I moved before I'd even formed a plan in my head. This seemed to be a running theme for my life, so why stop now?

Plans were for people who had time to think, and I was just doing my best to survive.

I burst from the undergrowth behind them, leaping over the fallen man as I rushed toward what I'd seen coming for them. The thing that had taken the opportunity this guy had given it and lunged to make a move while he was distracted with his friend.

The problem was, whatever it was they were up against; it was made of smoke and shadows. My blade cut straight through it, and it just kept coming. It didn't even flinch, let alone bleed. If it had a face, I expect it would have just fucking laughed at me.

"What the fuck?" a voice cursed from behind me. It was a voice that felt like it wrapped around me like a velvet blanket, and I never wanted to let it go.

His icy blue eyes met mine as I dived past him. The scar that ran through his eyebrow, over his eye and onto his cheekbone did nothing to detract from his beauty. It made him look dangerous like he'd seen the worst of the world and survived it anyway.

And then he smiled.

It was beautiful; it didn't belong in a place like this.

A laugh burst out of me, and I danced to the side, avoiding a tendril of shadow as it lashed out at the place I'd just been.

The man before me didn't even hesitate, and I watched as he lashed out with the magic-coated blades. I expected them to part the smoke the same as my own sword had done. Instead, they seemed to almost burn the shadow before us, and with a shriek, it pulled back in fear.

I wasted no time, going back in for a second strike. In my head, I knew it wouldn't make any difference. I couldn't cause this thing any pain; there was no injury I'd be able to inflict that would get us out of this situation.

But there was one thing I could do.

I could distract it enough for him to find a window to land a shot that made a difference. Something that would do some damage.

I aimed for the neck, falling back into my training and making sure that whatever blow I landed was a kill shot or at least enough to maim—if it had been a living thing in front of me, at least.

As I moved, passing through the smoke, the creature lashed out at me. I felt something clawing at my chest, and for a moment, I thought I'd made a crucial error, and yet, strangely, I was okay with that. If it meant the man in front of me could live, I'd trade my life for his.

The men behind me had different ideas, though.

As the force of the blow pushed me back, the one I'd vaulted over dived. His arms wrapped around my waist, and he collided with my side, pushing us both away from the fight and throwing me to the ground. It sounded like it hurt him more than me as he grunted from the impact.

My back slammed into the pebbly ground, and we skidded away from the creature. A shout of rage rose up from his friend, who was now trying to protect us both. I should have jumped back to my feet; I should have tried to help.

But I was trapped in my saviour's gaze.

There was a look of complete wonder in his soft brown eyes as he stared at me. His hands tightened at my waist like he was scared I'd slip away. There was no way I would. How could I? He was mine as much as I was his. They both were.

"She said we had to come when the watch told us. She said someone would need us on the other side, but I never thought... I never dreamed."

And then he kissed me.

We were two magnets pulled together. It would have been impossible to resist. We'd been made for this. Two pieces of a puzzle that could never be complete without the other.

Mate.

One of his hands moved to my head, and his fingers gently threaded through my hair as he tried to pull me closer. Not that it would have been possible. My thigh wrapped over his hip, and my hands clung to his shirt as I fisted the material, desperate to not let him slip away. It was only the clearing of a throat behind us that made us pull apart. A slightly embarrassed grin touched his lips before he glanced over his shoulder at his friend.

"Oh, don't mind me. It's gone, by the way. You know, the thing that was trying to kill us all. I sorted it out *all by myself* while you two were making out."

"You're just bitter that you didn't get the first kiss," the man on top of me joked, and that was the point when I realised I didn't know his name and just how ridiculous this whole situation was.

"Did you at least check she wasn't injured? That thing got a good hit in before you graciously jumped in with your manly dive and swept her off her feet."

"More like collided with and body checked to the ground," I playfully grumbled, quickly kissing the cheek of the man who still had me pinned. "And no, I'm not injured," I quickly added at the end.

He reluctantly lifted off me, reached a hand down and helped me to my feet. But he didn't let go of that hand. His thumb gently grazed across my knuckles as he pulled me closer to him like he couldn't bear to stay too far away.

"I suppose we should introduce ourselves, I'm Drystan, and the guy who won't let go of your hand is Xanth. You'll have to excuse him, he took repeated blows to the head recently, and I'm not sure if he will ever be the same again."

"Hey, asshole. I keep telling you I'm fine," Xanth snapped, but there wasn't any anger behind it. It was fairly obvious that these two had known each other for a long time by the way they acted. There was definitely a deeply established relationship between them already.

I took the chance to look at the two men who I'd stumbled upon, the two men I'd never be able to let go of now.

Drystan's dark hair was shaved around the sides but left long on the top to fall over his face as if he tried to use it to hide the scar on his face. The dark tattoos that peeked out of the neck of his shirt and around the cuffs of his sleeves intrigued me. My fingers itched to pull the material aside to see exactly how much of his skin they covered. Dressed in black, he looked intimidating, but the cocky smile on his face as he watched me check him out, said otherwise.

I knew I should have said something, like my name, but my eyes moved to Xanth instead as I gave in to the need to take in everything about him. He was the exact opposite of Drystan. His blonde hair fell in soft waves around his shoulders, and the simple white shirt he wore clung to his body, highlighting the toned body beneath. His thick muscular thighs received the same treatment from his brown leather pants.

It was like where Drystan tried to hide behind his darkness and severity; Xanth left it all out there on display. They were an unlikely pair, and yet that made them seem to go together all the more.

"Annnnd you would be?" Xanth asked, but he still grazed his free hand down his body, drawing my attention back to his abs showing through the soft shirt.

"Right, me, yes, Britt."

Wow, that was... just wow. Awkward did not even begin to describe me.

I felt all the blood rush to my cheeks and the heat radiating from them as a result.

"Adorable," Xanth muttered, and I spluttered in outrage at the accusation.

Before I could string two thoughts together to defend

myself, Drystan closed the two steps between us, one hand coming to my chin as he tipped my head back to gaze deep into my eyes.

"It's like a dream. One I never imagined. I never dared to hope."

He was so beautiful it almost hurt to be this close to him. My soul cried out for his lips to touch mine, and with it came a pain deep inside, a reminder that while my very essence rejoiced in finding the bonds with these men, there was also a missing part. A hole in my soul that ached from the loss of my wolf.

But then he kissed me.

And even though that pain remained, with every beat of my heart, that newly forming bond wrapped around it, not to take it away, but a promise to share the burden I'd held tight inside for what felt like too long.

"We should keep moving; if that thing comes back, I don't think we have the weapons we'd need to destroy it," Drystan said, licking his lips as he ran his thumb gently across my cheek.

"You're right. I need to keep moving before any of the angels catch up with me. They know someone survived, and I have to get to the river..." my voice trailed away as the weight of what was happening settled on my shoulders.

The loss of the Valkyrie pressed heavily on my shoulders. When you coupled it with the immense task ahead of me, I realised how much I'd been trying to push down and ignore.

"Hey, hey." Drystan bobbed down to bring himself back level with my eyes. "Whatever has happened, whatever is going on, you're not alone now."

It took a moment to sink in, but even then, I couldn't quite bring myself to hope that what I thought he was saying was true.

"You're coming with me?"

They didn't even know where I was going, let alone the suicide mission I'd set out on. And yet, as they both smiled down at me, I could see the absolute acceptance in their eyes. They didn't need to know. They were here for me.

"How... who sent you here?" I asked.

Drystan grabbed two packs from the ground that I hadn't noticed before, shouldering one as he passed the noticeable smaller one to Xanth. Even though I didn't know him, I could already see how much that irked him.

"How about we start moving, and then we can all take turns with story time?" he suggested.

I nodded despite my brain telling me this all seemed too good to be true.

We'd only taken a few steps before Xanth looked around, confused. "Wait, where's your stuff?" he asked.

Quickly grabbing the pack from the undergrowth where I'd dropped it, I shouldered it again, preparing for what needed to come next.

I sighed, knowing this was the part where I told them my story, but with it came a tidal wave of emotion I wasn't ready to deal with yet. It felt like explaining it to them all was the same as accepting they really were all gone.

Xanth seemed to sense the shift in my mood, and rather than waiting for my story, he started his own.

"We came from the Mage Library. It's basically empty now. The head families turned against us. They were feeding people to this fucking shadow portal. Like that thing back there. I came this close to being portal chow myself, but Echo and her mates saved me. They managed to get me back to Drystan, and this mad seer gave me a watch. She told me it would tell me when it was time, and when it did, we'd find someone who needed us."

He sounded so cheerful as he spoke. It was like he tried to gloss over the fact that all of the mages were dead. It sounded like he'd been living through tragedy as well. After a while, that sort of experience had a way of deadening you to the pain. How many must he have lost to be able to talk about it so casually?

But then I realised who he was talking about and an impossible smile touched my lips.

"Frannie? You met Frannie?"

"Yeah, she's a character. Do you know her?"

"You could say that."

"Sooooo... where exactly are we?" Xanth asked, looking around at the trees surrounding us.

The soft crunch of the dead leaves beneath our feet filled the gap in our conversation as I led them back through the trees and in the direction of the river.

"Valhalla." I looked around, taking in the forest that had once caused me so much unease until Geta had talked some sense into me.

"You still run and live and breathe. Honour the wolf you lost by living the life she wasn't granted. Besides, the trees aren't going anywhere; you might as well get over the things you can't change."

She always had a straightforward way of pointing out the obvious without making you want to hate her for it. Aria may have pulled my soul into this second life, but Geta had been the one who had saved me. She gave me a purpose, a family, a home and in the very end, she gave her life so I'd have this opportunity to move forward and do what needed to be done.

"So. Fucking. Cool," Xanth softly muttered, looking around again with wide eyes.

Drystan chuckled softly beside us, waiting for me to continue and supporting me in his silence as he reached out with his little finger, and hooked it around mine. It was a small gesture, but it was what I needed to forge on because I wasn't alone.

"Are we close to the Valkyrie camp? Are they actually real?" Xanth excitedly rambled. "I heard that the whole Valkyrie army came to the aid of the shifter packs with their warriors and slaughtered the demons trying to take the realm."

"Yeah. They did. We did."

It felt like a lifetime ago. The thrill of riding into that fight had made me feel invincible. With them at my side, it was like nothing bad could happen. We became one unstoppable wave of vengeance. It was the first time in my life I had a place where I truly belonged—at Aria's side, as a warrior.

"You were there?"

"Yes. But they're gone now. All of them. Dead." I wanted to stop. Just saying the word out loud seemed impossible, yet once it was out there hanging in the air, it just didn't feel right. "Odin sent the angels into the Valkyrie camp and slaughtered them all. I came back and..."

I felt the reassuring stroke of Xanth's hand down my back as they let me pause, waiting patiently for me to find the words to continue. But what more was there left to say?

"I'm heading for the river. I have a lead on a weapon that can take down Odin, and I'm going to find it."

"*We're* going to find it," Drystan corrected. "Wherever you go, we go. Whatever you need to do, we'll support you as much as possible."

"Why?" I rushed out.

They had to realise this was a suicide mission. Walking into Odin's palace with any kind of weapon would only end one way. Even if luck was on our side and we managed to take him out. He had an entire army, and who knew how many other gods were on his side, not to mention that crazy bitch Hel.

"Because you're the part of us we didn't even know we should be looking for. Why would we leave your side now that we've found you?"

My feet stumbled to a stop, and I stared at Xanth in wonder, not quite believing that I wasn't alone anymore.

"Don't you feel it too?" he asked quietly, suddenly looking unsure of himself.

"Of course I do." I walked straight into his arms, snuggling into his embrace. "But you realise that this is crazy right? The chances of us getting out of this are basically none."

I didn't know what I was doing. I didn't want them to leave. I wanted them with me; I was tired of being alone. And yet, I felt the same draw to them as they did to me. How could I not? They were my mates. But with that came a need to not walk them into an impossible position. If they were my mates, the two men I was supposed to cherish above all others, then surely I wouldn't lead them to their deaths; surely I'd do whatever it took to keep them safe.

"You're rejecting us?" Drystan asked softly.

"No! No, I would never. But I can't lead you to your deaths, either. You should go back. Rebuild. Live your life. Forget about Valhalla; things only come here to die."

Drystan laughed then. Pulling me from Xanth's embrace and spinning me around.

"Baby, where do you think we came from? You heard us say that the library is empty right? This world is filled with death and horror, and I have a feeling that the explanation behind that shadow portal lies with Odin. My friends, my family... my people. He has a lot to answer for, and I, for one, have more than a few questions for him."

Danger danced in his eyes, but it didn't scare me. If anything, it filled me with a sense of peace.

I wasn't alone.

More than that, they understood me.

And they were willing to do what needed to be done.

We're coming for you, Odin, and I might actually have something to live for now.

Chapter 5

Echo

As soon as we approached the gates of Thyellin, I felt a shift in the air. The pack was tired. There were so few left now compared to the day we'd set out for the academy, and they'd been through so much. It was impossible to look at them now and not see the terror, that resigned sense of inevitable grief in their eyes.

But as the walls of Thyellin appeared in front of us, a spark of hope seemed to rush through the air as the pack saw the possibility of a refuge appear before them.

Aubron immediately fell into the role of leader; this was his city, after all. He might have stepped away from his title and encouraged the fae to choose their own government, but they still looked to him with a sense of awe whenever he was nearby. He'd done the impossible, after all. He'd saved them from Haryk and freed them from the angels who would have hunted them for their blood.

"We're going to head through to the main hall. We'll arrange accommodation for everyone and get you settled. You will be safe here. Thyellin opens its gates to all in need. We will be your home until the pack can unite with your alpha," Aubron called out.

The Canidae pack, once the pack of the prime alpha, was nothing but the handful of shifters left in front of me. Our world had lost so much during this fight. And we hadn't even been the ones to start it. At least the Elites had joined them here to protect what was left of the pack.

I stared at my hands in wonder then, glancing around at the men standing by my side. Because we'd also gained so much.

True mates had returned to our world. We were taking down those who had puppeteered our downfall from the shadows. We might not be done yet. There might be bigger monsters waiting to feel our wrath as well. But we'd get there. The day would come when they'd feel the consequences of what they'd started here. And I, for one, couldn't wait to watch their blood spill on the ground for a change.

We led the pack to the great hall in the city's centre. It had already been set up to accommodate all of their needs. It wouldn't have been difficult. The fae and the angels who had joined them camped out here until enough of the city could be made habitable. We'd be looking for rooms in fae homes to settle the pack members, but we were fairly confident it could be done.

The Elites stayed vigilant as they surrounded them. I knew the pack found comfort in having them close, but there were so many who didn't have the same level of protection.

The city had been abandoned for longer than most people could remember. It should have been nothing but ruins, yet most of it had endured. I suspected there was magic here, and sometimes, in those moments between breaths, I could swear that I sensed something just on the edge of my senses, taunting me.

It was my first time at Thyellin. Coming here should have been a happy occasion, a new beginning for Aubron and his people. Instead, we were leading refugees and standing on the precipice of yet another battle.

It was exhausting.

The hate and the violence never seemed to stop. Who was to say that this would be the final battle? We were all assuming that Odin was it. That this would be the battle to end all battles. But I was starting to think it was a naive dream. When Odin was removed, another would take his place, and we had no one strong enough to stop them.

"You've grown quiet," Samuel murmured, coming to my side.

The soft caress at my shoulder let me know that he'd wrapped his wing around us, shielding us from view and giving an illusion of privacy. Apparently, it was what I needed, and I felt my body sag as the bravado seeped away.

It was amazing how much relief you could feel when you finally gave in to your exhaustion and let go of the illusion of holding it all together.

"I'm tired," I admitted. "Tired of fighting. Tired of this fucked up world and everyone's need to rule it."

"It is the nature of every living creature to crave what they don't have. The problem is when you have those who don't know how to stop taking it when they have a taste of it." Samuel's face wrinkled as he spoke, and I knew he was thinking about everything that had happened in Angelus, of all the angels we'd seen die over the last few weeks. "There has to be balance, or the world falls to chaos, but the only way to achieve that is for someone to stand at the helm and guide them."

"But who?" I asked, desperation lining my voice. "Who can we trust not to betray us, not to be swayed by the power and ultimately be driven mad by the need?"

Samuel's smile was wry, and it was more of an answer than his words could ever give me. Because he didn't know. I very much doubted anyone alive could answer that question. Because if they could? Well, the world would be the paradise we kept fighting to make it into.

"Is this a private cuddle session, or can anyone join in?" Stone's voice filtered through the mass of feathers and brought an impossible smile to my face.

He had that effect on a lot of people. His ability to smile no matter the situation was a quality most people would never be able to appreciate until they needed it. Plus, he had one of the sexiest asses I'd ever seen in my life.

Samuel lifted his wing, and we were graced with the sight of Stone's smiling face on the other side.

"We have something to show you," he told me, a faint blush touching his cheeks.

That intrigued me more than whatever secret he was planning to reveal. A bashful Stone wasn't something we saw every day, and it was actually kinda cute. Especially when Damon appeared behind him, propping his chin on his shoulder before lightly pecking his cheek. Stone's hand came up to tangle in Damon's hair, and he tipped his head to lean against Damon's.

They were impossible to say no to, not that I wanted to.

Holding out my hand, Stone grabbed it with his free one, the grin on his face reminding me that it wasn't all about the fight. There were people around me who were here to support me. We were in this together, fighting for the future we wanted to build.

Aubron and Tas quickly fell into step with us as they led me out of the hall. I had a momentary pang of feeling like I should stay, but when I glanced over my shoulder, I saw the fae helping the pack members get settled and realised I didn't need to be the one to do everything. They had this under control, and no one seemed to notice we were slipping away.

Stone stumbled to a stop as soon as we left the building and then glanced up down the street in each direction. It was obvious that he had no idea where he was going, and from the sag of his shoulders at that moment, I knew he was disappointed that everything wasn't going the way he wanted.

Aubron chuckled, taking up the lead. Glancing over his shoulder, he threw Stone a wink, and it seemed to ease some of his disappointment.

None of us had been to Thyellin before. We'd come straight from the packhouse; this was our first time setting foot in the city. I was surprised that Aubron seemed to know where he was going; he was a child when the fae relocated to Galvinae, and I hadn't expected him to remember this place at all.

Some of the fae had come directly to Thyellin while we ended up in a fight against the angels at the packhouse. In the following days, I hadn't wanted to rush away. Even though the packhouse was quickly becoming my least favourite place in the world. But I wanted to be there when we laid Frannie to rest. I wanted to be there when we honoured the sacrifices she'd made for us all to lead us this far.

I still couldn't believe she was gone. She'd guided us from the shadows, ensuring we were all on the paths we needed to see this through to the end. Yes, she'd had to make difficult decisions. She'd had to stand by and watch so many lose their lives when she could have intervened and saved them. But doing that would have thrown us into one of the paths that ended in disaster.

I didn't know how she'd done it. Perhaps that was what had caused so many cracks in her mind. It was a burden I wouldn't wish on anyone, yet she carried it without complaint.

Deep down, I was terrified I was destined to head the same way. I'd only just come into my kitsune powers. They may have helped me survive, but I wasn't sure if I was ready for that to be at the cost of my sanity.

I hadn't spoken to my mates about it. I should; I knew that. But it felt like saying it out loud was admitting it was a possibility, and living in denial was working for me for now. Maybe once this whole mess was dealt with, I'd speak with them, lay it all out there, and see if there was even an ounce of agreement in their eyes.

Aubron came to a stop in front of a house. Most of the front was covered in a thick vine, and it looked like it was on a quest to take over the building entirely. It was a cute two-story structure with a low surrounding wall that looked to have once enclosed a garden which was nothing but weeds and patchy grass now.

I didn't understand why we were here at first. Aubron's smile started to wilt as I looked between him and the house in confusion. And then it struck me.

"Is this ours?" I asked, excitement filling my voice as I stared at the structure again.

No one had lived in Thyellin for centuries, and even though the house didn't look like it had been abandoned for that long, it still didn't look like it was habitable right now.

"It can be." Aubron shrugged, and I knew it had more to do with the doubt of himself than me right now.

"Did you find us a house?" I asked; the smile on my face hurt my cheeks, but how could I not be happy about this.

I'd spent my entire life, or at least the portion I could remember, with nowhere to call my own. The coven hadn't wanted me there, and it was only because Aeryn had refused to let me go that they even allowed me to stay. Even my little room at the packhouse was shoved at the end of the corridor, a clear indication that there wasn't room for me anywhere else.

I'd loved that room; I'd loved having a space that was all mine. But it still itched at my need to feel accepted when I walked down that dark corridor alone, separating me from the wolves who truly belonged.

But this? This was a place my mates had found for us. A place that would be ours no matter what. No matter what happened, I'd always be able to return here.

Home.

It was such a foreign concept to me. Something I'd never had and hadn't realised I craved so hard.

"It isn't much, and it needs a lot of work. I wanted to build you a palace, to give you..." Aubron started, awkwardly shuffling on the spot as he looked at the house in front of us.

"It's perfect." I sighed, closing the last few steps between us and walking straight into his arms. "You have no idea how much it means to me that you'd do this," I whispered.

I could feel the tears wanting to form in my eyes, but I willed them away, not wanting to ruin this perfect moment with any sign of sadness.

"I would do anything for you," Aubron told me, his arms holding me a fraction harder. "We all would."

While we had our perfect moment, looking at the slightly broken house that needed some care and represented how I felt about myself so completely, we were suddenly interrupted by a screech—bordering on hysterical—as the front door flew open and an angel rushed outside.

Shaking on the spot, Chasan shuddered, shaking out his wings as a massive dust cloud seemed to emanate from him. He frankly looked hilarious with his cloth cap tied over his long blond hair and the full-length flowery apron over his clothes.

"Will you calm down?" Herchel grumbled, following him out of the door. Unfortunately, he wasn't kitted out in a flowery apron of his own, but he was inexplicably holding a feather duster in one hand. "It was one small rodent!"

"It was a nest! And it looked at me with *death* in its eyes!" Chasan shrieked before a full body shuddered preceded him, dancing in disgust on the spot.

That was when he spotted us, but he didn't look even slightly embarrassed by his antics.

"You're here!" he cheered, rushing down the garden path and straight to us.

I was suddenly enveloped in dusty wings as Chasan wrapped both me and Aubron in a hug, who fought it every step of the way and just made the whole situation even funnier.

Eventually, Chasan stepped back and dramatically threw his arm toward the house. "Do. Not. Go. In. There!"

Aubron flushed in embarrassment. "It might need some work before it's ready."

With one hand, I pushed Chasan away from Aubron, making sure that I had his complete attention because he needed to know how serious I was about it.

"It's perfect, Aubron," I told him.

Herchel came up behind Chasan, wrapping an arm around his chest from behind in a move that was shockingly more familiar than I'd ever seen him be.

"Leave them to be happy, you bloody pigeon. It was one single mouse. The house is solid."

Chasan leant back into Herchel's chest, and I couldn't help but watch them with a smile on my face. It would seem that the two angels were finally ready to accept what they meant to each other.

"Can we look inside?" I asked, bouncing excitedly on the spot. It was a complete turnaround from my earlier mood, but damn if I didn't need it.

"We should probably..." Aubron started, but Stone

quickly interrupted, cheering, "I want to show you our room."

Grabbing my hand, he pulled me out of Aubron's arms, and the two of us ran off giggling, knowing that we were supposed to be somewhere else and not caring if the world had to wait for us for a change.

Inside was dusty and cobweb covered, and it couldn't have been more beautiful if it tried.

Stone pulled me up the stairs, taking the steps two at a time and cackling like an idiot as Aubron started to shout at him to come back. It didn't escape me that several other sets of feet were rushing after us, so it seemed like everyone was on board with the idea of playing hooky, at least for a few minutes.

We rushed into a large room at the end of the hallway, and Stone spun around, throwing his arms wide. There wasn't any furniture yet, and it was just a big empty room, but the implication of this place blew me away.

We were going to make a life here.

All of us.

"There are a few other smaller bedrooms we can set up if anyone wants some space, but we were thinking we could make this a space for all of us," Stone told me, rushing over to another door in the corner. Opening it, he stuck his head in and then grimaced and closed it again. "Don't look in there. But we'll make it beautiful."

I turned around to find the others standing around the doorway, all waiting to see my reaction.

"How did you do this? We haven't been apart?" I realised out loud.

"We had some help from some friends. The Council wanted to offer us the palace, but it didn't feel right. Too many memories, and all of that feels tainted now." I knew what Aubron was trying not to say. He didn't want to be somewhere that reminded him of his father, and none of us would have made him do that, either.

"Aubron suggested that the palace be made into a place for the people," Tas told me, gently giving Aubron's shoulder a shove for not having admitted it himself. "There's going to be a school, a library, and a whole host of other things opened up. But for now, it's where we're settling the majority of those who haven't found suitable housing yet. It was one of the buildings that survived with relatively little damage."

That made sense, I supposed. It was probably the better-cared-for building to start with. Plus, all that space just for us seemed like a waste. I wasn't a palace kind of girl anyway.

But this? This really was exactly what I'd always dreamed of.

We all dragged our feet to the council meeting chambers. They'd taken over a suite of rooms in one of the palace's wings, and no one blamed them for it. From the sheer amount of activity going on here, it was clear that these people were eating and sleeping at work, trying to get a whole city repaired and functional for the people here. It wasn't a job I envied, that was for sure.

Maybe heading into Asgard and taking on a mad god wasn't that bad after all.

When we walked into the room with the new Council members directing other fae in tasks to be done for the day and hearing the report of how the renovations were going so far, I couldn't help but wonder if they felt like Aubron had ducked out and left them with the massive job of cleaning up after his father. That was completely erased when they saw him enter the room, though.

It was clear as day how much they admired him as they greeted him. I didn't recognise any of these fae, and yet they all knew my name and the names of my mates. I could see some of them looking just as uncomfortable about the whole thing.

"Echo, this is Leena. She's taken the head chair for the Council, and Treylor, Artin and Breton are assisting in Council roles until we can arrange for an election to take place amongst the people," Aubron said, introducing everyone in the room.

Again, I marvelled at just how much he'd been doing behind the scenes without any of the rest of us knowing.

"And we still can't persuade you to run?" Artin asked Aubron.

There wasn't a hint of sarcasm to his question. In fact, he seemed eager to change Aubron's mind.

My mate shook his head. "No. My family name does not belong in a position of power. I will, however, do all I can to help our people in any other capacity."

A pang of sadness hit my chest. Aubron had been through so much, and silently endured terrible horrors because he wanted to not only save his people but lead them. It might have been a selfish motive at first, but he'd changed as a person in the short amount of time that we'd known each other.

He'd literally bled for these people, time and time again. And now, as we neared the end of this whole thing, he was turning away from the one thing he'd wanted for his entire life.

"Come, I can tell by the look on your face that we have much to discuss," Leena said, leading us to a large table in the middle of the room.

There weren't enough seats for all of us, but Aubron directed me to one and sat at my side while the rest of my mates stood behind us.

"We've come to discuss the next steps in the battle," Aubron started.

It was then that I really looked at the Council's faces, and I saw a sad acceptance there that, whilst I hated, I completely understood.

"Yes. We've been discussing this at length over the last few days." Breton shifted uncomfortably in his seat as he spoke but didn't finish his thought. It would seem he preferred that someone else take up the task of letting us down gently.

"The fae has given much over the centuries," I started, looking to each of the Council as I did. "More than enough. And so have the other races. But no one will blame you if you decide that your time in this fight is done."

I could see the relief on their faces, and I could also see the way that Aubron tensed in his seat beside me. He didn't want to accept this; I knew he didn't. He wanted an entire army at his back when we marched into Asgard. But it was a selfish want. It was born out of a need to keep me safe and not to preserve what was left of his people. That didn't mean that Aubron didn't care deeply about the fae. It meant that he was just a man, and he was absolutely terrified about the task that lay ahead of us.

"We cannot fight by your side," Leena told us. Her face was lined with guilt, and when I went to speak to reassure her, she held up her hand to stop me. "I know you want to tell me that it's okay. But it isn't. Our realm stands on the brink of annihilation. We may have overcome one enemy, but we know the worst of them stands waiting in the shadows. Some have lost far more than us, and our prayers have been for the souls of the Valkyrie since we heard of their demise. But that unsurmountable loss cannot lead the fae into extinction with them. Our race is depleted. Our numbers are so low we may never recover. The magic we wield now is a shadow of what it once was. We have to take this time to recover; we have no other choice."

She was right. Samuel's soft scoff behind me spoke of how much the others wanted a different decision. But I couldn't fault them for their logic because their reasoning was sound.

After all, just a few hours ago, I'd been thinking the same thing about myself.

"That is not to say that we will not aid you at all," Treylor cut in. "We are pushing the housing plans as fast as possible to free up the space in the palace. Once we have the fae and the angels settled in the city, we will turn our attention to creating a space at the palace for all those who need it. We will be the refuge for your injured and all displaced by the conflict. Our engineers are working with the portal devices to try and create a remote system that will allow you to evacuate those in need directly to the city gates."

It was something the rest of us hadn't even considered. I knew through Aria that the rebellion in Asgard had a base which housed a lot of their people. I also knew that Odin searched for it every day. Those people needed some form of safety. Not to mention that if the battle didn't go our way, there would be many injured who would need a safe place to recover from their wounds.

"You realise that if we're not successful in this battle, we could be bringing the fight straight to your door?" Samuel questioned.

"Of course," Leena confirmed. "But, if you're not successful, we all know it will mean the end for all of us. If there is to be a final stand, Thyellin should be the place, and the fae will do all they can to stand beside you."

Of course, it would have been better if we had more numbers on our side. But tactically, this was a sound plan as well. Our plan had consisted of nothing but rushing into Asgard and picking a fight with Odin and his army. Having somewhere to fall back and regroup was actually a good idea. If we lived that long.

Aubron looked behind him at the rest of my mates, and they all nodded in agreement. When he turned back to the Council, it was with a grim smile.

"Thank you. Hopefully, it won't come to that, but no matter how the battle goes, there will be wounded who will need your help."

After that, we launched into discussions about the logistics of getting the wounded back and what the fae had planned for the palace to assist. There were a few areas where we offered some input, but the plan they already had in place was sound. I could see that the more we discussed it, the more relieved Aubron looked, and I had a feeling it had more to do with the proof that his people were in good hands than any battle retreat we were currently discussing.

The night was closing in by the time we finished. We'd eaten at the table, looking over plans and supplies lists.

"I know you have plans of making a home for yourself in the city, but will you take some rooms in the palace for the night? I feel you'll be far more comfortable," Leena asked.

"Thank you, and yes, we'd appreciate it. The house still needs a lot of work done to it, and we have a long journey ahead of us tomorrow."

"I wish there was a way we could convince you to stay." Leena sighed, and I could see the sadness in her eyes.

One thing I'd come to realise over the past few hours was the sheer amount of admiration these people had for Aubron, and I knew it must be difficult for them to watch him walk away to a fight he might never return from.

"I know. But this is something I need to see through to the end. My father may have been a monster when he died, but he was once a good man. I need to see the man responsible for taking that from us pay. The man who stole my mother from me stole so many lives. We will return, and when we do, it will be the beginning of a new era for more than just the fae."

He looked every inch the king he should have been as he addressed them, and I could almost see the stars in the Council's eyes. But it wasn't just Aubron that inspired it in them.

They looked at us all the same way. They saw the sacrifice we were willing to make for them, and they appreciated it more than any words could express.

And that made it all worthwhile.

It was enough to know what we were fighting for.

Chapter 6

Xanth

I couldn't take my eyes off how her ass swayed in those tight leather pants. I knew I should, but damn, she was absolute perfection personified, and I wanted to sink my teeth...

"Xanth!" Drystan shouted, startling me out of my thoughts.

"Hmmm?"

When I turned to look at him, he had the shit-eating grin on his face that I loved so much. The cocky fucker was trying to embarrass me for obsessing over Britt's ass, but there was absolutely no shame here. My magic thrummed inside me whenever my gaze fell upon her; I couldn't wait to see what happened once I'd stripped her of her clothes, and I wasn't ashamed of it.

"Were you even listening?" he asked; a hint of annoyance lined his voice, and I wondered what I'd missed.

"No, I was daydreaming about biting Britt's ass," I answered honestly.

I heard the soft snort of laughter from her, and it practically sang to my heart. I loved that she was the kind of woman who wouldn't be embarrassed about something like that.

Of course, she wouldn't. She was made for me, and fuck me if that didn't bend my brain.

A mate.

I'd fallen through a portal and come out in an unknown realm, faced with the most precious thing in all the worlds.

Me.

A nobody mage from The Lowers.

Part of me wanted to duck away and gossip with Drystan about the impossibility of it all. To actually question what the fuck was happening and how the fates had decided I was worth a gift like her. But even I didn't want to make her think I was that strange as I huddled with Drystan whispering about her like she wasn't there.

Because she was here.

And my brain didn't know what to do with that.

Apart from biting her on the ass, apparently. And damn, I bet it would be amazing.

"Can you just concentrate for two seconds?" Drystan snapped.

"Sorry, sorry, I got distracted by Britt's ass again."

She barked out a laugh that time and came to a stop, turning to face us.

"Good idea, hide it from view so my brain can separate from my dick for a minute."

Drystan was shaking his head at my antics; I didn't want to point out that I was being deadly serious right now. I may be injured but I wasn't dead. That ass should come with a warning label, and I couldn't wait to devote my life to worshipping it.

"I was asking if you needed to rest for a bit, but I'm starting to think that your injuries aren't bothering you half as much as I thought they were."

I could tell Drystan was losing his patience with me. But I could also see the smirk he was trying to keep from his face. I knew this man as well as I knew myself, and if these kinds of thoughts were running through my head about our beautiful mate, then they were definitely in his as well.

Drystan's eyes trailed across my body, and I felt the shiver that wanted to run down my spine. He'd always had that effect on me, and he knew it, even if neither of us had ever acknowledged it before.

"You look better," Drystan finally admitted.

"I feel better. Don't get me wrong, my ribs hurt like a bitch. But, it feels easier to breathe, and the pain is more tolerable."

I hadn't thought about it until now. Taking a deep breath, I was surprised at how much easier it was now.

Britt's face wrinkled in concern before she approached me.

"Can I?" she asked, holding out her hands toward me.

I had no idea what was about to happen, but the answer was what it would always be where she was concerned.

"Feel away," I told her. It was impossible not to grin.

She shook her head at my antics and then wrapped her hands around my lower ribs. "Deep breath," she instructed me. I did as she asked, taking the opportunity to stare at her while she was so close. "Again."

We repeated as she moved up my ribcage, and I watched every subtle change in her facial expression. I'd never spent much time around women; they weren't exactly common at the mage library.

My mother had stayed because she wouldn't leave her children. She barely had any magic, and her coven hadn't cared if she returned because of it. Most of the witches who came to The Lowers were the same, but most still thought they didn't belong with us. It wasn't like they could gain any political clout by being there. Most of them were sent as some form of punishment or trade deal, and they hated every second because of it. I supposed you couldn't blame them when deals were paid for with your own flesh.

I couldn't express how glad I was that Britt hadn't been subjected to such a fate. But as I realised that, I also realised that she didn't feel like a witch. Whilst my magic reached out for her, I couldn't feel anything reaching back.

"You're not a witch," I said, voicing my thoughts. "And you were in Valhalla."

She hummed in agreement as she checked my ribs, and because she wasn't looking at my face, she probably didn't see the rising panic there.

Looking over her shoulder, I saw the colour drain from Drystan's face as he came to the same conclusion I had, and it absolutely terrified me.

"I can't feel any breaks, but I've only done this twice before. You've either healed, or you only had bruising on your ribs to start. Still hurts like a bitch, but it at least heals much quicker than a break."

She looked up at that point and must have registered something on my face.

"What?" she asked, looking behind her at Drystan and seeing the same thing there. "The Valkyrie trained hard; it wasn't unusual for training injuries to occur."

"Are you... did you...?" I couldn't even get the full question out because the thought of losing her so soon after I'd found her was almost too much to bear. Except would I be losing her because she was standing in front of me breathing... alive.

"What? Oooh, are you asking me if I'm dead?" She smiled as she said it, and my heart surged at how ridiculous the question was. Until she followed it up with, "I guess." And my entire world shattered around me.

"You died?"

"Yeah. Ten out of ten do not recommend it, by the way."

Before I knew what I was doing, I wrapped my arms around her as I hauled her against me. I had no idea what I was thinking, but I was fairly certain it was something along the lines of keeping her forever and never letting her go.

"I'm confused about what's happening right now," she muttered, her words muffled by the fact that her face was now smushed against my chest.

It was only because I was worried she couldn't breathe that my grip loosened.

Drystan's hands came to Britt's shoulders as he gently pulled her from my grasp. My first reaction was to fight him; I had to keep her safe. But even in my moment of panic, I could see how ridiculous that thought was.

"Xanth is panicking at the thought of losing you, and we might need a better explanation about the whole dead and alive thing and what that means for our situation," he explained.

Her mouth opened in a soft 'O' as she realised what was going on, and even through the panic that was firing through my blood, my cock still hardened at the thought of slipping between her lips.

"Okay, so I was at Packlands Academy when the demons attacked, and I died in the battle for the academy. But Aria took me back to the pack, and at my funeral, she reaped my soul, and I ended up in Valhalla and became one of the warriors," she explained.

"So you're dead?" Drystan tried to clarify, and I didn't miss how he gulped at the thought.

"Yes and no. Think of it as a second-life kind of deal."

A breath of relief whooshed out of me, and I felt like all the energy drained from my body.

"Are you tied to this realm?" Drystan asked.

"I have no idea. I went to fight in the Blood Moon battle in the magic realm, but that was in answer to the Gjallarhorn.

Plus, if you think about it, Geta has me on this journey that will take me to the base of the world tree and then into Asgard, although I suppose Valhalla is technically part of Asgard..." Her voice trailed off as the thoughts rushed through her brain.

Somewhere along the way of her explanation about being dead but not dead, we'd started walking again. As we fell into silence, each of us considering what this meant, the subtle sound of running water filtered toward us. We were looking for a river, and it seemed like we'd found it.

"It doesn't matter," Drystan suddenly declared, and I looked at him like he'd lost his mind.

"I'm the one that's supposed to have a head injury, remember?" I joked, falling back on my usual defence mechanism.

"No, hear me out. So what if you're tied to this realm. What have we got waiting for us at the mage library? Nothing. It's a damn ghost town with far too many personal nightmares haunting it. I, for one, could do with a fresh start, so why not do that here?"

Okay, so I loved Drystan, and probably not in the strictly friends way, but I didn't have the energy to add that to what I was dealing with right now, but this who-cares-let's-see-the-bright-side version of him was kind of creeping me the fuck out.

"Who are you?" I gasped dramatically. "Why are you not brooding or threatening to stab something? If you're some kind of body-swapped portal monster, don't tell me, I can't take anything else right now!" I said dramatically.

Drystan rolled his eyes and then effectively ignored me as he turned his attention back to Britt.

"How about for now, we get through this craziness and then see where we stand at the end? There's no need for us to plan out our entire future the first day we meet," he suggested.

He kind of had a point, and even Britt was nodding in agreement. She didn't look even slightly upset by the idea.

"I'm just glad I'm not doing this on my own any more," she admitted, and her voice hitched as she spoke.

I could hear her pain, and it screamed how fresh it was for her. Drystan and I had lived through watching our family and friends being slaughtered for months. Something like that stayed with you. You didn't get over it. You did, however, learn how to repress it. How to shove it so deep down you could function still.

But looking at the beautiful woman in front of me, I didn't want that for her. I didn't want her to have to carry the burden of the pain Drystan and I tried to ignore every day.

And that meant only one thing.

There was only one way to work through the loss and the horror.

It came through blood and violence.

It came through revenge.

Chapter 7

Britt

Xanth had the strangest look on his face, but I didn't know him well enough to figure it out. He definitely seemed to be the fun-loving one of the two, and whilst Drystan's brooding had that bad-boy appeal to it, the glimpses of the caring heart he tried to hide were just as intoxicating.

Being so close to the two of them had my body spinning into overdrive. The need to hide them away from the world and protect them from what I needed to do was strong. If that time in hiding led to lots and lots of sex, well, I wouldn't be complaining about it any time soon.

But just looking at them now, I knew they wouldn't sit idly by while I ran off and took on an entire army alone. I didn't know these two men, but I could already feel that bond solidifying between us, and I had absolutely no intentions of fighting it. Why would I? This was where I was supposed to be, with them by my side.

I could hear the sound of rushing water nearby, and I knew we were nearing the edge of Valhalla. I had no idea what would happen when we reached the river. I just had to hope it was so obvious that Geta hadn't thought there was any need to leave further instructions—like a map and a detailed plan. Was that really too much to ask for?

My hand found the amulet hanging around my neck, and I held onto it like it was my entire reason for being. Except, it was. This was the thing that was supposed to show me the way to Odin, and I doubted I'd be able to go on without it.

I needed to see him dead. I wanted to tear him apart and listen to his screams while I reminded him about all the people he'd taken from me.

Was that really too much to ask for?

Every life had an end. That was the beauty of living. It was what made every decision too breathtakingly risky. And Odin had lived a life without that, without the reminder that everything could be lost in an instant—until now. It was time for his reign to be over and I was going to paint the halls of Asgard with his blood as I ended it.

"You've got a very stabby look on your face right now," Xanth pointed out.

I leaned into him as we kept walking toward our destination, for no other reason than I was finding the warmth of his presence comforting.

"Just thinking about what needs to be done," I answered honestly.

"Well, as long as it's not us that's invoking that emotion in you, then I'm definitely on board with it."

We emerged from the trees with the sun in our eyes as we squinted at the brilliance, trying to get a read on our surroundings. It was stupid, really. I knew I was being pursued, yet something about being with these two men had lulled me into a false sense of security.

"I can't believe the bitch actually walked straight to us," a voice laughed in front of us.

Frantically blinking to clear my vision, I braced for the inevitable attack.

Of course, it was coming. I didn't need to see him to know that the voice belonged to an angel. And I knew exactly what their job was.

Stupidly there were only two of them.

I didn't know whether to be insulted or amused.

Drawing the katana from my back, I wasted no time trying to talk them out of what they were about to do. We all had a role to play here, and theirs was to die because I had no intention of ending my journey before it had even really begun.

"You're not actually going to fight back, are you," the angel goaded. "It would be far easier on you to accept what's coming. You can't fight the gods. Sometimes you've got to accept the hand you were dealt."

My vision had cleared enough to see the two of them clearly now. Both were clad in the leather armour I'd seen on the angel back at the training grounds.

They looked like shitheads with smirks on their faces as they looked down on us, basically telling us to accept death.

But the one good thing about training with the Valkyrie was that I knew how to fight someone with wings and where all the weak points lay. Plus, these two were too arrogant to bring backup. One-on-one, they'd never have won against the Valkyrie; I'd never accept anything else. And they were about to learn their lesson about keeping the numbers in your favour.

I didn't wait to give them time to come up with a plan, and I dove just as the one on the left started to laugh at his friend's joke. It was a mistake he wouldn't have the opportunity to regret. He should have kept his eye on the threat in front of him.

Me.

Darting low, I struck out with my sword, quickly sidestepping and slashing at the base of his wings to disable them. The satisfaction I got as my blade sliced through the tendons on his back was almost sick. Hearing him cry out in surprised pain was almost euphoric.

"Stupid, bitch," the angel swore, diving toward me before he'd even drawn his sword.

He was so confident he could take me down; he didn't even think he needed a weapon to do it. That was his first mistake.

His second was that he didn't predict what calling me that was going to do to the two men travelling with me.

Drystan roared, throwing one of the knives in his hand. The blade caught in the light before it embedded into the angel's shoulder with a thud.

He screamed, throwing off his dive as he went for me.

I let myself drop to the ground, grabbing his shoulders and pulling him down with me as I planted my feet and flipped us. Gripping one of his useless wings with one hand, I threw my weight into the roll, grabbing Drystan's knife without even thinking about it.

I heard a faint yell behind me, but there was no way I could split my attention right now. I had to trust that the two of them could hold out long enough for me to finish this guy. Even if it was killing me not to make sure they were okay.

The knife in my hand warmed at my touch. I felt a tingle rush up my arm, and it brought a smile to my face, or maybe it was the grunt of pain beneath me as I drove it into the back of the angel's neck, slipping it up into his head. Either way, dang, I was feeling good.

His body slackened beneath me as his last breath seeped out of him, and I quickly popped back up to my feet, grabbing my katana from the ground where I'd dropped it.

Turning around, I was actually surprised by what I found. Drystan was staring at me, his mouth open in surprise. The more shocking thing was Xanth, though. He had the other angel pinned beneath him as he rained blow after blow down on his face.

"You. Don't. Get. To. Call. Her. That," he gritted out between each punch.

It should have horrified me—I think. I was pretty sure that would be the normal reaction. Was there something wrong with me that I found it kind of sweet?

"I think he's dead," I muttered, not really wanting to break the twisted mood but also conscious that Xanth had apparently been seriously injured not so long ago. The last thing he needed was to be nursing a broken hand as well.

"He was dead before he started," Drystan casually told me before he calmly walked to my side, picking up my hand and turning it over to examine my palm. "How did you handle my knife?" he asked.

"What do you mean?"

"My magic, the blades are imbued with a spell that should drain your energy if you come into contact with it."

"You mean the tingles?"

The corner of his mouth ticked up in a smirk. "Yeah, the tingles."

I shrugged. I had little to no knowledge about magic. Yeah, I had some friends at the academy who were magic users, and there was some information in the lessons we took. But I didn't really get a chance to finish my education, what with all the demons and the dying part. The pack wasn't really a magic-friendly place, even to our allies back then. Thank fuck, that bastard was dead.

As Xanth approached us, he wiped his hands off on a piece of material he seemed to have torn from the angel's clothes and then tossed it over his shoulder. Pushing the blond lengths from his face, he hit me with a blinding grin.

"We should probably get moving," he said like nothing out of the ordinary had just happened. "We don't know if any more will be coming or how long it will take before someone misses these two."

I looked back at the dead angel behind me and grimaced. We probably should have at least tried to get some information out of one of them before killing them. It was rash to walk into this without any kind of intelligence on Odin's operation. Or, at the very least, an idea of what the hell was going on in Asgard.

There was no changing the situation now though, so Xanth was right. The only option was to keep moving forward.

"Geta's letter said that once we reached the river, I needed to hold the amulet up into the light, and it would show me the way."

This whole thing sounded more like a wild goose chase now that I'd said it aloud.

"Do we have a destination in mind?" Drystan asked, not even questioning the insanity of the whole thing.

"A well at the base of the world tree," I explained as I lifted the amulet from around my neck and turned it over in my hands.

It didn't look like anything special. The silver twisted over and under itself, creating what looked like one continuous piece. In the centre, a deep blue stone sat. It wasn't until the light hit it that I realised it looked like there was something held in the centre of the stone. It sparked in the sunlight, and then I could have sworn it moved.

"Presumably, this will show us an exit from this realm then," Drystan added, looking down at the amulet in interest.

Neither of them tried to take it from me. They both stood patiently by while I stared at the object in my hands.

This was my last link to the Valkyrie; well, that and the breastplate I now wore. Looking back the way we'd come, I had a sinking feeling inside.

"What if I can't come back?" I asked quietly.

Up until this point, I probably would have said that I never wanted to see this place again. It was filled with too much horror, too many memories that had been twisted into haunting nightmares now that the friends that filled them had been stolen from me.

But Valhalla was the first place where I'd felt like I belonged. It was the first time I'd been accepted for just being me, and where someone had made space for me to grow into the woman I wanted to be rather than the shape of what someone had determined.

Aria had started this journey for me. There was a time when I would have done anything to go back to her side. But we'd both set out on different paths now. Maybe we'd meet again one day; I hoped with everything I had that we would. But the life I had back at the packhouse didn't exist anymore because I wasn't that person. I wouldn't fit back into the hole I'd left nor did I want to.

A soft wind rustled through the trees, lifting my hair from my neck as it swirled around me. There was something special about this realm, about this place. I couldn't let Odin take that from me and all the people who'd come after me that needed the opportunity to find themselves here.

"If you want to come back to Valhalla, we will. Nothing will keep us away. Not even if we have to find the magic to tear the walls between this realm and the next. We *will* find a way to return here," Xanth told me.

It wasn't the conviction in his voice that surprised me. It was the fact that even though he'd only just met me, he accepted so easily that he'd remain at my side. Even though we had no idea what was coming for us, or the fact this wasn't his fight, he would fight it with me anyway.

"I left them. I just left them where they lay, and I ran. I have to go back… I have to…"

I couldn't even end that sentence. The reality of what it would look like by the time I could come back to this place was more than my brain could cope with. But at the same time, I knew I needed to do it. I wouldn't leave them like their lives hadn't meant anything. They deserved the honour of someone caring enough to see them through their last journey to whatever afterlife Geta had arranged for them.

"We will," Drystan said, clasping my shoulder with his hand and squeezing it almost painfully. "I promise you."

I locked eyes with him as he did, and I saw something there. I saw someone who'd had to deal with this pain before. Someone who was still dealing with it. And hopefully, someone who knew how to make it stop.

Chapter 8

Drystan

Whatever was happening between us, I was pretty sure it would be the one thing that saved me.

This woman came charging into my life with a battle cry and brandishing a sword, leaping into a fight she had no idea about in defence of someone she'd never even met.

Before everything that happened in The Library, I would have rolled my eyes at her and told her how naive she was.

But now?

Fuck, I couldn't be more in awe of her.

She was so fierce, so unquestioningly brave. I couldn't even imagine what she'd been through, what she'd seen, and yet she didn't even hesitate when she saw we needed help. Even with the heavy burden on her shoulders.

I'd never have admitted it before, but I'd been so close to giving up. Xanth was the only thing I had left to fight for. He believed with every ounce of his being that whatever we found, where that crazy woman sent us, was where we needed to be. He didn't even question it.

And here we were.

With her.

And she *was* everything.

Those little glimpses of vulnerability she tried to keep inside were driving me insane. My fucked up magic practically begged for me to wrap her safely in my arms and unleash it on the world to keep her safe—and I was actually tempted to do it.

This fucked up curse I'd borne my whole life. The thing that had me hiding in The Lowers and hated by everyone who found out about it. Every day was a risk that someone would spill my secret to save themselves. So I spent my days helping, moving through the shadows they'd relegated me to and finding the things they needed the most. I made myself indispensable until the thought of losing me was worse than having me around. I never did quite get used to stepping out of the background, though, to being part of the crowd. I much preferred the secret paths I'd found where I could be alone, in the silence, in the darkness. Some days it felt like that was where I belonged, and others, it was the place I wanted to dissolve away into, a place where I could leave everything else behind.

Britt lifted the necklace up to the light, twisting and turning it like she was trying to see something inside. Her head tilted to the side as she frowned, almost like she thought if she concentrated harder, it would reveal its secrets to her.

As she moved it around, a flash of light appeared before her, quickly disappearing a second later.

"Do that again," I told her, stepping around her, trying to figure out what I'd just seen.

She rotated the necklace again, and this time, when the flash flared into existence, I wasn't the only one who saw it.

"Fuck!" Xanth rushed out, taking two steps closer as he saw the same thing I did. "Was that a crack?"

"What?" Britt turned around to try and see what we were talking about, but of course, it wasn't there any more.

"It was like a crack, a tear," Xanth tried to explain.

Britt lifted the necklace above her head, slowly twisting it in the rays of sunlight as she stared at the same spot we were.

When the crack came back into view, it wasn't just a flash this time; it gradually materialised right in front of us as Britt slowly changed the angle of the stone. Almost like she was focusing on the image in front of us.

Once it was whole and real before us, we all stood and stared at it in silence. For me, it was because I couldn't quite wrap my brain around what I was seeing; I had no idea if the others felt the same.

"It's... what is it?" Xanth asked before tearing his eyes away from the sight and looked at both Britt and me.

I didn't answer because the only one I had was that it was a tear between this realm and the next, and I didn't know if I wanted to admit that such a thing was possible.

"It's our way out of here," Britt said grimly, looking around once more. "We don't know if this is a one-time thing or how long it will take to come back. We should go through now."

"Fair enough," Xanth responded cheerfully, already walking toward it.

"Stop! Will you think first for once?" I sighed in exasperation.

Seriously, keeping this guy out of trouble and alive was becoming a full-time job. I barely had time to grab the packs we'd prepared when the portal appeared in front of us to bring us here. He'd walked straight through without a second thought, and I swear the thing closed, skimming against my ass as I dived in after him. Thank god we'd thought to pack and be ready to go beforehand, or we'd be wandering around out here with no supplies or anything.

"I'm with Xanth," Britt told me with a shrug. "No time like the present, and we don't exactly have anything to test whether it's safe or not."

"Oooo, I could throw one of those guys through," Xanth offered, sounding far too excited about throwing a dead body through a rip in the wall between realms.

I opened my mouth to object and then silently closed it again because, unfortunately, it was the only thing we had.

"Fucking hell," I swore, glancing back over my shoulder at the two bodies behind us. "Well, I guess we should grab the small one then."

This had to be one of the weirdest and also grossest things I'd ever done in my life. I swear if this guy exploded and I got dead angel on me, I was gonna be pissed.

"Works for me." It worried me that Xanth could sound so cheerful about the most fucked up things.

"Are we actually doing this?" Britt asked with a grimace as Xanth and I hauled the body up between us.

"Might be easier if we take the wings off," Xanth mumbled.

I looked up at him in shock. "Sometimes the things you say completely go against your happy, fun guy exterior."

"I'm an enigma." He shrugged and then hauled the dead angel's arm over his shoulder as we started to drag him toward the split in the realms.

Britt had stayed as still as she could, keeping the amulet held above her head so it stayed open.

"So we're just gonna shove him through then?" I asked, not quite sure if we were tripping into psychotic territory here. Still, if anyone was going to explode, I'd much prefer it to be this guy than any of us.

"Whoopsie daisy," Xanth cheered, launching the guy off his shoulder and nearly dragging me along with it.

"For fuck's sake!" I swore, untangling myself just in time.

"Sometimes I wonder why I even put up with you," I grumbled, patting myself down to make sure everything was still there.

"It's my sweet, sweet ass," he taunted, giving it a little shake as he walked away from me.

Britt was just laughing her ass off at us by this stage, and who could blame her. But fuck, if it was going to bring that sweet sound out of her, I'd be the butt of Xanth's jokes every day—I just wasn't going to promise not to punch him every so often.

"Well, it seems to have worked," Britt said, peering through the crack at the angel that now lay on the other side.

I took the opportunity to study the edges of the strange phenomenon in front of us. It was almost like a portal, but it didn't have that natural shape magic seemed to create. It quite literally looked like a crack in the wall.

"I wonder how this happened and how long it's been here. Do you think these are all over the realms?" I didn't know why I was asking them because there was no way they could know the answer but the thought of these cracks existing in other, more dangerous places was pretty terrifying.

"I wonder if this is how Frannie was able to move around so easily?" Britt theorised, moving to my side.

And then she just stepped through.

"What the fuck?!"

My hand snapped out to grab her, but it met nothing but thin air because she'd already moved through the other side.

"I thought we were waiting to see if it was safe." I sighed.

Xanth happily skipped through after her, trying to look at the edges as he passed. When he missed whatever it was he was trying to see, he stuck his head back through the crack, squinting at the crack itself.

"Will you just..." I shoved his head back through and then quickly jumped through myself.

I could already tell that the two of them together were going to give me a heart attack.

"We threw the angel through, and he didn't explode," Britt said, looking at me like I was the crazy one. "It seemed fine."

I raked my fingers through my hair, sighing. It was official; one of them was definitely going to be the death of me.

"Let's just act with a little bit more caution from now on, shall we?" I suggested. "It will do wonders for my heart condition."

"He's joking." Xanth laughed. "If he had a heart condition, I'd have killed him years ago."

I turned around when I heard the strain in his voice, only to find him rolling the angel back through the crack. It quickly snapped closed as he did, and he jumped back, shaking his hand with a cackle.

"Woah, that was close."

"Imagine if you'd have had your head still stuck through," I snarked, trying to make a point.

"Yeah, I'd probably be running around like one of those headless chickens." He laughed like the lunatic he was.

"No, Xanth. You'd be dead. Like a normal person, expect slightly less normal," I deadpanned back.

He shook his head at me like I was the crazy one before he slid up to Britt, wrapping an arm around her shoulders.

"Now that we're here, we should probably start thinking about making camp," he said. It was the first sensible thing he'd said all day.

Looking around, I tried to figure out where we were. When it had looked like a forest on the other side of the crack, it didn't quite look right now that we were here. Crouching down, I realised that the ground was actually made of wood.

"Where are we?" I asked, peering up at the leaves above us.

I could see the sky, so we were definitely still outside.

"If I had to guess, I'd say we're on the world tree," Britt said, almost like those words were the most normal thing in the world to say.

She pointed over my shoulder, and when I looked behind me, my jaw just about hit the ground. Because the strange wood surface I was standing on also formed a wall behind me, and now that I was looking at it, it was starting to look more like bark.

"A problem for the morning," Xanth decided.

Grabbing the bags, he sat on the ground beside me, pulled out some food and started to prepare a meal for us. I'd always been envious of the way that Xanth could just roll with the punches. Deep down, I knew it bothered him more than he showed. That he kept all of the pain locked deep, deep inside. He had to. He'd lost so much more than I had. And some days, I didn't know how he went on.

Britt slowly sank to the ground, leaning back against the tree behind her; she bent one knee and braced her arm against it. Staring around at her surroundings, I watched as she catalogued what information she could. I could practically see her brain spinning as she quickly evaluated what to do next. Britt might seem like somebody who didn't have a plan, someone who was going through the motions to do what needed to be done. But I could already tell she was thinking three steps ahead. And there was no doubt in my mind that she'd succeed in this journey, in this impossible task that we'd decided to do at her side.

Most people would probably think we were crazy, but at the end of the day, there was one person responsible for everything that had happened around us. One person who had moved all of the pieces into place to allow those at the library to decimate the population and take those that we loved away from us.

Everything flowed back to Odin, and I, for one, was practically giddy at the thought of him finally getting what he deserved.

And what he deserved was a very slow and very painful death.

Chapter 9

Britt

The world tree posed a practical problem to us that I didn't think the others had appreciated yet. Namely, how the fuck we were going to get down to the ground. Geta had told me to find the eagles at the top, but how we were supposed to climb this thing was beyond me. It would also mean adding time to our journey that I didn't think we could afford. But she'd also mentioned the possibility of another way. And it was that possibility I was hoping like hell would become a reality.

An idea was forming in my mind, but it completely relied on chance. And recently, I wasn't so sure that luck was on my side.

I remembered the story that Aria had told me of her journey to Valhalla. More specifically, who had helped her climb the tree. Our best chance at this point was to hitch a ride down. Since none of us had wings, what else could we do?

I was surprised that the guys were still with me if I was honest. That they'd accepted so easily to go on this quest. Because let's face it, the chances of us surviving were slim to none. All we could hope for was to take Odin down with us.

I should be trying to discourage them from coming. But deep down, I didn't want to be alone. I didn't want to leave behind yet another thing that made me happy. I hardly knew these men, and yet how could they not bring a smile to my face? How could they not make the darkness seem just a little bit brighter?

"Here."

Looking up, I found Xanth standing in front of me. In his hand was some kind of sandwich and what looked like a bag of dried fruit.

"Oh, thanks."

As I bit into the sandwich, Xanth smiled before moving away and making some food for himself. It should have made me smile. It was a sweet gesture, after all. Instead, it just made me sad. My wolf would have been preening over this if she was here. She'd love that he'd made food for her. It made that hole inside me seem wider, bleaker. It was hard living a life with only half your soul.

"So, next steps?" Drystan asked.

I was starting to realise that he was the sort of person that needed a plan. He needed to see the steps laid out in front of him and to weigh up all the risks and possibilities. What I was about to say next was probably going to infuriate him.

"We're going to have to hang out here until we find someone to hitch a ride with down the tree."

I almost wanted to count the number of times his eyebrow twitched at that, but I decided it was best to look away. Mainly because I was fighting to keep the smile from my face.

Damn, he was adorable.

"So what you're saying," Xanth started, and I could already hear a purr starting to form in his voice. "Is that it's just the three of us hanging out here with nothing to do but entertain ourselves."

Now this was an idea I could get on board with.

"Yep. Just you, me, and a lot of time to fill."

He grinned as he met my gaze, his food forgotten as he shoved it back in his pack and slowly crawled toward me.

"Hi, I'm Xanth," he said, a cheeky smile covering what was no doubt a laugh at his own joke I didn't quite understand yet. "I once had a pet frog when I was a kid, and I really hate tomatoes."

"I know your name."

I couldn't help but laugh at his antics because he'd put a sway in his hips, and Drystan was fighting to keep his eyes away from his ass. Good luck with that.

"I'm just making sure that you can't say you don't know me yet. Bolstering my chances of you letting me kiss you again."

"Oh really? Maybe it's Drystan's turn for a kiss," I joked.

"Drystan, get over here now," Xanth barked. "Because that sounds hot as fuck, and I want to watch."

Given that his eyes were still fighting to not look at Xanth, he didn't see the serious look on his face. His initial laugh soon drifted away when no one joined in with him, and his eyes widened ever so slightly when he saw the way I was looking at him.

Because this was exactly what I needed.

Was it the most sensible thing to be doing right now? No.

I didn't really know anything apart from the most basic of information about these men. We were strangers.

But everything inside me hurt. And I needed this. I needed a moment of selfishness to feel something else, something that wasn't the overwhelming grief inside of me, something new and pure.

I needed to get lost in my mates, and as soon as Drystan stood to walk over to me, I knew he'd give it to me. Because I saw on his face just how much he needed it too.

They both did.

The world we lived in was a cruel and heartless place. But as he reached out a hand and pulled me to my feet, wrapping his arms around me, I could forget it for a while. I could pretend this was all there was, nothing but the heat of his body, the soft feel of his lips as he tentatively brushed them against mine.

Drystan pulled back, gazing into my eyes as if he was trying to reassure himself that I wanted this. Whatever he saw there seemed to satisfy him because in the space of time between one breath and the next, his lips descended to mine, and he devoured me.

The heat rose between us as I sank into him. I didn't fight for control, to dominate the kiss; I let him take over. His hands came up to bracket my face as he tilted my head to the angle he needed, and his tongue drove into my mouth. He licked against my tongue as his fingers sank into my hair, and a soft growl rose from his chest.

I never wanted it to end. I wanted to stay here in his grasp, feeling his chest pressed against mine as his bruising kiss went on forever. This was the world I wanted to be lost in. This was the safe place I could hide while my wounded heart tried to fix itself.

Another set of lips softly brushed against my neck, and I whimpered. My hips pressed back to find Xanth behind me, and he ground himself against my ass before he moved closer.

"You look so fucking beautiful right now," he whispered into my ear. "Both of you do."

My hands clawed at Drystan's back as I bunched his shirt in my fists, hoping with everything I had that this would never end.

I felt Xanth's hand wrap around my throat before he pulled me away from Drystan. Need slammed into me. I was separated from the feeling I needed most, and I could feel a whimper of distress wanting to escape my mouth.

"Don't worry, I've got what you need," Xanth told me as his hand subtly tightened on my throat, pulling my back against his chest and pressing my head to his shoulder. "Look at those beautiful breasts, Drystan. It's a shame not to give them the attention they deserve."

Drystan's tongue swept across his bottom lip as he stared down my body. His chest heaved as he panted, and I could see the hard bulge in the front of his trousers that screamed how much he wanted this.

"Tell me now if you want to stop," Drystan groaned out. His gaze moved back to mine.

I didn't say anything because who the fuck would want to stop now when they'd only had a taste of what was to come?

"We need your words, sweetness," Xanth whispered in my ear. "Tell us that you want us; tell him how much you want him to devour your sweet body. He's not going to move until you do."

It was something I'd never been told before. Something that was never freely offered in the world I'd grown up in. And it was one more thing that told me these men were made for me. Because I'd needed to hear it so badly, and I hadn't even known.

"Don't stop," I told them, finding my voice. "Don't ever stop. I want it all. I want everything you'll give me."

They both seemed to move in unison then as their deft fingers slid across my body, loosening the ties and straps that held my armour in place as they pulled the chest plate and the rest of my clothes away.

Xanth's hand stayed wrapped around my throat, and he only let me move a fraction away from his body if it was absolutely necessary.

Drystan dropped to his knees in front. He stared up at me like I was a thing to be worshipped. His hands wrapped around my sides before they gently trailed down my body in reverence.

I squirmed in Xanth's grasp. I wanted to feel his lips on my skin, his teeth closing around my nipples. I wanted his fingers to slip inside the wet heat between my legs, but his teasing touch denied me.

My breasts heaved as I panted. Drystan's hands traced another path back up my body, avoiding all the areas where I wanted him the most. My nipples beaded almost painfully, begging for his attention, and I could feel the wetness sliding onto my thighs.

I was desperate for him. Desperate for them both.

And they knew it.

Before I realised what was happening, Xanth pushed two fingers into my wet pussy from behind, and I gasped in ecstasy as it felt like a wave of need surged across my body.

"So fucking wet," he groaned, pulling his fingers free.

I whimpered in protest at the absence. I wanted to ride those fingers until I came. But it was almost worth it when he tilted my head to the side, and I watched up close as he sucked them into his mouth instead.

"So fucking sweet, just like I knew you would be." Finally, he looked down at Drystan, still kneeling at my feet. "Don't make the lady wait; it's just rude."

It was apparently what he'd been waiting for. As Drystan dove forward, his tongue swept up my crease before he closed his lips around my clit and sucked.

I shot up onto the tips of my toes as that subtle wave of sensation slammed into me with a force I'd never felt before. A groan fell from my lips as I sank back against Xanth, closing my eyes and letting myself sink into the feeling of Drystan's tongue circling that needy bud before he gently scraped his teeth against it.

"You make the most beautiful noises," Xanth told me. His

lips came to my ear as he sucked the lobe between them and then bit down. "I can't wait to hear what it sounds like when you come."

I could already tell that he wouldn't be waiting long. That familiar feeling grew inside me, and my heart pounded in anticipation.

Drystan pushed his fingers inside my pussy as his tongue concentrated on my clit. He didn't let up for a second as he lashed against it, pulsing his finger in time with every move of his tongue.

My hips cantered forward. It was impossible to hold still. I was chasing that promised high of orgasm, and when it came, I fell into the freefall of ecstasy and screamed out my satisfaction.

I didn't hold back as my cries echoed in the silence around us. This was what my mate wanted to hear, and I was going to give it to him.

"On your back, Drystan. Our beautiful mate is going to ride your cock," Xanth told us.

We moved without question. Why wouldn't we? It was exactly what we wanted, and the way that Xanth was ordering us about was hot as fuck. Both men tore their clothes from their bodies, and I licked my lips at the sight of what lay before me.

Once he was settled on the ground, I swung my leg over Drystan's hips and leaned forward, kissing his lips and savouring the taste of my release on them.

I felt Xanth's hands come to my hips as he moved me over his friend, lining me up as Drystan pushed up, sinking his cock into the wet heat of my pussy.

The sudden sensation of a tongue swiping against my ass had me yelping and sitting up, which only made me sink further down on Drystan's cock. It was swiftly followed by a slap to my ass as Xanth pushed me forward back into Drystan's arms.

"Back into position, mate," he growled, and I felt my pussy clench as I complied.

Drystan groaned at the sensation. "Fuck, she likes that."

His hips rocked up, pushing himself impossibly deeper and tilting me back to his lips which I happily kissed again.

This time when Xanth's wet tongue ran along my ass, I didn't startle. It wasn't something I'd had done to me before, but I didn't hate it as he slowly licked around my asshole.

When he moved away and Drystan suddenly groaned in surprise against my lips, I smiled. Apparently, I wasn't the only one getting attention, and from the way his cock twitched inside me, I wasn't the only one enjoying it either.

Xanth's hands had stayed at my hips, and as I went to slide up Drystan's cock they tightened, preventing me from moving. Before I could protest, he pulled me up, dragging me up Drystan's cock before pushing me back down again.

"Damn, now that's a sight I'm never going to forget," he murmured.

"Fuck. Xanth, stop being a dick and trying to be in charge. I need..." Drystan didn't finish his statement. He didn't really need to; we all knew what he needed.

I needed it too.

I needed to fuck him. I couldn't cope with this slow pace, I needed to let go, and I wanted to feel Drystan tensing beneath me as he tried not to come from the things I was doing.

Yep, I definitely needed that.

"Fine." Xanth sighed. "But you better spread these cheeks for me because I'm going to come all over this ass."

I groaned at the suggestion, not realising how much I needed that as well until he suggested it.

"Yes, sir," Drystan joked, his hands moving to my ass and pulling my cheeks apart.

Xanth finally released his grip on my hips, and I pulled up

on my knees, sliding right to the tip of Drystan's cock before crashing back down again. He swore under his breath, his fingers digging into my ass cheeks as he did.

So I picked up the pace, moving how I wanted now that I was finally free. I let my head fall back as I sank into the sensation, feeling his thick length slide in and out of my body. When Xanth's hand came between my shoulder blades to push me forward, I let him slowly push my chest down.

I knew what he wanted. He wanted to watch. He wanted to paint my ass with his come while he watched Drystan sinking into my body.

It was dirty, and I was so fucking here for it.

The new angle made it harder to keep up my rhythm, but I didn't need to worry. As soon as I slowed, Drystan was there taking over and fucking me as hard as he could.

My hands came to his shoulders as I held on for the ride, each thrust of his hips pushing me higher and higher as that wave started to build again inside me.

"So fucking beautiful," Xanth groaned again, and I felt his hand reverently stroke against my ass as he did.

I could feel the beat of his hand as he worked his cock over, keeping in time with Drystan's pace as he fucked me. When his thumb came to my asshole, I found myself pressing back against him, wanting to feel him breach that ring of muscle more than I realised.

When he finally pushed inside, my eyes rolled back, and the orgasm I'd felt just starting to build suddenly exploded to life inside of me.

Pinned between the two men, I had little choice but to let them take control of my body while they pushed me through wave after wave of sensation. I was so lost to it that I barely heard the grunt of Drystan as he came deep inside me or the warm ropes of come as Xanth followed through on his promise.

Sagging forward into Drystan's arms, I felt spent. My body was wrung out, and my eyes were already starting to flutter closed. It was the last overload of emotion my body could take, and I listened as Drystan whispered soft words to me before slipping from my body.

In the back of my mind, I registered Xanth's gentle movements as he cleaned me up before tucking something soft around me as Drystan continued to hold me.

It was probably the best sleep I'd ever had in my life. It was deep and dreamless and exactly what I needed to escape what would be waiting for me in the morning after this one perfect night.

But I wouldn't say I'd be happy if this was all we got because even though it had been perfect, I'd had a taste of what could be now. And why would I ever want to let it go?

Chapter 10

Aria

I held the Gjallarhorn loosely in my hand as I stared up at the door to Valhalla before me. It was still exactly the same as the last time we'd been here; the only difference was that now we were standing before the doors of a tomb. It was no longer the place of hope it had once been, for me or for anyone else.

Kyle stepped to my side, his hand seeking out my other hand as he held it firmly in his grasp. I could feel the soft reassurance that came whenever he was near, whenever any of them were close by. And right now, the rest of my mates stood quietly at my back, waiting for me to prepare myself for whatever we were about to find on the other side of those doors.

"You *can* do this," Kyle told me quietly. "We'll do it together."

I didn't know if he was right, but what other choice did we have? Valhalla was our way into Asgard, and even if it wasn't, a part of me needed to see the devastation here to believe it was true. Because it felt so impossible. Like fate couldn't really have let something so terrible happen.

But I couldn't let my mind go there. Because I knew as

soon as I did, I'd grab hold of that idea and never dare let it go. Then whatever we found on the other side would be so much worse.

It was better to have no hope than to have it ripped away from you. Without hope, the rage could burn brighter, and the need for revenge was the only thing keeping me going right now.

I wanted to tell him I couldn't; that it was all too much. But the reality of our situation was that it didn't matter. This was something I *had* to do, and the Valkyrie who had so easily accepted me the last time I walked through these doors deserved it, too. They deserved to be remembered, to be honoured. Their sacrifice should be felt, and I wouldn't let them down by shying away from it.

I raised the horn and blew that now familiar bass note, the reverberation through my body no longer holding the same feeling of relief that it used to.

The great doors shuddered, it almost seemed like the giant valkyries embracing the door were about to move, but instead, the portal shimmered into existence just as it had the last time.

It was time to go back to the home I'd never had a chance to know, time to return to Valhalla.

The guys didn't move; they waited for me to step forward first. It was one of those polite moves you wished people didn't make because I didn't want to be the first one through, and I also didn't want to admit it out loud.

Instead, taking a deep breath, I strode forward. Kyle stayed at my side, holding tightly to my hand, and I loved him even more for it. None of them would have made me do this alone.

The wet sensation of the portal washed over my skin as we stepped through, and then it was like we were being catapulted forward until we finally exited the other side. It was almost not as bad as the other times I'd had to travel through a portal, and a distant part of my brain wondered if I was getting used to the strange way to travel. Well, it was either that, or it just wasn't as bad when you weren't running for your life.

Stepping out onto that training sand, the memories of the last time slammed into me. The loss of control as I slipped into the bloodlust, and the only way out was to fight the Valkyrie who thought they were training with me. It had been one of the worst moments of my life, seeing those women who looked at me with respect and awe and then hurting them.

But this? This was so much worse.

Because they weren't getting up this time.

My eyes moved from body to body. The story of how brutal this battle had been was written in the splashes of blood across the ground.

Kyle's hand tightened in mine as he reminded me that he was there. That I wasn't as alone as my broken heart was telling me right now. I could sense the others standing at my back, lending me their silent support.

But it wasn't enough to deal with the sight in front of me.

My fingers slipped free of Kyle's hand as I stepped forward. I didn't know what I intended to do as I came to a stop at the first fallen Valkyrie on the ground.

What could I do?

My magic roared inside me, feeding off the pain and the crushing guilt of not being here with them.

In the back of my mind, I knew my presence wouldn't have saved them. Maybe there was a part of me that wished I'd died beside them; I wasn't quite brave enough to acknowledge it, though.

As I stared down at the body at my feet, all I could focus on was the sword still held in her hand. Looking around in confusion, the pain built and built inside of me.

They were just lying where they fell. Of course, they were. There was no one left to bury them. But something about it felt so wrong. Not only had they been cut down in some kind of senseless revenge move, but no one had cared enough to even bury them.

But then my eyes found a single person lying in a clearing next to a hastily constructed wooden X which had been staked into the ground.

My feet were moving before I could even get her name to slip past my lips.

"Geta!"

I tried not to think about the things on the ground that I stumbled over as I rushed to her side. Dropping to my knees, my hands seemed to drift over her. I didn't know what to do, if I should even touch her.

She was gone.

She never would have looked this at peace if she was alive. Her hands were crossed at her chest, holding her sword as it lay down the length of her body. She'd been so fucking fierce. So full of life, and at every single moment, she was ready to go, ready to help. She gave her entire life to those around her, and then they took it so easy in some kind of tantrum.

"Why does she look like this?" I asked the guys.

"She's..." Brandon stopped and then knelt beside me, reaching out for Geta and then looking at the wooden cross that ominously loomed over her. "Someone took her down," he said, looking at the marks around her wrists where she'd clearly been tied up.

"Someone survived?" Sykes asked, and I could hear the tinge of excitement in his voice.

Even now, amongst all this death, we were all looking for a positive. A single ray of hope that not everything had been torn away from us.

Climbing back to my feet, my eyes scanned over the fallen. I tried to disconnect my heart from the process, to push aside the pain it caused so I could focus on the hope.

Because I really, really needed this.

But there were so many on the ground, so many cut down and just left there to rot.

It was so senseless. So fucking senseless.

The people lying here were more than just warriors. They gave their lives fighting for those who needed them. They'd come when we'd needed them; they'd been prepared to lay down their lives for us because it was the right thing to do. They weren't from our world, they didn't know us, and yet they fought for us anyway.

I was supposed to be looking for signs of a survivor, but I couldn't. All I could see was death and needless violence that our world had broken down into.

And I was so fucking angry about it.

The magic inside me roared, and it shook me to my very core. My wings burst from my back with so much force that I dropped down to my knees. They burned hotter than I'd ever felt before, and I let it soak into me. I let that fire dance along my body just to feel something other than the pain and rage that clawed at my mind.

Once the magic was given free rein, it lashed out at the bodies around me. It burst out of me in righteous waves, seeking out the people we were supposed to protect, our people, my people. But everybody it touched was missing that spark of life it was searching for.

I felt it graze across my mates, brushing over them as their magic reached out to greet it in return.

But the absence of any other life in the area didn't sadden it—it just enraged it more.

There should have been so much more here. There was a reason why Valhalla existed, why the valkyrie had been created in the first place, and Odin had lost sight of that in his madness. He'd turned away from his people chasing his own greed, and the descent into madness had cost his people everything.

We had paid the price.

And I was so fucking tired of it.

Tired of paying for the crimes of those in power. Tired of sacrificing for the greed of others.

And the magic agreed.

It really agreed.

So it did something about it.

The fire crept out from my wings, it arched across the sky in blazing ribbons, hitting each valkyrie and flowing inside of them.

I felt it. I felt every single one of them as a piece of my magic broke away, nestling inside them.

And then it flared to life.

The collective pulse as that piece of magic called out into the universe the wrongness of the realm, and it made it just a little bit better. As everybody around us took a breath, muscles tensed, and hearts burst into life once more.

I was the Phoenix General, and these were my people. I carried the eternal flame, and this was what it was made for.

I was tired of losing. It was time for a win.

"What the fuck?" Kyle breathed as he looked around at the valkyrie, slowly starting to move on the ground.

"*Zombies*! Are we up against zombies again?" Sykes all but screeched.

All the others just laughed, and even I felt the urge to smile. The tears in my eyes burst free just as the overwhelming wave of relief threatened to overwhelm me.

"Aria?" a voice croaked from the ground beside me. "How... what?"

The Valkyrie beside me groaned and then rolled onto her side.

"Try not to talk yet. We should probably check you over to make sure you're not still wounded." I had no idea what I was doing, and the fact that I was talking to someone who had been dead literally moments ago was more than my brain could take right now.

"Considering my last memory of Valhalla involved a sword sticking through my chest, I think I'm good."

She groaned as she sat up, her hands roaming over her chest as she double-checked it was indeed healed.

"I had the worst fucking dream," she groaned, finally stopping her search and looking out at the other Valkyrie starting to move around us. "I was in the Elysian fields, and they wanted me to *relax*," she spat like it was the most horrifying thing she'd ever heard.

The noise around us slowly started to rise as more of the Valkyrie and their warriors sat up, looking at their friends around them and checking they were okay. It wasn't enough to cover the voice beside me, though.

"No! No, no, no, no, no. I'm not supposed to be here," Geta's voice wobbled as she started to scramble backward as if she was trying to get away from us.

"Geta! Geta, calm down. It's okay. You're back. The angels are gone, you're safe now," I told her, holding out my hands and trying to comfort her like she was some kind of wild animal rather than a traumatised woman. God knew what they'd made her watch when she was tied to that cross.

"You don't understand," she rushed out, her wild eyes searching the crowd of rising valkyrie and warriors. "There was a price. I wasn't supposed to come back. I was going to fade away as penance for what I did."

"What are you talking about?" Dread was filling me at what she was implying. Had Geta been involved in the slaughter? It seemed impossible. She loved her people; she'd never do anything to hurt them. I knew she wouldn't. But the way her eyes moved from person to person, muttering about the price and how she wasn't supposed to be here. Seeing her broken like this was carving a hole inside me that I was terrified she was about to fill with betrayal.

When her eyes came back to me, I watched as the tears slowly poured down her face as she shook her head in denial.

"I... I didn't want to come back. I didn't want to face them, to face you."

"Geta, what the hell are you talking about?" I snapped.

Slowly climbing to my feet, I stood over the terrified woman. My hands itched to reach for a weapon, and even though I knew it was the panic making me want to do it, I was still horrified that I would even think about drawing a blade on her.

Geta sighed, I saw the resignation fill her gaze as she breathed deeply, preparing to confess her crimes. When she started to speak, I didn't think I was ready to listen because if she said what I thought she would, then it would fall to me to pass judgment, and I really fucking didn't want to.

"She came to me decades ago. She told me what was going to happen. That there would be one who would lead the realms to salvation. She told me about all the terrible things that would come to be, and then she gave me a choice. I could try and fight to save who I could, or I could wait. I could sit by and wait for her arrival. Help push her to the right path so that she could save the world. And I... I chose the world. I knew what would happen, and I did absolutely nothing to stop it. Because our sacrifices, all those sacrifices would mean we could leave behind a world for the generations that came next, and it would be a *better* world."

She found her resolve toward the end, even though she hiccuped through the last of it. I saw the fire building inside her as she explained what had happened, and I saw the guilt trying to smother it.

"Frannie," I realised. "She came to you with what she'd seen."

Geta nodded just once. "She knew you would need to find a way into Valhalla and that I held the Star of the Valkyrie that would lead you back to us. And I gave it to her. She helped me broker a deal for the souls of Valkyrie to move on to another afterlife, and I was supposed to fade away. It was the only thing I asked for. That if I was going to do this thing to them, I should pay for my crime."

Fucking Geta.

"Are you fucking kidding me?" I snapped. The fire built in her eyes again, and I saw her bracing for the blow that would strike her down like she thought she deserved. What she hadn't anticipated was my falling to my knees and wrapping her in my arms. "How could you think that you should leave us? That we'd let you go. We need you, Geta. I need you. I wish you hadn't had to do this alone. That I could have been here to help you. What Frannie asked you to do was an impossible task, and you shouldn't have had to carry that burden alone," I told her firmly.

When I pulled back, the shock on her face showed just how much she hadn't expected to find any forgiveness here. The other Valkyrie had gathered around us as she'd told us what she'd done, but none of them looked even slightly angry with her.

"You didn't really think that the Elysian fields would have been able to hold us, though, right?" the Valkyrie I'd been talking to earlier said. "That had to be some kind of sick practical joke, surely."

The laughter that rippled through the crowd lightened the mood, and I sighed in relief. The Valkyrie were back. I'd... I'd brought them back.

I looked down at my hands and tried not to panic at the thought of what I'd just done. But then a smile flickered across my lips.

I wasn't just made to kill. I could give life too.

Maybe this was my penance for the things I'd done.

Whatever it was, I was so fucking glad.

"I can't believe it's not over," I whispered as Geta's words whispered through my head. "I thought I was done. I thought I'd fought my fight, and now you're telling me I still have more to do."

Geta looked at me in confusion, frowning as she tried to figure out what I was saying. "No. Well, yes, there's still a fight to be had, but I wasn't talking about you."

I looked at her in surprise, and if I was being completely honest with myself, relief as well.

Then she said the words that struck fear into my heart.

"We need to talk about Britt."

Chapter 11

Xanth

Waking up, my back had cramped and the dull ache in my ribs, which had finally started to ease, was just a mere annoyance now. But I couldn't have been happier. Because in my arms was the most important person in the world to me and I'd finally found her.

As I opened my eyes, I stared dreamily at my mate before Drystan snuggled in closer to her other side, drawing my attention.

"Hey."

His eyes widened as he looked at Britt like he'd thought it had all been a dream, and then the cutest blush I'd ever seen swept across his cheeks. I knew exactly where his mind had gone. To last night. To the feeling of my tongue sweeping across his balls.

Drystan and I had been dancing around our feelings for years. It wasn't something that wasn't really accepted where we'd come from, but there had always been this inseparable bond between us. It all made sense now. But I didn't think those feelings were just because we happened to share a mate. I truly loved him, even if I'd never had the balls to admit it before. The time just never seemed right for us.

"So, last night," he started, before awkwardly clearing his throat.

I suddenly had one of those moments of doubt, the kind that plagued you in your weakest times. But then I shoved it aside. This was Drystan. I'd seen the love in his eyes for years now and there had been no mistaking it when he'd spent the last few days nursing me back to health.

"Yeah, can you believe we waited so long?"

I wouldn't give him a chance to back out of this because of nothing more than awkward embarrassment.

The Drystan that the world got to see was gruff and harsh. He was fiercely protective of the people he cared for. And he had reason to be. He'd lost so much in the short life he'd had. We both had. The library had been a living nightmare for a long time. It was a miracle we'd made it out of there. Even if it had been more by luck than skill on my part.

Dumb fucking luck.

Story of my life.

"I... I can't," he finally admitted and all the tension I'd been trying to hold inside drained out of me.

"We can take it slow. Do whatever feels right. We're going to make sure we have all the time in the world to explore this, okay?" I didn't know if I was trying to reassure him or myself. Either way, I thought we both probably needed to hear it.

Britt stirred between us and immediately had our undivided attention.

"Will it be weird if she wakes up and we're both staring at her?" I asked, realising how creepy this looked.

Drystan opened his mouth to say something, but Britt's sleepy voice beat him to it.

"Depends on what you're doing while you're watching me," she joked, her eyes blinking open.

She was the most beautiful woman I'd ever seen, and I was pretty sure that every time her eyes met mine, it would take my breath away.

"I'd prefer to talk about what we're going to do now that you're awake," I purred.

I had no idea where this side of my personality was coming from. I was the jokester, the one in the group that refused to take life seriously. It was hard to hold on to a fun side when your entire world was on fire. So I'd done it for those around me that hadn't been able to. I'd done it for Drystan. I pushed all the pain, fear and self-loathing as far down as I could and I covered it with a layer of laughter just to see the darkness fade in his eyes.

Britt playfully shoved me before sitting up and stretching.

Yeah, obsession had already hit me hard, and I'd never get enough of the woman before me. I had no idea what I'd done to get this lucky, but I was taking hold of life with both hands and there was nothing I wouldn't do to keep it.

"We need to talk about what happens next," Drystan pointed out. "What's the plan?"

"Geta told me I need to get to the seers well at the bottom of the world tree. She suggested we seek the eagles at the top, but if fate was on our side, another option would present itself. I think I know what she was talking about. I just have no idea how we find them."

Britt looked around like she was searching for something, but my brain was still stuck on what she'd said.

We were currently sitting on a branch of the world tree that was bigger than the entire lowers had been back at the mage library. If this was the size of just one branch, the idea of climbing to the top of the tree seemed impossible. Surely it would take us months to do it.

Yet, the idea of going down seemed all the more terrifying. How high up were we in the first place? And now that I thought about all the falling I'd be doing if we reached that point, it was the only thing on my mind.

"If she said it was down to fate, then I'm guessing it's more of a they-find-you type of situation," Drystan pointed out. "We should go through our supplies and eat while we have the time."

From the look on Britt's face, she wasn't entirely on board with this idea. I had a feeling it was the whole waiting on fate thing that she had the issue with. From the little time we'd spent together, I'd definitely call Britt a woman of action. Leaving it up to fate didn't feel like her style.

"Fate isn't exactly my favourite person right now," she grumbled.

She sounded so broken and I hated it. She should never have to feel like that, not when I was around.

Wrapping her in my arms, I kissed my beautiful mate. Fate had been cruel to her, and she'd been through more than any person should have to experience. But things were changing, right? We'd found each other and now she had us at her side. She'd never be alone again, and we'd never let anything hurt her.

My hands came to her cheeks as our soft kiss deepened. I could almost feel the heat building as her lips moved against mine. I trailed my fingers through her hair, needing to pull her closer, the back of my hand brushing against... fur?

I froze.

Flipping my hand, I reached out for what I'd felt and when my fingertips pressed against soft fur; I lurched back, taking Britt with me.

"What the fuck is that?" I screeched, staring at the monster in front of us that had been getting an up close and personal view of me making out with my mate.

"Oh, thank god," Britt sighed in relief, clearly having lost her mind from my amazing kissing skills.

The giant squirrel in front of us made some kind of strange chattering noise and bounded a step closer. Britt reached out a hand like she was going to pet the fucking thing and I pulled her back safely to my chest as I tried to scuttle us further away.

"Erm... what is happening right now?" Britt asked. I could hear the laughter lining her voice, but I didn't care in the slightest. Couldn't she see the same thing I could? The monster in front of us had to be some kind of demon pet, right? Look at it! It was the size of a cow and there was no way that had happened naturally.

"Don't touch it! It could be rabid or something." Then it cocked its head and squinted in annoyance at me. "I think it can understand me," I whispered to the others, like that made a difference.

It was only then that I realised Drystan was pissing himself laughing at me and I knew I was definitely missing something about this situation.

Britt carefully extracted herself from my arms, giving me a little pat when I tried to cling to her even tighter, which only made Drystan laugh even louder.

"Master Ratatoskr, it's an honour to meet you. My friend Aria told me how you helped her, thank you." Britt nodded respectfully at the squirrel and it nodded back at her. "We're trying to find a way down the world tree and we would be honoured if you could help us."

Oh fuck. She had to be joking, right? Maybe she meant some kind of secret passage. Yeah. That sounded right. She couldn't possibly be suggesting what I thought she was.

The squirrel turned around and bolted for the tree, scampering up a few feet as he chittered loudly. It didn't take long before two more appeared, hurrying down the tree trunk like they could defy gravity.

Britt and Drystan were already gathering up our packs and

shoving in the blankets we'd used last night as I stared at them in shock.

Why was I the only one that seemed to have an issue with this?

My eyes went back to the three creatures as they happily bounced closer. Three? Hopefully, a coincidence. Yeah. Definitely didn't mean what I thought it meant.

And then Britt climbed onto the squirrel closest to her.

Fighting the urge to sit down and refuse to move, I watched in horror as Drystan eyed up the other squirrel before climbing on.

That left one for me.

The one I'd pissed off earlier.

Huh, I never thought falling to my death from a mutant squirrel was the way I'd go out.

"Stop messing about and just get on already," Drystan sighed.

I knew what he was doing. And it grated that it was fucking working. Because if there was one thing that would get me moving right now, it was the need to not be the one standing here like an idiot in front of my mate because I was worried about mounting a giant squirrel.

Hmmmm, poor choice of words maybe.

"Okay, okay," I mumbled, swiping my now sweaty palms against my trousers. "I can totally do this."

The way it shuffled closer, dipping lower as I grabbed the soft fur in my hands, didn't fill me with confidence. It should have. But there was no way this was a good idea. We were putting our lives in the hands of these rodents, and I knew it couldn't end well.

But I wouldn't be left behind because I was too afraid to get on this damn squirrel. So I sucked it up, and I swung my leg over the top, climbing onto the damn glorified rat. Like a man! Maybe.

Drystan was still pissing himself laughing at me, and I would definitely make him pay for it later.

"Okay, well, I guess we're ready then." I could hear the suppressed laughter in Britt's voice, but at least she tried to hold it back.

Pity from my mate. That was definitely where I wanted our relationship to go at this super early stage.

"This is all your fault, you know," I quietly grumbled to the squirrel.

We started off at a slow pace, ambling down the branch of the world tree. This wasn't so bad, I guess. I mean, the size of this thing meant it was pretty much like riding a horse and there was at least a bunch of fur for me to hold on to.

"How exactly are we getting down the tree?" I called out to the others over my shoulder.

Britt shrugged and I could see them both looking around like they were searching for an answer.

Then I turned back in the direction we were heading.

And the fucking devil rat I was on glanced over its shoulder at me and smirked.

That was the moment I knew I was in trouble.

That we were about to be betrayed in the worst possible way.

And I was about to come dangerously close to wetting myself in fear in front of my new mate.

The squirrel shot off at top speed and all I could do was scream and cling to its fur like it was the only thing that would keep me alive.

Because I was pretty sure it was.

The edge of the branch we'd all failed to see before grew closer and closer.

"No... no... no! Don't you fucking dare!"

Then it launched itself over the edge and I squealed like a

six-year-old little girl seeing a unicorn for the first time... if that little girl believed she was about to be murdered.

A whoop of glee sounded behind me before Drystan gruffly swore.

I couldn't concentrate on that though because I was currently plummeting to my death on the back of a suicidal squirrel.

But then it stretched out its legs and suddenly caught the air and... we were gliding.

Releasing my death grip from its fur, I felt the squirrel shudder beneath me as it rolled its muscles like it was trying to shake off the pain. I nearly felt bad about it, even if I was fairly certain this creature had put me through hell for the fun of it.

Taking a deep breath, I blew it out slowly, letting the tension leak out of my shoulders as I took in the view in front of me. Now that we were out of the world tree, it was like the world was laid out before us and a great forest covered the ground as far as I could see.

This wasn't our world. It couldn't be. So where exactly were we?

The squirrels banked back around, heading back to the tree, and for the first time I got a glimpse of the world tree in all its glory.

And it was magnificent.

The world tree stood taller than the eye could see. Its branches disappeared into clouds that shimmered like galaxies. A hint of gold ran down the bark. It was easy to imagine that this tree could hold entire worlds. Its size was more than my mind could comprehend.

So many lives depended on this one thing. And it was the one thing that linked us all to Asgard and the man who was systematically destroying everything he touched.

Chapter 12

Britt

The rush of gliding to the ground with the squirrels nearly made the whole thing worth it. Couple that with Xanth's girlish squeals of terror and I was in an amazing mood. Even if I did feel bad that it was at the expense of my mate.

I watched as Xanth scrambled off the squirrel, falling to the ground as he scuttled further away. He squinted in anger at the squirrel, which I was pretty sure was laughing at his antics.

"Thank you for helping," I told the squirrel at my side.

It was strange having my feet back on solid ground.

"That was incredible," Drystan cheered, coming to join me. "Oh man, I hope we get to do that again."

He wrapped me in his arms, and I took a moment to sink into his joy. It was the first time he'd seemed so relaxed and it made me wonder what type of man he would have been if he hadn't seen so much pain and misery in his life.

The squirrels gathered around us as Xanth shakily joined us. "That was... that was... please, can we *not* do that again?"

I tried not to laugh. I really did. His pale face and the slight tremor in his arms as he reached for me really weren't amusing at all.

Drystan, however, clearly didn't have as much self control as I did. "Man, that was hilarious. I've never heard you scream that high before."

Xanth squinted in annoyance at him. "I preferred you when you were grumpy and brooding."

Drystan laughed and shoved him playfully, and I had a glimpse of what these two must have been like growing up together.

Ignoring their antics, I turned back to the squirrels, who were waiting patiently. Master Ratastok approached, chittering happily. I had no idea what he said, but when he pointed one paw behind us, I knew he was telling us where we needed to go.

"Thank you." I dipped my head respectfully to him. "We wouldn't have made it down here without you."

He crept slowly closer to me, his little paw coming to my cheek as his black eyes stared into mine. For a moment I thought I saw them fill with pain, but then he turned and scampered away, running up the side of the world tree like it was the easiest thing in the world to do.

I had no idea what that had meant, but I had a feeling if we ever needed to call on the squirrels for help again, they'd be there. I only hoped for Xanth's sake it wouldn't be too soon.

As I watched them disappear up the tree, I realised how similar this journey was to the one Aria had taken. She'd had an impossible task, and I was sure there must have been times along the way when she'd wanted to give up. But she didn't. She'd pressed on. Because she knew it was important that she did.

Without her, none of us would be here. I'd never have been reaped and sent to Valhalla. Echo would never have been at the Mage Library to save Xanth and I doubted

Drystan would have lasted long after losing the man he loved.

Frannie had been right to do what she did. It was so easy to see how all the threads wove together into one intricate pattern now, the picture it created hopefully being one that would show us our salvation.

How many had carried the burden of knowing what needed to be done? How many others like Geta had suffered in silence, knowing they wouldn't be around to see the whole thing through, but made the ultimate sacrifice, so the rest of us had a chance?

As the thoughts of the friends I'd lost filled my mind, I blinked the tears away from my eyes and focused back on the here and now. And as I did, the world tree came into focus in front of me.

"What's that?" I asked the guys, moving closer. I knew even though I'd asked the question, neither of them would have the answer.

"What?" Drystan stepped to my side as he asked, following me over to the tree while I silently stared at the bark.

My hand reached out to touch the dark stain spreading across the bark, but Xanth's grip on my wrist stopped me. My gaze skipped over the surface as I tried to make sense of what I saw.

"Is it some kind of parasite?" Drystan asked, leaning closer but being careful not to touch anything.

But that didn't seem right. It didn't look like something on the surface of the tree.

"It's rot," Xanth told us somberly.

Was the world tree sick?

"That can't be a good thing," Drystan mumbled, shuffling closer and moved to look at the darkness from the side, almost like he hoped Xanth was mistaken.

But he wasn't.

Now that he'd put a name to it, I could see it, too. The world tree was crumbling away, dying right in front of us.

"What happens if the world tree dies?" I asked, my voice quiet and scared.

"Everything disappears," a soft feminine voice said from behind us.

Turning around, I saw a woman standing there. Despite the fact she was covered with a heavy cloak, the hood pulled down to cover her face, there was nothing threatening about her.

"Is it true?" I asked. "Is the world tree dying?"

There was a desperate tone to my voice and I could feel my heart racing as my mind filled in the blanks of how dire our situation truly was.

"Yes and no," she answered cryptically. "Come. We've been waiting for you, Britt. This journey of yours is more urgent than you know."

"No pressure," Xanth mumbled, as the woman turned and walked away from us.

"I guess we're following then," Drystan quipped. Taking my hand, he squeezed it gently and then we did just that. There was no doubt in my mind that this was one of the seers we'd set out to find. She had the answers we needed, even if we weren't ready to hear them.

We followed her silently through the forest that surrounded the world tree. Everything was too silent here. There was no birdsong, even the breeze seemed to have disappeared and stolen with it the sound of rustling leaves.

We probably should have been worried that she was leading us into some kind of trap. After all, it felt like everyone was out to get us at the moment and we had no way of knowing who could be trusted.

But there was a serenity to this woman, and the forest that made this place feel sacred. Violence didn't feel like something that had a place here. Besides, I was done playing. I had a job to do and a massive fucking grudge to bear for those who stood against us. Maybe there was a part of me that wanted someone to stop us. To give me an opportunity to ease that lingering rage which threatened to pollute my heart.

I understood Aria so much better now. How she struggled with what needed to be done. Not because of the lives she'd have to take, but because of the fear of what it would turn you into when you were done.

Just how dark was I about to stain my soul?

We approached a clearing with a strange collection of stones in the centre. I didn't know what I'd expected, but it hadn't been this.

The well was more like a pile of rocks that held a great golden dish cradled in the centre. Two other hooded women stood at the edge of the stones, staring into the golden bowl and talking in hushed tones.

At first, I didn't think they would acknowledge our presence. But when our guide joined them, they gently grazed their hands down her arms in greeting before all three lifted their heads in unison to look at us.

Something about the synchronised move sent a shiver down my spine.

I could feel the magic in this place. The significance of what we were about to do. If my wolf had still been with me, I knew she'd have bowed her head in respect. But even without her here to guide me, I could feel how important the women before me were.

Dipping my head respectfully, I waited for them to speak, knowing that whatever happened here would be on their terms.

The silence seemed to grow thicker around us and an icy chill swept down my body as I waited. I could feel the gentle caress of magic as it reached for me, before quickly retreating, finding nothing but a human standing in its midst.

And for the briefest of moments, I hated myself for not being enough.

"You've come a long way and suffered much to stand before us," one of the women finally said.

"A body containing half a soul. An impossible burden to carry. But carry it you must," the second one added.

Tears came to my eyes. I didn't know what I had come here to hear, but there was a tiny part of me that had hoped they'd have an answer to how I could be reunited with the missing part of myself.

Xanth's hand slipped into mine, and he silently offered me his support. I felt Drystan reach out and brush a hand over the small of my back giving me his.

It reminded me I might have lost a part of my soul, but I'd also gained something else. That enormous hole inside of me wasn't as vast as it had once been. Two men had taken up residence there, showing me I wasn't as alone in this world as I'd believed.

"You seek the way to the ravens," the third woman said. "The raven claw is the only weapon that can accomplish the task before you. Only the reigning raven can wield the weapon. Where the ravens are held, the weapon resides. Find them and you will have your weapon."

All three of them stared at me expectantly. This wasn't really news to me. I knew I needed to find the weapon and the ravens. Whichever of them was the reigning raven would need to be convinced to join our cause, and I was hoping they'd be holding enough of a grudge that they'd take up our fight without question.

It was probably ridiculous considering how things seemed to go for us. But a girl could hope, right?

"Do you know where the ravens are?" I asked when I

couldn't take the silence any longer.

All three women laughed. It was like a ripple that flowed through the three of them until only the one who had led us here giggled at the ridiculousness of the question.

"We are the Norns. We know all," she finally told me.

"Right, yeah. I knew that. I guess it just seemed like you were waiting for me to ask."

The only part of her face that was visible through the dark shadows of her hood was her chin and her pale lips. I saw them quirk into a wry smile and I hoped it was because she found me endearing rather than infuriating.

"Hel holds the ravens. Odin gifted them to her when they tried to abandon his side. For their betrayal, he sent them to be her playthings."

"Of fucking course they'd be with that crazy bitch. Why make this easy?" I sighed.

She laughed then, except the other two didn't join in with her this time.

"Hel will not be easy to convince to part with her prizes," the first one told us.

"You will need to seek the aid of Nidhogg to find a way into Hel's realm," the second one added.

"The dragon lives at the base of the world tree, feeding from its roots and transporting the wretched condemned souls to Helheim." I couldn't be the only one who heard the grimness in her tone.

Then a thought struck me. "Is Nidhogg the reason the world tree is dying?"

"No, he has lived entangled with the roots for an eternity and has never caused Yggdrasil distress before. The rot you saw is a consequence of Odin's insanity. His magic is separating from his body and it seeks to feed, to grow, to consume everything in its path. It knows nothing but the pain of a hunger that will never be satisfied."

"Well, that's not terrifying," Xanth muttered.

She reached into the golden dish, her fingers trailing through the water that pooled there. As the ripples danced across the surface, all three of them leaned forward and stared into the depths.

"If you defeat Odin before the madness can separate from him fully, the world tree will recover," she told me. "But do not worry about Yggdrasil. If you fail in your task, you will die long before the world tree fades and the realms collapse."

It wasn't exactly the comforting idea she thought it was, but she had a point.

"And what about after we get the raven claw?" Xanth asked. "Where do we go next? What do we need to do to defeat Odin?"

"We cannot give you all the answers, young mage. Playing with fate is a dangerous game. Our sister likes to have the upper hand and whilst she allows us to have glimpses of what will come to be, she doesn't give up all her secrets at once."

His hand tightened in mine, and I could feel his frustration. It would have been too good to get all the answers we needed. To have a map laid out for us of what we needed to do to actually win this thing.

"Do you want a glimpse of your future, young mage?" one of the Norns asked.

Before Xanth could answer, Drystan snapped, "Keep your fortunes to yourself, witch."

I was surprised by the venom in his tone, but the women in front of us seemed nothing but amused.

"Not even tempted for yourself, dark one?" one of them asked.

"I make my own path in life. I don't need you trying to steer me in the direction you want me to go."

She smiled happily, stepping back from the well, the other two women moving in unison with her.

"There are always forks in every path, and only you can make the choice of which direction to travel," the one who had led us here pointed out, indicating for us to follow her. "The lonely path you've travelled to bring you here was paved with hardship, but the prize you'll find at the end of it is the reward for all you've endured. I may not be able to show you how to accomplish this task, but I have every faith that you will. I've seen the things you've been through. I've watched all of you overcome so much with more strength and grace than most possess."

She picked her way through the trees, leading us back to the world tree. I had so many questions for her, but part of me was terrified that she might actually have the answers to them. Drystan was right that knowing would inevitably influence any choices we made, and there was something about having my life mapped out for me that didn't feel right. I kind of liked the chaos. It was the not knowing that made you feel alive. Even if I was terrified of what sat waiting for us on the horizon.

Everything that Frannie and Geta had been through was to ensure we stayed on the right path. As tempting as it might be, if we let the Norns influence us now, it would have been for nothing. And even if there was the chance of an easier path, no matter the temptation, I trusted Frannie and Geta with my life and I wouldn't stop now.

The Norn stopped in front of us, pointing out a path that looked to run around the world tree. "Be careful when you bargain with the dragon. He's used to transporting the souls of the dead. This needs to be more than a one-way journey for you."

I gulped in fear. Just going to negotiate with a dragon for a way into the underworld. What could possibly go wrong with that? Oh right, he might steal our souls as well.

Chapter 13

Drystan

As we reached the tree, I watched the old witch turn her back and return to her sisters. She might seem like a young, kindly woman, but I could feel her. I could feel her magic and how ancient it was. I knew the games that seers played. Sitting on the sidelines, watching life from a distance had a way of breaking a mind. They couldn't be trusted. The only fun they had was leading people away from the things they needed the most.

Fate was a bitch, and all she did was play with your life, throwing every hardship she could at you, saving the easy path for her chosen few. Mortals had long been the playthings of gods. Even if we had forgotten how much influence they had over us, they'd never stopped playing the game. Not when we sealed them inside their own realm, and not when they no doubt found out we were on a journey to take one of them down.

It seemed we'd spent the best part of a day coming down the world tree and then meeting with the Norns. It felt like it had only taken a few hours, but the sun was already beginning its descent through the sky.

"We should make camp for the night. I don't like the idea of trying to bargain with a dragon in the dark," I told the others, dropping my pack to the ground and leaving them with no choice.

I could see Xanth and Britt exchanging looks like they had questions, but didn't want to voice them.

Xanth would probably know what had made my mood so foul, but he wouldn't spill my secrets unless he thought it was absolutely necessary.

Dark one.

She'd called me it so easily and I fucking hated that.

My magic was always going to be the one thing in my life that kept everything I cared about as far away as possible. People couldn't help but be afraid of me because of it. And I despised it.

Magic was so ingrained inside us that losing it would cost a mage his life. We simply couldn't exist without it. It was that entangled in our souls. And there were days when I would have been okay with that. When I would have given it up without a second thought, embracing that cost as easily as it was to take my next breath.

But now I had Britt.

We hadn't had a chance to get to know each other, but I already knew she was perfect for us both. The perfect balance to each of our craziness.

Then the Norn dropped the dark one name so casually in front of her. And now she would hate me. Because before I'd had a chance to persuade her I could be a good guy, my fucked up magic would ruin it, like always.

"I'll get firewood," I huffed out, intending to escape the conversation as quickly as possible.

"On it!" Xanth cheered, jogging off into the trees before I could even stop him.

Fuck.

This was him trying to be helpful and making me face my fears. Sometimes it really sucked having someone know you better than you knew yourself.

Britt sat down, fidgeting through her pack like she was trying to look busy. I knew I should say something to her. Was it really so wrong to keep it to myself? I just wanted her to look at me like she did before. I didn't want to see the pity in her eyes and I sure as hell didn't want to see fear.

"You doing alright?" Britt asked quietly.

I cringed. I couldn't help it.

It felt like this was the moment my entire world was about to collapse around me and I'd been through it so many times before that I couldn't stomach it one more time.

"Sure. Fine. I should check that Xanth doesn't need any help."

Before she could respond, I was up, slipping away. Not looking back to see the disappointment in her eyes. I wouldn't be able to keep moving if I saw that, and I really needed to get away from this moment.

It took me less than a minute to find Xanth. He was leaning against a nearby tree, arms crossed, listening like the jackass I knew he was.

"You ran out of there way quicker than I thought you would."

"Yeah, well, you're supposed to be collecting firewood, so I guess I'll be picking up the slack like always," I snapped, storming past him and angrily grabbing some dead wood from the ground.

I heard his footsteps following behind me, but carried on with my angry chore. With every branch I grabbed, the anger inside me grew. I knew it was a bad idea. Control was key when you had the issues I did.

"She won't judge you about this," Xanth told me quietly.

I knew he was trying to reassure me, but it only had my teeth grinding.

"Is it too much to ask that I get to have this one thing? Just for a little while, before my magic fucks it up like it always does?"

I hated how small I sounded right now. Like that little boy hiding in the shadows and begging his parents to love him. But how could they love a monster like me?

"Drystan..."

"Don't," I snapped. I'd heard this attempt at comfort from him so many times that I could recount it word for word in my head. It still didn't make me feel any better. If anything, that inner voice had turned it into some kind of taunting threat and it had exactly the opposite effect now.

Xanth sighed, and I listened as his footsteps faded away, back toward where my mate was no doubt waiting for an explanation.

I guess one night had been all I'd get. One perfect moment of her looking down at me with love in her eyes as she came on my cock. I'd never get that again once she found out what I could do. She'd probably never let me touch her again. That's how it usually went. That love would turn to fear and I'd be left sitting on the sidelines watching Xanth get everything I wanted and not even being able to hate him for it.

Britt deserved someone like him. He'd never treated me differently. Never judged me, never recoiled from my touch. Even when others had warned him away from me, he'd just laughed at them like it was the most ridiculous thing he'd ever heard.

My mind filled with images of her. Every memory I'd collected of her smiles. The easy way she reached out to touch me. That perfect laugh when her head tipped back and pure joy seemed to radiate from her for just a moment. She was even beautiful when she was sad. In those moments when she thought no one paid attention, she let the weight of the world sitting on her shoulders crush her for just a second before she steeled her spine and gritted her teeth, preparing to fight back. How she ever thought she could stand amongst people and not be seen baffled me. We'd been powerless to her pull the moment we saw her.

So maybe... maybe she'd understand.

I shook my head, I grabbed another broken branch from the ground and added it to my pile. Hope was for the blessed, the rest of us wallowed in the reality of life and prepared for the inevitable disappointment that was to follow.

Chapter 14

Echo

"Are you sure this is a practical use of our time?" Tas asked, "Wouldn't we be better travelling to Asgard and meeting up with Aria to prepare for the battle?"

Stone shook his head and stared at the towering building in front of us.

Everything around the Mage Library seemed dead and rotten. Had it always been like this? What had once been considered the centre of knowledge in our realm now just looked like a haunted nightmare. Which I guess it was for all the people who'd lost their lives here.

"Stone." My hand came to his shoulder, and I felt the tension in his muscles ease a little. "Do you want to go inside?"

We'd been standing here for nearly an hour now. When Stone had suggested we come here, none of us had objected. The last time we'd been here, we'd fought for our lives and Stone had trapped his father in an inescapable magical trap, fully prepared to take his place inside as well, if that was the cost.

The library had been like a ghost town then. Surely any

who had survived would have abandoned this place as soon as they realised they were free?

But this was something that Stone needed to face, and even if we were here in the guise of seeking help for our cause, we could take whatever time he needed to get through this.

"Come on," he finally said, striding forward like he hadn't been standing there for an hour staring at the building in dread. "Any survivors will probably be in the stacks. Hopefully, the lowers have been abandoned."

"Xanth and Drystan seemed like they were preparing to organise people. Perhaps they'd be a good place to start," Samuel offered.

"If they're still here," Aubron added. "Frannie gave them the pocket watch. It seemed like she knew they'd have a role to play in all of this, and I doubt that involves sitting here waiting for us to return."

He had a point. If Frannie had taken an interest, then they definitely had a role to play in the battle to come, and an important one at that.

"They won't have left without making sure that everyone else was organised. Drystan might seem like he sits on the outside of everything, but they'd have turned to him for answers once the ruling families fell," Stone told us. "He might not see the sway he has in the library, but he's respected more than he realises."

I remembered the pair of mages we'd come across at the mage library when we'd snuck inside. Xanth was on death's door, about to be fed to whatever monster Stone's father sacrificed his people to. If Frannie had a role for him to play, then he must have survived. Drystan though. I couldn't figure him out. He seemed to be preparing for an uprising, but who was left to fight?

As we climbed the stone steps to the wooden door on the tower, I felt a shiver rush down my spine. This wasn't a place

I'd ever thought we'd come back to. And if I was honest, it freaked me out. Something about it had the hairs on the back of my neck standing on end and every nerve in my body screamed at me to run. Even my Kitsuné seemed to shrink back in my mind. I didn't understand why at first, but then I realised what I could smell. This whole place reeked of death.

And when Stone used his magic to push the massive front door open, the reason why became apparent.

We all stumbled to a stop, not having expected the sight that met our eyes.

The once grand entrance was nothing more than a tomb. Lines and lines of covered bodies lay on the floor, each draped with a white cloth to hide the person beneath. At intervals down the rows, incense had been lit and small altars of offerings placed. Hundreds of candles lined the walls, making the shadows dance around the room with their flickering flame, casting an eerie beauty across the whole thing.

"Maybe we shouldn't go inside," I whispered.

It felt wrong to intrude in this place. Especially when we were coming to ask them to fight with us. The evidence of everything they'd already lost was right in front of us. How could we ask them to give even more?

A familiar figure emerged from the shadows, the kind smile on his face not suiting the surroundings we found ourselves in.

"Master Stone," Nathaniel said quietly, nodding his head respectfully. "I've been waiting for your return. If you could follow me?"

He indicated off to the side, and we followed, keeping to the edge of the room so as not to disturb those in the centre.

Stone's hand slipped into mine and I gripped it tightly, needing the comfort of one of my mates close by. If I was feeling like this, I couldn't imagine how Stone felt right now.

Nathaniel looked exactly as he had when he'd helped us. I

hoped like hell that he'd been able to reunite with his family and they weren't under one of those white sheets that I couldn't get out of my head. Yet, I didn't dare ask, because I didn't think any of us would survive if the answer was no. We should have stayed, or at the very least, we should have come back quicker. There had to have been a way we could have helped and at the moment, it felt like we'd just abandoned the mages to their fate.

We followed Nathaniel into the library itself. Great stacks of books surrounded the room, and it had left a large open space in the middle. It looked like this was once filled with desks, but all the tables had been hastily pushed to the side, leaving just a few in the centre which several people gathered around quietly discussing whatever was laid out before them.

A woman I didn't recognise looked up, her eyes widening in surprise when she saw us. Nathaniel moved to her side and when she slid beneath his arm, cuddling into his side, a sense of relief filled me.

"They actually came back," she murmured, more like she was talking to herself rather than anyone else.

"Yes, but we can't stay long," Aubron told her gently, and it made me want to reach for him. I knew him so much better now and I could see how what had seemed to be his usual abrupt manner was him stepping in to shoulder the disappointment so others wouldn't have to.

Stone gave him a grateful smile, and I realised then how close we'd all become. It wasn't me and my mates. We were a unit. A family. Everyone shared bonds with each other. They didn't solely exist through me.

"Aubron is right, I'm afraid. We're on our way to Asgard to join the final battle," Stone filled them in, softening the blow.

It didn't have the effect that I'd been expecting. I'd assumed they'd thought we were here to help them, but when the excited chatter started and the woman in front of us smiled in happiness, I had no idea what was happening.

"We can be ready to move in a few hours," she told us, striding away without even waiting for a response, barking orders at those around her who immediately jumped into action.

The guys standing around me watched in surprise, none of us really knowing what we'd walked in on.

Nathaniel chuckled.

"I have no idea what's happening right now," Damon admitted, voicing what the rest of us were thinking.

Now that everyone was moving, the table they'd been clustered around was empty, and I realised it held an enormous map. I couldn't stop myself from moving closer and trying to figure out what seemed to have had their attention. It was the strangest map I'd ever seen. It looked similar to a star chart, but every so often, there were indications of land masses. Almost as if someone had laid the night sky over a topographical map, but there were layers and layers of different versions. Lines and measurements swooped across the paper, seemingly indicating that the stars would be in constant motion. It made absolutely no sense to me.

"We've been trying to figure out a way inside," Nathaniel told me, moving to my side. When he saw the confusion on my face, he added. "Traversing the realms isn't easy without a guide."

I saw it then. The small scribbled words that labelled places, one standing out more than the others.

Asgard.

The mages were already trying to find a way to join the fight.

"You're coming with us?" I asked.

"Is that not why you came here?" Nathaniel actually looked worried for a moment. "We just assumed. We have lost much here, and at a certain point, hope was the one thing we never thought we'd get back. But then you came, and you stopped the murders, the crimes against our people. There may not be many of us left, but we have a grudge to bear and a right to fight against those who have stolen so much from us."

I was shaking my head before he'd even finished. "No, no! It's not that. I don't know what we'd thought we'd find when we got here, but willing volunteers definitely wasn't it. I thought we'd at least have to persuade you to help us. And I'm not sure if I ever expected you to agree," I admitted.

But I saw it then, not only in Nathaniel's eyes but also in how the people around us were gathering supplies and securing weapons to their bodies.

These people were angry. And they deserved a chance to strike back.

Wasn't that why we were here in the first place?

We were heading toward an impossible battle, and we needed them by our side.

But all I kept thinking about was what the fae had said and as I looked around this room, I realised there were far fewer people here than there were in Thyellin. The mages couldn't afford to lose anyone else, but if this was all that was left of them, then it would seem that the damage was already done.

"Do you have..." The words froze on my tongue.

I'd seen the lines of bodies in the entrance and from what I knew of how the portal operated, there would be countless others who there wasn't anything left of to warrant a pristine white sheet.

My mind turned back to the hundreds of candles lining the walls and I hoped like hell that they didn't signify what I was now pretty sure they did.

How did so many people die with no one else noticing? Why wasn't our entire realm outraged by this?

"If you need supplies, we may be able to help," Nathaniel

told me, not understanding what I was about to ask. "We have access to all the upper floors now and there is still much which can be found in the higher chambers."

I shook my head. My gaze darted around the room as I tried not to look at the people around me getting ready to walk into a battle they probably wouldn't come back from. Getting ready to end the race of people we called mages.

But as awkward as it was to ask this man who'd done nothing but help us, I needed to know the truth of what I was about to do to these people.

"Is this all that is left?" I asked, my voice dipping low as my shame practically dripped from it.

I felt Stone stiffen at my side and I knew the inevitable answer to this question was going to hurt him. Gripping his hand tighter, I hoped he could feel the silent support I was trying to give him. He'd done so much to fight for his people, to find out who was hurting them, and in the end, it had all been for nothing.

Nathaniel looked around at the others, who were going through the motions of preparing to leave the library behind.

"We may not be many, but we're strong. We can be useful to you in this fight," he told me, misunderstanding me again.

"I'm not questioning that. Truly, I'm not. I'm asking if we stood on the sidelines and did nothing as mage after mage was murdered. If I stole Stone away when you needed him the most. If I had the audacity to call myself an Elite, believing I was standing up to fight for what was right, all while a monster ripped through the mage library and killed an entire race of people." I was panting by the end of it and I could feel the tears burning in my eyes as my failure wrapped around like the antithesis to a security blanket.

Nathaniel shook his head, moving forward to lay a reassuring hand on my shoulder.

The first of my tears slipped free and I let it slide down my face unashamedly. I'd never felt like such a failure as I did right now. I'd thought the battles we'd fought had been for the good of the realm when, in reality, we'd abandoned the mages to die silently in the shadows.

They deserved for us to feel their passing.

"Do you know how the mages have survived as a race?" Nathaniel asked. "How a race of men came to thrive in this place?"

"You make bargains with the witches, and alliances are involved that include them bearing children," I answered, confused about what he was trying to say.

He looked at his wife then who'd stopped what she was doing and stared at him with so much love in her eyes. She nodded, like she was giving him permission to continue, and a small spark of hope burned to life inside of me.

"We in the lowers have learned how to survive, through necessity more than anything else. The ruling families thought they had the weakest of us cast down into their pit, unworthy of their time and attention. But all they did was group the most desperate of us together. And in the shadows, we learned, and we adapted. We may not have all been born with the same strength as them, but we found different ways to harness our magic, ways to make it grow, to cultivate it inside ourselves and make us strong. And with that strength came a desire to live in the light. To live how we wanted to live and not how those in the higher levels deemed us worthy of. The witches who came to us were considered weak. But when we fell in love with them, when they chose us over the covens that had cast them aside, we showed them what we'd learned and we helped them nurture their own magic. And through that love, that mutual respect, we built families who turned into armies. Did you really think we gave up our daughters? Those who wanted to leave did so with any daughter they bore. The sons were never given that chance.

But most didn't want to send their daughters back into the poison they'd been forced to live in. When you live in the shadows, you become good at hiding in them. Yes, we lost more than we ever dreamed possible to the demon that surged through the tower, but we also saved countless others."

Stone stepped forward then, the hope on his face a beautiful thing to see.

"How many? Where... I... Why did you never tell me?" he stammered.

Nathaniel wrapped him in his arms, a fatherly smile on his face. "You always were the best of them, Stone. You may not have been my son, but I always felt like you were. I would have told you in time. I didn't want to put you in any danger when your father was one of the worst we fought against. We were preparing for an uprising before all of this. We would have brought you into the fight when the time was right."

Stone buried his face in Nathaniel's shoulder and I watched as his shoulders heaved with his sobs. His hands bunched at the back of the other man's shirt as he sank into his pain and finally let it out into the world.

I hadn't realised that he'd kept all of this inside. He'd hidden it so far beneath his happy exterior, I wondered if he'd even realised the depths of his pain.

When his sobs slowed, he reluctantly pulled away from Nathaniel, swiping angrily at his eyes as he did.

"I won't fail you again," he swore. "It ends in Asgard. There's no other option. What happened here, at the pack, to the fae, to everyone in all the realms, it stops now."

Nathaniel beamed with pride as he watched Stone build himself back up, the fire burning in his eyes, one that I knew wouldn't easily be put out.

"The others are safely hidden?" I asked, and Nathaniel nodded in confirmation. "Then how long do you need to prepare to leave? We need to join with the others in the mountains of Asgard and plan our next move."

"There are others?" one of the other mages asked, stepping forward shyly with a look of relief on their face.

"Yeah, we're not in this alone. We'll march into Asgard with an army of the abused at our back. Every single one of them has a reason for revenge, and we're going to give it to them." I felt my mates move up to my back as I spoke and I leaned back into Tas' protective embrace.

They knew what it was like to feel loss. They knew what it was like to have someone take something they had no right to.

For the first time, I started to think that maybe we could actually do this. It had seemed so impossible before, but looking at everyone before me now, I saw their burning need for vengeance and I knew it lived inside every single person ready to stand up and fight back.

That had to mean something.

Everyone leapt into action again, pulling on heavy packs. Sparks of magic danced between people as they felt out the power they had to fight with.

Xanth and Drystan weren't here. I might have only known them for a brief period, but I already knew the pair of them would have been excited about the fight if they were. I could already imagine Xanth bouncing about in excitement.

If they were missing, it meant only one thing. Whatever task Frannie had given them was already happening. She'd said they'd find someone who needed them, and I hoped it was more than that. I hoped wherever they found themselves; it was with someone they needed too. It would be nice to have a happy story to think about whenever this place came back in my memory. For the thoughts of a hidden generation, safe from the madness, and a love story that spanned across realms to overtake the pain and the misery that had lingered in this place for so long.

Chapter 15

Britt

Xanth and Drystan had been on edge ever since they'd emerged from the trees last night. I could see a sadness warring inside Xanth every time he looked over at his friend. Drystan seemed to have shut down and was in the process of trying to push us all away. It was like he was preparing for rejection and I hated that this all felt like a familiar routine for him.

I wasn't an idiot. I knew it had been something the Norns had said. His attitude had changed so quickly when we were at the well. He went from the carefree man he'd been on our journey here to cold and closed off in the matter of seconds. And I had a feeling I knew what it was.

Dark one.

That's what she'd called him.

I'd felt Xanth stiffen in surprise as soon as the words so casually slipped through her lips. It was a knee jerk reaction to something he knew would cause his friend pain. And it had. Drystan had lashed out and walled himself away from the rest of us. From me.

And I wouldn't let him do it.

We'd had an awkward night around the fire. Xanth's sadness made this hurt even more as he'd watched his friend silently try to deal with his emotions on his own. If I had to guess, he'd tried to reason with him in the forest and Drystan hadn't been ready to accept his help.

But we were about to go to find a dragon to ask it to take us to the underworld so we could bargain with a bat-shit crazy goddess who seemed more likely to condemn us than help us. And we couldn't do that if we weren't strong. If our group was fractured, fighting our bond.

Drystan angrily snatched his pack from the ground, throwing it over one shoulder and turning his back on us.

I fucking hated this.

What we'd started was something special. And I wasn't prepared to lose that.

No.

I *refused* to lose it.

I was done losing everything in my life. I goddamn deserved some happiness for once.

"Put the pack down," I snapped.

Drystan's head whipped around as he looked at me in surprise. When he slowly dropped the bag to the ground, I was more relieved than anything because I was seconds away from ripping it off his shoulder and I didn't want this whole thing to turn into an argument.

"Now, both of you sit your asses down."

Xanth happily took a seat on the ground, leaning back on his hands as he watched in fascination. It was only Drystan who seemed like he would rebel. One eyebrow twitched up, and I just knew he was thinking about how far he could push me. But then, slowly, almost as if to prove the point that he was only doing it on his terms, he sat down.

Except now that I had their full attention, I had no idea what I should say to straighten this whole mess out.

So, of course, I paced. Every so often, a moment of inspiration would strike me and I'd stop, look at them, and chicken out. So the pacing continued instead.

"Erm, Britt..." Xanth started, as he shuffled uncomfortably.

"This is not acceptable!" I snapped, hating how I'd somehow adopted some kind of mom voice.

Drystan smirked at me, and I could see Xanth trying to hold back the laughter.

Yes, I was spiralling right now. But I didn't need them to laugh at me about it.

"You!" I waved an accusing finger at Drystan. "You don't get to do this. Not now, not ever, and especially not to Xanth. I... well, you don't know me, so maybe I don't matter..."

"Of course you matter," Drystan growled. He climbed to his feet and stalked closer to me. A darkness brewed in his eyes that I was sure would have had most people running for their lives. But it only made me sad for him. Because I could see his pain and I hated he was having to go through whatever this was. "You're the only thing that matters. I won't survive losing you, Britt. So it has to be this way. I'll break, but maybe there'll be enough pieces of me left to be of some use to you."

My mouth opened and closed, giving that attractive fish-like quality I was sure wouldn't have him dropping to his knees and confessing his love.

"I... I..." Sucking in a lungful of breath through my nose, I felt the fire inside me push that confusion to the side. "You. Are. So. Full. Of. Shit," I seethed.

He reared back, shocked by either the anger in my voice or my refusal to just accept what he was saying.

"Britt..." he said with a sigh. I could tell he was going to try to reason with me about why I shouldn't be around him, but I wouldn't give him a chance.

I'd had a taste of what life with Drystan could be like, and I refused to accept anything less.

"Are you my mate?" I demanded.

"Yes, but..."

"And am I some weak, pathetic creature who doesn't deserve to have an opinion and make her own choices in life?"

His eyes widened comically, and I didn't give him a chance to answer me.

"Or am I strong enough to stand by your side? Someone you can trust to have your back and support you when you need it, regardless of my sex?"

He practically deflated on the spot. "That's not what I'm saying, Britt. It's just safer for you if I'm not around. My magic is dangerous and I won't risk you. It was stupid to think otherwise and I'm sorry for letting you think..."

"I'm going to try not to be insulted here," Xanth cut in, his lighthearted tone completely at odds with how I felt like my chest was caving in on me right now. "I've been around you for years and not once did you think I needed to be saved from you."

Drystan cut a glare in Xanth's direction as he stood and slowly approached us. "You know why it has to be this way." He all but pleaded with his friend.

"No. I know the voices in your head that are telling you it needs to be this way. The ones that echo all the shit people have spouted at you over the years. I also know that they're wrong. Never! Not even once in all these years have you even made me feel unsafe, let alone hurt me. So why do you keep punishing yourself with this? Why are you so stuck in your own bullshit that you can't see how much you're hurting our mate with it?"

Drystan turned to me then, his eyes big and round as his gaze moved across my form. Part of me wanted to turn away. This was one of those things that society trained you to be ashamed of. But that wouldn't help him. It wouldn't make him see. So instead, I took a deep breath, and I sank into that feeling I usually tried to bury deep inside. I opened up the box and I let it out, the tears immediately welling in my eyes in response.

His arms banded around me as he pressed his face into my hair. I could feel the tremor running through his body. As Xanth's arms came around him from behind, meeting in the small of my back, as we sandwiched Drystan between us.

"I hate it," Drystan whispered as he clung to me even harder. "It takes everything from me. I don't want to live like this anymore."

Xanth pulled us all closer together and as Drystan's knees seemed to fail him, we all sank to the floor together in one collective embrace.

I knew how it felt to feel like your life was a curse, not to see any possible way of escaping the inevitable. I didn't want Drystan to ever feel this way. But hurt and hatred ran deep inside a person. The scars it left on you were impossible to set down and walk away from. Even if you had people standing beside you telling you that none of it was true. Drystan was the only person who could save himself from the pain that his past had left him with. We could show him the way to the light, but it would be up to him if he chose to walk toward it.

"You don't have to," I told him gently. "You can choose to live a new life, with me, with Xanth. Nothing about you could ever be wrong or dirty. You gave me a glimpse of the man you truly are, and I refuse to accept any difference."

At first he didn't speak. I listened to his soft gasps of breath, praying that he'd give us a chance. It went on for long enough that I started to think this was the beginning of the end. That he was getting ready to say goodbye.

"My magic... it's... it's wrong," he finally said.

"No, it's not," Xanth told him. The force of his voice only

confirmed how much he believed what he was saying. "There is nothing wrong with what you can do. Just because evil men in the world have tried to subjugate and kill to possess it doesn't mean that you are like them. Your power is a part of you, Drystan. And I don't see how it could ever be considered wrong, just because of that one simple fact."

Drystan finally lifted his head, and his watery eyes met mine. I could tell by the look on his face that he wasn't ready to just accept the things that we were trying to tell him. But there was a glimmer of something in his eyes that made me think that maybe, for the first time, he was actually willing to consider it.

"I take," he finally said. "I drain power, I steal life, I take... everything. And then when it finally stops, I leave behind nothing but a desiccated husk that once held a life."

I knew he was trying to scare me. This was his final push to see if I'd run. Clearly, he didn't know me very well yet.

So I faced his confession, and I gave him one of my own.

"I died. I drifted away into nothingness and then, when my friend pulled me back, she left a part of me behind. My wolf is gone. That part of my soul was sheared away and never found a way back. I have a great cavernous hole inside myself and sometimes I want to fall into it and never find my way out again. Because it hurt so much. It felt so... wrong. I actually thought I was being punished at first. That it was my penance for refusing to join with a pack and be their mate, even though I knew they were not fated to be mine. That they were trying to force a bond on me so they could control me. But then I found you, Drystan. You and Xanth. And for the first time in what feels like a long time, that hole inside me feels smaller. And I can finally breathe again without hoping it's going to be the last breath I take. How could you ever believe that there's something wrong with you when you're everything to me?"

Xanth moved then. Sliding from Drystan's back so he

could get closer to me. The look of concern on his face would have been enough to break me if I hadn't been expecting it.

"Don't look at me like that," I whispered, turning back to Drystan so I could make sure he was really listening to what I was trying to say. "I'm not telling you this to make you feel sorry for me, or to compete against your pain. I'm telling you because I want you to understand how important you are. You're not some evil, dirty thing that was put in this world deserving to be forced out of it. You were put here to help a wretched, broken soul like mine find some peace. You're a part of me, Drystan. And I need you. Both of you. I don't know who's responsible for us being here or the way we are. Well, apart from one crazy Kitsuné who could see the possibilities the future could hold. But I believe there's a reason I lost my wolf, a reason you have the magic you hold. And it's not because we're being punished. It's because we have an impossible, no, an almost impossible, job to do. And we're uniquely qualified to do it. Drystan, if you and your magic were made to save me, to save the world, how could you ever think that it was anything but perfect?"

A tear slipped free of his dark lashes and slowly flowed down his cheek. He didn't even blink as he stared into my eyes, weighing the truth of my words and deciding just how much he'd let himself believe them.

"You truly believe that, don't you?"

"Of course I do." I hadn't realised it before, but as the words had flowed through my lips, I felt the rightness in them. There was a reason we were here, and it was to put right a terrible wrong that had happened across the realms. Even if that was the sole purpose of our existence, if we were fated to meet our end at the conclusion of it all, I had to admit it all seemed worthwhile. I'd been given a second chance at life. If the cost of that was to fight for the people I'd been forced to leave behind? Well, I'd be okay with that. But I'd be asking for something in return, because there was no way I'd accept that fate for the two men in front of me.

"Most people see nothing but evil when they see a necromancer," he grimly told me. And like a play being acted out in front of me, I imagined how terrible life would have been for a young Drystan when he realised what his magic was made for and experienced the reactions of others to it.

How many years had he witnessed the revulsion and fear in his community whenever they looked at him? I could understand how that would chip away at you over time. Making you believe maybe it was true if every single person you met told you exactly the same thing. That you were evil. Wrong. Didn't deserve to exist.

But now that ended. Because he had me and Xanth. And we wouldn't let them hurt him ever again.

Chapter 16

Xanth

I'd known Drystan for a long time—practically our entire lives. So I could see the change in him where no one else would have been able to.

For the first time in his life, he'd listened to someone say something positive to him. And he actually heard them. He didn't brush it to the side. Those voices from his past that haunted his mind hadn't drowned it out.

He heard her.

And he was going to let her save him.

Drystan's fingers entwined with Britt's as they walked a few steps ahead of me. I couldn't take my gaze away from their interlocked hands. It felt like a sign. There was no way we were through the worst of it. The task which had been laid at our feet would be one of the hardest things we'd ever done, and none of us had it easy to begin with. But suddenly, it didn't feel all that impossible.

We'd find a way.

We had to.

Because I wasn't ready for this to end and Drystan deserved a chance at a life where he finally understood that he was loved. He deserved to experience what it felt like to wake up in the morning and not wish the darkness had claimed him in his sleep.

"We should make camp here for the night," Drystan said, breaking the silence.

We'd spent the entire day walking around the base of the world tree. It was big enough that I was starting to think we could spend an entire year doing so and still not get back to where we started.

"Works for me," I told him gratefully, and shrugged the pack from my back.

It wasn't heavy, but the boring monotony of walking with nothing happening had made me irrationally tired.

"How are we going to know when we find the right place?" Britt sighed, throwing her bag down on the ground and sagged next to it. "If Nidhogg is entangled in the tree's roots, then surely that means he's underground. How do we know we haven't passed him?"

"I doubt the Norns would have sent us off without more instructions if they thought we'd stumble past where we needed to be," Drystan said as he stretched out his muscles. An audible crack rang out as he twisted his head to the side. "Knowing our luck, we'll surprise him when he's trying to take a shit and he'll hold it against us."

"Well, that's a lovely thought." Britt giggled, and the sound had my cock going harder than stone.

But Drystan was right. We'd no doubt stumble on the dragon at the most inconvenient moment if our past luck was anything to go by. Being buck naked with my cock in my hand wasn't exactly a position I wanted to be in if I was about to face a soul-sucking dragon down.

Drystan excused himself to get firewood, and I quickly stole his spot next to our mate, throwing an arm around her shoulders and pulling her against my side while I had the chance.

"Thank you," I told her earnestly.

She seemed surprised and looked up at me in question. "What for?"

"He's never felt accepted before. No one ever fought for him. It won't be easy. He's a stubborn ass and you'll probably have to keep beating him over the head before he remembers that he's loved. But I promise you he's worth it."

Britt turned her head to look out between the trees where Drystan had disappeared, and a soft smile curled across her lips. "I know he is."

It was a sweet moment, and I knew what I was about to say would ruin it. But I needed to say it, nevertheless.

"What you told us..."

"I'm okay," Britt quickly cut in. Before I could say anything else, she continued. "I know how it sounds, and I promise you I'm not trying to put your mind at rest. Strangely, I actually am okay at the minute. I meant what I said before. You and Drystan make that emptiness inside feel easier to bear. I was working on it with Geta before all this happened and... it doesn't feel so impossible anymore."

I tucked her under my chin and just held her. I couldn't imagine what it must feel like to lose such an important part of yourself. It would be worse than losing my magic. My magic was something I could do, and whilst it was still a part of me, it didn't have its own thoughts and feelings. I hadn't shared my body with another soul. She would have been one with her wolf for as long as she could remember, and now it had been torn away from her.

But there was something else that she'd mentioned when she was talking to Drystan, and I desperately wanted to talk to her about it.

"About the pack you mentioned..."

"You don't want to listen to my sad stories, Xanth." She sighed and burrowed herself against me, seeking comfort. "This entire realm isn't that great a place, really, is it? Makes you wonder if it's actually worth saving sometimes."

"Would you walk away if you had the chance? If you could give this task to another, would you?"

She thought about it for a moment and then eventually she shook her head. "No. I have to believe that there was a reason for everything that's happened to me up to this point. And going up against Odin might be terrifying, but at least it makes all the shit that we've been through seem almost worth it. If we can do this, if we can save them, maybe..."

I knew what she was trying to say, and I could understand the sentiment. I didn't know if I could ever agree, though. When I closed my eyes at night, I still heard the laughter of my sisters. I saw their smiles and those few brief happy moments we had as a family. I'm not sure any amount of good deeds could make the cost of losing them seem any less painful. They never had a chance to grow up, never fell in love and had their hearts broken. They never got to see the world or make enough stupid mistakes. It had all been stolen from them. The only motivation I could get from this whole thing was the chance for revenge. Maybe that made me a terrible man, but it was enough for me.

"What do you want to do when all this is over?" I asked her instead, not wanting to share the shame of my darkened heart when hers seemed so pure.

"I don't know. I always thought I'd spend the rest of my days in Valhalla, but now that the valkyrie are all gone... I'm not sure I have a place in this world anymore."

I clung to her tighter as a wave of fear rushed through me at the thought of her not being here. "You'll always have a place, Britt. We'll make sure of it."

"What do you want to do when all this is over?" she repeated the question back to me.

What did I want to do? She was right about not feeling like she had a place in the world. The mage library wasn't a place I wanted to go back to. It probably stood abandoned now, anyway. I doubted anyone would want to stay there after what we'd all witnessed. Not that there were many mages who had come through the other side of it all.

"Huh, I guess that's not such an easy question to answer," I admitted now that I was thinking about all the possibilities. "Nothing I can think of seems..."

"Good enough?" Britt suggested.

She was right. How did you admit you just wanted to have a quiet life away from the world when you had such a momentous task in front of you? It felt like we were supposed to declare that after we'd dealt with Odin, we'd set out and deal with the rest of the wrongs in the world. In reality, there was nothing I wanted to do less.

"I think I just want to live for a bit. Wake up wrapped up in you and Drystan. I want to feel the sun on my skin, eat because it tastes good and not because I'm starving. I want to laugh, to dance. To stare at the stars and dream up stories to tell our children. Then I want to fall into bed and lose myself in your touch before you fall asleep in my arms. And then do it all again in the morning."

"That sounds like an excellent plan," Drystan said from behind us.

We both turned to see him walking toward us with a pile of wood in his arms. Britt sighed at the sight, and the cocky smile that came to Drystan's face in response was the first glimpse of the future I wanted to have.

It didn't escape my notice that he hadn't said he was going to be there with us. Maybe it was enough that we wanted him to be. Besides, it would take us time to find this weapon and destroy Odin. We had time to wear him down.

"Do we have anything to eat? I can try to catch us something," Britt asked.

Her pack was nearly empty. She'd run out of Valhalla with little in terms of supplies, and we'd already had several meals while we'd been together. Hunting for food was probably a good idea while we had the option. We could reserve what little rations we had left for emergencies. But since Britt had confessed about the loss of her wolf, asking her to head out to hunt for us seemed too bitter of a pill to swallow.

"We're fine for now," Drystan told her, probably thinking the same thing I was. "We should probably take shifts to keep watch tonight. I don't like how quiet it is around here."

I hadn't noticed it until he spoke, but Drystan was right. Had it always been like this? There was no birdsong, not even the rustle of leaves in the wind.

Britt looked around us as she pulled some wrapped bundles from her pack. "It got like this in Valhalla sometimes, too. You get used to it."

A shiver of unease ran down my spine at her words. We all knew what had become of Valhalla and everyone in it.

"Was it always like that in Valhalla?" Drystan asked. His attention seemed to be over Britt's shoulder as he spoke. When I looked to see what had drawn his gaze, I spotted another patch of the black rot on the bark of the world tree.

Was it spreading? Just how bad was the problem? The Norns had told us that Odin was inadvertently responsible for the damage to the tree, but what if it was too late? What if killing him now wouldn't stop the damage that was already done? It didn't seem like the realms would survive the death of the world tree. So what would it mean for the rest of us?

"I don't know. I wasn't there for long, really. You think it could be another symptom of whatever damage Odin is causing?"

Drystan shrugged. This was so far outside of our experience that there was no way any of us had an answer to that question. We probably should have asked the Norns more questions, but at the time none had come to mind. It was hard to think calmly when someone told you the world was ending and the only way to stop it was to kill a god. Not any god, but the All Father. The god that all other gods feared. Oh, and did we mention that he'd gone insane as well?

Laughter suddenly bubbled up inside me, spewing out of my mouth as I clung to my stomach and let the ridiculousness of our situation sink in for a moment.

Britt and Drystan looked at me like I'd lost my mind. Britt's beautiful pouty lips parted in surprise and even grumpy ass Drystan, who still firmly felt sorry for himself, was trying to suppress a smile.

"We've got to kill an insane god that's possibly the strongest that ever existed," I wheezed. "And to do it we've... we've got to ride a dragon into Helheim, where we're probably going to lose our souls."

I was wheezing now as I tried to draw enough air into my lungs. My sides hurt and my arms were wrapped around my stomach like I could contain my sanity if I just held on long enough.

"Are you okay?" Britt asked, a soft laugh following the question. "I'm not really sure that any of those are actually funny."

Drystan barked out a laugh in response, and I felt like my insanity was catching.

"We're so fucked," Drystan suddenly blurted out, only to sit down on the ground and devolve into a fit of giggles that did nothing but make me laugh harder.

"Are you guys high? Did you snack on some mushrooms when I wasn't looking or something?"

Britt's smile lit up her beautiful face as she watched us laughing like we didn't have a care in the world. And that thought made me laugh all the harder.

But then she tensed, her head tipped to the side as she listened and her body seemed to coil, ready to spring into motion. The strange, hysterical joy of our situation fled from me as I reached for the sword at my hip, ready for whatever it was she'd realised was heading our way.

Drystan fell silent as quickly as I did. He raised to his feet, so he was crouching on the ground, prepared to leap in whatever direction she pointed him in. He didn't reach for his sword. Instead, the dark glow of his magic coated his hands and I knew he was ready. Drystan rarely ever reached for his magic. He hated it that much. But just the idea of a threat coming anywhere near our mate had him ready to fight with everything he had. It was a sentiment I could fully get behind. I just wished I could be as deadly as he could be.

Britt's hand reached over her shoulder, and she grasped her Katana, silently pulling it from her back as she slowly rose to stand. Her eyes searched the darkness between the trees before her and then she stilled, her gaze fixed on one spot ahead.

I strained trying to hear what she'd heard over our laughter, but there was nothing there. Considering that she didn't have her wolf any more, I couldn't understand how she'd been able to tell danger was nearby. Even so, there wasn't a single part of me that doubted she was right.

As Britt took a step forward, my hand snapped out unbidden to stop her. She raised an eyebrow in silent question, and I reluctantly pulled my arm away. Britt was an accomplished fighter. I knew she was. Trying to keep her behind me was probably insulting, considering the fighting skills she would have developed with the valkyrie would be far superior than mine. And yet, I still grit my teeth in dreaded anticipation as she took another step forward.

A rustle of leaves had me certain that something was about to happen, but if this was an attacker, they were terrible at it. They could have leapt when we'd least suspected it. Instead, they'd lingered out of sight. And now that they'd obviously been spotted, it was almost as if they were doubting what to do next.

"Wait, wait. I... I mean you no harm," a male voice called out from the shadows.

Britt tensed, but I didn't know if it was because she knew who this voice belonged to or if she was preparing to fight.

Drystan slowly drifted away from Britt, moving out to her side. I slowly mirrored his movements, even if moving further away from Britt felt so wrong. It made sense to spread ourselves out. It gave us the tactical advantage of being able to confront an attacker on three sides rather than clustered in front of them. I hated every second, though. It left Britt far more exposed than I was comfortable with.

Four men slowly emerged from the treeline and I nearly cursed aloud. We were outnumbered, but maybe with Drystan's magic we could still have the advantage. He would never forgive himself for using it on someone again though, even if it was in defence of his mate.

The guy in the middle raised his hands, and an uncertain smile crossed his lips. "I kind of thought you'd relax a bit when you sensed our wolves, Britt."

His words didn't really register until Britt slowly lowered her sword, but her eyes still moved between them warily. Then I realised what he'd said. These had to be men from her old pack. It wasn't exactly a comforting thought. Not when I knew that someone had tried to force her into a mating when she'd been a part of that pack. Either these men were involved, or they'd turned a blind eye when she'd needed help the most.

"Trent," Britt acknowledged. "What are you doing out here?"

The four men in front of us relaxed as soon as they knew she recognised them. Trent stepped closer, but the other three wisely stayed where they were, regarding Drystan and me with barely veiled suspicion.

"Aria and Kyle sent the pack to shelter with fae. They tasked us to round up some of the satellite packs and escort them to the new fae lands," Trent explained.

"That doesn't explain why you're here," Britt pointed out.

There was a creak of leather as her hand gripped her Katana tighter and Trent's eyes nervously moved between the three of us.

"I feel like I'm missing something here," he murmured instead of answering.

I pulled a dagger from the sheath at my back, letting my magic coat the blade as he spoke. Something didn't feel right.

"I need you to very clearly tell me why you're *here*," Britt told him slowly as her sword raised again and a panicked look flashed across Trent's eyes.

"We didn't want Aria and the others to fight when we couldn't be there to support them. We're pack. Pack is supposed to stay together. So we figured after we did the job we were supposed to, maybe... we'd try to follow them." He sounded nervous as he spoke, but the sheepish look at his admission had some of the tension draining out of my muscles.

He wasn't here to confront us. He was just nervous because we had caught him going against his alpha's instructions, even if he had technically followed them through.

Britt huffed out a breath of relief and poor Trent looked

like he was going to piss himself in relief. "Fucking hell, Britt. I really thought you were going to kill us there for a minute."

The three men at his back chuffed out nervous laughter, proving he hadn't been the only one who was starting to worry.

"It's good to see you, Britt," one of the others murmured as they drew closer.

"You too, Ellis." She turned back to Trent and gave him an uneasy smile. "It's been a tense time around here. Come and sit by the fire and we'll talk."

I pulled back on my magic, letting the amount that I'd called fade into the air before slipping the dagger back into the sheath at my back. Drystan seemed more reluctant to trust these men who had apparently just happened to stumble across us. His gaze moved to Britt, and the magic didn't fade from his hands until she gave him a nod. Even then, I could see his need to refuse.

The four shifters moved to the fire, and it soon became a situation of us sitting on one side and them on the other. They looked at Britt in confusion, no doubt not understanding her reluctance to trust them.

"Harrison, get the deer we brought down. We might as well eat while we talk," Trent said, and one of the men slipped back between the trees.

My stomach growled embarrassing loud at the thought of having something fresh to eat. Trent sent me a wry smile, but quickly turned his attention back to Britt. "Kyle is going to be pissed when he finds out that we've tagged along, but we won't let our pack face this fight alone. We moved the shifters to Thyellin and they're as protected as they can be. But we should be allowed to choose to fight if we want to."

"You don't have to persuade me," Britt told him as she pulled up her legs and rested her arms across her knees. "I'm not one of you anymore. I don't have any say in what you do."

"You'll always be pack, Britt," Trent said quietly, and she winced, but said nothing to correct him. "At least we can travel together now."

Britt shuffled uneasily, and I could tell that she didn't want to have to tell these men about her wolf. She shouldn't have to. It seemed deeply personal and I, for one, didn't think she owed them anything. From the sound of it, Aria had been the only one to stand up for her when a group of men had tried to force her to be their mate. All the other shifters would have a lot to answer to when we finally met up with them, as far as I was concerned.

"We aren't travelling to the same place as you, and trust me, you don't want to head to where we're going," Drystan told him dryly.

"O-kaaaay. So you're not joining the fight?" Trent clearly couldn't take a hint, and pushing us when we were clearly not his biggest fans wouldn't end well. "Odin has to be stopped. We heard what happened in Valhalla and it crushed Aria. This is the right thing to do."

And that was all it took for me to snap.

"What the fuck do you know about the right thing to do?" I seethed.

Chapter 17

Britt

Meeting other shifters before we reached Asgard wasn't something I'd considered. In fact, if I was honest with myself, I hadn't considered what it would be like seeing the pack again at all. I'd briefly had time in this realm after the Blood Moon battle, but I'd spent that with my grandmother and the Elites.

The worst part was that I hadn't considered what it would be like for my mates to face the pack after they knew some of the details of my past I didn't particularly like to think about.

"What the fuck do you know about the right thing to do?" Xanth suddenly yelled.

Trent reared back like he'd been slapped and I caught the subtle sound of Ellis' growl even though he was trying to hold it back.

The confusion on Trent's face hurt more than I thought it would.

I didn't know whether they'd been unaware of what had happened to me, or if it was just that they didn't think it was a big deal. I supposed it was common back then.

"You stood by and allowed a pack to attempt to force *our*

mate to mate with them," Xanth shouted at Trent. "And now you sit here expecting her to greet you with smiles and skip into a battle with you. I wouldn't trust you at my back, and I sure as fuck wouldn't fight to save your worthless hide."

Trent and his packmates leapt to their feet at his words, and Xanth and Drystan quickly followed. Blades were drawn and the dark glow of Drystan's magic coated his hands again.

And here I was, still sitting on the ground, hugging my knees like some kind of broken little girl.

"Will you stop your fucking posturing and sit your asses back down?" I snapped. "I'm tired. I just ran for my life after seeing all of my friends slaughtered and I'm being hunted by psychopathic, murdering angels. And *that's* not even the worst of my problems."

They, at least, had the decency to look embarrassed and if Trent hadn't taken that moment to wilt on the spot in defeat, I doubted any of them would have listened to me. But was it terrible that finally having someone, or two someones, fly into a fit of rage on my behalf over something that was done to me made me feel whole again? Aria had been the first to do it and then she'd given me so much more. Now, I had these two beautiful men, snarling at my side, ready to slaughter armies on my behalf—well, four shifters. It gave me the warm fuzzies, which was exactly what I needed when the weight of the world was trying to crush me again.

"He's right," Trent admitted, dropping to his knees on the ground, his head hanging low as he spoke.

No one else moved. Xanth and Drystan still looked ready to tear down the rest of the men in front of us and Ellis and Ian were looking around, unsure what to do. It was only when Harrison came back with the deer slung across his shoulders and looked at the scene in confusion that the tension seemed to break.

"Did I miss something?"

I didn't know what to say. Before, at the academy, I'd hated the situation I was in. Before Aria had stood up for me, there was a kind of reluctant acceptance that there was nothing I could do about it. Yes, I raged, and I pushed back against Isaac and his pack, but I never expected anyone to stand up for me. It just seemed so inevitable, even though it was so unbearably terrible.

Then Aria came and tore me out of a situation I was pretty sure would claim my sanity and then my life. She gave me a chance at a life I hadn't dared to dream of. Even when I died, she didn't give up on me. I owed her more than I could ever express. But why had I never expected any of my friends—the men I'd grown up with at the pack—to do the same?

"I'm sorry," Trent whispered, his voice breaking as he did. "We saw what was happening at the academy, and I suspected the truth, but I should have spoken to you. I should have... Fuck! I should have done something. But the four of us never stood a chance against Isaac, and I told myself that I was protecting *my* pack. It was just an excuse to turn a blind eye to the terrible things that were happening around us. We failed you, Britt. Our entire pack failed you, and there are no words that will ever make it right."

At first I didn't know what to say. It was an apology I'd never expected, even if it was an apology they desperately owed me. But I could also see the world through his eyes and the impossibleness of the situation.

"It's not okay, but you have nothing to apologise for." I didn't even realise the truth of it before the words were coming out of my mouth and from the grumbles of disagreement that came from Xanth and Dystan they weren't as willing to let the men in front of us off so easily. "We lived in a broken world for so long that we were starting to accept it as inevitable. It wasn't until Aria came into our lives and raged against the unfairness of it all that we even realised we'd reached the place we had. We have so many problems now. So much blood has been spilled and lives ended. It all feels so long ago now. And even though at the time it felt like the end of the world... Well, I think we've experienced enough death now to see the truth. There was nothing you could have done to change what was happening."

"That's not true," Ellis told me, and for a moment, the regret that shone in his eyes made me wonder if my suffering back then hadn't been as unnoticed as I'd assumed it had seemed. "Aria changed everything, and she was just one woman. If we'd wanted it enough, if we'd fought hard enough, we could have made a difference."

I laughed then, and it was only when I felt Xanth's arm wrap around my shoulders that I realised he and Drystan had finally returned to my side. I leaned into him, my hand reaching out to Drystan and entwining my fingers with his.

"Aria will never just be one woman."

They laughed because if there was ever a fact that had been so blatantly true; it was that one. I didn't have words to describe the amazing woman she was. I just hoped that when we reached the end of all this madness I'd be able to live up to half of the example she'd set.

We sank into a comfortable silence as the memories of what had happened to us over the last few months consumed us. The world as we knew it had changed. We stood on the precipice of something great. Failure might mean the end of everything, but I didn't see it as an option. How could it be when we had Aria and her Elites fighting for what was right? We wouldn't stop until we'd achieved our goal. We would be ceaseless in our revenge. And when the smoke cleared, and the world was bathed in the blood of our enemies, we'd raise a new world. One where girls didn't have to fear a pack claiming her against her will. It would be a world where everyone stood a chance to live the lives they wanted to, and if anything tried to stand in their way, the Elites would fight back the shadows for them.

And that was when I knew what I wanted to do. When I finally saw what I wanted the end of this whole thing to look like. The beginning of a dream started inside me and I knew without a shadow of a doubt that it was what I'd been made to do.

Trent nodded and even though I could see how much he wanted to argue with me, he didn't. He had given his apology, and in my own way, I'd accepted it. Well, I'd rejected it, but not in a bad way.

Harrison prepared a haunch of venison and cooked it over the fire we'd made earlier. Conversation was stilting at first, but eventually we fell into a mixture of reminiscing about our time at the pack as unruly pups and what Aria and her mates had been doing while I was gone.

I was worried about her, and I could tell that Trent was trying to downplay how the battles had left her. It was clear she was hurting. I wanted to go to my friend, to reassure her that everything would be okay. But before I could do that, I needed to find the weapon that would end this thing. It was the best thing I could do for everyone right now—find a way to slay a god.

"So where exactly are you heading?" Ian asked as he bit into the perfectly prepared venison.

"Heading out to search for a dragon that steals souls so it can take us to Helheim," Drystan grunted.

Oh good, we were on to the male posturing part of the evening.

Drystan and Xanth still glared at the four shifters I'd once been friends with. They were angry on my behalf, and I was kind of grateful that someone was. It was lifetimes ago for me and I didn't know if I had the energy to keep holding a grudge for my shitty past with everything we had in front of us. What was the point of wasting time on terrible memories when there was nothing you could do to change them? Aria and her mates had torn down that world and the men responsible for what had happened to me. Continuing to hate everyone connected to my past life seemed like more energy than I was prepared to expend right now.

"How are you intending to get into Asgard?" I asked, not waiting for them to comment about the journey we were about to go on and why we were doing it.

Trent shuffled awkwardly on the spot while Ian, Ellis and Harrison suddenly became very interested in their food.

"You don't know," Xanth realised.

"We were following their trail, but lost it at the base of the tree." Trent looked at the world tree behind us with wide questioning eyes. "We've been trailing around the base trying to pick up their scent again, but so far we can't find a trace of it."

Damn it. We couldn't take them with us. It was too dangerous and frankly, I just didn't want to. But that meant finding them a way into Asgard, and I had no clue how to do that. I wasn't even certain if I knew a way back into Valhalla at this stage.

I looked at Drystan and then at Xanth. They'd found a way through to the outskirts of Valhalla, but that had been Frannie's doing. Maybe they had some ideas, though.

"Don't look at me." Xanth shrugged. "We came through the portal when the Kitsuné's watch told us to. You're the one with the amulet."

"And the amulet leads you out, not in," I pointed out.

"It could still work for them," Drystan said with a frustrated sigh. "If they enter Valhalla through the tear, they could travel to Asgard that way."

"Valhalla is full of angels that will kill them as soon as they see them, and they don't know the way into Asgard from

Valhalla. Not to mention they'd still need to find a way up the tree," I pointed out.

As we bickered, the four shifters wilted more and more on the spot. It truly seemed like an impossible task, even if it was kind of noble that they wanted to be part of the battle to support their friends.

"The squirrels would know the way in," Xanth pointed out.

He was right. They would. But we had no way of contacting them.

"You hit the end of the trail and then just kept wandering, right?" Xanth asked Trent, who nodded in response. "I bet if you follow it back to where you lost them and wait it out, the squirrels will find you. How else did the others get up the tree?"

It was a sound idea. It was better than having them following us around. Worst-case scenario, they camped at the base of the tree for a while before heading home.

I could tell by the look on Trent's face that he didn't like the idea. It involved a lot of sitting around and it felt like he had something to prove, even if it was just to himself.

"It's the only idea we have," I told him quietly.

I could see his reluctance in the way his eyes moved between the three of us, gauging which would be more open to persuasion to let them accompany us. He wouldn't find it in Xanth or Drystan, who looked at the shifters like they could barely tolerate their presence. Nor would he find it with me. I might not hold the past against him, but I didn't want to be responsible for his life, either.

Maybe that made me a terrible person. Aria would have stood and fought for them. She never would have considered abandoning them in this place. I'd just have to keep telling myself it was the safest option. Perhaps that would assuage the guilt I was trying to ignore that built inside.

"We should get some rest," Harrison said, growing uncomfortable with the tension. "You no doubt have a long journey tomorrow and if we shift and run fast enough, we can probably make it back to where we lost their trail in a day and a half."

Trent mumbled some kind of agreement and we tried to get comfortable around the fire. The flames separated us and them. It was the stark reminder that the pack was no longer an option for me. I'd lost the very part of me that made it possible. Perhaps if I'd still had my wolf, I would have been more open to them staying with us. To seeing the possibility of strength in numbers. But that hole inside me echoed with a feeling of disinterest, and it was all I had for those I called family in my past life.

Chapter 18

Drystan

Britt's breaths had slowed to an even pace, indicating she'd finally slipped into sleep. She'd spent the last few hours tossing and turning and it was only when Xanth drew her close that she'd settled with his chest pillowing her head.

I'd chosen to take the first watch. I knew in reality I'd take the entire watch. There was no way I'd be sleeping, and I didn't want her to have to look at the men who'd done nothing to save her.

The shifters slept more peacefully than they deserved. Deep down, I knew they weren't entirely at fault for what had happened to Britt. I could even appreciate that there was probably little they could have done to prevent it. It wasn't wholly dissimilar to the uselessness we'd all felt back at the Mage Library as we watched our friends and family be dragged away. But still. They were there. And a part of me could never forgive them for that.

I definitely wouldn't trust them to watch our backs while we slept.

It wasn't like sleep came easily for me, anyway. Most

nights, the memories of everything I'd lost haunted me until I gave up trying to find the peace that sleep could bring.

I scanned the treeline for anything that could hide in the darkness. At least, the tree at our backs afforded us enough cover that we didn't have to be worried about being surrounded. Unfortunately, if an attack were sprung on us without warning, we'd quickly find ourselves pinned down with nowhere to go.

The angels had been off our trail for too long now. We might have rolled that dead angel back through the tear, but what if they could sense it, too? The hairs on the back of my neck stood on end as I surveyed the trees again and then the sky above us. It had been days. There was no way they'd just let us walk away.

I didn't know if it was the spiral of the thoughts running through my mind, or if I really did sense that there was something out there, but without drawing my eyes away from the treeline, I reached out to Xanth. Grabbing his foot, I gently shook it, not wanting to wake Britt if there wasn't a need to.

"Hmmm," Xanth mumbled. It took only a few seconds for him to snap into awareness.

"I think I should check the forest," I whispered to him. "Are you okay watching the camp while I go?"

He didn't answer, instead he gently slid out from beneath Britt. I was about to walk away when his hand snapped out and grabbed the back of my collar, hauling me back to him.

"What the?"

"That wasn't me saying yes," he hissed. "What's wrong? Did you hear something?"

Sometimes I forgot people needed things like explanations.

With a sigh, I turned back to him, even if taking my eyes away from the trees felt wrong. "It's nothing. I just... I have a weird feeling."

"Explain more," Xanth said, slipping into one of his rare serious moods.

"Don't you think it's strange that the angels haven't figured out where we are by now? It's not like they'd just let her walk away. We left those bodies so they know someone made it out." I felt like I needed to pace from the frustration bubbling away inside me. My body was practically vibrating with the need to move.

"But why now? What's made you so jumpy?" Xanth asked carefully.

"I was just thinking..."

"You're always thinking, Drystan. What's different this time?" Xanth asked as he grabbed my shoulders and turned me around to look at him.

It was only then that I realised I'd been staring out into the trees again. What was different? Yeah, I could get caught up on things at times, but why was this sudden urgent need taking hold of me now?

"Something isn't right," I muttered, answering my own question more than Xanth's.

But Xanth being Xanth, that was all that he needed. He didn't question if I'd lost my mind, even if I was firmly in that camp right now.

"Britt, sweetheart, I need you to wake up," he said, rushing to her side.

The words were barely out of his mouth before she was on her feet, her hand reaching for her sword.

Xanth moved through the shifters, gently waking them with a finger pressed to his mouth, indicating for them to remain quiet.

My eyes frantically searched our surroundings. I knew without a shadow of a doubt that something wasn't right, but I didn't know how to explain that to everyone without them looking at me like I was crazy in about two minutes.

The shifters climbed to their feet, acknowledging Xanth's insistence that they remain quiet. They clumsily pulled swords they didn't appear to have much experience with, yet it didn't stop them from fiercely staring out into the trees, ready for whatever was coming.

Except nothing came, and it didn't take long for them to look at each other in confusion.

Xanth was back at my side before I could let the doubt take solid root inside me. His hand clasped my shoulder in support. "Trust your magic," he told me. "Let it do what it's always wanted to do. Let it be free."

I reeled back from him. How could he say something like that? He knew what my magic could do. He'd seen the effects on the very few occasions I'd unleashed it to its full potential. Of all people, he should understand why I kept it locked down as tightly as possible.

My gaze moved to Britt. But instead of the look of abject terror that should have been on her face, there was nothing but a peaceful smile.

"It's okay, Drystan. You won't hurt me."

I shook my head before I even realised it and had no idea which denial had made me move. Of course, I'd never hurt her. Not consciously, at least. But surely they could see that was why I couldn't just let my magic free to cause havoc on the world?

She slowly moved to my side, reaching out for my hand as she entwined her fingers with mine. Xanth grasped my other hand, and I felt my heart race with panic.

"We do it together," Britt said.

I wanted to hold it back. I had no intention of doing what they said, but my magic had other ideas. It seeped out of me, slowly moving out across the grass at my feet even though I tried to hold it back.

Stepping back, I tried to pull my hands free of the two

most important people in my life, but both of them held firm. There was nothing but calm understanding on their faces, and it should have made me feel better. When a wave of power flooded out of me, I gritted my teeth, trying with every ounce of strength that I had in my body to claw it back inside. But it was free now, and had no intention of being contained.

"Breathe, Drystan. This magic is a part of you. Don't be afraid of it. Feel it. Make peace with it. It won't betray you or do anything you don't want it to," Xanth breathed like he knew what the fuck he was talking about.

Of course he didn't.

He might have been at my side for years, but he wasn't there through my childhood when everyone I touched died. He wasn't there when my own family looked at me like the monster I was because I couldn't stop the magic from clawing its way out of me when I slept.

As the power that I'd kept chained away inside of me slowly seeped into the world around me, the ground shook and we all stumbled from the sudden movement.

"What the fuck?" one of the shifters mumbled behind me.

"You should be running," I whispered, finally looking up and locking eyes with Britt.

I wouldn't survive hurting her. I couldn't live in a world without her in it. Not now that I'd had a taste of her love.

"There's nothing to run from," she told me as she moved closer, stepping beneath my arm and cuddling against my chest.

I held my arms out to the side, not daring to touch her. How could she not understand the seriousness of the situation we were in? Even the world around us could tell my magic had no place amongst it.

"Tell me what you can feel," Xanth demanded, moving closer, too.

I stared into his eyes, finding nothing but love and respect there. There was no sign of the fear he should have been feeling. No reflection of the emotion that tore at my insides.

But then, as the ground shook again, and we rode what felt like a ripple that waved across the surrounding grass, I realised one important fact. My magic hadn't permeated the ground of this place. It lay across the soil, reaching out and listening to the world around it.

And it wasn't my magic that was drawing this feeling to the front of my mind. It was my magic warning me of what lay beneath the ground. The thing that even it was afraid of. The power that had drawn it out of me, not to exact some kind of terrible price, but to protect me and those I'd come to care for.

"Death," I whispered. "There is nothing in this place but death."

Britt whirled around. At first I thought she was pulling away, and even though it had been what I wanted moments before, it still tore apart what little remained of the heart inside me.

"Run!" she yelled at the men from her old pack. "Run and don't come back. Follow Aria's trail for as far as you can and then stay by the base of the tree until the squirrels find you."

"You can't expect us to leave you here," Trent shouted at her, finally stepping up now that she had men who would fight to the death for her.

Well, it was too little too late. She was ours now and there was no way we'd let her go.

I bared my teeth without even realising, a growl echoing in my chest that seemed ridiculous considering that the man in front of me contained the soul of a wolf. One of his eyebrows raised in surprise, but then rather than challenge me, he spun to his companions instead.

"You heard the lady. We're leaving."

The other three quickly grabbed their bags, heaving them

onto the shoulders and took off at a run toward the trees without question.

Trent looked back at Britt one more time. "You're sure about this?"

She nodded grimly, giving him no words of parting, and he didn't wait for any. Turning in the direction his friends had gone, he ran and suddenly we were alone again.

Or at least alone with the creature who we hadn't even realised had slumbered beneath our feet the whole time we'd been here.

The ground shook again, and Xanth and I reached for Britt at the same time to keep her steady. A great rumble filled the air, but it didn't come from the groaning ground that was splitting at our feet, but the creature that was pushing itself to the surface.

I staggered back, dragging Britt with me as I did. The ground crumbled around our feet, and there was no way staying in one spot could end well for us. But with the world tree behind us, we didn't have anywhere to retreat to.

My eyes widened in horror as the grass suddenly exploded upward and a great scaled head surged into the air. Obsidian scales glinted in the sun as the dragon turned toward us, its eyes squinting as it focused on us backing up against the tree.

"Who dares disturb my sleep?" it grumbled.

I felt the great tree at our back quiver from the vibrations that ran through the ground as the dragon pulled its body to the surface. And for the first time since we'd arrived on the ground, I laid my hand against the bark of the trunk.

I felt it then. The rot that was setting in. The yearning ache of the tree as the energy that fuelled it was slowly being leached away.

Tearing my hand away in shock, I rubbed my fingers together, trying to dispel the sensation. The wrongness of the whole thing. The world tree was dying. We already knew that.

But it was suffering too. And that was something I didn't think any of us had realised.

"I did," I mumbled, still staring at my fingers in confusion. "I woke you."

Xanth's head snapped in my direction as he looked at me with wide, astonished eyes. I couldn't blame him exactly. This was one pissed off dragon and when I looked up and locked eyes with it, I could already see why. I could see the same pain that wracked through the world tree reflected in its eyes.

"I didn't mean to. I think our magic has some similarities, and they were drawn to each other."

The dragon exhaled a stream of steam from its nostrils as it dipped its head, moving closer to us. I didn't dare look away. The need to check on the others felt like claws dragging across my mind, but I knew taking my eyes off the predator in front of me was a mistake. At least, until he'd decided if he'd accept my reason for disturbing him.

I could feel a huff of his breath race across my skin before the dragon finally spoke. "You command the magic of life," he stated.

And my mind froze.

I'd never looked at it that way. I'd only ever seen the death that came when I pulled the life force from another, whether or not I'd intended to do so.

"I... suppose so."

The dragon cocked its head to the side as it stared at me. "You don't know your own nature."

"I know I take the lives of the people around me, sometimes when I don't even mean to."

The dragon nodded. "You lack control. It will come with time. If I allow you to live, that is."

If it was possible, the dragon smirked at me and then turned to my friends. I stepped in front of Britt without even considering the risk to myself. All I could see was her standing in front of a dragon who could swallow us whole and it was never a situation I wanted my mate to be in.

The dragon looked at me curiously, squinting again in annoyance. This probably wasn't the best way to convince him not to eat us.

"We need your help," Britt said, stepping around me as she addressed the dragon. "The Norns sent us to find you. We need passage to Helheim, and they think you can assist us."

The dragon snorted a laugh and the sulphur on his breath was a stark reminder that this was a dragon we were facing down and there were so many ways he could end us.

"Helheim is a place for the dead and I am not some beast you can call to hitch a ride." The dragon snorted in disgust and Britt's mouth dropped open in shock. We hadn't considered that he might refuse.

The Norns had told us to find him, not that we'd have to convince him that helping us was the right thing to do.

"We seek passage to Helheim so that we can petition Hel for the raven's claw," Britt forged ahead.

"You seek the god killer?" At least we had his attention. The problem was we didn't know if he would be in favour of us killing Odin or if this was signing our own death warrants. "Hel will not be easily parted from her favourite pets."

Chapter 19

Britt

I needed to think. Things were moving faster than I'd expected, and it hadn't occurred to me that getting Nidhogg to agree to help us would be this difficult.

The dragon appeared to have some kind of mutual respect for Drystan's magic, but that didn't feel like the right way to go in this situation. Drystan barely tolerated his magic and after what the Norns had said to him, there was no way I would warp that to my advantage.

Drystan needed to see that people weren't afraid of him, but he also needed to realise that whatever power he held was his to control, and we wouldn't try to use him as a weapon, either. It was a delicate line and when we were so new in our relationship, I wouldn't risk it all just because it felt like the easiest path.

"Yes, we seek a god killer," I said in as strong of a voice as I could muster, given that I stared down a dragon. "Odin's madness is killing everything, and he has to be stopped. This is the only way."

"The only way? So you have no other motivations?

Revenge has not taken root in your soul? Admit it. This quest you find yourself on is just an excuse to see the blood of your enemy stain the ground at your feet."

Nidhogg's eyes flashed silver and for a moment, it felt like he was inside my head. That he could see into the very essence of me and he was judging the weight of the rage that now lined my soul.

"They don't need to be mutually exclusive motivations," I said with a shrug of my shoulders.

There was no point in lying. I could already tell that he saw deep enough inside of me to see the truth.

The dragon snorted out a laugh, throwing his head back in mirth as he did, and I felt the breaths of relief heave out of Xanth and Drystan.

"I like you, little one. You have a fire inside you that will serve you well. And you'll need it. Hel will not want to relinquish what you seek. There will be a price to pay and it won't be one that you can easily agree to."

My mouth ran dry as he told me what I already knew. I'd witnessed Hel on the battlefield at the Blood Moon and I didn't hold out much hope that she was going to be easy to deal with. In fact, she seemed to despise us all and I couldn't think of a single scenario where she would actually help.

"There has to be something she wants," I muttered, more to myself than Nidhogg, but he answered me anyway.

"She wants what all gods want. Power. While she holds a god killer, she has that. None of the other gods would dare stand against her when she has the ability to end them. And because of that, she can do whatever she wishes. You'll need to offer her something of greater value to persuade her to part with it, and I doubt such an object exists."

Shit! Why hadn't we considered that? Obviously Hel wouldn't want to give us the weapon that assured her control over the other gods.

"There has to be a way," Xanth said, his brow furrowing in thought. "The Norns wouldn't have sent us to her if we didn't already have what we needed."

Drystan scoffed. He didn't trust the Norns, and I didn't quite understand why. I got that calling him the Dark One was a pretty shitty move. But the level of distrust he had for them had to come from something else. It was a level of hatred that needed time to brew deep inside a person. Not that I'd ever judge him for it. We'd all been dealt a pretty crap hand in life and it was going to take time for us to talk through it. I just hoped that he'd come to see me as someone he could lean on when he was finally ready to talk.

"But we don't exactly have anything," I pointed out, not drawing attention to Drystan's sudden change in mood. If brooding was what he needed, I could deal with it.

It was then that I realised we were essentially chatting with a dragon whose main role was to drag souls to the underworld, and I started to question the sanity of the whole situation. Not to mention the fact that Nidhogg hadn't exactly agreed to take us yet.

As I turned to look at the dragon, who now seemed to be patiently waiting for us to decide what we were going to do, I realised he seemed more like he was about to fall asleep than drag us anywhere. My gaze moved across his dark scales, taking in the dull gleam and the bare patches where his scales seemed to have shed, leaving angry sores behind. His glazed eyes were red with veins and he squinted at me in annoyance when he realised I was staring at him.

"Something you'd like to say, human?"

The label had me rearing back in shock, mostly because I realised he was right. I couldn't call myself a shifter anymore. I'd lost my wolf and all that remained was the human side of my soul. It was a fresh wave of grief that I hadn't even realised I should have been expecting.

For a moment, a flicker of regret seemed to pass through his gaze before he resorted to raising his lip in a half hearted snarl instead.

"You're sick," I realised aloud. "Is it because of the world tree? You live in the roots, right?"

Nidhogg snorted a cloud of smoke but then tucked his legs beneath him as he laid on the ground with a huff. "I have slumbered in the roots for millennia, only rising to drag the unwilling to Helheim, and never has Yggdrasil turned against me until now."

We all glanced at the world tree, its shining patch of black rot gleaming in the early morning light, almost as if it wanted to make sure we knew exactly where the blame should lie.

"The tree is dying," Xanth said sadly. "Odin's madness is killing it, just like it's killing everything else."

Nidhogg sighed, and it seemed like a sound that held a thousand lifetimes of emotion. His massive head came to rest on the ground like he barely had the energy to hold it up anymore. "When Yggdrasil perishes, so too will I. We are eternally linked in life and in death."

"When Yggdrasil dies, everything dies," Drystan corrected him. "And it's why Odin needs to be stopped. Death comes to everything eventually, but not now, not on Odin's timeline. The realms deserve a chance. A chance to learn, to grow, to build new foundations over the tragedies of our past. We can't let this be the end. Not when we have the capacity to move on to something so much better."

It was possibly the most positive I'd ever heard Drystan sound, and clearly Xanth felt the same as he slung an arm around Drystan's shoulders with a dopey grin on his face.

But was the dream of a better future naïve to hope for? Did people really have the capacity to be better or would we just find new and devastating ways to subjugate the many to the benefit of the few? We'd all lost so much, and it was enough that rebuilding felt nearly impossible, especially in a single lifetime.

Nidhogg looked between the three of us, weighing his thoughts before finally speaking. "I will take you to Helheim to meet with Hel, but I make no guarantee that she will give you what you want or even set you free after you speak with her."

"Will you be okay?" It seemed laughable to be concerned about this massive beast being able to transport the three of us when we were so small by comparison. But I could see the glimmer of pain and exhaustion in his eyes, and I was worried about how much time he actually had left.

"I have lived for countless lifetimes. If this is to be the end of me, then so be it."

Nidhogg clambered up to his feet, swaying heavily before he seemed to shake it off. He dipped down on his front legs and with a flick of his head indicated for us to climb onto his back. It wasn't the easiest thing I'd ever done, especially while trying to avoid the sore patches of skin that shone through his missing scales.

Xanth jogged across to where we'd left the packs, passing them out and hauling himself up between Nidhogg's shoulder blades. He reached down and offered me a hand to help me up the last of the way. As I settled between Nidhogg's neck spikes, looking for how I'd stay on, Drystan moved behind me and leaned over my shoulder. Thankfully, the packs were nearly empty now, and he could press close against me.

"Hold here," he instructed, pointing to the two lines of smaller spikes which ran down either side of Nidhogg's neck spikes. They angled outward and offered more of a handle to hold on to, but I'd been worried about hurting him to take hold of them myself. Nidhogg had lost enough scales, and I didn't want to contribute to the problem.

Drystan then reached past me, grabbing the spikes in front

of me and effectively caging me in between his arms. With Xanth seated in the row of neck spikes in front of me and Drystan making sure I had no way of slipping off the side, I felt secure enough not to worry when Nidhogg flared his wings out to the side.

I was strong enough to hold myself in place, and I wasn't exactly scared of heights, or flying, whichever it was that Xanth had been so terrified of when the squirrels helped us down the tree. But it felt nice to have someone care enough about my safety that they put my needs above their own. It was a foreign feeling for me, this acceptance to lean on someone other than myself.

And not one I was ready to risk, I realised.

"Maybe you two should stay behind," I quickly spluttered out before Nidhogg could set off. His massive head turned to look at us and he raised one scaly eyebrow in question, no doubt annoyed that we couldn't have had this conversation earlier.

"That's not going to happen, sweetheart. It's not even worth discussing for how unlikely it is that you're going to persuade us to leave your side," Xanth all but laughed.

"Yeah, do we look like the type of men that would leave you to take on all the risks on your own? If I'm being perfectly honest, it's taking everything in me not to throw you off the back of this dragon so we can do this without you. If I didn't think it was important that you were involved in whatever batshit crazy negotiations we're about to enter, your ass would already be sitting in the mud," Drystan scoffed.

Okay, that warm fuzzy feeling I'd been having a moment ago was quickly fading. Especially when Nidhogg snorted a laugh at Drystan.

"You realise I am a strong and capable woman, trained by the valkyrie and the phoenix general herself? I don't need to be left behind for the sake of saving my poor feminine soul. I am a warrior in my own right," I snapped.

Nidhogg turned away, almost like he was trying to give us the illusion of privacy. This probably wasn't the sort of conversation one was supposed to have whilst sitting on the back of a dragon ready to ride into the underworld.

I expected Xanth to be the one who turned around to convince me that I was seen. He was the people pleasing comic of our group. Even in the short time I'd known him, I could see how important it was to him that everyone was happy. Instead, it was Drystan whose hand raised to pinch my chin between two of his fingers and tip my head back so I'd meet his eyes.

"Never doubt that we know your strength. We will never make you cower in the shadows. You were born to fight in the light and we would be lucky men to stand at your side while you do it." His eyes blazed with the truth of his confession and it was impossible not to believe the words he spoke.

I didn't have time to respond. To tell him how his confidence in me was something I'd needed to hear when that voice inside my head told me all the ways I was lacking because Nidhogg was apparently done waiting for us to get our act together.

Climbing to his feet, the dragon flared his wings out to the side. I caught a soft eep of surprise from Xanth followed by a sigh of relief as the wings folded closer to the dragon's body.

We shouldn't have relaxed though. We should have been holding on for dear life. The one thing none of us had considered was the location of Helheim. And as I felt the dragon's muscles beneath me coil in preparation, I had a brief moment to wonder what was happening. But before I could open my mouth to say a thing, he dived headfirst into the hole he'd emerged from and Drystan suddenly flattened me to Nidhogg's back as the ground surged up around us.

With the sound of Xanth's muttered prayers drifting toward us, we dived deep into the darkness of the ground as Nidhogg snaked his way through blackened tunnels none of us could make out. I felt the brush of dirt tumbling onto my skin and then suddenly a rush of cold air blasted over me.

Drystan's grip around my body softened, but I didn't dare look up at first. Only the soft sound of wonder slipping through his lips had me glancing up in question. The sight I saw when I did took my breath away. Because Nidhogg might have been burrowing beneath the world tree to take us to Helheim, but an entire galaxy of shining stars shone around us. Nebulous dust clouds dripped from the tips of the world trees' roots into the void we'd somehow entered and as we looked around in wonder, it was almost like we were staring at the beginnings of a new world. At a universe that was in the process of being born.

"What is this place?" Xanth asked, reaching out almost as if he thought he'd be able to touch one of the stars that felt so far away and yet within reach at the same time.

"This is the place where all things come to be. The birthplace of every possibility and where the forgotten choices are left to linger." Nidhogg's voice rumbled beneath us and yet it seemed to come from every corner of the vast expanse we found ourselves in as well. "It is nothing, and it is everything. Soon to be the only evidence that life once existed if you can't complete your mission."

It was a sobering thought to have the fate of an entire world sitting on your shoulders. But then, it also wasn't. Because I wasn't in this alone. I had two men at my side that would support me through it all, and I knew without a shadow of a doubt that I had friends out there who were also fighting for everything we loved.

Yes, this was scary, and fuck me, did it feel impossible at

times. But as I stared at what looked like a world being born, I knew we couldn't let this be the end. Not when there was still so much I wanted to do with the second life I'd been gifted.

Chapter 20

Aria

Valhalla may have been decimated, but its people, its fighters, still lived. Leaving so soon after everything that had happened hadn't been easy, but Geta was already making arrangements and preparing for war. There would be no persuading the Valkyrie to sit this one out. It was personal now and some of them even seemed excited about that idea.

The next leg of our journey was too short to have time to worry about what we'd find. It was only as we approached Asgard that the thought of Odin having struck out at the rebellion entered my mind. Why hadn't I considered it before now? We hadn't heard from my father since before the angel attack. It wasn't completely unreasonable to assume the rebels were hit at the same time as the valkyrie.

"I'm going to scout ahead for the entrance and make sure we won't have any problems like last time," Braedon told us as he moved away from the group.

The other guys looked between themselves, and I knew they were discussing who would go with him via the bond. It didn't take long before Virion peeled away and followed Braedon into the trees.

The mountains towered above us, and the trees in this part of the forest partially covered the side of the mountain we were currently waiting to climb. It was a stark difference to how we'd approached it the last time. Moving across the open ground to the cave mouth wasn't something I'd quickly forget, and I doubted the others would either.

Thankfully, as we'd been told previously, the location of the entrance frequently changed and this new one at least afforded us some cover. To be honest, I'd have been okay with anywhere as long as it wasn't the same one where I'd shattered one of my wings. Definitely not something I wanted to do again anytime soon.

A shudder rippled down my spine just thinking about the pain of it all and the events that followed. So much blood. Always, so much blood.

Every move I made was always coated in the same thick, red shame.

How could I consider myself the hero in any story when it was always covered in so much death?

I felt a reassuring hand brush up my spine, and Kyle moved closer. His lips brushed across my ear. "I can feel how nervous you are. We're right here, Aria. We've always been right here. Lean on us and let us help shoulder the burden of these feelings you let crush you."

Sykes and Liam moved closer. Each of them reached for me, and for a change, I found myself reaching back.

Kyle was right that I'd been holding this inside. It wasn't that I didn't trust them with the pain I felt, or that I believed it made me weak. It was more that I didn't want to see *them* crushed beneath the weight of my feelings. They felt so overwhelming, so all-consuming, that I couldn't see past them at times. I didn't see how anyone could ever live with the weight of the guilt I felt for the things I'd done, the lives I'd taken.

"I'm going to be okay," I told them, knowing that the

smile I tried to give them didn't quite reach my eyes. "We just need to get through this, and once it's all behind us, we can build a life together. A life where we can make amends for the things we've done."

Sykes looked worried. He was like that more and more nowadays. He couldn't mask his concern anymore when he caught me in those weak moments, and it was bleeding into every second we had together now.

"Aria, you have nothing…"

"We're clear," Braedon announced as he emerged back through the trees. "But we should move fast before we lose this window."

I quickly moved toward him, hoping to escape the same conversation we seemed to always be having. The one about blame. The one they never seemed to understand.

God, I didn't know how they put up with me these days. Even I was bored of my attitude.

"Let's do this. The sooner we get in there, the quicker we find out how close we are to staging the attack. We need to loop my father in on the situation with Britt before they make a move, and make preparations to move the valkyries here."

Britt. I hoped she was doing okay. What Geta had told us back in Valhalla felt impossible, and yet it made so much sense. It should have been a relief. It should have been the opportunity I needed to take a step back and see that not everything was on my shoulders like it always felt.

But Britt deserved so much more than this. I knew what it felt like to have everyone look at you, expecting you to save the world. It wasn't something any one person should ever have to shoulder alone.

And that was why I needed to get to the base and make preparations as soon as possible.

Because I wouldn't let her do this on her own. I was going to build her an army and be at her side every step of the way.

I glanced back over my shoulder at my mates as I felt their concern radiate through the bond we shared. "It's going to be okay. We finish this fight for our friends, for our family, and at the end of it all, we're going to change the world."

For the first time since this whole thing had begun, I could feel a glimmer of the girl I'd once been. The one who saw the injustice in the world and decided she wanted to change it.

Virion looked around at the group of us and I could feel his and Braedon's confusion about what they'd walked back into. The thing was, it was the same thing we were always talking about. The same reassurances that I hadn't been ready to listen to when we were back at the pack house. But now that we were in Asgard, stepping back into what I hoped like hell was the final fight, maybe it was starting to sound right to me.

When Frannie had held me back that day, telling me that my role was done, I'd thought it made sense. If I was honest, the sense of relief was overwhelming, but all it had really done was give me time to think about the things I'd done. We might have had a victory in the battle of the blood moon, but it wasn't enough. It wasn't an end. And without seeing that something good had come from all the fighting, all it did was leave me wallowing in the blood I'd spilled.

But that could change now.

Yes, we had one more fight to survive. But it was a fight that would see us standing at the side of our friend and supporting her in ending the madness once and for all.

And maybe, just maybe, it would mean it had all been worthwhile.

Perhaps saving the world would make the dark shadows that crowded my soul feel a little less like a burden.

It had to. I couldn't let it be anything less.

"Well, at least this entrance is in the treeline," Braedon rambled, a feeling of unease flowing into our bond. "You don't want to see where the next one would have been. We should really get moving before we lose our chance of entering the camp the easy way."

"How did you know the entrance would be here, anyway?" Liam asked, peering up the side of the mountain where Braedon and Virion had just come from.

"The entrance moves to help keep it hidden. It appears random, but after a while you can see the pattern if you're looking for it. This is one of the easier locations and the next one would add another day's travel onto our journey," he warned.

"Personally, I always felt the chasm entrance was the most fun." My father's voice cut through the silent forest around us and my mates spun to find Thor watching us in amusement.

It was easy for the God to move silently in his own world, which was fortunate considering he headed the entire rebellion against Odin.

"Father, you're making sneaking up on us a habit."

"Perhaps if you studied entering the ether like you promised, then I wouldn't have the need to." He walked to my side, dropping a kiss on the top of my head, and I felt a warmth flow through my body.

I never thought I'd have a relationship with a parent. These brief moments where we pretended we were like any other family meant more than I could ever say. It was one more thing I was fighting for in the future, which felt so unsure right now. I wanted the chance to know him, to know my mother. For us to have the opportunity to work through the lifetime of memories we'd missed.

"Chasm?" Kyle asked, the subtle smile stretching across his lips at the show of fatherly love he'd never experienced himself as a child.

"There's a ravine in the mountain face about halfway up. The trick is to take it at a running jump and hit the entrance shoulder first, which is about twenty feet down." Thor grinned like he'd just explained a trip to a theme park rather than a jump to your death, and Kyle's alarm flowed down the bond to me.

"Perhaps we should get moving then," he muttered, rousing a chuckle from my father, even if my other mates were quick to agree with him.

Wings really came in handy when you had a life like mine.

We set off up the mountainside at a slow pace. Kyle and the others concentrated on our surroundings to ensure we didn't run into the same problem as last time.

I fell into step beside my father, content that he'd know before any of us if one of Odin's soldiers was heading our way.

"Your mother is waiting for you at the entrance," Thor said quietly. "She's eager to see you again."

I nodded, keeping my eyes cast to the ground like I was concentrating on where I stepped. It wasn't necessary. I could move silently through these trees with little effort, but I needed this brief moment to organise my feelings. Thankfully, my father was happy to give it to me rather than point out that I was clearly trying to buy myself some time.

It wasn't that I didn't want to see her. I would have left the magic realm to burn so I could save her from Odin's dungeon if that had been the cost. But, after everything, she hadn't reached out. She'd hidden at the rebellion camp with my father, and I hadn't heard a word from her since she'd been rescued. I understood. I did. She'd been through so much and even after we'd pulled her out, she could never truly escape the things that had happened to her. The absence of her wings was a constant reminder. But deep down, every passing day that she hadn't tried to contact me pressed down on that little girl hidden inside that was abandoned by her parents. And the whispers about how she wasn't wanted grew louder and louder.

Facing my mother would mean facing whether she wanted me in her life. And I was scared. Scared that she'd turn away. And, if I was completely honest with myself, scared that she wouldn't. Because then I'd have to prove that I was good enough. That everything she'd suffered through had been for something. And I didn't know if I was.

My father's hand slipped into mine, and he squeezed it gently. "Talk to me," he whispered as he slowed his steps and my mates pulled ahead, giving us the space to talk.

With a sigh, I finally pulled my gaze away from the ground. The understanding look on his face was reassuring. It didn't immediately make me want to run like it did whenever someone else tried the same with me. It felt different coming from him.

"How is she?" I asked, delaying what I really wanted to say and even though he no doubt knew it, he humoured me anyway.

"She's physically recovered. It took time to regain her strength and our doctors were able to remove the rest of the wing joints on her back, which had been causing her pain. We've talked a lot about what happened and I think she's working through the trauma of it as well as could be expected in our circumstances. She needs this war to end before she gets the chance to make any meaningful progress, though."

"I know how she feels," I muttered.

"She talks about you a lot," he told me and I winced. "She likes to daydream about what life will be like when this whole thing is over and a lot of those dreams include you."

"Really?" I couldn't hide the hope in my voice and the soft smile that broke across his lips was proof of it.

Thor wrapped an arm around my shoulders and drew us both to a stop. "She loves you fiercely, Aria. But she didn't want to stand in front of you as the broken woman she felt she was when she walked out of that cell. She wants to be strong for you. She wants to fight for you. Myra may not have her wings, but she is still the fierce Valkyrie she once was. And she wants you to be proud of her."

It was sobering to hear all your own fears being echoed back to you by a parental figure. Talk about realising they were still people, too.

"I think I need to speak with her," I said, realising aloud that my father was not the person I needed to persuade that Myra's fears were completely unfounded. Maybe if I could convince her, I'd finally believe it myself as well.

Looking up, I saw my mates standing at what was no doubt the entrance to the rebel hideout. It was nothing more than a slight depression in the cliff face, but I remembered with eerie clarity the last cliff face I'd flown into at top speed.

This should be traumatically fun, and wasn't that the damn story of my life!

Braedon locked eyes with me. A crooked smile touched his lips and then he stepped back, disappearing into the rock face behind him. The others followed until it was just me and my father staring at the rock in front of us.

"I fucking hate portals," I sighed before holding my breath and stepping into that wet, slippery feeling of magic. I wasn't quick enough to escape the amused laugh that burst from Thor before I did.

It always felt like an age of travelling through the nothingness when, in reality, I probably only took about six steps before I was emerging from the other side. I blinked my eyes at the surprising brightness of the cave on the other side, temporarily blinded as I did. It should have alarmed me to feel the sudden burst of anxious energy that flooded through the bond toward me. But it didn't surprise me to feel the concern of my mates when faced with my mother waiting for us as soon as we'd arrived.

What did surprise me, though, were the arms that were

thrown around me and the fierce embrace I found myself in. I was doing pretty well at holding myself together until I felt my father approach us from behind and wrap his family in his arms. I didn't know who started, but in the end, all three of us dissolved into tears as my mates silently moved away to give us the time we'd desperately needed together.

I soaked up the attention I'd spent my entire life dreaming about, but never believing would ever be real. Every fucked up situation, every hurt and pain faded into the past as I finally let myself be part of the family that fate had prevented me from having. I knew it would all come back again as soon as it was over, but the brief respite allowed my soul to finally breathe. It didn't feel so impossible anymore. The past was the past and even if we found a way to work through what had happened, it would always be a shadow of a memory that we couldn't escape. But with the potential of a future together, we at least had a chance to build something that would outshine it. We just had to make it through this final thing.

"I'm so sorry, my love. So sorry that I couldn't be enough to save you from all of this," my mother finally said as she pulled back enough to see my face.

I hated every tear on her face and all the reasons they were there. She didn't deserve the things that had happened to her. She shouldn't have had to hide her child away from the world just because one insane god determined that I shouldn't exist. But most of all, Myra didn't owe me a single apology, and it hurt me to see the same pain on her face that had plagued me all this time.

"You have nothing to be sorry for. None of this was your fault; was any of our faults. We're here because of one person only. Don't take on the responsibility of his actions. All that matters is that we're together now and we can finally be a family... if you want to be."

"Of course I want to, my sweet girl." Her hand came to my

cheek as she stared into my eyes and my heart felt like it would burst from the sheer presence of my mother alone. "I should have gone straight to you once I was free. But my wings... it took time to deal with the damage that was done to my body. It hadn't been easy to build my strength back and I'm ashamed to admit that my mind was just as broken as well."

Myra couldn't hold eye contact with me as her gaze cast to the ground under the weight of her confession. I could practically see the shame bearing down on her. She looked different from the last time I'd seen her. The image of her chained to the ground in that filthy cell still haunted me some nights. But I could see the weight and muscle she'd built back, and the healthy glow that had returned to her skin. Her dark hair held the same auburn shine that mine did and for the first time in my life, I could look at someone and see the proof of where I'd come from.

"You're allowed to take time to heal. It's what I've been trying to do as well," I admitted. "It's been difficult accepting the things I did."

Her head snapped up in surprise and she hauled me back against her chest as she clung to me tightly.

"Don't. I know the pain of taking the lives of your enemies. It's confusing to mourn for those you fought against, but it's because you have a kind soul and you see them for the people they were and not the faceless soldiers of your enemy. We might not like to admit it, but none of this is within our control. We're all just players in Odin's game and you're right when you say that the blame should lie solely with him. But I could have done more. I should have done more. This war started so quietly that we didn't even know we were fighting it at first. It came on the backs of gradual oppression and our friends and families disappearing in the dead of night. Whispers of rebellion weren't loud enough to be heard over the subtle ways we used to be controlled, and those who spoke the loudest were never seen again. By the time we realised what our lives had become, it seemed almost impossible to escape. We should have paid more attention, fought harder when we saw what was happening. This was never a fight which should have been laid at your feet. It was never your pain to take over. As your parents, our generation should have done the work to make sure the future held every possibility for you. Instead, we watched a madman set fire to the world and were too afraid of the smoke to put out the flames."

Thor clearly hated seeing his mate in pain and was quick to cut in. "We did what we could, my love. But if there is to be any fault, it should lie with me and my kind. We had the power to stop this when it started and yet we did nothing."

The three of us were alone now. The others had left to give us some privacy and without someone else entering the base at this exact moment; it seemed like I could finally get some answers to the questions I'd never dared voice before.

"Why didn't you stop him?" I asked, hating how accusatory it felt.

Thor sighed. His arms dropped from around me and for a moment, I feared I'd gone too far. I hadn't meant it to sound like I was accusing him of anything, but it was something I was sure I wouldn't be the only one questioning. How had we reached this point when there was supposed to be an entire world of gods here that could have stopped him? Were they really that apathetic with the fate of the rest of us?

"In the beginning, Odin ruled with a heavy fist, and he was harsh, but he was fair. We called him the All Father for a reason. There were few who did not respect him. When he started to lose his mind, we didn't see it at first. We may have doubted or questioned even if only to ourselves, but the answer was always the same, Odin would have a reason that we didn't yet understand. It was our complete trust in him that was our undoing. It started out small, even for me. I heard the whispers of my fellow gods going missing. Of punishments that seemed too harsh to be true. By the time we knew we had a problem, it was already too late. The god realm was already losing its magic with the doors sealing us away and there weren't enough of us with any real strength that had a chance of standing against him."

Thor sighed and walked over to the side of the cave, leaning back against the wall as my mother walked into his waiting arms. It was nice to watch them being so freely affectionate with each other. It would have been something they'd never had the chance to do when they were forbidden to be together.

I couldn't help but stare at Myra's back as she leaned into his chest, taking a moment to soak up the strength he was offering to her. There was no sight of the charred wing stubs now. The shirt she wore laid flush against the skin of her back. If you hadn't known she once had wings, you wouldn't be able to tell. I couldn't even fathom how that must feel for her. The loss was one I didn't know if I'd be able to bear, and I'd only had my wings for a matter of months as opposed to entire lifetimes.

"He has to have a weakness, something we can use to weaken him," I murmured, not really realising that my thoughts of loss had turned to ones of revenge so quickly.

When my mother turned to face me, it wasn't the sadness of her face that worried me; it was the defeat. They'd been fighting this war for so much longer than I had. Of course, they'd been through all the options time and time again, probably before I'd even been born.

"The only option we have is to face him and defeat him. Odin must die." The fierce tremor in her voice might have sounded like weakness to some, but I could tell just how much she needed this to happen.

We all did.

Everyone hiding inside this mountain had lost something or someone because of Odin. The entire realm was void of life because of his actions. If everything died and the realms collapsed, he'd go with it. So was it really so bad to end him before it happened and let everyone else survive? Given the plethora of crimes he'd committed against us all, I doubted the world would blame us. But the guilt I'd felt from the lives I'd taken all stemmed from questioning why I felt I had the right to end them. I knew it didn't make any sense. If I hadn't, they would have killed me, probably without even a second thought. Yet, it would always be something I'd find difficult to reconcile. That was the type of person I was.

So why was it so easy to imagine plunging a sword into Odin's chest and watching the light fade from his eyes? And what did it say about me that I knew without a doubt that I wouldn't regret it for a single second?

I was losing myself, and yet it felt so justified that it scared me. And maybe that was where Odin would win. Because even if we succeeded in removing him from this world, he would always hold some kind of power over us. He'd have changed us to be ever so slightly more like him and we were all willingly walking toward it.

Chapter 21

Britt

The sound of Nidhogg's claws scraping against the rock echoed around the cavern he'd landed in. Somewhere along the way, the newly birthed worlds gave way to dirt and rock and somehow we'd inexplicably ended up in this enormous cave.

Xanth and Drystan quickly slid off the dragon's back, and I followed straight into Drystan's waiting arms.

I looked around at the bleak cave, not quite understanding where exactly we were. Nidhogg had said he would take us to Helheim, but this wasn't what I'd pictured.

"Is this where you tell us there's no turning back?" Xanth joked, his voice eerily echoing around us like an ominous warning.

"You're far past that point, mage. You should have run when you first felt me rising like your friends did if you thought turning back would ever be an option."

Nidhogg's voice faded away as he left the cave in a sweep of wings without any further word.

"I guess we're here then," Drystan muttered. "Kind of thought he'd at least have some advice for us."

"Run." The quiet whisper of Nidhogg's voice reached us. "You never should have asked me to bring you here."

And then he was gone.

"Anyone else feeling like we might actually be fucked right about now?" Xanth joked again.

None of us laughed. I doubted we had it in us. I could feel the stillness in the air that had every inch of my being, screaming that something wasn't right here. There was the subtle smell of smoke in the air and my hand automatically raised to the hilt of my Katana as my gaze moved around the cave walls. As soon as I realised what I was doing, my hand stalled, and I ran my fingers across the breastplate I'd barely taken off since I'd found Geta's letter. She'd told me it would keep me safe and knowing that it had come from her had a level of comfort to it. It almost felt like if I looked over my shoulder, she'd be standing there with that confident smile on her face. The one that actually made me want to take on the world just for the fun of it.

The soft scrap of stone against stone was our first sign that we weren't alone. When the hulking figures peeled away from the stone face, I realised just how right Xanth actually was.

None of us moved. Indecision crashed around me as I watched the stone sentries pull themselves to standing. They had to be three times the size of a person and they resembled the demon we'd encountered back at the academy, except rather than a strange brittle looking fur covering its body, this one was made entirely out of stone.

The dark pools of energy that glistened where I'd expect it to have eyes squinted in intelligence as they regarded us.

How were we supposed to fight something made entirely from stone? Were we even supposed to fight? We'd come here to find Hel and negotiate for the ravens. Surely bursting in there, threatening her life and the life of her... subjects, wasn't the way to do it.

Or maybe it was.

I'd seen the craziness in the goddess' eyes when I first encountered her. Something about it made me think she'd maybe respect a show of bloodshed to gain her attention.

But this wasn't a fight we could win. Or at least I didn't think we could.

The dark glow of Drystan's magic coated his hands and as it sparked to light, one of the stone demons stepped closer with nothing but interest in its eyes.

"Tell them why we're here," I whispered to Drystan. He looked at me in confusion, so I explained. "It recognises your magic. It might listen to you."

He nodded in agreement, but there wasn't the sad acceptance in his eyes that I'd come to expect whenever his magic was the subject of conversation. He looked ready to fight, almost like he wasn't even questioning whether he wanted to use his magic. And this wasn't the first time I'd seen that look on his face. I realised I'd seen it before. Whenever he was having to fight for Xanth and me, he was ready to do whatever was necessary and he never seemed to question himself about it. He fell into the natural feel of his magic and I wished with all my heart that he could feel like that about it all the time.

"We need to speak with Hel," Drystan announced without a shred of doubt in his voice. His back pulled straight, and he confidently stepped ahead of us, facing down the two giant stone demons like it was nothing.

The glow of his magic cast light around the cave and he stood there like the powerful mage he was, unafraid of the monsters facing him down.

I could feel my heart slamming against my ribs in worry as both sides regarded the other with no outward sign of emotion. Xanth shuffled closer to my side and, for the first time since I'd met him, I felt the buzz of magic radiating from his body.

It was enough to break my attention, and I looked at him with interest. Xanth had been injured when we'd first met and wasn't in any condition to fight, let alone raise his magic, it seemed. But now there was definitely a subtle sign of something and I could feel a power starting to radiate from him.

He turned to me and gave me a cheeky wink before his attention was back on the two demons in front of us. Reluctantly, I did the same. Now wasn't the time to ask questions, and I was surprised that it hadn't been something I'd thought to ask before now. Maybe it was one of those questions you weren't supposed to ask, but Xanth was my mate and I didn't want him to think I wasn't interested in every single thing about him.

For a moment, a pit opened in my stomach because I hadn't done enough to get to know the cheeky man at my side. I immediately cast it from my mind. It might feel like we'd been together forever, but that was just the reassurance of the bond we shared. It had only been days, and we had all the time in the world to get to know each other later. I'd make sure of it.

Suddenly, the stone demon who'd stepped forward turned and pressed his hand against the cave wall behind him as the other moved away to the side. A crack rent the air and the ground shook as a gate etched into the wall in front of us. Stone crumbled to the floor as some kind of magic carved the image of an ornate gateway in what had once been blank stone.

The demon pressed both hands to the surface and then leaned his whole body into the wall, pushing as the wall split open, each gate swinging wide and revealing the extent of Helheim behind it.

All the breath left my lungs in shock at the strange and beautiful world in front of us. Helheim was so much more than I'd imagined. Carved from stone was a vast world that stretched further than my mind could fathom. Lights embedded into the roof of the cave glittered like stars casting blue light down on a rolling field of black grass dotted with glowing white flowers. Beyond the field was an entire city, some buildings carved into the walls of the cave and others sprouting from the ground itself.

It was impossible to take the whole thing in at once.

What I'd expected was nothingness, of blank arid expanses of tortured souls and raging pits of fire. But what we'd found instead was an entire civilisation. One that had built homes and roads, that had fields which looked like they grew strange crops I'd never seen before.

The stone demon walked through the grass, heading toward the city before us. It didn't say a word, but assuming that it was leading the way, we fell into step behind it. It wasn't difficult to realise where it was heading. Because whilst the city seemed to be built to follow the curve of the cave, the buildings which were built further from the walls were low, single story structures, almost like they didn't dare to stand taller than what could only be described as the palace that stood in the centre.

A palace that had no doubt been built for a goddess, and one that I hoped wasn't about to be the place where our journey came to a sudden and abrupt bloody end.

As we walked through the city, there wasn't a single sign of life. Yet, it didn't feel deserted. There was something about the way the air shifted that made me feel like there had once been life here, even if I couldn't see it. Were they hiding? How could they have possibly cleared out all these buildings in the space of time it had taken for us to step off Nidhogg's back to now? It wouldn't be possible.

So if they weren't hiding from us, what were they hiding from?

The palace loomed in front of us, its doors hanging open.

That same pale blue light that shone from the ceiling of the cave illuminated the inside. It's cold radiance didn't feel welcoming at all. It felt like a cold warning of what we could expect inside. It reminded me of the pale goddess who'd looked down at us on the battlefield and decided we were nothing but worms to her.

Stepping onto the steps that led up to the door, the stone beneath our feet turned to black marble polished to a high sheen. Even the doors were made from the same material.

The stone demon waited at the bottom of the steps, one hand pointing toward the door as he gestured for us to go inside. His reluctance to step through first didn't exactly fill me with confidence.

Drystan and Xanth either didn't hold the same reservations or had already realised that there was no alternative path for us. We'd come here for one thing, and it lay inside this creepy, cold palace. Turning away now wasn't an option, no matter how sensible it might seem.

With a sigh, I followed them further up the steps and through the already open door. We came into a long corridor. The blue light I'd seen from the doorway appeared to be coming from another set of doors at the end. There were no other doors, no other ways to turn, just the one long corridor leading to the light at the end. No wonder we didn't need an escort.

Xanth glanced back over his shoulder and when he saw me standing in the doorway, held out his hand. Taking it felt as natural as breathing and a warmth flooded through our emerging bond that felt like a reassuring hug.

He squeezed my hand as I slipped it in his, before turning and following Drystan deeper into the palace.

Part of me wondered if I should take the lead. If I should be the one making a show of strength since it seemed I'd be the one asking for the raven claw which Hel was unlikely to part with. Getting my mate to ask on my behalf felt weak, and she wasn't the type of person who would respect that sort of thing. But I didn't have it in me to stop Drystan and call him back. He strode so confidently to our assumed destination that all I wanted to do was follow.

We stepped through the second set of doors, and the cold light clouded my vision. Clasping Xanth's hand, I continued walking on, giving no sign of my sudden blindness and the unease it filled me with. It was like walking into the lion's den with a pork chop tied around my neck, although from what I'd already seen of Hel, being eaten might not be the worst possible scenario right now.

The sound of our footsteps echoed around us and, with each one, my vision slowly cleared a little more. It didn't take long for me to make out the dais and the monstrosity of a throne sitting atop it. Okay, in reality, it wasn't that bad. A substance that looked like black glass was ornately sculpted to resemble flames erupting out of the ground. Cradled between them, looking like an avenging ghostly mirage, was Hel, and from the look on her face she wasn't pleased to see us, but she was excited about something. Unfortunately for us, I had a growing suspicion it was from all the ways she planned to fuck with us, and the growing smile on her face screamed how much she'd enjoy it.

The men on either side of me didn't make a sound. Their steps drew them closer to my sides, and I knew they were preparing to shield me in whatever way they could. I doubted it would do us any good, but the sentiment was appreciated even if I had no intention of cowering behind them.

My gaze darted around the room, looking at the potential angles this could go wrong. Considering the size of the palace and the vast hall we'd walked into, it was strange that it also appeared absolutely devoid of life.

Except, no. The creak of metal drew my gaze up to the ceiling, only to find two metal cages hanging there. They'd been spaced far enough apart that the occupants shouldn't have been able to touch, but somehow they'd swung close enough together for one of them to wrap an arm through the other's bars. The shadows collecting in the vaulted ceiling hid the occupants from view, and I knew better than to let my attention linger on them. Especially when that brief glimpse of a person inside had my heart surging against my rib cage and a feeling growing in my chest that made me certain I didn't want any harm to come to those inside.

Because they were... mine.

The sensation of panic built inside me then. There was nothing about this situation which was an advantage to us. Even with the plan I'd cooked up involving what I'd thought could be the ultimate bargaining chip, I didn't see any way to sway Hel to give us everything we wanted. And if I faced a choice between the raven's claw and the occupants of those cages, I didn't know if I had the stomach to hold true to saving the world.

If I chose a man I'd never even met over the entire world, what did that say about me? And how did that not make me just as bad as the god I'd sworn to destroy?

Before I had time to consider what I was about to do, I was already at the bottom of the dais and staring up into the face of Hel. Her skin was so pale that the blue of her veins almost glowed through. Painfully thin, she looked half-starved, with sunken cheeks and dark shadows collecting around her eyes. In fact, the more I stared up at her, the more changes I noted. Hel looked ill and now I couldn't help but wonder if her decline had started before that day on the battlefield. Her half-starved appearance and the strange emptiness of Helheim had me wondering if perhaps more was happening here than anyone else was aware of.

I opened my mouth to speak and then suddenly realised I

had no idea what the respectful way was to address a goddess and there was no way starting off by insulting her would win us any favours.

Instead of any words, a strange squeak left my throat and the corner of Hel's lips ticked up in amusement.

"I see you find yourself struck down by the awe of my presence." Hel's pale lips curled up in a satisfied smile as her eyes darted between the three of us. "Walking into my realm is not something many have dared to do."

Drystan dropped to one knee, pulling me down with him. He dipped his head respectfully and even though it turned my stomach to do it; I copied his movement.

The woman in front of me considered the entire realm beneath her. None of us were worthy of her time or attention and definitely not her compassion.

And here we were to ask for her help.

What could possibly go wrong?

"It is hard for us mere mortals to stand in front of a goddess such as you," Drystan told her, and vomit immediately filled my mouth.

Damn, I couldn't do this.

"Of course it is. It's always hard to look at your greatest mistake and realise it will cost you your life."

Yeaaaaaah, this wasn't going that way. I had absolutely no intention of kneeling to this woman. If she was going to kill us anyway, then I'd rather die on my feet.

"Fuck this," I muttered, climbing back to my feet even if Xanth and Drystan's frantic hands tried to keep me down. "I'm not dying on my knees in front of someone like you."

Shockingly, Hel only smiled wider, leaning forward in her throne as she stared at me greedily. "Oh, I do love it when the worms start to squirm, thinking they can fight back."

The urge to reach for my sword was strong, but I at least had the smallest amount of common sense to hold back from that. Belligerent was definitely something I was happy with being. Some might even call it suicidal, but I wasn't about to invite her to kill me before I had the chance to at least say what we'd come here to say.

"The Norns have sent us to collect the raven's claw from you. You will give us the weapon and the ravens and allow us to leave Helheim so we can slay Odin."

There were two seconds where we stared into each other's eyes and every stupid decision I'd ever made flooded through my brain at once. Surprisingly, there weren't as many as you'd think.

Then Hel tipped back her head and laughed. She didn't have an evil genius laugh like I'd expected. It was one of those annoyingly tinkling sounds that drilled into your brain as it tried to claw a migraine to the surface.

"And why would I do that? Just because the Norns have sent you on this foolish quest doesn't mean I will give you what you want. The raven's claw is the only thing that protects me. I'm not about to give that up." The malice flaring in her eyes was almost as expected as the rejection. We already knew she wouldn't want to help us.

But then I took another look at how sick she seemed. This place was empty, abandoned, and that shouldn't be possible. It was an afterlife, and you didn't get to decide to move to a different one just because you didn't like it. The world didn't work that way and Hel didn't exactly seem like the type of person who would agree to it, even if it did.

"You will do it because despite the fact that you have the raven's claw, Odin is slowly killing you and you don't have the strength to stand against him, even if you have a god killer in your hand."

The slight widening of her eyes was the only sign that I was right, but I knew it still wouldn't be easy to sway her. She couldn't make us feel like we'd won. Hel would never be the type of person to roll over and admit weakness. In fact, I was pretty sure she'd rather wither away and die on her throne than give us the one thing that could save her.

No, we had to find a way to make it seem like she was winning. If she could save face, I had a feeling she'd give us the raven's claw to save her own hide. After all, she was used to thinking she was immortal, so this sickness had to be scaring her. Evidence that you weren't as invincible as you once thought was never an easy thing to look at.

"Or you could do it in return for a prize no other ruler of an underworld has ever claimed. Something like the soul of the All Father?"

Hel squinted in interest. Her mouth opened to say something, but she just inhaled and then quickly closed it again.

I had her; I knew I did.

But then she settled back on her throne and I knew she wouldn't let this slide quite as easily as I hoped. I'd made an error in judgement. I'd baited the hook with our biggest prize and she wasn't done negotiating yet.

I heard a soft scoff come from one of the cages above me and knew whoever it was up there had realised the same. I was nothing but a child playing at the games of gods and I was going to lose.

"I'm intrigued enough not to kill you immediately." Hel's hands steepled in front of her as she thought and my stupid heart had the nerve to actually hope this wasn't about to go horribly wrong. "My pets will show you to somewhere less comfortable while I consider your proposal."

That soft scoff from above turned into a vicious laugh, and Xanth and Drystan shuffled close enough that their arms pressed against mine. I wasn't about to hang out in my own little bird cage while Hel decided if she wanted to help us, but what choice did we have? She looked sick, weak even, but I wasn't foolish enough to think we'd be able to fight our way out of here. The only thing we could do was go along with what she wanted, and let her dictate what happened next so she felt in control enough that whatever happened was enough of a win for her.

The stone demons from before herded us away from the throne as Hel leaned her head on one hand, a look of complete boredom crossing her face. This was a problem. We couldn't linger in a prison waiting for her to find us interesting enough to play with. We didn't have that kind of time.

"Thank you," Xanth suddenly blurted out, dipping his head in reverence. "You will look magnificent on the throne of Asgard." And then he turned and confidently walked back toward the doors we'd entered through, leaving the rest of us, demons included, to pick up our pace so it didn't look like we were chasing after him.

What the fuck had he just done?!

Chapter 22

Xanth

We weren't taken far until the stone demon pushed us through a door entering into a surprisingly opulent suite of rooms. As soon as the door slammed behind us, the telltale click of a lock quickly followed. Drystan whirled to face me, his brow pinched in that adorable annoyed look I loved to put on his face.

"Have you lost your mind?" he whisper-yelled at me. "We're supposed to be taking a maniac off the throne, not replacing them with another one."

Britt looked white as a sheet as she stared at me with her mouth hanging open in surprise.

My gaze darted between the two of them, going from angry to shocked and almost questioned myself for a split second before the grin stretched across my lips instead.

"I think you'll find I'm getting us a god killer with the only thing that's going to entice a goddess to actually give us her playthings."

They were still looking at me like I was crazy and even though the urge to explain myself pressed against my mind; it flitted away just like most of my sane ideas did. The hanging silks in the corner of the room distracted me and I strode over with only one thought left in my mind—Britt would look incredible with these draped across her skin.

I heard Drystan sigh from behind me before his hand gripped my shoulder and whirled me around. "Concentrate!" he snapped. Grabbing both of my shoulders to hold me still as I tried to turn back to the bed hidden behind the silk.

"Xanth?" Britt's soft voice flowed over me and my gaze immediately snapped in her direction. "We need you to finish your thought."

"Gods crave power and what's more powerful than the throne of Asgard? Look at this place. It's empty. If I had to guess, I'd say Odin is fucking with her. She's probably pissed him off. But if Hel is stuck here, then it's a solid bet that the souls in Helheim are what fuel her magic. Even if they don't, then she must have some kind of connection to the realm itself if she rules over it. Odin's madness is feeding from everything. This place won't be any exception. She looks like crap, she's dying and she knows she is. What better way to screw him over than take his place?"

It made total sense to me. We had marched through an abandoned city. Hel wasn't the type of ruler to sit on a throne in an empty throne room. She'd want her sycophants at her beck and call. Even if she didn't, she'd at least want a show for whatever poor soul faced her wrath that week. And the two dudes hanging out in the cages clearly didn't count. She wasn't playing with them. She was already bored with them, otherwise she wouldn't have them hanging around out of sight, but close enough that they knew they'd never escape.

"That... actually makes sense," Drystan said almost reluctantly.

I'd try not to take it personally. I might get distracted by the shiny things in life, but I could have good ideas as well.

His grip on me loosened as he turned to Britt, probably to

talk it out. But as soon as I knew I was loose, I dived at that soft-looking bed to see if it had as much bounce as it looked like it did.

My ass hit the heavenly softness, and I giggled like a child.

If we were going to be stuck in this place for an undetermined length of time, I could think of something to keep us occupied.

When I looked up with a grin, Drystan and Britt were talking seriously about the Hel situation, totally oblivious to the naughty thoughts taking over my mind.

Or at least I thought they were.

Drystan's gaze darted to me. "Stop it."

Britt looked confused, and my grin stretched wider. "Stop what?" I asked, interrupting him before they could start talking more about the cages and who could be contained inside. It was pretty obvious when you thought about it. But it didn't matter right now. There was nothing we could do until Hel had fantasised enough about taking over Asgard so much that she'd throw that damn raven's claw at us and shove us out the door.

Ah greed, predictably motivating.

"You're being purposefully obtuse," he snarked.

"I don't know what you mean."

"Exactly."

"What is happening right now?" Britt interrupted, huffing in annoyance.

It just had me raising up on my knees on the soft mattress and licking my lips as my attention became firmly fixed on her.

"Xanth is bored... and horny," Drystan told her.

I didn't miss the little gasp of breath or the way her pupils dilated at the information. The little minx was more on board with my plan than Drystan's incessant need to talk over every single potential problem that could arise.

But then she shook her head like she was trying to talk some sense into herself.

"We can't do that," she suddenly gasped. "We don't know how long we're going to be here. Or if someone will walk in. They could be watching!"

Damn, she was just making this seem more and more like an excellent idea.

"You're only encouraging him." The sly smile on Drystan's face gave him away. I wasn't the only one who liked the sound of this.

"We could be here for days, or hours. Going over all the 'what ifs' again and again will only drive you mad. You need to loosen up. Relax. Let your body rest if you want to be ready for what could comes next. Overthinking will only end in making mistakes."

The fact that I was making so much sense right now should have been our first warning that something was amiss. But instead, all I could think about was how much I wanted them both. We had a bond forming between the three of us and we were heading toward a fight we might not even survive. We owed it to ourselves to take these small opportunities and bask in that bond. To intertwine ourselves closer together.

"Strengthening our bond will only make her stronger," I whispered, knowing Drystan wouldn't be able to resist.

I could already see the need taking him over. He was too far in his head, like always, listening to those voices that told him he wasn't good enough, that he couldn't have what he wanted. He needed this just as much as we did. Drystan needed to be reminded that he had everything he could ever possibly need at his fingertips if he'd only let himself be brave enough to reach out and embrace them.

I watched as his fingertips trailed across Britt's cheek before he cupped her chin and tipped her head back. Drystan's lips softly brushed against hers and she wilted against him at the barest of touches.

Watching them together was one of the hottest things I'd ever seen. Drystan and I had always had a strange relationship. He was the best friend I'd ever had, and I'd always found him attractive. I'd go as far to say the feelings I had for him were developing into something far more than friendship. But with the world falling down around us, I didn't know if it was something I should push for, or if waiting when the future was so uncertain would be an even bigger mistake.

Britt's hand came up to cup my cheek, and I found them both looking at me curiously.

"Kiss me, Xanth." Her words came out breathy and needy, and I didn't hesitate to pull her into my arms.

Her hands came up to tangle in my hair as she whimpered against my lips.

Damn, this woman was perfect, right down to the little noises she made.

Hooking my hands under her thighs, I picked her up and carried her over to the bed. Drystan followed in our wake and soon we were both joining her on either side.

Britt shifted up the bed, her eyes hooded with lust as she watched us stalk after her. Leaning down, I kissed her deeply, my hands trailing down her body as I did. As I pulled my lips away from hers, I gripped her chin, turning her head to Drystan, and he was immediately pressing his lips to hers.

My hands worked swiftly as I pulled the clothes from Britt's body. As my fingers moved to the last strap of the breastplate, they stalled. A hazy memory tickled at the back of my mind about something important to do with this piece of her armour, so instead of pulling it away from her body, I left it in place.

Drystan worked his way down her body, his hands running over her bare skin until he reached the waistband of her trousers. Peering up her body, he paused, seeking permission like we'd always promised we would.

As Britt bit her bottom lip and nodded, I felt my cock throb. She looked so fucking sexy, and as Drystan peeled the leather down her legs, the stark contrast of her creamy white skin against the dark armour of the breastplate made me want her even more.

Drystan threw her trousers over his shoulder, not pausing for a second before he was burying his face between her thighs. Britt's breath hitched, and she almost shot up the bed as he suddenly sucked her clit into his mouth, but Drystan's hands clamped around her thighs as he held her in place, then hauled her further onto his face.

He worshipped her pussy in a way that had Britt's eyes rolling back in her head, and I watched every expression of bliss that crossed her face with rapt attention. I'd never get enough of seeing her like this. Watching Drystan bring her to the precipice and then make his way to her thighs, kissing and sucking, leaving his mark behind before her whispered pleas had him returning to what she begged for the most.

Drystan's fingers slipped inside her sweet pussy, and Britt ground down on them. I knew she was desperate to come and it wouldn't be long if Drystan was going to let her this time.

Her fingers scrambled against the fastenings of my leathers as she frantically reached for my cock. I didn't need her to ask twice as I quickly shed my clothes and she wrapped her hand around my length. I wanted to sink between her lips, but I knew if she came with my cock in her throat I wouldn't be able to hold myself back and I had something else planned for us tonight.

"Get her nice and wet, Drystan," I told him. "I've got a very interesting idea I want to try."

Britt's eyes flared wide and when I looked down at

Drystan to see him staring up at me from between her legs, I cursed and nearly came there and then.

I saw the smirk on his face, knowing what he was doing. He rolled, picking Britt up at the waist and sat her straight on his face.

"Fuck," I cursed again as Britt looked down at Drystan in surprise. "Ride his face, sweetheart. Take what you want from him."

I wanted to lie back on the bed and watch. To memorise the way her thigh muscles flexed as her head tipped back in bliss. Drystan's fingers dug into her ass cheeks as he pulled her closer, his tongue moving across her clit as she worked herself against him.

My hand gripped my cock as I slowly worked myself over, watching the show they put on for me. My own personal fantasy in live action.

A desperation tore at my mind. A need that felt like it would never be fulfilled. I wanted a taste. I needed it. It was the only thing that could take me from this moment to the next. Without her, I truly thought I wouldn't be able to go on.

Magic banked around the room. The silks lifted on a breeze of power and none of us paid it any attention. It registered as strange somewhere inside my mind, but I dismissed it without a second thought, completely consumed by my need for the woman in our bed.

Britt came with a scream. She lost rhythm and only Drystan's grip on her ass, tugging her back and forth over his face, kept her moving.

I couldn't take it any more and I seized her around the hips, picking her straight up off him and throwing her back on the bed.

"My turn," I growled, sinking to my knees between her legs.

She was so wet that her come coated her perfect pussy and

dripped down her thighs. Drystan knelt on the bed at her hip as he watched me run my fingers through the mess he'd made. His cock bobbed level with my head and my mouth watered with need.

My brain misfired having both of them in front of me and not knowing which I wanted more.

"Clean her up, Xanth," Drystan ordered, making my toes curl. "Look at our mate. Overloaded with pleasure. Show her it's just the beginning."

I sank down into her pussy in relief. My tongue swiping through her juices as they coated my chin. She tasted like heaven. She tasted like a future that would be lived well and full of every pleasure we could ever imagine.

As I teased her sensitive clit, Drystan slipped off the bed and circled behind me. I felt his hands trail over the bare skin of my back and I shuddered. He ran his hands up my body, his fingers tracing across the muscles in my back like he was memorising them for the first time.

He'd never touched me like this before and when I felt his lips kiss the small of my back, it was my turn to whimper at the feeling.

"You're beautiful, Xanth. I always noticed you, watching me when you thought no one was looking."

He leaned against the backs of my thighs as his hands ran up over my shoulders. I could feel his hard cock nestled between my ass cheeks and it made me desperate for more. I doubled down on my efforts between Britt's legs, my face pressing into her flesh as I sucked her clit into my mouth, dipping two fingers inside her pussy as I did.

Peering up her body, I saw her watching intently as she gasped and moaned at the sensations I was pulling from her.

Her hips started to move as she rode my fingers, and I knew she was starting that climb to orgasm once more.

Drystan's hands trailed back down my body until he

gripped my waist and Britt licked her lips. This was no doubt what we'd look like if he took me. And from the way her pussy gripped my fingers she loved the idea.

Nearly as much as I did.

As his hand slipped underneath, I added a third finger to her pussy and the gasp from Britt's mouth was echoed by the moan from my own as Drystan finally gripped my cock in his hand.

My hips flew forward at the feeling, and I fucked his hand, desperate for his touch but also not wanting to come. He was getting me so close, just from a single touch. It was my desperation that pushed me to the edge, but I wanted to come inside my mate; I didn't want this to end so soon.

He dipped his head down to my ear, his body pressing against my back as he whispered in my ear. "How does it feel, Xanth?" His hips moved back and forth as he ran his cock through the crease of my ass. "Do you want to come?"

It took everything in me to shake my head no. "Not yet," I gasped, tearing my face away from Britt's beautiful pussy.

But the feeling of Drystan's body against mine, the way he gripped my cock so tightly, watching as I worked a fourth finger inside my mate, it was all nearly too much.

Britt's back bowed as I filled her. "Get her there," Drystan whispered. "I need you both, and I can't hold back much longer."

My tongue lashed out at her clit without mercy as I worked Britt up into a frenzy. I could already feel her thighs shaking and I knew she was seconds away from giving into the pleasure growing inside.

"So fucking beautiful," Drystan murmured as he pulled away and I felt his hands trail across my body again.

And then she came, shuddering and screaming, her head thrashing from side to side as I refused to relent on her clit, pounding my fingers mercilessly into her as her walls rippled against my digits.

I only stopped as she pleaded. "I can't. I can't take it anymore."

I couldn't wear her out. The best part was about to come.

The need still clawed at my mind to have her. It felt completely natural. I'd always wanted Britt. As soon as I'd seen her, I knew she was mine, and it was hell not to touch her whenever she was near. But something about the desperation that lined that need now was unlike anything I'd ever felt before.

"Do you feel strange?" I asked neither of them in particular.

"I feel like if I don't come soon my balls are going to explode," Drystan answered cheekily, his lips softly kissing my shoulder in a way that he never had before.

All concerns and worries left my mind as Drystan moved up the bed, lying down at Britt's side, and all I could focus on was what came next.

As Drystan laid back, I could already see the picture forming in my mind. Reaching out my hand to Britt, I smiled as she took it, her eyes glinting in question.

"I have a feeling that you know exactly what you want to happen right now," she told me, a grin breaking out across her lips.

"He does love to boss us around." Drystan laughed, his fingers trailing around the edge of the breastplate she still wore.

"So give us our orders," she sassed, her eyes glinting in challenge.

Damn, she really was perfect.

I guided her up to her knees and then helped her straddle Drystan's hips.

"Do you think you have it in you to ride him, sweetheart?" I asked.

She glanced at me over her shoulder, one eyebrow cocking up in question. But then she was sinking down on Drystan's cock, and her head tipped forward as he slowly filled her up.

It was so like the last time we'd been together, but there was going to be one big difference. I wanted to join in with them this time.

She set a slow pace, rising and swivelling her hips as she sank back down. Drystan's hands came to her hips as he helped her, both of them moaning at the sensation of being joined.

My hands came to her shoulders as I moved myself over Drystan's legs. "Lower yourself down," I told her gently, and she happily leaned forward. Drystan looked at me in question, and I grinned in response. "Do you think you can stay still?"

Britt hummed in confirmation, and then her lips met Drystan's and she kissed him slowly.

I could see his cock nestled inside her beautiful pussy and I ran my fingers through the wetness that had collected there before slowly pushing one finger inside her, trailing up his length as I did.

Britt gasped and then groaned in pleasure as I gently withdrew a little before pressing deeper inside.

"Fuck," Drystan swore, as I added a second finger. "That feels incredible."

"Do you think you can take more, sweetheart?" I asked, knowing exactly what I wanted but worrying about hurting her.

"Don't stop," she gasped. "I want... I want it all."

Her breathy words were music to my ears as I lined my cock up with her entrance, leaving one finger inside her to help with the initial sting.

I took a deep breath to make sure I had a tight rein on my

control and then slowly eased my cock inside. It was tighter than anything I'd ever experienced before and I could feel every ripple and quiver of her muscles, along with every detail of Drystan's cock.

It was the closest we'd ever been to each other, and it felt like everything I could ever want and more.

The urge to drive myself into her was nearly overwhelming, and I had a tight hold on my need to stop it from taking over. If we did this wrong, we'd hurt her and then we'd never get to do it again.

As soon as I was fully rooted inside her, we all panted in need and Britt squirmed, needing us to move.

"Be careful," I warned Drystan between gritted teeth. "Go slow to start."

He slowly drew himself out of her pussy, his cock dragging along my length as he did, and I nearly went cross-eyed at the feeling. Britt whimpered and moaned between us, helpless but to let us do all the work.

As Drystan pushed back inside, I carefully pulled back, and it was his turn to thrash his head from side to side as he mumbled words of encouragement.

None of us would last long like this. It was too good. It felt like it tugged at the very soul of me and I could feel my magic seeking the bond between us all.

"More," Britt pleaded. "I need you to... I want... harder," she gasped.

Her words fractured my control, and I shoved myself deep inside as her pussy clenched and rippled, like she was trying to hold me inside.

Drystan and I picked up the pace. Once we started, I didn't think we'd be able to stop. Our cries of ecstasy echoed around the room as we became nothing but the sensations we could pull from each other's bodies.

I could feel the sweat gathering in the small of my back as I desperately tried to stop myself from coming. My balls drew up so tight they burned with the need to explode. But I didn't want this to end. I never wanted to stop. I'd live in this moment feeling the both of them beneath me if I could.

Britt fell over the edge first. She came screaming and her pussy clenched down on me so hard that it was impossible not to follow. I could feel the twitch of Drystan's cock as he came deep inside her, too. His hands reached around us both as he grabbed my ass and pulled me deeper as he did.

The devastating relief of the orgasm that flowed through me made it impossible to breathe, to think. My entire existence boiled down to the pleasure that filled every inch of my body.

I didn't know how I ended up laying on my side on the bed, Britt pinned in an embrace between Drystan and I. We were all half asleep with exhaustion as we explored each other, dragging fingertips across overly sensitive skin as Drystan and I told Britt how incredible she was.

I could already feel that need clawing at the back of my mind again. As if she could feel it too, Britt's hips twitched and Drystan groaned as she must have brushed across his cock.

"Sleep first, and then we can let Xanth come up with some more good ideas," he joked and I could hear the same exhaustion in his voice that I felt, too.

Britt sleepily objected, but then her breaths evened out and she finally relented. My own exhausted body was the only reason I could ignore the need for her already growing inside me.

And as I drifted off to sleep, a thought at the back of my mind flared to life that I couldn't quite grasp hold of before I slipped into a dreamless sleep.

Chapter 23

Drystan

There were no windows in the room they'd locked us in and as my eyes fluttered open, I had no idea what had awoken me. I was pretty sure it hadn't been a sound, and it wasn't like the morning sun could have because there wasn't any sunlight here.

Britt's body pressed against mine and I knew without a shadow of a doubt that Xanth lay on her other side.

From the soft sound of their breathing, they were still asleep, but something had definitely disturbed me.

I stayed as still as I could, cursing myself for opening my eyes and not taking the time to listen before I did. I'd lost my element of surprise if someone was watching us, although, even now, I could tell that wasn't exactly what had troubled me.

Sitting up in the bed, I was certain we were still alone. This corner might have been obscured by the hanging silks, but they were sheer enough to give a glimpse of what lay on the other side, and it was the same empty room it had been when we'd fallen asleep.

I carefully slipped off the mattress and padded across to

the door, pressing my ear against the surface to listen for anything moving around outside. Part of me was tempted to try the handle and make sure it was actually locked, but I knew it was pointless. Even if it wasn't, those stone beasts we'd encountered on our way in would definitely be waiting outside. Hel wasn't stupid enough to risk us wandering around her realm. Not when she seemed to have so many secrets to hide.

What Xanth had said before made so much sense. She was visibly ill and for it to have reached a stage where even we could tell; I had a feeling she'd been weakening for some time. There had to be a way to use that to our advantage.

Britt stirred in the bed and I returned to her side, slipping under the covers again and basking in the heat of her skin against mine.

Xanth was a pushy little shit. I knew what he was doing; taking over to stop me from second guessing my choices when it came to her. I hated that it was actually working. It was a welcome break from listening to the voices screaming in my head and an opportunity to let go and finally feel something for a change.

There was still that lingering doubt that she would be better off without me. But as she rolled over and clung to me, her head resting on my chest as she let out a little sigh, I knew I'd never be able to let her go now. I'd never survive losing her. I wouldn't even want to. Britt would always be everything for me.

"You're thinking very loudly," she mumbled, not opening her eyes and trying to burrow deeper against me.

"I thought something woke me, but there's nothing here. You should go back to sleep and get some more rest."

It was the worst possible thing to say, and she suddenly snapped upright in bed.

"What was it? A noise? A presence?"

Gently gripping her shoulders, I attempted to pull her back into my arms, but she was having none of it as she tried to wriggle her way down off the bottom of the bed.

"It was nothing, Britt. Come back to bed."

"Why is our mate trying to escape? What did you do?" Xanth sleepily accused.

"I didn't do anything! I just told her that something woke me, but I already checked and..."

And now Xanth was doing the exact same thing Britt had, except there was definitely more flailing than wiggling going on.

"Did you check the door? The window?" he rushed out, grabbing his trousers as soon as he was free of the covers.

"There aren't any windows. And weren't you the one who was all 'let's relax, don't overthink the life and death situation we're currently in'?"

Being the calm one was a definite change for me, but maybe it helped that I'd already got up and decided there was nothing to worry about.

Xanth tripped as he quickly tried to shove his leg into his trousers and then hopped over to the door which he flattened himself against, one leg in his trousers and the other still trying to find its way inside. He was making more noise than a small elephant, and yet somehow he looked like he was convinced he knew what he was doing.

"Stealthy," I joked, and Britt snorted out a laugh before she could cover it.

As Xanth whipped around in outrage, falling back against the door as he did, he stuck his tongue out at me and then finally seemed to remember how to dress himself as he pulled the trousers up his leg.

"I can't believe we fell asleep. How long were we out for?" Britt asked.

Xanth started looking around the room for some way to

gauge the time, but there was nothing. The two of them were definitely acting weirdly, even if it was all kinds of amusing.

"What is going on with you two?" I leaned up in the bed to watch them closer and not because I was imagining what round two would be like.

Okay, maybe I was, but it was also the fact that the atmosphere in the room had definitely changed from earlier.

Xanth was struggling into his shirt in a way that made me think he needed a refresher lesson on how to dress himself, and Britt's gaze was darting around the room like she was just waiting for something to jump out and attack her. Periodically, her hand would dart for her breastplate, almost as if touching it gave her some kind of reassurance.

"Okay, stop," I said, getting out of bed as the concern built inside me, but neither of them paid any attention. "STOP!" I barked, and they both froze.

Something strange was going on, but why was it not affecting me, and had it affected us all before?

Britt's eyes were wide as she stared at me, and I hated the look on her face. It came far too close to fear, and that was one emotion I'd never be okay with her feeling.

"Take a breath and then think. How do you feel? What's making you feel like that? Something seems to be influencing you both?"

Britt opened her mouth as if she was about to object but then closed it again. Her brow furrowed in thought and she quickly pulled on the last of her clothes before spinning on the spot.

"Something..." she trailed off as she turned to look around the room again.

"... doesn't feel right," Xanth finished for her.

I carefully climbed off the bed and grabbed my own trousers. Confirmation was all I'd needed. There was definitely something off about this place. I wouldn't say that last night, or whenever it had been, wasn't incredible, but it wasn't exactly like us. This place wasn't safe, no matter how much it might feel like it was, and Xanth and I wouldn't put Britt in such a vulnerable position if we were in our right mind.

Someone had been playing with us. The question was how and where were they now?

A soft growl flowed from Xanth, and I saw a flash of his magic cross his eyes. He was nearly back in control. It had taken him longer than I thought it would. Coming here with only my magic as protection had been foolish, except we hadn't exactly had a choice. We hadn't done too badly so far, but once we had Xanth back at full power, we might stand a chance.

A soft laugh flowed through the room and I reached for Britt before I even thought about the fact that my magic blazed to life across my skin. I quickly snatched my hand away and Britt gave me a strange look before she pulled her sword and stepped fearlessly beside me.

For the first time in my life, I felt my magic recognise the person standing next to me. It didn't pull or surge. It didn't sense a weakness or a meal for the taking. If anything, it seemed to look outward, looking for threats to protect the mate at our side. Was this a result of the bond forming between us? Or had I finally wrestled my magic under control?

The sheen of magic in Xanth's eyes flickered and then faded away, but he still moved to Britt's other side, ready to fight. We should have brought him better weapons, or rather any weapons at all, not that he'd really know how to use them. Mages had become so reliant on magic that fighting with any other means had been frowned upon. Swords were nothing but collector's items in our society. The rarer the better, especially if it was enchanted. Hoarding power was what we'd done best, after all.

But until Xanth had fully recovered and had a chance for

his magic to recharge, he was more vulnerable than the rest of us. Whilst his physical injuries seemed to have healed more quickly than should have been possible, his magic was still taking its time. Maybe that was another thing this growing bond was helping along? We'd spent so many years being told that mages didn't have mates that I didn't think any of us fully understood how a completed bond would affect us. Or even how long it would take to complete.

But we didn't have a chance to think about forming bonds and recovering magic as the walls and furniture around us slowly faded away. The subtle scent of magic filled the air, and I cursed myself for not being more cautious in this place.

Slow clapping echoed around the large chamber we found ourselves in and as I turned toward the sound, the sight of the monstrous throne caught me with Hel smugly sitting atop.

The cages that had once been high above were lowered, and I got my first glimpse at the men sitting inside. Both were looking at us in disgust, their dark eyes filled with nothing but judgement. There was no way to know how long they'd been contained inside them, but from their dishevelled appearance and the gauntness that seemed to be starting in their features, I'd warrant this wasn't a new situation.

"Wonderful! What a show," Hel chirped, sitting back on the throne as she stared down at us and laughed. "I haven't seen such a show of emotion for millennia. It was quite delicious."

I realised then that the dark circles around her eyes were slightly lighter and the flushed look on her face wasn't just from the satisfaction of humiliating us. She'd somehow fed from having us perform in front of her. It was an affront to the mate bond to manipulate it like this for your own benefit, without the agreement of all the parties involved. Not even the gods were supposed to do such a thing. It took something rare and precious and sullied it.

Surprisingly, Britt didn't immediately leap into action and drive her sword through the goddess' chest like I would have expected her to do. I caught the tightening of her jaw as she ground her teeth to control her temper. But then she stepped forward. A false smile stretched across her lips that would have seemed genuine to anyone who didn't know her well. Dipping down into a bow at the base of the dais, Britt straightened and locked eyes with the goddess.

"I'm glad you could enjoy the show. Now, back to our negotiations. We will take the raven's claw *and* the two ravens." She dismissively flicked a hand toward the two waiting men in the cages, having come to the same conclusion as I had. "In exchange, you will be allowed the opportunity to take possession of Odin's soul when I end him. What happens to the throne of Asgard from then will be up to whoever is strong enough to seize it. That's what this was all about, right? A little snack to boost your reserves while you had the chance?"

Hel looked impressed, and I doubted it was a look that crossed her face often. She'd clearly played us, but from the way Britt acted it almost seemed like we'd been willing participants and that we weren't all reeling from how dirty the vindictive goddess above us had made us feel.

Unfortunately for us, she also didn't seem like she was done playing with us yet.

"That might seem like a fine bargain for you, but from where I'm sitting, I'm the only party assuming all the risk here. What happens if you fail? Odin will know I gave you the sword and I won't have a weapon to protect myself with... or my favourite pets to play with." She licked her lips and my stomach rolled at the insinuation.

I wasn't the only one disgusted by the thought if the rattle of cage bars was anything to go by. I didn't dare look at the two men again for fear that my real feelings would cross my face. The more we looked like we wanted to take them with us, the less Hel would want to part with them.

"True. But at least you won't look like some weak-ass fool sitting on your pretty throne in an empty realm as you slowly wither away." My magic surged to my hands as the words slipped through Britt's lips. This was an enormous risk. If we pissed Hel off enough, we wouldn't ever leave here, let alone with the raven's claw in our hands. "Right now, Odin sits in Asgard, thinking you're nothing but a worm beneath his feet. He's humiliated you and everyone in Asgard no doubt knows of your fate. They're *laughing* at you. You've become the cautionary tale of why you shouldn't cross the all powerful All Father. This gives you the opportunity to show him that not only are you not afraid of him, but you're stronger than him, too. It shows the rest of Asgard you're what it takes to be a true leader. And without assuming hardly any of the risk yourself."

Hel tipped her head to the side in thought. It was nearly victory enough to know we'd reached this far. I doubted many before us had done the same.

Movement to the side caught my attention, and I watched from the corner of the eye as one of the men in the cages sat back on his haunches. He looked across at the other and something passed between them as he subtly shook his head and then returned his gaze back to the group of us.

His shaggy dark hair fell over his eyes as he watched Britt negotiate with the madwoman in front of us. I couldn't tell if he was trying to hide his hope for us negotiating his freedom or if he truly was as disgusted about the thought of going with us as he seemed. The sneer on his lips as he looked Britt up and down made me want to stab him despite who he was. I, more than anyone, should know that appearances could be deceptive. Most saw the scar on my face as evidence of the wrongness of my soul. Like someone had marked me as a warning or because I'd been deserving of the treatment. Even if they found out the true cause, most seemed to think it had been done for a valid reason and not just because my own people could be the worst the world had ever seen.

"Fine, I will give you the raven's claw and one raven. I'll even allow you to choose." Hel grinned as she waved a dismissive hand at the cages, and a soft growl flowed from one of the men.

He needed to calm the fuck down or he was going to make this even harder than it already was.

"You know we need both. It isn't in your interest to set us up to fail," Britt pointed out.

"I'm also not about to give over the only two souls I have left in my kingdom to sustain me. Perhaps you have no intention of ending Odin. Perhaps this is a ruse to deprive me of my greatest weapon so you can seize the throne of Helheim for yourself."

She was just spouting shit now, and it was obvious why she'd done it. She was trying to save face. There was no genuine sacrifice on our part and at the moment, from the outside, she seemed like the weaker party. Apparently, her own pride was enough to make her give up her only chance of survival.

Sacrifice. That was the only way she was going to agree to our terms. She had us on the hook and now we needed to give up something that made her feel in control.

I looked at my two mates, and a surge of protectiveness flowed over me. All my life, I'd always felt lesser, like my place in the world was for nothing but suffering. I didn't see how my magic could ever be seen as a force for good. But there was one thing about the curse I had—it was strong. I'd never had to practise to develop the strength that most wished for. It was what had made most of my childhood so unbearable. Yet right now, standing in this throne room, I realised that for once in my life, I had something that had been worth the suffering for all this time.

"Take mine," I answered loudly.

You could have heard a pin drop as Xanth and Britt both whirled to look at me in shock. It was pure madness. No sane person would ever willingly make such an offer. But when I looked at my two mates, it was an obvious sacrifice that I'd make time and time again if it meant they could have what they needed to be safe. To live a long and happy life.

"My magic and my soul will be more than enough to sustain you." I let my magic flow as I spoke. For the first time in my life, I withdrew the ironclad will I had wrapped around it and let its full strength flow. It covered my hands in a blue light that drifted up my arms before spreading to cover my entire body. "I will give you my soul if we should fail."

Hel finally stood from her throne and slowly walked down the steps of the dais. She moved around me without an ounce of fear as she carefully looked at the deadly magic that now coated my body.

"Interesting," she murmured. She reached one hand out to touch it before seeming to think twice and slowly pulled it back to her side. "You have a gift I haven't seen for centuries. But tell me, why do you hoard the life force you have gathered? It won't strengthen you any more than you already are. If anything, it will just make your magic more volatile."

I looked at her in confusion and she grinned when she realised I didn't know what she was talking about.

"Oh, now this is even better. Yes, I will accept your bargain." She turned back to the throne and ascended the dais once more, delicately sitting down with a grin on her face that finally screamed that she knew she'd won this round.

Fuck! I couldn't ask her what she meant. There was no way she'd tell us and she'd find it nothing but fun to have me beg at her feet and then deny me. She knew something about me I didn't even know myself and if that wasn't a kick in the nuts; I didn't know what was.

Before I could think what to do next, Hel waved a hand and one of the stone beasts from before walked to her side. It gave no sign of being anything but her puppet, and I wondered if it was actually alive or just the last show of power that she had.

As it climbed the steps, I could hear the grate of stone every time it lifted a leg. Its hulking body overshadowed the petite goddess on her throne, but it showed absolutely no sign of considering crushing her. That had to be the biggest sign it wasn't actually alive. I doubted anyone could exist around Hel for an extended period without some kind of outward show of wanting to kill her.

Before I could consider the many ways this beast could end the goddess in front of me, her hand darted out and plunged into the chest of the creature that knelt before her. As she ripped it out, pulling free a sword of pure black metal, the creature crumbled before our eyes, becoming nothing but a pile of rock and dirt. It didn't even make a sound as it seemingly ceased to be. Only Britt gave a gasp of shock and the caged men in front of her eyed her curiously for her response.

Hel transferred the sword to her lap before she clapped her hands together to shake off the dust. "Damn, dirty creatures," she scoffed to herself before picking up the sword and examining it more closely. "Handy though."

No one else dared move. I hardly felt like breathing. We were so close to getting what we'd come here for and yet it felt like it could still go wrong so easily.

"Here is my final offer," Hel finally said with a sigh, like she was growing tired of this whole situation now. "I will allow you to take the Raven's claw and both of the ravens to use in your fight against Odin. If you are unsuccessful, however, I will claim the soul of every single being in this room to do with as I please."

Hel's greedy eyes looked over our rag-tag group and a satisfied smirk settled across her lips. We didn't really have a choice but to agree. Curiously, she had made no stipulations for if we were successful. Perhaps she didn't think it was possible. Either way, it was a loophole we needed to make sure we could exploit.

"We can seal the deal with magic," I suggested, allowing the magic I'd called to form around me in a binding circle. It was something I'd only done once before. Few mages wished to come anywhere near my magic, let alone allow themselves to become bound with it. But I knew the flashy blue sparks that danced around me on the ground were distracting enough to the goddess who seemed to covert the power I knew little about. "In exchange for you providing us with the raven's claw and setting both of the men formerly known as Odin's ravens free, we agree to allow you to take possession of all our souls should we be unsuccessful in our task by Odin besting us in the final battle."

"To do with as I choose," Hel added.

"To do with as you choose," I agreed.

It was obviously an important clause for her, and I saw no harm in adding it. We would no doubt face a painful and torturous existence if we failed, but it was just one more thing to show that failure wasn't an option for us. Besides, what choice did we have? This was the only way.

"Then I agree." Hel dipped her head. She would have been the picture of a benevolent ruler if not for the satisfied smirk on her face.

"And it is bound," I answered.

I kept my face as plain as I could. There was no point in antagonising her, and she still held the sword in her hand. On the outside we'd agreed to her deal, and she was satisfied that she had some kind of huge payoff at the end. But what she hadn't accounted for in our bargain was that wording meant everything, and she'd just agreed to give us the sword and the ravens with no implied stipulation that we would return them. The sword we might part with, although a god killing weapon would be handy to keep around, but the two men before us deserved a chance to live free.

Chapter 24

Britt

One second I was striking the bargain we needed, and then Drystan jumped in and bound all our souls in a magical agreement without a word of warning. I trusted him but, what the fuck?! That was the sort of thing most people discussed first.

Hel waved her hand, seemingly oblivious to our shock, or more likely not giving a shit either way, and the doors to the cages popped open. Both men contained inside took a second before they moved. Glancing at each other first, they slowly unfolded from the cramped conditions she'd kept them. There wasn't a smile on their face. Nothing about their demeanour screamed gratitude. If anything, they looked at us like we were beneath them. Perhaps they weren't as happy with the fact that we'd gambled their souls.

There also wasn't a glimpse of recognition on their faces. I could feel the telltale pull inside me as they stepped free. The same one I'd felt as soon as I saw Drystan and Xanth. I was certain they were my mates. But from the looks on their faces, they either didn't feel it or didn't care.

Nearly identical, both men took a tentative step closer.

They didn't approach us, and made no show that they would stand with us. The only thing they seemed to care about was each other. It made sense. I had no idea what they'd been through, but I was assuming they'd been together for a long time. The bond they held with one another was definitely stronger than anything they had with me at this point.

Hel laughed as she saw the way they both distrustfully glanced at us. She knew something we didn't. No surprise there. It seemed like she was constantly one step ahead of us.

"Here." Hel tossed the raven claw as if it was nothing but a meaningless toy, and the sword clattered down the steps of the dais before it skidded across the stone floor, coming to a halt at one of the raven's feet. "Take it and leave before I decide that I have more need of you."

"The bargain is already struck," Drystan reminded her. "It's time for the game to begin, no?"

She smiled cruelly and then, with a simple wave of her hand, the stone demon we'd first encountered walked away.

"Follow him and leave this place. You'll be back soon enough."

Hel's laughter followed the five of us as we walked out of the throne room, the double doors closing before we'd even cleared them. The ravens took the lead, their heads held high as they strode away from their place of captivity. Neither said a word, but a cloud of anger hung over them. They were pissed, and I had a feeling it was with us for whatever reason. Sitting outside the doors were the packs we'd arrived with and we quickly grabbed them, even though the contents were hardly worth keeping around now. Next to them, leaning against the wall, was a black sword scabbard, and I passed it to the nearest raven, who didn't even meet my eye as he took it.

Following the stone demon through the twists and turns of Hel's palace, I was lost before I even glimpsed the first window. Given that she'd had us spend the night in a room that didn't even exist, I doubted we'd be able to find our way back to the throne room even if we wanted to. But then, when we rounded the corner and found a portal shimmering in front of us, I realised it wasn't the throne room she was trying to hide.

This shouldn't be here. There shouldn't be a way into Helheim that was this easily travelled. Judging by the way the ravens both came to a sudden stop at the sight, they thought the same.

I wondered how long she had held them here with a chance of freedom sitting so closely by. It was the sort of thing that Hel would do. Give them the freedom to walk the palace, knowing they'd never be able to find the one place that could take them away from whatever hell she'd put them through. It would have amused her to no end that the portal sat open and ready to use if only they could find it first.

The stone demon pointed at the portal and then turned and walked away, not waiting to see if we'd actually step through.

"What do you think is on the other side?" Xanth asked, just as I thought the same.

"Freedom," one raven muttered, his voice grating with lack of use. "Either on land or in death. Either is better than staying here." And with that, they both stepped through, not leaving it to chance that something could snatch away their escape.

"I guess we're following them," Drystan muttered before following them through.

Strangely, it was watching Drystan disappear from view that had my feet moving for the portal as Xanth pulled my hand into his. The ravens leaving hadn't elicited the same response, and I couldn't help but feel guilty about that.

Why had I been given multiple mates? Was this some kind of consolation prize for the half of my soul that had been ripped away from me? Given that two of them didn't seem to notice I existed, I wasn't sure it was a bargain I would have agreed to. Not that I'd ever chance losing Drystan and Xanth.

The wet slippery feeling of the portal pressed against my skin as I stepped through it, and I mentally cursed myself for even thinking that. The ravens were hurting, and they needed understanding, not impatience. And at the end of the day, just because we had the potential to be mates didn't mean we had to be. I knew what it felt like to be forced into a position you didn't want and I'd never do that to anyone else. Even if a bond was fated, you should still be afforded the chance to walk away. Choices were what made us. They shaped our pasts and our future. They moulded us into the people we were. I wasn't about to take that away from them. I wouldn't be the one to force them into the future I wanted rather than the one they should be able to create on their own.

As the portal propelled us forward, I let one tear of sadness touch my cheek. Here, wrapped in the portal magic that threw us from this realm to the next, I let myself have a moment of pity. One single moment of hating the path that fate had laid at our feet and then I stepped through with the mask of the woman I was supposed to be firmly in place. The one who had been fated to kill a god. A woman who was picked up off the floor by the Phoenix General and moulded into what she'd always wanted to be.

A fighter.

A survivor.

Chapter 25

Xanth

Something was wrong with Britt. As soon as my hand touched her, I felt a sadness smothering the light I'd always been able to see just behind her gaze.

My growing magic surged, and for the first time since I'd nearly lost my life at the mage library, I felt it move inside me, pushing against the surface. Yet instead of it pushing to be set free on the world, this time it was trying to reach our mate.

I hadn't spoken with Britt about the magic I contained yet. She'd been through enough facing Drystan's hatred of his own power. I didn't hold the same level of disdain as he did. I actually loved the magic I held. But it still frightened people and if there was one thing in this world that I'd never be able to stand, it would be my mate looking at me with fear in her eyes.

The sound of shouting hit us as soon as we stepped free from the portal, and I saw Drystan squaring off with the two ravens.

"A little gratitude wouldn't go amiss," Drystan shouted, looking the two men up and down like they were dirt.

What could possibly have happened in the few moments it had taken for us to follow them through?

"Gratitude?" One of them growled. "You're like everyone else. Gambling and bartering with the lives of the ones around you."

"In case you didn't miss it, she already owned you. All I did was sentence us to the same fate."

It was a good point. From an outside perspective, I could see how someone would be pissed at what Drystan had done. But they didn't get it. Where he went, we went. The three of us were in this together. I didn't even need to ask Britt if she felt the same. I already knew it was true. Besides, there was no way we were going to fail and even if we did, everything would end. Helheim would be no different.

"Okay, clearly we missed something, but arguing between ourselves won't make this situation any easier. We have a mission to accomplish, and that's the only thing that matters right now," Britt interrupted.

Unfortunately, all it did was pull the ravens' ire directly to her.

"You! I don't know what you think you're going to accomplish with whatever spell you're working on us, witch, but it won't work. The raven's claw stays firmly with us. If it was possible to strike down Odin, don't you think we would have done it?"

Britt shook her head, and I couldn't fault her. It was a lot to separate. "Okay, first I'm not a witch and no one is working a spell on you. Second, the Norns sent us for the raven's claw and told us it was the only weapon that could kill Odin. *You* must be mistaken."

"Mistaken?" he growled, taking a step closer to Britt, only to have Drystan shove him back. "Do you not think we would have struck him down centuries ago for his misdeeds and abuses if we could? Do you think we would have become the pets of that mad bitch if we'd had a weapon that could have stopped it?"

He was shouting now, but beneath the anger and rage, there was a sadness in his eyes. I knew what it looked like when someone tried to stay strong and mask the abuse they'd suffered. I'd seen that look on Drystan's face for years. He'd been one of the few at the mage library to stand up and fight in the shadows for our people. The very same people who wouldn't even look at him. Who barely tolerated his presence amongst them.

"I think we all need to calm down and take a step back. Shouting at each other and hurling accusations gets us nowhere," I pointed out. "We're heading to Thor's rebellion base. Will you come with us? It's the best place for everyone with what's going on right now. Even if you don't want to fight beside us, Thor will be able to explain more about the situation to you."

Drystan scoffed. "All they're interested in is running away."

Britt's eyes widened in surprise and I realised what had happened before we'd arrived. The ravens were planning on leaving, and given that one of them had the raven's claw strapped to his back, it seemed like they were intending to take the sword with them.

"Is that true?" Britt asked, the hurt lining her voice unmistakable. "You were going to leave. Don't you care about the rest of the realms?"

The raven who'd been arguing with us looked like he was ready to take on the world for the pain that he'd suffered. Unfortunately for the rest of the world, he seemed to place the blame firmly at their door rather than where it really belonged. The one who'd stayed quiet until now, though. I could see a glimmer of doubt on his face. If we were going to persuade them to come with us, he was the way to do it. Especially with the wince he'd given at hearing the hurt in Britt's voice.

"Where was the rest of the realm when we were thrown in Helheim for having the audacity to tell Odin he should protect his people? When we stood up and spoke for those who were suffering only to be cast out, humiliated and tortured for years? Where were they?"

The only sound that could be heard was the panting of his angry breaths as he shouted his rage into the world. This was the same situation thousands faced across the realms. We'd all been trampled beneath the feet of those who were supposed to protect us. Should we have stood up and fought sooner? Probably. But we didn't have the means to do it. It was only when we were well and truly broken, when all hope seemed lost, that those who fate had deemed heroes had finally found the strength to stand and fight, too. Maybe we'd needed to see the devastation to truly realise what we'd be losing.

Maybe we were no better than those who seemed to reap the benefits of the pain and suffering of others. But we were doing what needed to be done now. We were putting our lives on the line because someone had to do it. Nothing else mattered. We'd all made mistakes. We'd all suffered. But now we had the pain and the rage to make us fight harder. To win.

"They were dying," Britt whispered.

The ravens fell quiet. It was hard to argue in the face of the brutal truth that was the state of the realms right now.

"Valhalla has fallen. The valkyrie have been wiped out. Asgard is mostly abandoned and empty. Odin's madness has already consumed most of his people, and the magic realm isn't any better. The wolf shifters stand on the brink of extinction, as do the mages. The fae have returned to the old cities, but even their fate is unknown. Even if we win, we might still lose. It might all be for nothing. But don't stand there shouting about your pain, thinking that the rest of us aren't suffering right alongside you. I'm not saying you don't deserve the hurt and betrayal you feel. I'm not even saying you're wrong to be angry about this fucked up world we've found ourselves in. But what I am saying is that letting it all end for some kind of vindictiveness isn't the way. *We will fight.* We'll even give our lives doing it if we have to. But what we won't do is lie down and accept what feels like the inevitable over a sense of bruised pride. This is it. *Don't you get that?* There are no more second chances. No more tomorrows to delay until. There's barely anyone else left to expect to fight in our place. But I refuse to accept that everything ends. I *refuse* to let him win without making him fight for it. Even if all I do is piss him the fuck off and make him work harder for the end of the realms. Well, I'm petty enough to do it."

The quiet raven chuckled, and I couldn't help but join him. It was a hell of an argument. Fight back just to spite the bastard that was trying to end it all. Not only that, but it was a fucking convincing one as well.

He stepped forward, bypassing the angry man, who still clung to his anger. "My name is Bran, and this is Corvin. Perhaps we should start this introduction again?"

"Britt." She held out her hand for him to shake, but he grabbed it and pulled it to his lips instead. When Bran peered up at her through his lashes, it was proof he would be the easier raven to get along with.

Britt cleared her throat uneasily before turning the attention to us. "And this is Xanth and Drystan."

Bran nodded, straightening but didn't let go of Britt's hand. "Mages. It's been a while since I have heard of your kind being out amongst the rest of the realm."

"Yeah well, when the Council turns on its people and starts feeding them to the portal monster Odin sent after us, it kinda makes the library feel a touch less homey," Drystan snarked.

From the way he held onto Britt and the accusation Corvin had thrown at us earlier, I was starting to put two and two together and come up with a mate bond. And I didn't know how I felt about that. Britt deserved all the love in the world and I wouldn't begrudge her taking two more mates, I wouldn't let them treat her like crap though. The ravens were going to need to get over themselves and step up if they wanted to join our family.

The two ravens locked gazes, and Corvin finally sighed in defeat. "Don't look at me like that."

"What can it hurt to talk with Thor?" Bran suggested.

Corvin shook his head but didn't respond. Instead, he looked around him, turned in a specific direction, and walked.

"Ermmmm." Britt shuffled uneasily, clearly not wanting to fight again but as curious as I was about where he was going.

"He's heading into Asgard," Bran said helpfully before he followed his brother, still holding Britt's hand and pulling her along with him.

Drystan looked at me and then shrugged. They had the weapon, our mate, and were heading to the same place as us, so we didn't really have any choice but to follow. Still, now that we'd gotten off on the wrong foot, I could already tell this would feel like a long journey. Nothing like snark and sarcasm to get to know two men who were supposed to be sharing your mate.

It didn't take much time with us walking in silence before Bran broke and spoke .

"So, you're not a witch," he said carefully.

It was the safest way of asking Britt what she was without coming out and saying it. Unfortunately, it wasn't exactly the easiest subject for our mate.

"No, not a witch." She didn't elaborate any further, but from the tension I could see in her shoulders from three steps away, I could tell she knew she wouldn't get away without saying anything else.

"Whatever your feeling is real. We've done nothing to influence you," Drystan added, trying to be helpful. Had he come to the same conclusion as me?

Corvin hummed a sound of disagreement and in the space of time it took to take two steps, Bran had clearly decided to get straight to the point.

"What are you?" he asked quietly. "I can tell you aren't from Asgard."

"I came from Valhalla," she told him, and I guess it was the truth, even if it didn't completely fill him in on her situation.

I wasn't about to criticise Britt for not being completely honest. She deserved to get to know these men more before she shared her most painful secrets. When she'd been met with nothing but aggression and accusation, she couldn't be blamed for not being an open book. I mean, we'd barely got the names out of the two of them and they weren't exactly forthcoming with their story, either.

There was a lot of anger and pain in our group, and it wouldn't help us achieve our goal. It was going to be hard enough. Not being able to bond and work together was just lining ourselves up for inevitable failure. If we couldn't get our crap together, we might as well hand the raven's claw over to Odin and ask him to kill us with it.

"It's true then? The valkyrie are all gone?" Bran asked.

"Yes. Odin closed the gates of Valhalla and forbade them from leaving, but there was a great battle in the magic realm which would have wiped out the entire shifter race t. The Phoenix General opened the gates, and the valkyrie responded to her call for aid in the battle. Odin apparently wasn't a massive fan of that. He sent the angel armies and wiped them out as punishment."

"Not all of them," Corvin cut in. "You apparently somehow escaped."

Bran had the decency to wince at the accusation, but he didn't exactly jump to Britt's defence either. I could reluctantly admit that it did sound suspicious, but that didn't give them the right to interrogate her.

"Yes. I wasn't there at the time. A seer in the realm has been helping. She's been moving the pieces behind the scenes to put us all on the right path. We wouldn't be here right now if it wasn't for her," Britt explained.

I knew the loss of the valkyrie had hit her hard. How could it not? She'd lived and trained with them for months, but you wouldn't know it listening to her now. She'd pushed that pain down as far as she could and I worried how it would affect her when we got to the end of this. We didn't have time to sit down and grieve our losses, but there had to be another way.

"We'll talk to her later," Drystan murmured in my ear, and when I turned to look at him, I saw him watching our mate just as closely.

At least I wasn't the only one looking out for her. Britt had a support system now. She just needed to learn how to lean on us when she needed it.

Chapter 26

Corvin

She was hiding something. Looking back over my shoulder, I saw her holding my brother's hand as she calmly told us about the annihilation of an entire race of people.

Why wasn't she angry? Broken? These were her people, but she might as well be telling us about the best way to butcher a pig.

I didn't trust her.

As soon as the doors to the throne room had opened, and I'd been hit with her delicious scent, I knew it was another trick Hel was playing on us. She'd taken great enjoyment in making us watch the two mages take her, even if she didn't know that my brother and I were reeling from this woman who felt like our mate. Hel would never have let us go if she'd suspected. The bitch just thought we were going insane from the length of time it had been since we'd enjoyed the touch of another. And I wasn't counting the unwelcome touches that had come from her.

We'd been Hel's playthings for far too long, and I didn't know if I'd be able to do that with another again. Not without seeing the look on my brother's face when she'd made him perform in front of me. It was no doubt the same one he'd seen on my own.

Hel had broken us. We liked to argue otherwise, but it was impossible not to be after being in her tender care for so long. There was only so many times you could push your emotions beneath the surface before you lost touch with them entirely. And mine had sunk into the bottomless black hole inside of me decades ago.

I'd tried to protect Bran from the worst of it. He was the gentle one between the two of us. But it had been impossible. Not with the length of time she had imprisoned us there.

I didn't realise that he'd left her side until I felt his hand on my shoulder. "How long until we reach the mountains?"

I shrugged. It had been so long since we'd travelled through Asgard that even the feel of fresh air on my skin felt foreign. I was fairly certain any rebellion force would have taken residence in the mountains. There had been whispers of it before we'd tried to abandon Odin and been banished for the audacity of thinking we had that level of freedom. Hopefully, they were not only still there, but they'd intercept us along the way. Otherwise, I had no idea how we were going to find them, and I sure as hell wouldn't ask the three people behind us.

"I like her," Bran suddenly blurted out.

My head snapped to the side to look at him in surprise before I peered back behind us to make sure the others hadn't heard. The three of them were several steps behind us, talking between themselves. I could see the two mages trying to draw the female into a conversation, but she seemed distant for some reason. It wasn't my problem. This was probably what she did with all the men she trapped in her net, toyed with them until she got bored. If anything, I felt sorry for the pair of them who'd so easily fallen under her spell.

"Don't," I warned Bran. "We obviously can't trust them. She's hiding something from us and trying to influence our emotions with whatever this damn spell is."

Bran was silent as he walked at my side, but I knew he had more to say. It didn't take long for him to break, it never did. He hated conflict.

"Maybe... what if it's not a spell, and she is our..."

"She's not," I snapped. I couldn't believe he, of all people, would start with this. "You know the prophecy. You heard it from the Norns themselves. Our mate will be the reigning raven. Whatever she is, she isn't one of us."

Bran nodded reluctantly, picking his steps carefully as we entered a patch of woodland. I could feel his sadness through our bond. He wanted her to be our mate. He wanted it to be true. And I hated her even more for it.

"We should think about where we want to make camp for the night," Xanth said, his voice raised to include us in their conversation. "We're going to need cover and somewhere to potentially hunt for food. These trees could be the best opportunity we have for a while."

He was right, but I didn't want to admit it. If we were where I thought we were, we'd emerge from these trees and have nearly an entire day walking through the grasslands before we came to any more cover. The sun was already high in the sky and we definitely wouldn't make the next treeline before nightfall. Not on foot at least, but there was no way Bran would agree to leaving these three behind and taking to the sky.

"Let's make it through the trees to the edge of the grassland," Bran told them. "It will give us sightlines across the plains to see if we're going to have any unexpected company from the direction of Asgard."

We could go around the plains, but it would add days to our journey and I didn't like the idea of spending time walking through Asgard when we weren't fully in the picture of Odin's condition.

He'd sent us to Helheim because after millennia of service, we'd disagreed with him and stepped away from his side. Bran and I were his ravens, his most trusted advisors, and whilst we didn't always agree, we'd never considered leaving him before. Not until we'd seen the extent of the madness he'd shielded from us. Not until we saw the empty streets, and the broken bodies of the people he was meant to protect. It was only then that we knew there would be no saving the man we thought of as a father.

But what could we do to stop him? We had the raven's claw, but no way to truly wield it. We were just the keepers of the sword, waiting for our mate to take its possession, and there was no way Odin was ever going to let that happen. So he'd cast us down into the one place where he'd known we would never find her, and let Hel believe he was gifting her with the ultimate weapon as a reward for her loyalty in keeping us contained. She had no idea that the raven's claw would be nothing but an ordinary sword in her hands. Either that or she was just egotistical enough to think she'd be able to make it work, anyway.

"You can't push this away with no proof, Corvin. The entire world isn't waiting to stab you in the back. This could be our chance to finally find a place somewhere."

"How can she possibly be our mate, Bran?" I hissed. "She isn't one of us."

"Stranger things have happened in our world, brother," Bran told me before he turned his back and walked back to the others.

I could hear them chatting easily with each other while I stormed ahead, looking for somewhere to camp for the night. Finding something to eat shouldn't be too hard. We'd passed enough tracks in these trees for me to know it was still teaming with wildlife. But sitting around the fire, eating and talking wasn't something I wanted to do right now. No matter how much the thought of sitting under the night sky might appeal to me. To finally see the stars again and feel the night breeze on my skin. It was something I hadn't realised I'd even missed. Yet it would all be tainted because I'd be sitting with *her* and there was no way I could trust her to be who we needed her to be.

Chapter 27

Britt

"You don't like me much, do you?" It hurt to even think, let alone let the words slip past my lips.

Corvin looked up from where he skinned a brace of rabbits. We'd found a place he deemed an adequate campsite a few hours ago, and then he'd disappeared back into the trees, telling us he'd hunt for tonight.

Bran had watched him walk away with a mixture of confusion and sadness on his face, and even though my first instinct was to pump him for information on the grumpy one of the pair, I'd refrained. Drystan had looked like he'd have to physically restrain Xanth at one point, who appeared to find it equally difficult.

Corvin didn't trust us, or rather me, more specifically. And I couldn't really blame him. We had no idea what the two of them had been through and throughout the entire time we'd travelled to this spot, Bran had regaled us with stories or their time in Asgard, but not a single one had been while they'd been in Helheim. I dreaded to think about what had happened to them at the hands of Hel. And it wasn't my place to judge them for being affected by it.

I'd tried to stay away. I told myself that I'd busy myself on the other side of the fire, and leave Corvin to do the task that seemed to occupy his mind away from the shadows that kept creeping into his eyes.

But I couldn't.

I didn't even realise I'd been creeping closer to him until I found myself sitting on the grass at his side.

Corvin scowled at my question but didn't answer. His usual scowl was firmly in place as he concentrated on what he was doing and desperately tried to ignore me.

I didn't mind. It gave me the opportunity to really look at him without feeling all that bad about it. To the outside observer, I looked like I was waiting for an answer to my question. In reality, I was greedily soaking in the details of a man that I was certain was my mate, but who wanted nothing to do with me. This could be my only chance to be close to him and I'd take it while I could.

I knew it would hurt if they rejected me, but after everything he'd been through, what kind of mate would I be if I couldn't give him this one thing to help heal his heart?

"You're staring at me," Corvin gruffly commented as my eyes greedily took in his shaggy dark hair and the way it fell into his grey eyes.

His strong hands made quick work of preparing the rabbits and from where he'd rolled up the sleeves of his shirt, I could see the strength in his arms. His was a body that had been carved through centuries of fighting and training. I'd seen it in the warrior camp in Valhalla enough times to recognise it. I'd bet his hands had the callouses formed from the years of wielding a sword as well.

It was obvious from the way his clothes hung slightly too large on his frame what he'd lost from the years of neglect, but he was still a beast of a man.

His eyes darted to Bran as he made sure the other raven

was still where he could see him. Ever watchful. I wondered if he'd always been like this or if it was a habit he'd developed during his time with Hel.

"I was waiting to see if you were going to answer my question."

With a sigh, he laid his knife on the ground. Well, it was actually my knife, but he'd taken it to prepare his catch when he'd refused any other offers of help.

"No. You were staring. You already knew I wouldn't answer your inane question because you already know the answer to it. No, I don't like you. You're lying to us and I don't like people I can't trust."

His answer took me aback, and I stared at him in surprise. Some people might find him rude, but his honest way of getting to the point was brutally refreshing.

"My friend, Aria, is going to love you," I mumbled, already seeing the similarities between the two of them.

Corvin peered up at me through his lashes as if I wasn't worth the entirety of his attention and then continued with his work. Either he hadn't been expecting that answer or I'd perhaps found a way to get to know my mate. Forced conversation it was then.

"I'm not lying to you. Everything I've told you is the truth. But if you're so intent on believing that we have some kind of hidden agenda, then why not just ask me what you want to know?"

The others had fallen silent on the other side of the campfire, giving up the illusion of giving us our privacy.

"That goes for you too, Bran," I told the other raven. "If there's anything you want to know, just ask. We don't have any secrets and if we end up heading into this fight together, then we need to find a way to trust each other."

Bran nodded thankfully and I could already see that he was carefully considering what he wanted to ask.

I didn't miss the proud look on Drystan's face. For the man who'd tried to push me away himself, he'd been the one advocating getting to know the two new men to our group before making any judgements. He and Xanth were both worried that they were going to reject me. It showed how good they were that they were more concerned with me being rejected than hoarding me for themselves. It couldn't be easy to look at the two ravens and know that they'd have to share a mate with them when they were practically strangers. In fact, maybe this was something we all needed.

"What are you?" Corvin asked, his direct question holding a hint of malice.

So this was what he'd thought I was hiding from them and had been winding him up all this time.

"I don't know anymore," I told him honestly. "This is what's been bothering you since we left Helheim? Why didn't you just ask?"

"Because it was obvious you were avoiding answering the question when Bran asked you earlier, which you're doing again now."

I guess he was right.

"She doesn't owe you an explanation," Xanth hissed. "Some people prefer not to talk about the things that cause them pain."

Corvin's head tipped to the side in thought and, for the first since we'd met, his trademark scowl slipped.

"It's okay. I was a shifter," I explained quietly. "I had a wolf, but then I died, and when my soul was brought to Valhalla, they left my wolf behind."

The only sound that reached me was the light night breeze as it rustled through the trees. For a fleeting moment, I realised that she would have loved this. Sitting beside the campfire surrounded by her mates. But my wolf had never got to experience something like that. The only thing she'd had in life when it came to mates was pain, when they tried to force us into a mate bond with someone we didn't accept and wasn't fated to be ours.

"I'm sorry," Bran whispered. "That must have been a horrible thing to experience."

I shrugged. Xanth was right that it was painful to think about. For a while back in Valhalla, I'd been so pissed about the unfairness of it all, even though I was grateful that Aria had found a way for me to have a second chance at life. But now, sitting here with them, I realised it didn't hurt like it used to. Yes, the ache and the emptiness still sat in the centre of my chest, but it almost felt bearable now. Like I'd grown so used to it that it didn't have the same hold over me anymore.

"So you don't know what you are because..." Corvin didn't sound mean when he spoke, just like he was genuinely trying to understand.

"Can I really call myself a shifter when I can't shift and I don't even have my wolf anymore? Nidhogg called me a human and I guess he's right." My face wrinkled in disgust, even though I had nothing against humans. It just didn't feel like the right label for me and I didn't want it. I wanted to be a shifter. It was the only thing I'd ever known.

As I stared into the flames, pondering the reality of my existence, a hand came to my knee and gently squeezed. It was only when I saw the surprised look on Xanth's face that my gaze trailed up the arm attached to that hand and realised that it was Corvin.

"Oh, don't look so shocked. I'm not completely fucking heartless," he grumbled, but his hand never moved.

Bran chuckled, and it didn't take long for it to flow around our little group. This was nice. It was a glimpse of what we could have had if we didn't live in a broken world and had the fate of existence sitting on our shoulders.

"So, I think you can agree that my poor little, potentially

human soul couldn't have placed some kind of fake mate enchantment on you," I told him sarcastically. Hopefully, it came across in the playful way I meant it. "Besides, don't you think it's ever so slightly conceited to think I'd go through the trouble to do something like that?"

"Hey!" Bran protested. "I'll have you know I'm a catch."

And the laughter came that little bit more easily this time.

It was the first time the word had been uttered aloud and my eyes darted to my mages realising we hadn't had time to discuss this yet. They both smiled broadly at me, not an ounce of upset on their faces. Somehow they'd already worked it out, but I still planned to check in with them later. Something I should have already done.

I didn't miss how Corvin gently withdrew his hand. It stung a little. But at least he didn't withdraw from the group. He didn't turn his back on us. He seemed to open up a little as he came closer to the fire, sitting the rabbits on the spit that Bran had already built.

And that was how we spent the rest of the evening. Eating, talking, making as much fun of Corvin as we dared. I think I even caught the sight of a slight smile on his lips at one point. It was obvious from the very beginning that he was fiercely protective of Bran. But what I hadn't realised before was how much he needed Bran as well. He was the one that reminded Corvin to let go and enjoy the moment. The dynamic between them was so similar to Drystan and Xanth that it was almost like looking in a mirror.

Maybe we were just a collection of broken souls, but what better way to feel whole again than to find someone who's broken pieces matched up with your own?

Chapter 28

Bran

I'd never felt more free than I did at this moment. It would be easy to underestimate the meaning of those words considering I'd just spent the better part of a century locked inside a cage. But as my gaze found Corvin and how he actually walked with our group rather than storming ahead, I realised how much he'd needed this just as much as me. And I wasn't talking about a way out of the cage Hel had us locked inside.

Corvin had always been my protector, which was strange because it wasn't like I needed it. I'd bested him in battle many times. In fact, I'd go as far as to wager that I could take him right now if I needed to.

But ever since we'd come into existence, Corvin had wanted to shield me from the ugliness of the world. He saw me as an innocent who needed protecting from the horrors and realities of life, and no matter how much I'd implored him to stop, it only made him fight for me harder.

In a way, I think standing in front of me was his way of protecting himself. That if he did what he could to stop any harm from coming to his brother, then it would excuse him for the things he had to do on Odin's command. From the things we'd both had to do.

I didn't remember being a child. I remembered nothing and then just existing. We didn't have parents. We didn't have a family outside of each other, and with our birth came all the knowledge of the realms.

Odin called us his thought and memory. We were forever at his side, witnessing his rule over Asgard and advising him on matters that no one else could. There was a time when he had trusted us. When he listened to our reasoning and actually considered what was best, not just for his own people but for all the realms.

The throne of Asgard was a heavy burden for the All Father. He held a power that made others quake in fear, but there was a logic to it. For how else did you prevent war after war, atrocities and senseless death, if you couldn't strike fear into those who would even consider such a thing?

The All Father stood at the pinnacle of good, watching over everyone and everything.

Until he didn't.

Until he rose his hand against his own people and the beginning of his spiral into madness began.

We'd warned him of the consequences of closing the realm of the gods, but his ego had pushed his decision when the mortals looked at the gods as the cause of all their problems. And when the mortals turned their backs on him, he responded in the only way his machismo would allow. He turned his back on them as well and closed the doors, abandoning them to their own fate.

It didn't take long for us to see the consequences of sealing the gods away. It was small to begin with. Senses were dulled, and it took a little longer to use the magic we'd become so used to having in everyday life.

By the time the people questioned what was happening,

Odin had slipped so far into believing that what he'd done was right that he couldn't fathom changing his mind.

Corvin and I were oblivious to what happened next. Whether Odin had purposefully shielded the truth from us or not, we'd never know, but by the time we received an anonymous note to inspect the dungeons, the damage Odin had done was more than most could ever forgive.

Dungeons were never meant to be a pleasant place, and in an attempt to hide what he'd been doing, Odin had closed them off to nearly all his soldiers. They'd been cast into darkness and the smell of stale, dank air and unwashed bodies hit us strongly as we'd descended the stone steps. Every cell was full. Some prisoners had died long before we'd known what was happening, and the smell of rot and decay made me gag as we swung open the main door.

Corvin had grabbed a torch from the bracket on the wall and we'd walked the length of the pathway between the cells, our eyes cataloguing every atrocity that Odin had committed in secret. By the time we'd reached halfway, I hadn't thought I'd have the stomach to walk all the way to the end, but I'd forced myself to. I'd needed to see what my complacency had allowed to happen, and the sight would stay with me until my dying day.

Somehow Odin had found a way to drain the citizens of Asgard of not just their magic, but their connection with the realm. Of course, he'd consumed the majority for himself. He'd let no one think of him as weak. The rest he seemed to send back out into Asgard to fix the slow degradation happening around us.

It took us nearly an entire day to open the cells and provide those inside with the necessary medical aid. It was too late for some, and those who looked like they would survive would never be the same. They were strangers in a place they had once called home, and there was no way they'd ever feel safe again after what they'd suffered.

It was the start of the rebellion. Corvin and I had contacted Thor, knowing he was already displeased with Odin and was the sort of man who would protect those that had been abused by Odin's hand. We knew what we were doing, what we were putting into motion. You might have thought that after centuries of service we'd have had more loyalty to Odin than that, but there was no coming back from what he'd done.

Unfortunately, the rebellion wasn't the only thing we'd put in motion that day. Because now Odin was desperate to maintain the balance and without the people he'd been draining in the dungeons the raids of Asgard soon began.

There was no talking Odin out of it once he had his mind set. He'd clung to power with a desperation we'd never witnessed in him before, and with it came a disgust for those he thought were wasting what little magical reserves the realm still had.

We'd intended to join Thor once we'd finally admitted to ourselves there was nothing else that could be done from Odin's side. We couldn't even warn the people of what was coming. Odin had become too suspicious of us, and any information we'd once been privy to before, he hoarded for himself.

We should have done something then. We should have made moves to bind his power, to remove him from the throne. It was a mistake I'd never be able to forgive myself for. We could have ended this before the worst came to be. Perhaps it was a remnant of loyalty that we'd clung to or the hope that he'd finally see what he was doing and become the man we once knew him to be. Either way, we'd found ourselves ambushed in the night by Hel's demons and dragged to Helheim before we had a chance to fight back.

But that was just the beginning of our punishment.

Presiding over her own realm, Hel had retained every drop of power she'd always had. We knew we'd weakened along with the rest of Asgard, but facing Hel had been an awakening we'd never expected. It was brutal and unending. I didn't know how long she had tortured us until she finally deemed us broken. Then we'd had the privilege of becoming her pets, on display for all of her people to mock and pity. We'd fallen so far from our previous position at Odin's side and by the time it was done, I doubted we cared.

Because Hel was right, except we'd been broken long before we fell under her tender care and attention. It had happened when we'd failed our people, and when Corvin and I had personally buried every person whose life had been ripped away by Odin in that dungeon. It had taken us two days, and I remembered every face of the people we'd failed, and their children who'd died at their side. Entire families snuffed out because of greed and madness.

My heart was heavy by the time I'd finished telling our story. Britt, Drystan, and Xanth said nothing. There were no weak placations as they tried to convince me we held none of the blame for what had happened. Whether it was because they believed it, I wasn't sure. But there was one thing I did know for sure when I looked at each of their faces. We'd all been through something that had torn at the core of our being and whether it was deserved or not, they knew the pain of that type of guilt because they bore it themselves.

We were a group of people who'd witnessed the worst of what people were capable of, and every one of us regretted not having made a stand earlier.

"Do you ever wonder why fate brought us together?" Xanth asked. "Like, do you think she matches mates together because they're the only people in all the realms that could ever truly understand you? All of you. The parts you bury deep and don't want to admit, let alone have to look closely at."

"Fate turned her back on this world a long time ago," Corvin said from Britt's side. He'd given up striding ahead and trying to stay separate from the group. In fact, he never strayed far from her side and I believed my brother might actually be accepting the bond he'd been so adamant couldn't possibly be real.

"Maybe fate is trying to help us fix things?" Xanth said half-heartedly, a remnant of hope lining his voice.

Corvin looked at him like he'd lost his mind. He needed to remember that they didn't have the same experiences with gods and fates that we did. They didn't know the faces behind the whispered names, they also didn't know the shitty attitudes.

"We make our own fate," Drystan said gruffly, effectively shutting down the conversation.

He was more like my brother than I doubted Corvin would admit. I saw his soft looks and the smile he thought no one noticed whenever it came to Britt. You only had to look at the scar on his face to know something had happened in his life to give him the same outlook on fate as we had. There was something about his magic that felt familiar to me, but I couldn't quite put my finger on what it was. I'd spent too long swinging in that cage trying to forget about the world that had forsaken us and it was taking longer than I cared to admit for my senses to come back online.

Chapter 29

Britt

It felt like we'd been walking endlessly, when in fact it was only two days. As we approached the centre of another forest, which quite frankly seemed exactly the same as the first one, Corvin announced we should start looking for another place to camp for the night. For all I knew, we were walking around in circles. Strangely, I wouldn't mind it. Walking through the day, and swapping stories had been rather nice. We were slowly relaxing around each other, even if we were trying to avoid the subject of the mate bond. I couldn't figure out if the ravens were accepting it, or rather accepting me, or if our time together was about to come to an end.

"We should reach the mountains tomorrow," Bran said as he helped me slip the pack from my shoulders. It barely contained anything now, and it was more a reassurance than anything else. "Hopefully the rebellion finds us before Odin's soldiers since we have no way of contacting them."

That was another topic we'd avoided until now. We had a vague idea of where we were going, but that was it. Plus, it wasn't like we could storm into Asgard alone. We'd need an army at our back to have a chance of even making it to Odin.

Unfortunately, we didn't have one of those packed away ready for use, and none of us had been inside Thor's camp or knew how to find it.

Bran and Corvin told us they'd hunt for the night and then disappeared into the trees. I saw the suspicious look on Drystan's face and knew he didn't wholly trust them yet.

"They'll come back," I told him, maybe needing to hear it aloud more than I wanted to admit.

"They were going to ditch us at the portal. I don't trust them not to do it now." Drystan started kicking aside the debris on the forest floor, clearing a patch for a fire, no doubt. With the annoyed look on his face, it only made him look like a little kid about to have a meltdown.

"Then maybe this is a way for us all to show that there is trust between us," I suggested. "We trust them to come back and they trust us to still be here when they do. They've been locked away in Helheim, for I don't even want to think how long. They no doubt think this is some scheme cooked up by Hel. Let them have time to be together. No one understands what they've been through more than each other, and they need to have time to talk about it."

"So, mates," Xanth started, starting the conversation we hadn't been able to have yet.

"Yeah. I don't know what to say about that. I feel like I'm betraying you both somehow and..." The guilt was more than I'd realised once I finally acknowledged it.

"Hey," Xanth said softly, his hands coming up to cradle my face. "There's no betraying anyone going on. They were fated to be yours, sweetheart. Just like we were. We will never object to you having more people to love and protect you."

I could see the certainty in his eyes and surprisingly it was even in Drystan's eyes, even if something else was clearly bothering him as well.

Drystan pulled off his pack with a huff and dropped it to

the ground beside the patch he'd cleared. Crouching, he sorted through the contents. It was as empty as mine and I had a feeling this was his way of trying to shut the conversation down.

"I'm going to get some firewood," Xanth unhelpfully told us.

He was doing the exact same thing he had before. Leaving us so we could talk through whatever was bothering Drystan. Last time it had ended with Drystan deciding he needed to step back as my mate, so I wasn't exactly thrilled to have a second go at his meddling tactics.

"He does that a lot, doesn't he?" I murmured after Xanth had all but sprinted away.

It at least made Drystan bark out a laugh, and from the look on his face, it had surprised him as much as me.

"Xanth hates conflict. He's the happy jokester who wants everyone to get along. He's also experienced enough of my moods to know when he needs to get out of the firing line."

"So, he's setting me up as an unwilling sacrifice?"

"No. He knows you're the only one I wouldn't take a shot at." Drystan looked up at me and I could see his pain and confusion in his eyes. Something was bothering my mate more than just the two ravens being suspicious of us and I hadn't realised it until now.

Urgh, I really sucked at this mate stuff. I still hadn't formed a full bond with Drystan and Xanth and I was too afraid to admit that I had no idea how. I was starting to think that I'd lost the ability along with my wolf. But I also hadn't realised that something was bothering him this much. I could blame it on the bond not being completed, but I knew deep down it was because I was so tangled up in what we needed to get done that I wasn't taking the time to get to know my mates enough.

"I'm sorry, Drystan." I dropped to sit on the ground beside him. "I'm really crap at this, aren't I?"

He looked taken aback as the words slipped through my lips, shaking his head in denial before he said anything.

"No! Why would you say that?"

"Because you're hurting and I didn't realise it until now." I took a deep breath, getting ready to admit my suspicions to him, but before I could speak, he blurted out the problem.

"I'm so used to people leaving that I can't even imagine them wanting to stay." He stared into my eyes and I saw guilt that I didn't understand. "You're the most amazing woman I've ever met, Britt. You're strong, determined, selfless, and you deserve everything in this life, including four mates who absolutely adore and worship you. But I'm worried they'll take one look at my magic and leave because of what I am. What if I'm the one who pushes them away from you? How would you ever be able to forgive me for something like that?"

I shuffled across the ground and closed the gap between us so I could duck under his arm and lean against his side. Drystan had spent a lifetime being pushed away from people, and he needed to know that none of us were afraid of being close to him.

"They've already seen your magic," I reminded him. "They were there in Helheim when you were prepared to use it to defend us. If they leave now, Drystan, it has nothing to do with you and everything to do with them. It's not your responsibility to bear the guilt of someone else's actions. Besides, they're coming back. I don't think they'd abandon us here. At the very least, they seem like men who would escort us to the safety of Thor's base and if they decide to part ways with us then, we'll deal with it."

Drystan's fingers trailed across my breastplate, almost like he was trying to reassure himself that I had something that would protect me while we were so out in the open. None of us had really voiced how dangerous it was for us to be travelling on foot through Asgard right now with the only weapon we'd been told could win this fight.

Xanth sat down next to me holding two sticks and not kidding anyone that he'd been gathering wood rather than listening in.

"Does it strike anyone else as odd that we've seen no sign of Odin's soldiers?"

I cocked my head to the side because no; I hadn't thought about it until he'd just mentioned it.

"Maybe he's keeping them close to the city?" Drystan said. "If the realm is pretty dead, he might think he has nothing to worry about this far out. Or, you know, he's not thinking at all because he's as mad as a cat in a rainstorm."

Xanth and I both looked at him like he'd never said stranger words in his entire life. "Who are you?" Xanth gasped dramatically, only for Drystan to shove him playfully.

"I can be all Xanthy when I need to be!"

Xanth frowned, mouthing the word 'Xanthy' to himself before he shrugged. "Taking it as a compliment," he decided before dramatically flopping back to lie on the ground.

"A patrol came through here about two days ago." Corvin's voice cut through the playful atmosphere as he emerged from the trees with two rabbits and a sullen look on his face.

I resisted the urge to poke Drystan and tell him I'd told him so. Mainly because the idea of a patrol being nearby was enough for us all to sober. We'd let our guard down, thinking we were taking a pleasant walk through the countryside rather than the reality of our situation.

"Do you think they're still in the area?" Drystan asked, suddenly on full alert.

Corvin shrugged. "Can I borrow your knife again?"

I was already holding it out to him before he asked and he

gave me a smile before taking it and getting to work. "Bran is following the trail to see if he can figure out where they are heading."

"What? Should he be doing that alone?" That sounded like a terrible idea to me and worry immediately slammed into me.

Corvin looked surprised by my sudden outburst. "He'll stay in the sky. They won't be able to get anywhere near him and he can travel further without one of you on the ground."

I frowned at his words, confused for a second, until it finally sank in. "He's flying?"

All the guys laughed at my confusion and I could feel the blush heating my cheeks as I realised why.

"They don't call us ravens for nothing." Corvin laughed as he spoke and my embarrassment was pushed to the side as I watched the carefree happiness on his face. I could survive saying something stupid if it gave him this.

"How come you didn't go with him?" I asked. This could have been their chance to leave us behind, and perhaps I needed the reassurance just as much as Drystan that they weren't considering it.

"Couldn't have you going hungry." Corvin shrugged. "Besides, we've got the raven's claw to worry about. If it really is going to end this whole thing, we can't leave it in the forest for anyone to find."

He unfastened the sheath strap around his chest and took the sword from his back before he frowned down at it in his hands. Then, without warning, he thrust the thing at me. I was confused at first. We'd gone to Helheim to get the sword, but Corvin had refused to let it out of his sight for a single second. In fact, this was the first time it hadn't been secured to his body.

But why was he giving it to me?

Corvin must have seen the look of confusion on his face

because his head cocked to the side in question. "This is what you came for. The weapon you need."

"Yeah, but, the reigning raven has to wield it, which I'm assuming is you." I frowned as I thought it through. Corvin definitely seemed the dominant of the two ravens but maybe that wasn't the determining factor. "Is it Bran? I didn't mean to insult anyone or anything. I guess I'm used to pack hierarchy for this type of thing."

Corvin laughed then, still holding the weapon out for me. "No. It's you."

My mind went blank as that one word echoed around my brain... you.

"Me?" I screeched.

"Of course. The reigning raven will always be our mate."

I slowly reached out and took the weapon. My fingers closed around the worn leather of the sheath as my heart tripped over at finally having it in my hands. The Norns had said the reigning raven would use this to end Odin's life, and that raven was supposed to be me. Holding it now brought it all screaming to the front of my mind. And, for the first time, it brought with it an ounce of fear. Yes, I wanted with nothing more in my heart than to end Odin, to have my revenge for everything he'd done. For all the friends he'd taken from me. But for that to happen it would mean actually fighting, not just a god, but the All Father. The man who stood above them all because none of them dared to challenge him. I was just a girl. I wasn't even a shifter anymore. How was I supposed to do this?

"We've got this," Drystan said softly. "We'll be at your side every step of the way."

I looked up and locked eyes with him. Was it so obvious that I didn't think I could do this? Or was everyone else just thinking the same thing?

Corvin cleared his throat and uneasily told us. "Once we

reach Thor's base, we'll start training. Nothing needs to happen straight away. We have time."

I nodded slowly. It was the first time he'd implied that they'd stay by our side. That they weren't planning on leaving at the first chance they got. It should have filled me with more confidence than it did, but while the fear of what was to come was still filling me, all I could think was that they didn't believe I'd be able to do it, either.

Chapter 30

Drystan

Bran had returned not even an hour after Corvin had, telling us he'd lost the trail several miles out from our location. And even though he'd scanned the surrounding area, he hadn't been able to pick it up again.

We'd all been in a strange mood throughout the evening, and Britt had pressed herself firmly against my side all night, clinging to me even in her sleep.

I knew she was afraid, and it was so unlike her, I didn't know what to do with it.

We broke down camp in silence, and even the two ravens seemed able to tell that something was wrong with our mate. The concern on their faces was at least evidence that they weren't completely unfeeling toward her. It was strange to look at these two men and think of them as her mates. They didn't act how Xanth and I had done when we'd first seen her. Hell, Xanth had been kissing her within minutes and even I'd wanted to do whatever it took to be close to her. That they could fight the bond so easily was concerning.

Britt needed them and whilst she'd seemed confident last night we'd be able to deal with it if they left, I wasn't so sure she was right. The more she got to know them, the more she'd be able to feel it. They might have some way to turn it off, but she didn't. If they were intending on abandoning her, then they shouldn't be giving her even the slightest hope that they'd stay. It was cruel.

But maybe there was something we could do about it. We were all supposed to be in this bond together, and whilst Xanth and I hadn't been through half of what they had; we understood what it was like to suddenly find yourself on the other side of your personal horror and not know if you were ready to accept that it was real. Or at least I did.

Not to mention the fact we were going to be together for the rest of our lives.

I wanted to shake myself. I wasn't the mushy one in our group. Xanth should have already thought of this and be cozying up to the pair of them. That it was me thinking of extending a hand had to mean there was something terribly wrong with one of us... or Xanth was fucking with me.

I scowled over at the man in question. He was walking with his arm wrapped around Britt's waist and whispering in her ear. When her head tipped back with a laugh, I had to begrudgingly accept that he wasn't fucking with me. He was looking after our mate. Damn it, if I'd thought of it first, I could be the one snuggling up to her and he'd be left with the two grumpy ravens.

Slowing my steps, I dropped back so Bran and Corvin would be walking by my side. My mistake was not thinking through what I would say before I did.

Before I could utter a word, Corvin beat me to it. "Is this where you warn us to stay away from her?"

He sounded amused enough that I wasn't worried about this suddenly ending in a fight.

"She needs you to be honest with her." I was the worst possible person for this conversation. "If you're not planning on sticking around, you need to stop making her think you want to get to know her."

They both looked surprised by my directness. Hell, even I was slightly surprised by it. I guess it was a natural extension of what I'd done at the Mage Library. I'd stood up for the people there who needed me to. It was obvious that the need to protect those around me would extend to my mate, even if it would mean that I'd have to act in ways that seemed completely against my character.

Neither of the ravens spoke. I didn't know what I'd expected. Who was I kidding? Of course, I knew. I'd thought they'd adamantly deny even considering walking away from her. She was perfect. What idiot would even consider it? Well, me. But it was a momentary blip in my sanity and I wasn't even sure I meant it even when the words passed my lips.

Part of me wanted to push them to respond, to admit they couldn't live without her. However, Xanth's shout of surprise cut through the air before I'd had the chance.

My head snapped in their direction, and I couldn't believe the sight before my eyes. They'd fucking found us!

Xanth grappled with an angel on the ground who tried to run him through with a sword. I could see his magic flickering in his eyes as he attempted to desperately draw on it, but couldn't quite get it to rise to the surface.

Britt had her sword drawn, and I could see her gaze darting to Xanth in distraction as she faced the two angels flanking her.

My magic raged to life and flowed across my arms, but before I could take a single step forward, Corvin shouted. "Behind you!"

I dropped to the ground as I felt the rush of air over my head as a double-headed axe swept through the place where my head would have been.

Damn it! Why hadn't we learned our lesson to keep an eye on the sky? How many of them had gotten a drop on us?

Thankfully Britt had returned the raven's claw to Corvin earlier, not being able to carry both swords, and he pulled it from his back and leapt at the angel attacking me. They traded punishing blows with their weapons as I quickly took stock of our situation. Five angels had ambushed us without us even realising it. But given where we were amongst the trees, it felt strange they'd been able to spot us from the sky. Were they the patrol Corvin and Bran had spotted signs of last night? Was it only a coincidence they'd discovered us before we could reach the mountain base?

All the questions flew through my mind as I dived for the angel that had the upper hand with Xanth. I could see his growing frustration that he couldn't quite reach his magic while he struggled to stop the angel from running him through with his sword. Both of them grappled at the weapon, but it was only a matter of time before Xanth's arms would tire and the angel could push the blade down.

My rage flared hotter at the sight of the angel straddling Xanth as he towered over him, the tip of his short sword growing steadily closer to Xanth's vulnerable throat as he desperately tried to push it away.

I didn't have to think, and I doubted I'd even regret it later. My left hand closed around his wing and I let my magic flow. I could feel the way it tore through his body, binding to his very essence and draining it away. It happened so much quicker than it usually did, but I wasn't fighting it this time. If anything, I was pushing to make it work faster. It was the first time that I reached for the magic willingly rather than the enchanted blades I'd relied on for so long.

The angel cried out, his back bowing in agony as I stripped him of his life. He didn't even have time to turn and fight me off.

It was the first time I'd purposefully used the power that had horrified me since I was a child, and it was the first time I hadn't hated it and the thing it turned me into. Because it might have been a terrifying weapon, but Xanth had been right. I hadn't used it accidentally in years. It was under my control and I could make sure I only used it for good. And there was no better reason than protecting my mates.

Once I realised I wasn't a monster, even as I watched the angel fall to the ground dead, I whirled around, looking for the others and what I needed to do to help. Corvin and Bran had dealt with one of them and whilst it looked like Britt had also ended another, the second who had been attacking now held her clutched to his chest with a sword at her throat.

His wide, horrified eyes fixed on me and his dead friend behind me. The only other remaining angel had moved to his back now that they were outnumbered, and they'd seen a glimpse of what I was capable of.

For a brief second, I actually thought we could still make it. All we needed to do was free Britt, and we could overpower them. There had to be a way. If only that sword wasn't already at her throat. Then six more angels touched down on the ground behind them and I knew we'd lost. All we could hope for now was to get Britt out of this alive.

"Give us the raven's claw and the bitch doesn't have to die," the angel shouted, pressing the edge of his sword further into Britt's throat as a thin line of blood trailed down her neck.

We all tensed. We couldn't risk her, but were we willing to condemn all of existence to save her? The answer was obviously yes, but our beautiful mate had other ideas.

She struggled feebly, downplaying her skill as the angel laughed at her. I gritted my teeth at her reckless move and my heart just about leapt into my throat as I saw her fingers slowly dragging the knife from her hip that she could barely reach.

"We don't have time to play with you, little girl," he mocked, his sword digging further into her skin.

"Here!" Corvin blurted out, holding out the sword toward the angel. "Take it. Just set her free and we'll be on our way."

"On your way? Hel wants her pets returned to her. They'll be no going free for you. You should be grateful Odin allowed her to keep you in exchange for taking the raven's claw for himself. He was quite keen to be reunited with the traitors who were trying to end his reign when Hel filled us in on your plans."

"She never gets to touch them again!" Britt roared, suddenly twisting to the side.

As she plunged the dagger into the angel's side, she somehow got her other arm between her neck and the sword. It sliced deep as blood poured down her arm as the blade hit bone and then started to cut the flesh of her arm away. It didn't deter her. Twisting further to the side, she pulled the dagger free, only to plunge it into the angel again.

The rest of us all dived forward at the same time. I grabbed his sword arm, my fingers brushing against the skin of his hand before the angel had time to pull away. Not that he could. My courageous mate had him caught in her grasp and there was no time for him to untangle himself even if he dropped his sword.

I felt myself sway as my magic leapt into action. My ears rang and my vision went blurry as it latched onto his life and pulled it from his body. I'd never used so much, so close together, but rather than feeling drained, I felt like my entire body buzzed and my head was about to burst. I sank to my knees at the same time the angel dropped to the ground, dead.

Britt cradled her arm as she knelt at my side in concern. I heard a roar of rage as I tried to pull her behind me to shield her, but my arms didn't want to cooperate.

I could feel consciousness quickly escaping me, and I knew I couldn't fight it. I desperately wanted to, though. At least until I knew she was safe. I opened my mouth to tell her to run, but the sound never came and I pitched forward, the darkness taking me instead.

Chapter 31

Xanth

Everything went to shit so quickly I felt like my head was spinning, but right now my only concern was the fact that Britt was injured and Drystan had passed out at her feet.

Britt had already grabbed her sword from where it had fallen and was protectively crouched over Drystan despite the blood flowing down her arm.

I scrambled over to the pair of them, ready to do whatever was needed to keep them safe. I was already cursing my stupid fucking magic for failing me again. It was so close to the surface, but I couldn't quite grasp it. And that fucker had nearly been successful in running me through before Drystan saved me.

As I reached for Drystan's pulse, I felt the strong beat beneath my fingers and sighed in relief. I couldn't lose him before we'd even had a chance to explore this thing that was growing between us. Not when we'd only just found the peace in our life that Britt had brought. But we weren't out of danger just yet because there were still seven of these angel fuckers who wanted us dead and the ravens back inside their cages.

My eyes caught one of the dead angels' swords on the ground, and I made to dive for the weapon when a roar split through the air. My gaze immediately snapped toward the sound and caught the rage in Corvin's eyes as he stared at the blood that dripped from Britt to the ground.

"You dare," he growled, "to injure our mate?"

Bran stepped to his side, and it was like a cloud of darkness fell around the pair of them as they faced down the seven remaining angels. It was clear the angels didn't know what to do. Clutching their weapons, not a single one of them dared make a move toward the enraged ravens. Instead, their fear froze them to the spot as Corvin and Bran stepped forward.

"We are not pretty pets to be placed in cages and toyed with. You forget our true names in your complacency, blinded by your fragile egos. We are the darkness, the harbingers. We bring justice and we bring death to those who stand on the wrong side of fate, those who work against the interests of Asgard." Bran's voice echoed out across the land, and wind picked up around the pair of ravens as they took another step closer to the terrified angels in front of them.

"Raising your swords to us will be the last mistake you make in this life," Corvin sneered.

And then everything moved so quickly that it was almost impossible to track with my eyes.

Black wings exploded out the backs of Corvin and Bran and they darted forward at an impossible speed. Corvin slashed at all who stood before him with the raven's claw. The ground staining with the crimson blood of his enemies. But Bran was unarmed still. Not that he needed it. Resorting to nothing more than his hands, he tore into the angels in front of him. Screams filled the air as bones broke and wings were torn asunder. The screaming didn't last long, as Corvin quickly gave them their end at the edge of his blade.

By the time they were finished, both ravens stood barely

out of breath in a circle of death and destruction. Corvin's head lifted, his gaze moving to Britt, and I almost had the urge to pull her behind me. Not that there was any need to. The darkness lifted from them, and with it, the wings at the ravens' backs disappeared once more. Britt was pulled into Bran's arms as he gently lifted her arm to inspect the injury.

The relief of the danger being over quickly disappeared as the realities of Britt's injury came to light. I could see the bone flashing white through the ravaged wound on her arm. The pale cast of her skin was evident of how quickly she had lost blood so I reached for one of the packs, looking for anything I could find to stop the flow.

"We need something to tie off that arm, now!" I gasped out, looking up to see the same panic mirrored in Bran's eyes.

"Take a strap from the breastplate," Corvin gritted out, his fingers already moving to the first buckle he could find.

"No! It has to stay on her." I could see the confusion on their faces so I explained, "I don't know why, I just know she was told it would keep her safe."

Bran nodded like that made perfect sense. "The lace in your arm brace," he said, nodding at Corvin's arm. "It's the best we have for now."

Corvin quickly worked the knot out of his lace as his gaze dropped to Drystan. "Does he need any assistance?"

"He overloaded his magic," I explained, kneeling to check on my friend again. "He's never used it much in the past, and it must have overwhelmed him. I think he'll come around fine."

"You think?" Corvin sounded sceptical, and I couldn't blame him.

I shrugged. "I have no idea what's happening with him. Like I said, he doesn't use his magic much, so this has never happened before."

Corvin hummed in response, his eyes not leaving Drystan

as he handed Bran the lace he'd freed. "It's quite something to witness. I suppose I can see why he wouldn't have had many occasions to use it to its full potential."

This was the first time someone had seen Drystan use his magic and wasn't absolutely terrified of him. Corvin actually seemed impressed.

"He won't be happy when he wakes up. Drystan doesn't have the best relationship with his magic."

Bran glanced down at my friend and his gaze moved across his face. I knew he was looking at the scar that ran through his eyebrow and down across his cheek. He'd been lucky not to lose his eye at the time. That scar represented the darkest time in Drystan's past, and the fact that he had a reminder on his face for everyone to see had taken a long time for him to deal with.

Corvin grunted almost like he knew what that would feel like, but his face crumpled in concern as Britt hissed in pain.

"Fuck, that hurts," she gasped.

"I know, but we need to slow the bleeding until we can treat this," Bran told her as he quickly tied a tourniquet around her arm.

Britt's eyes rolled as he twisted it tighter before she shook her head. "It's a good job I'm fucking badass then," she muttered, and we all chuckled in amusement. "We should try to find somewhere with more cover. At least until Drystan wakes up."

"I might know a place," a female voice sounded from behind us.

As I sank to the ground and grabbed a discarded sword ready to fight, Britt pushed herself out of Bran's arms and staggered forward. Corvin looked like he would dive on her and push her to the ground until Britt and the newcomer did that strange thing girls do where they laugh and cry at the same time.

Clearly, we were missing something here.

But the white wings spanning this woman's back marked her as an angel. Unless...

"Aria," Britt gasped, falling into the other woman's arms. "You have no fucking clue how glad I am to see you."

They both embraced before Aria gently grasped Britt's wrist and examined her wound with a tut.

"Well, you must be happier than I am right now. You couldn't have left at least one of them alive for me?" she joked.

And I knew it was a joke, even if poorly made, because this was Britt's friend and she'd already told us how worried she was about how the effects of fighting had affected her emotionally.

"They annoyed us," Corvin answered gruffly, and stepped forward, his head cocked to the side as he took stock of the woman in front of him. "We were told that the Valkyrie had been wiped out."

"I wasn't there at the time..." Aria started as pain flashed through her eyes.

"That seems to be a common theme around here," Corvin snarked, clearly suspicious of Aria even if he seemed to have put aside his suspicion of Britt for now.

Aria's face broke into a grimace as her wings flared behind her before they caught fire. The flames leapt from the wings but surprisingly didn't scorch the surrounding trees. "If there's something you want to say, then get on with it," she snarled.

Bran gasped at the sight of Aria's flaming wings, stepping forward as he did. His hand reached out for the fire until he seemed to think twice and let it drop to his side instead. "The Phoenix General. We didn't know they had found you."

"Stop hounding her," Britt snapped. "We need to get out of here. I take it you're here to show us how to get into the mountain base." Britt turned back to her friend, and I knew the ravens were on her shit list for not being nicer to her. I had no problem with them joining our mating circle, but that didn't stop a slight amount of satisfaction from flowing through me at not being the one in trouble.

Who'd have thought it? Me, the sensible one, and Drystan the inoffensive one. The world truly was turning upside down. Of course, Drystan was currently unconscious. That guy caught all the lucky breaks.

"I actually came here because Heimdallr told me there was going to be a battle and you'd need help. YOU'RE GETTING SLOW, OLD MAN," she shouted up into the sky.

I didn't know what I expected to happen then, but it wasn't for a portal to open up just metres away from us. I flinched before I could stop myself, expecting the black shadowy tendrils to snap out and attack us. Aria eyed me curiously, having seen my reaction but said nothing and I tried to push it off as normal considering everything we'd been through. Afterall, I'd nearly been eaten by the damn thing twice now.

No one moved. It was almost like we were waiting for the catch. Nothing had been easy up until now and the thought of stepping through a portal and finally getting to where we needed to be felt... wrong.

"Finally!" Aria cheered, throwing her hands up in the air before she wrapped one around Britt's shoulders and guided her toward the portal. "I knew it wasn't just me that fucking hated these things."

The wings on Aria's back shimmered and then disappeared. Just before she stepped through the portal, she shuddered and then shouted over one shoulder, "You might want to pick that other fella up off the ground and catch up."

And then she disappeared with our mate.

It was only once Britt was out of view that the three of us sprung into action. We had no idea how long the portal would stay open, and there was no way I'd separate from her. As I turned to Drystan intending to drag him through the portal if I had to, I caught sight of Corvin throwing him over one shoulder.

"You heard the lady," he said, striding to the portal as I hurried to catch up.

As the wet slippery feel of the portal brushed over my skin, I couldn't help but think that Aria was right. These things were pretty gross and when you coupled it with shadowy tentacled monsters... Well, I definitely wasn't a fan.

Chapter 32

Britt

Aria.
Aria was here.

And Corvin and Bran had just torn through a squadron of angels because they'd hurt me—literally in Bran's case.

Was it wrong to admit I was impressed? It probably was, right? Death and blood definitely weren't sexy. Nope, nope, it was probably the blood loss making me woozy or something. Definitely no swooning going on over here.

"You've got that weird look on your face that means your crazy is screaming too loudly in your head," Aria said, drawing my attention to her smirking face.

I'd been sitting on the hospital bed for a few minutes waiting for a doctor to arrive and given that it was little more than a cave—an admittedly well-equipped cave—there wasn't exactly much to catch my attention. So, instead, my head had been crowded with thoughts of what had just happened and maybe Aria was slightly right about what was going on with me right now.

The guys were leaning against the opposite wall, looking between Drystan and me in concern. He still hadn't woken up, and I was desperately trying not to think about it. Thinking about it would lead to freaking out about it and I'd only just apparently won over Corvin and Bran. I had to keep the crazy contained for at least a short while.

"I don't know what you're talking about. Definitely never had crazy thoughts. You must be thinking about yourself," I blurted out in panic when I realised they'd heard what she said.

Thankfully at that moment, the doors to the clinic burst open and the doctor rushed through, followed by Kyle, Sykes and a big ginger guy who looked suspiciously too happy considering the situation we were in.

I was only slightly insulted when he strode past me and pulled Corvin and Bran into one of those weird man hugs they all seemed to universally know how to do. What was with that? Damn, how did a person hold the crazy at bay again?

"Generally, they keep it inside their head," Kyle said with a grin and I felt what little blood I had drained from my face as I realised what I'd done.

Aria cracked out laughing, but then did her best to smother it when she saw the look on my face. "I'm sorry. I've just missed you so much. Don't worry, it's just the blood loss making you loopy. I'm sure you'll heal soon enough."

The doctor tutted and eased Aria out of the way before he grasped my wrist and lifted my arm in front of his face. "I think I'll be the judge of that." He gave Aria a side eye like he was fully aware of how much of a difficult patient she could be herself. I dreaded to think what the poor guy would go through if it was one of her guys sitting here.

"It's deep," he murmured, and I mentally questioned his medical qualifications. "You'll need stitches since you're showing no signs of healing this yourself."

My face flushed in embarrassment. It hadn't been said

with any kind of tone, but it had felt like it might as well have been.

I heard a growl of upset from Xanth at his choice of words, and Corvin and Bran seemed to look at him in confusion before they suddenly understood.

But they weren't what I was afraid of right now.

Because as soon as those words slipped through his lips, Aria, Kyle and Sykes crowded around me, trying to peer at my arm as well.

"What's going on?" Kyle asked, taking the arm from the doctor and angled it around as if he could see why it wasn't healing. "This isn't healing."

Aria looked panicked and whirled around to my guys. "What did he cut her with? Did we leave the weapon behind?"

I could see her panic building, and I reached out with my good hand for her. When she felt my hand brush hers, her wide, panicked eyes met mine, and I realised they were all waiting for me to answer.

I knew exactly why it wasn't healing. What I didn't know was how I'd tell her the truth. Right now she looked like the same girl I remembered from when she was thrown into the academy—totally outraged by the world she'd found herself in and determined to make a difference. That felt like so long ago now. And this would crush her. I didn't think I could bear to see that look on her face again.

My gaze darted to my mates, who were standing against the wall behind them. They shuffled uneasily and Xanth stepped forward like he would take the burden for me.

I was almost ready to let him do it, even if it felt like a betrayal of our friendship. Then the doors to the clinic slammed open and, given what we'd been through recently, my head snapped in that direction as I ripped my arm from Kyle's loose grip and reached for my sword, ready to fight.

My hand paused midair as I froze at the sight in front of

me. My mind couldn't comprehend how it could be real, my heart racing at what it meant. Dropping my hand, I held them both out and stared at the blood that coated my palms.

Always covered in blood.

Mine.

Hers.

All of my friends and the people I loved the most.

This was my curse. Watching the blood of everyone I loved slip through my fingers and never being able to do anything to stop it.

I welcomed the darkness as consciousness fled. It might have been the blood loss. It might have been the overwhelming need for my mind to turn away from reality for a while. But whatever the cause, it was silent here. It was dark. And if I was alone, that meant no one else needed to get hurt anymore.

Chapter 33

Aria

Kyle caught Britt as her body pitched forward and she nearly fell from the examination table she'd been sitting on. The doctor rushed to her, ordering us all from the room as one of Britt's mates helped him lay her flat on the table.

Something was going on. I hadn't been in Britt's life for as long as I'd wanted to, but I knew that girl as well as I knew myself. Mainly because we were so alike. And I could tell, without a shadow of a doubt, that she was hiding something from me.

Kyle gently laid a hand on my shoulder, and my gaze moved from where I'd been staring at Britt to him. "Come on. We can wait outside if you want, but he needs room to work."

I nodded numbly. I hated seeing her hurt, but it was the confusion of what she could be hiding that distracted me.

Her mates argued that they wouldn't leave her, and even when the doctor bargained that one of them could stay, they didn't back down. The sight brought a smile to my lips. It was about time Britt had someone like them in her corner. I'd always have her back, and god help anyone that dared to raise a hand to my girl but they'd love her in ways I couldn't. And after everything, Britt deserved that. More than most people in this realm.

I'd always thought I'd been dealt a hard hand in life when I was forced on this journey to save the shifter packs. But Britt? She'd died to take the first step on this journey. She'd lost so much more than I had, and now, as we were hopefully reaching the end, the greatest risk fell on her shoulders. It was so unfair that even after everything; I was trying to figure out some way that I could take her place.

"I know that look," my father's voice rumbled from behind me as Kyle led me out of the clinic.

I spotted Geta pacing restlessly in the corridor after her dramatic entrance looking like she'd seen a ghost.

"Yeah, you could have dealt with that a bit more gently," I pointed out, but then as I turned to look at Thor, I realised he was actually talking to me. "Wait, what? What did I do?"

I was like a child about to protest my innocence, and clearly Thor felt the same as a huge grin stretched across his lips. We'd missed out on this in our lives, and every time we accidentally slipped into a family dynamic, it always made him deliriously happy.

Kyle and Sykes stepped away, probably knowing things were about to get mushy. Ordinarily, I'd protest that they save me as well from the gushy stuff, but not when it came to Thor. This time with him was something I hadn't realised I'd needed, and it was healing some of the guilt and pain I couldn't seem to shed.

My mates murmured between themselves, so I turned back to my father and Geta, who looked at the pair of us curiously.

"You're hatching a plan that's going to involve swords and possibly fire… I haven't figured out your 'set it on fire' face yet," Thor told me, his face scrunching at the seriousness in his tone.

"My 'set it on fire' face?" I wanted to laugh and deny that it was even a thing, but unfortunately for me Sykes wasn't as distracted as I'd thought he was.

"It's more angry but with this little evil smile," he butted in.

The audacity! I'd show him a 'set it on fire' face. I knew where his human realm snacks were hidden back at the packhouse and as soon as we...

"Oooo, like that! Wait... why do you look like that?" He sounded concerned, even more at the laugh that slipped out in response.

Maybe I could accept I had a 'set it on fire' face, after all.

Thor, of course, found the whole thing hilarious, and it took me a moment to realise what had started it.

"Britt's hiding something. Why isn't she healing?"

I looked at Geta because out of all of us, she'd spent the most time with Britt recently, and given the flash of guilt that touched her face, I was right to think she knew the reason.

"It's her story to tell," she answered non-committedly.

The first thing that hit me was worry. If Geta wouldn't tell me, then that meant it was bad enough that she respected Britt's need to keep it private.

I looked back at Kyle and Sykes, and saw the same looks of concern on their faces as well.

I wanted to argue, but reluctantly I had to admit that Geta was right. Britt should be allowed to tell us on her own terms. She didn't need to worry about us when she had so much weighing on her already. So, instead of standing here, worrying about something I couldn't change, I decided to do something productive instead.

"Britt and her mates have the raven claw. We need to start preparing for our first move. We won't be able to do anything until she's healed, but it at least gives us more time to prepare and train."

I could see the respect in Thor's eyes when I didn't challenge Geta. Hell, before all of this had happened, I probably would have pushed her for answers. But I understood personal pain on a level I'd never experienced before, and I appreciated it when they'd given me the time to work through the thoughts in my head. I could do it for them, too.

Thor nodded. "I'll call a meeting with the squadron leaders and see if Heimdallr can get us any up-to-date information on Odin's troop positions." He walked away before any of us could even comment.

Geta looked at me thoughtfully. "I'm surprised to see you working so well with Heimdallr after everything that happened on the blood moon."

I shrugged in response. It had been hard at first, and if he'd approached me before I'd had time to work through my pain, it probably would have ended differently. But I could appreciate that he had to do what was necessary to get us through to this point. Frannie had given him a role to play, and he'd played it. Now he had to stand back and deal with his guilt at the things he'd been party to.

I could see it in his eyes that he was struggling. Part of me even thought he deserved it. But then I'd realised that this entire journey had asked the impossible of so many people and we were all trying to deal with the consequences any way we could. Heimdallr could redeem himself if he did the right thing now. We might not have agreed with his actions before, but if he hadn't done as Frannie had needed him to, none of us would still be on this path.

We'd all been assigned a role, and he'd been given one of the worst. Now it was time for him to prove he wasn't a villain in this story and I had to begrudgingly accept that we needed him, too.

"It's been difficult. But who between us hasn't had to do things we don't regret? He deserves a chance to show us that when he has a choice, he can make the right one."

Geta nodded thoughtfully, a look of pride crossing her features. "You've grown into an incredible leader."

I wanted to deny that I'd done anything of the sort because I didn't feel like a leader. I felt like a broken shadow of a person who stood up when needed. Except that wasn't exactly true anymore. I was dealing with my shit and I was stronger because of the things I'd done. Life meant so much more to me now and I could see the world in more than the black and white that used to exist for me. Life existed in all the varying shades of grey, and it was there that you truly proved the type of person you were.

CHAPTER 34

CORVIN

I paced the edge of the room. Every so often stopping so my gaze could move to my mate and assess if she was any closer to waking.

"She's lost a lot of blood. Even with the wound closed and the bleeding stemmed, it's going to take a while for her body to recover from the shock," the doctor told us.

So now we waited.

And it was the most painful thing I'd ever experienced in my life.

This woman lying so small and pale on the examination table had burst into my life, and even though I'd felt the pull, the need, I'd denied myself the hope she could be who she seemed to be.

After living so long in the darkness with the pain of watching my brother's suffering, I didn't believe a creature such as me was worthy of something as pure as hope. His pain had hurt more than anything they could do to me. Unfortunately for Bran, Hel had figured that out, and he'd paid the price for it.

But this? This was so much worse. I felt more helpless now than I ever had, and I hated it.

"She's going to wake up," Bran told me unhelpfully.

I knew she would eventually. The doctor had told us as such. She wasn't in any kind of life-threatening danger. She'd had treatment quickly enough, and now she needed to rest. It didn't make any difference, though. I wouldn't feel whole again until she opened her eyes.

The door to the clinic opened, and a man we hadn't met yet stepped inside. "We have a room prepared for you if you want to get cleaned up."

I looked at him like he was insane. He couldn't really expect us to leave her side.

"Sorry, I'm Braedon. We haven't met yet." He strode into the room and held his hand out, which Xanth politely shook. "I've been in your exact place and trust me, I know it's killing you right now. Aria just wanted to let you know you had the choice if you wanted it."

A groan came from Drystan as he rocked to his side and nearly rolled off the table we'd left him on. "Fuck my life. What happened?"

Xanth practically skipped to his side, happy to see the mage finally regaining consciousness. I could admit to being slightly relieved myself. I didn't understand enough about his magic to know if his reaction was unusual, but we couldn't afford for a repeat when we faced Odin, which meant we needed to find a way for Drystan to practise his magic, and that posed a whole host of problems.

Drystan struggled to sit up, and his gaze fell on Britt. "What happened?!" he shouted, scrambling to get off the table even though Xanth stubbornly kept him where he was. "What's wrong with her? Why isn't she waking up?"

"She lost consciousness when the valkyrie walked into the

room but the doctor assures us she just needs the rest," Bran told him.

Xanth froze then at Drystan's side. Both of them looked like they'd seen a ghost, which I didn't understand because Xanth had been here when she'd walked in.

"Valkyrie?" Xanth asked in confusion. "I thought... I don't know what I thought. Angel maybe?"

I shook my head at the mage. I was about to accuse him of not being able to tell the two apart, but thankfully remembered my own confusion when I'd seen Aria and thought better of it.

Drystan's gaze returned to Britt and he frowned in concern. "It's no wonder she was shocked. We never saw the destruction of Valhalla, but Britt did. She saw all the dead and had to leave them behind. I think it killed a part of her to walk away from them. At least she's not the only survivor. Maybe that will give her some peace."

The pain in his voice proved that he knew how it felt to feel guilty about surviving.

"Erm..." Braedon interrupted. "There's... there's probably something you need to know."

And then he launched into a story that sounded too incredible to be true. Every so often, we all glanced at Britt before our attention quickly returned to the man telling us about the resurrection of an entire race. I didn't know if we were checking to see if she had woken or hoping that she hadn't.

"How are we going to tell her this?" Xanth asked worriedly.

"I'd say she probably suspects after seeing whoever rushed in here earlier," Bran said.

He had a point. Damn, this whole situation was getting more and more complicated and we still had the issue of the raven's claw.

The sword was strapped firmly to my back once again. Drawing it in a fight had felt so familiar and yet also wrong. There was something different about it. Bran and I had safeguarded the sword for centuries. It was given to us by fate herself when we'd begged her for a mate of our own. That was the problem with never having actually been born and just coming into existence. We didn't have a place in this world really, not like the ones who were made to be here. There was no string of fate running through our lives and even if it had taken us a while to realise, we soon came to believe that meant there would be no way for any other threads to intersect with ours. Which meant that a mate was something that would never happen.

Obviously, we could have looked for a partner, anyway. Choosing to bond out of love instead. But that wasn't what we wanted. We'd seen the beauty of mates coming together and wanted it for ourselves. After our service at Odin's side, we'd foolishly thought it was unfair to be denied.

We'd sought her out. Beseeched fate to tie us to the realm with one of her threads and grant us a chance. She'd warned us what it could mean. That by tying ourselves with a thread, we'd also risk such a thread being broken. But back then, the chance of mortality seemed like such a small price to pay for the happiness that had been denied us.

What we hadn't realised was that fate always had a price for the things she did, and whilst she'd granted our request, the mate we'd dreamed of never appeared. At least when we knew it wasn't a possibility it didn't hurt as much, but with every year that passed without finding her, that price felt so much larger than we'd first believed.

And then Odin had betrayed us, and we'd been banished to Helheim. That thread that we'd once begged to have became stretched so thin that we'd become a shadow of the men we once were. Because it didn't just bind us to our missing mate, it bound us to the realm that had birthed our existence. How Odin had known about it was something I'd never been able to figure out, and I hoped it didn't mean that fate was on his side. This would all be for nothing if she was.

Drystan groaned as he swung his feet off the edge of the table and tried to stand. "This feels like a hangover from Helheim," he grumbled.

It was then that Braedon stepped forward, looking at him curiously. "If you try to expel the energy, it should help you feel better."

From how Drystan looked at him, I could tell he didn't know what he was talking about. "Erm... I can maybe help you if you want," Braedon offered.

Xanth was about to say something before Drystan cut in. "I'd appreciate it."

Braedon nodded happily before reaching out a hand for the mage. Strangely, it had me darting forward protectively. We didn't know him or what he was about to do. How did we know we could trust this guy?

Bran stopped me with a hand on my chest before he gave me that dopey grin I hated so much, and usually meant I'd done something that proved I was a normal person and not just the grumpy asshole I liked to pretend to be.

"This is going to feel strange. I'm going to pull the soul energy you're holding onto, but I'll separate the threads from your own, so you don't need to worry about it draining you."

Why was no one else freaking out about this?

I went to step forward again, and this time Bran pushed me back. I didn't understand him. We might not know these mages well, but they were Britt's mates as well and we couldn't let some stranger mess about with his soul. It definitely had nothing to do with the pair of them growing on me. Even if they were kind of amusing to have around.

"Let him work. We're among friends here," Bran reassured me.

It should have been enough to have me backing down, but after hanging in a cage watching your brother be tortured for so long, it kind of made a man hesitant to trust in those around him.

"We don't know that. He could do anything to him..."

"There. How does that feel?"

My eyes snapped up as I realised it was too late. Not only that, but they were all staring at me and grinning like idiots.

"Fine. Let some stranger rip out your soul. See if I care." I stormed back to Britt's side, letting my fingers brush through the dark lengths of her hair. I knew I was sulking, but at least they all had the decency to ignore it.

I wasn't used to having people around me that I gave a crap about and I couldn't decide how much to hate the feeling. It was a vulnerability I'd never considered. They had used Bran against me for so long, but I'd never regretted my attachment to him. He was like a mirror to my soul. My brother in every sense of the word. But now those attachments were growing, and after seeing Britt and Drystan both incapacitated so easily, I felt the panic setting in at the idea I wasn't enough to keep them safe. How could I be? I hadn't been able to save Bran. In fact, I was the reason he'd suffered as badly as he had. *I was the liability.*

"That feels... strange," Drystan admitted, drawing the attention away from me.

Reluctantly, I peered over at them. Not wanting to be a part of it, but also not wanting to miss a thing.

"I didn't have any magic most of my life, but my bond with Aria brought it to life. It's taken some time to get used to, and it hasn't been easy to learn. There aren't many books about soul magic and I've never met another person with the same power that I have before. I'd love to talk more to you about your experiences with it," Braedon explained happily.

I could see the shock on Drystan's face. His mouth opened as if he wanted to say something, then it closed, and he frowned in thought before repeating the process again.

"What Drystan is trying to say is that he would love to do that," Xanth added helpfully, nudging his friend playfully.

Drystan scowled at him, apparently still shocked into silence for some reason I didn't understand.

Bran looked as confused as I did. This was the problem with being thrown into a bond with a bunch of strangers. We'd all had lives before this and when were we supposed to find time to share them with each other? The past always clouded the future, and right now the clouds were so thick they were impossible to see through. We needed time together, but how did you tell someone to put an end of the world fight on hold so you could hold hands and chat with your mate?

"How about Drystan and I get cleaned up while you stay with Britt and then we can swap? She's going to be out for a while if the doc is right, but I know we'd all prefer she wasn't alone."

It was then I realised how much Xanth needed to hold Drystan up, and I could see the exhaustion around his own eyes as well. We probably all looked like shit.

"You should catch a few hours' sleep as well. We can wait," I offered, surprising myself.

Bran grinned again, and I resisted the urge to punch him for his amusement at the fact I was concerned about someone who wasn't him. I'd never hear the end of this. Maybe I could persuade them to take him with them so I could at least get some peace for a few hours.

"Thanks, man," Drystan replied, slurring his words slightly.

Braedon looked at him in concern, especially once he

caught the scowl I sent in his direction. If he'd fucked around with Drystan's soul by mistake, there'd sure as fuck be a price to pay.

I didn't even have time to growl out a threat before he showed them out of the room and Bran's grinning face was suddenly in my line of sight.

"I knew you had a heart in there somewhere," he mocked and I scowled in response, not giving him the rise he looked for.

Instead, I turned back to Britt, reaching out and running my fingers through her hair again. Hopefully, when she woke up, she wouldn't be completely outraged by the action. I hadn't really been receptive to the idea of mates when we first met and hadn't given her any sign that this was something I wanted. For all I knew, she didn't want me as a mate. That hurt more than I'd thought it would.

"She's vulnerable." I didn't know why I'd said it. It was clear to anyone who saw her that Britt was a fierce warrior. "We have to protect her."

Bran said nothing and when I finally dragged my gaze away from our unconscious mate, it was to meet his eyes filled with the same sense of resolve.

"She's going to hate that," he pointed out, and I snorted out a laugh. That was one thing I'd definitely come to realise about her as well.

"How is she going to wield the raven's claw?"

He didn't respond. Of course, he didn't. There was no denying she was our mate. I could feel the bond already reaching out to entwine around my soul. There was no question about whether it was real. But fate had told us that only our mate would wield the raven's claw and that she would be the reigning raven. Only Britt wasn't a raven. She was as weak as a human. None of it made sense.

"Maybe fate was wrong," Bran finally said.

I looked at him like he'd lost his mind. The woman bound the entire universe in her threads and even if she swore she didn't manipulate them, there was no diverting from the path. Not without consequence, at least. You could follow the thread or you could break it. That wasn't really a choice at all.

"No. There has to be something we're not seeing."

I stared down at the woman who'd stolen my heart without even having to whisper a word. Who was she? She wasn't a human, she never had been, but how were we going to turn her into the raven she needed to be? The reigning raven all the realms needed her to be, if they were going to have any chance of survival.

Chapter 35

Britt

The throbbing in my arm was the first thing I felt when I came to. With it came the memory of what I'd seen, and the pain that accompanied that sight was more than anything I'd ever experienced. Considering my past, that was saying something.

I groaned and tried to sit up, an awareness flooded my body that I wasn't entirely sure I wanted. I hadn't ached like this since I'd first trained with Aria. Back then, I'd welcomed every ache and pain. It was evidence I was growing stronger. That she was moulding me into a survivor. But this pain... this felt more like a reminder of everyone I'd failed to protect.

A gentle touch at my back helped me to sit up and my eyes fluttered open; they focused on a glass of water being held in front of my face. I readily accepted it, realising then how dry my mouth felt. I gulped down the fresh cold liquid, and took in my surroundings. It wasn't too much of a surprise I was still in the clinic. Xanth's concerned face was the next thing I noticed and then Drystan standing behind him, who looked nothing but relieved.

My eyes scanned his form, checking to see if he looked harmed at all. The last I'd seen him, he'd been unconscious on the examination table beside me. Now his hair was damp from a shower and he wore a fresh set of clothes. It made me itchy with the realisation of how desperately I needed one.

When I noticed the lack of two other people in the room, I couldn't keep the disappointment from my face as I passed the glass back to Xanth.

"We could only convince them to leave your side half an hour ago. They've stood watch over you for nearly a day," Xanth told me.

A wave of relief swept over me, even if I wasn't entirely sure it was a good thing. At least it wasn't a rejection. I remembered their rage at seeing me hurt, but this would have been their first opportunity to leave us behind. A part of me still thought they might.

"Yeah, you should have seen Corvin clucking all around you. That ones going to be clingy," Xanth joked when he saw the relief on my face.

I chuckled at the thought, even as I found myself being pulled into his arms. "You scared us there for a minute," he whispered, burrowing his face into my hair. "Let's try not to do that again, yeah?"

I clung to him as he held me, taking the comfort from his embrace that I desperately needed. When he let go, Drystan took his place, and tears came to my eyes.

"I thought I saw Geta," I whispered. "I thought…"

I knew how ridiculous it sounded. Logically, I knew it was impossible. She'd died in my arms and I'd left her body in Valhalla while I'd fled. The hope and the guilt that simultaneously struck my heart had been more than I wanted to bear.

As Drystan's grip loosened on me, he gently pulled away, and I was already waiting for the blow to land.

"Aria went to Valhalla first. Her magic... she raised them," Drystan told me.

I didn't understand what he meant at first. Then tears of relief flowed down my face, and I couldn't even articulate the words of how I felt right now. It was only when I was back in his arms that I realised I didn't need to say anything. Of everyone in all the realms, he'd understand how this made me feel, and my heart broke that he'd never had the chance to experience it himself.

"She's waiting for you with Aria when you're ready to see her and she wanted us to tell you she was sorry for bursting in here. She cares for you a lot, sweetheart. When she heard you were injured, she couldn't stay away even though she knew she should," Xanth explained.

"I think I might want to take a shower first and maybe eat something," I decided.

My stomach growled loudly at the idea alone. I was so numb that hunger hadn't registered with me. It had been more of a stalling tactic, if I was honest. I just wanted time to deal with the reality of it before I saw Geta and did something embarrassing like cry on her. She wasn't a tears type of person.

What would she say when I saw her? Would she be happy that we'd made it this far? Or would she be disappointed, that even though we'd found the raven's claw, we had no idea how to use it?

We'd come so far and yet, in some respects, it felt like we were still standing at the starting line. What use was a weapon you didn't know how to use? Especially when you were up against the All Father and whatever army he'd pulled around him.

"Maybe we should find Aria and go over what plans they've made so far?" I suggested instead, realising how much work was left to do.

As I went to move from the examination table, my arm twinged with pain when I put weight on it. I gasped, pulling it up in surprise. For some reason, the fact I was still injured surprised me. I guessed it came from going through my entire life relying on shifter healing. I might not have been able to fully heal something like this in a day, but it would've been close.

"They can wait," Drystan told me as he reached for me to help me off the examination table. "Let's get some food into you first."

"Yeah, Aria would probably appreciate you taking a shower, too," Xanth joked.

Drystan snorted as a look of outrage crossed my face. "Rude!" I gasped.

"Hey, I'm merely telling it like it is." Xanth had one of those looks on his face which he no doubt thought gave him an air of innocence. Instead, I kicked out the back of his knee, so he stumbled and huffed in outrage as I strode past him.

In reality, it was more like a slow shuffle, but I'd definitely got my point across.

Xanth laughed, jogging to catch up with us, and then threw his arm around my shoulders and pulled me close. "You know I'm only joking. I love you, stink and everything."

Without responding, I turned to Drystan. "Would you stab him if I asked you to?"

He looked thoughtful for a moment before asking. "Where are we talking? Because if it's something like a thigh, I might get on board, but I feel like straight in the gut might be going a bit too far."

"You make a good point," I responded, pretending to actually consider it.

"Hey, I'm the charming one, remember!" Xanth protested.

It was nice to have a playful moment even if my arm burned like someone had set it on fire and I was dead on my feet, even after being unconscious for a day. We had no idea what tomorrow held for us, and ignoring that fact was exactly what I needed right now.

Xanth and Drystan led me through a series of tunnels which weren't half as depressing as you'd expect a secret rebellion mountain base to be. We were obviously in some kind of living quarters, and the sounds of life echoing around us were comforting. Children laughed, darting between rooms as they chased each other. Their weary mothers ran after them, looking exhausted, and yet happy all at the same time. We saw people dressed in fighting leathers with weapons strapped to their bodies, and the elderly moving at a slower pace, looking like they were distributing supplies.

These people looked like they'd been here for a while. They were comfortable enough to be making the best of the situation they'd found themselves in, but it was still hard to look at. These kids deserved to be running through the fields with the sun on their skin and the wind in their faces. This had been going on for far too long. Longer that most in the magic realm were aware of. And yet they'd not only endured it, they'd found a way to flourish. It gave me hope I hadn't realised I was missing. One that saw the packs back in their packlands, pups running around carefree once again. These were the people we were fighting for. We were all the same, after all. Just trying to get through life with the people we loved at our side.

By the time we'd stopped at a door that looked exactly the same as the last dozen we'd walked past, I had a newfound sense of resolve, despite the exhaustion that currently pulled at me.

Xanth swung it open, stepping inside, muttering about how no one appreciated his role in the group. I followed him through into a surprisingly comfortable looking bedroom that was more than big enough for all of us.

A blush rushed across my cheeks as I took in the sight of Bran sitting on the edge of the bed, shirtless and rubbing his wet hair with a towel. But that was nothing compared to when he gasped, "You're awake," and Corvin darted into the room wearing only a towel wrapped around his hips.

Was it suddenly getting hot in here?

Xanth snorted at the look on my face, and I resisted the urge to poke fun at him even more in retaliation.

"You're awake," Corvin repeated, striding toward me.

When he pulled me against him, my face pressed against his wet chest, I didn't know what to do with my hands. Well, I did. I wanted to grab that towel and rip it off to get a peek at what was underneath, but that felt inappropriate for some reason.

"Is this weird?" Corvin asked quietly, realising what he'd just done.

"Not at all," I reassured, finally letting my arms wrap around him and shuffling as close as I could get.

It was the first time he'd properly touched me, let alone held me, and I was going to soak up every second while I had a chance.

For a moment, the world stood still. His chest moved in time with mine and I almost thought I felt a bond stir inside my chest. It was followed by an ache in the emptiness where my wolf had once been, but it was a reminder of her, one that wasn't entirely unpleasant. Because I was still alive, and even though part of my soul had been sheared away, I was still here. Living. Loving. Making the best of what fate had dealt us.

When we separated, I found a sheepish-looking Bran standing next to us. "You got one of those for me, too?" he asked quietly.

It was all I needed to throw myself into his arms.

"I was so worried," he whispered against my hair as he held onto me as tightly as he could.

"It's going to take more than that to take me down," I joked.

It fell completely flat and had the unfortunate side effect of ending the hug far faster than I would have liked.

"Your training starts this afternoon," Corvin told me gruffly.

The girl I'd once been probably would have sighed in defeat at that, but I wasn't that person anymore. "Is Aria training with us?" I asked, bouncing on the balls of my feet despite the exhaustion I felt.

"She had exactly the same reaction. There's something wrong with the two of you," Xanth grumbled, clearly not as excited about the prospect as I was.

"Just wait. Training with Aria is something else. She's got this weird valkyrie general thing that makes you awesome," I told him excitedly.

It was enough of a step back toward what had been my normality that it made me feel almost reassured.

"First things first..." Drystan said.

"Yeah, I know, I stink and I need a shower," I grumbled.

Corvin and Bran snapped to attention at the tone in my voice and looked ready to throw down on my behalf. Awww, sweet.

"I swear no one gets my humour," Xanth sighed dramatically before flopping down on the bed and throwing an arm over his eyes.

Drystan shook his head at his antics, but I caught the look of relief on his face. We all needed this. Not just time together, but time to be... people again.

"I'll grab some food while you shower," Drystan offered, and I grinned in happiness.

Bran moved across the room and grabbed his shirt to pull on. "I'll come with you and we can grab something for everyone. Maybe take some time to relax and talk before we head off for Britt's training."

I snorted at the sentiment. Not that he wanted to get to know me, but that he thought he wasn't about to get pulled into said training as well. The guys all looked at me like they were worried it was a sign I'd collapse again, but I decided to let them think what they wanted. It would be better to leave it as a surprise anyway.

"Pick up your feet!" Aria shouted across the training hall.

Xanth attempted to scoff in outrage, but it sounded more like a wheeze than anything else. The ravens were keeping pace so far, but I could see the tiredness setting in. They'd been shut inside cages for whatever amount of time they were currently trying to hide from us. Running wasn't exactly something they were used to, and the smugness they'd started out with at thinking this would be easy had worn off about three laps back.

I'd been spending the last two laps cursing the fact my arm was killing me and I still hadn't had enough sleep. Exhaustion was already pulling at me, and it shouldn't have been. I was in better shape than this. I should have had at least another three miles in me.

"Bring it in, that's enough for today," Aria shouted a moment later. I didn't want to stop, and as the thought of pushing into another lap entered my head, Aria added, "If you push too hard today, you won't make it back tomorrow."

The academy flashed back in my mind at the reminder of those earlier training sessions, but then with it came the screams, the blood, and the smoke from that last fateful day. My feet stumbled to a stop, and I nearly tripped as I shook my head, desperate to stop the memories that wanted to take root in my mind.

"You doing okay?" Bran asked, walking beside me as we headed to the other side of the training hall. "To be honest, I'm surprised to see you up and about so quickly. I thought you'd need at least a few days to recover."

"I feel better when I'm moving. It filters all the everyday crap out of my head and I think clearly. Besides, it's been forever since I could train with Aria and I've been looking forward to this. One minor scratch won't stop me from doing that." I tried to put on a brave face. My arm hurt so much that I was pretty numb to it now, but I knew I'd regret this later. I was just hoping I'd be able to cover it up enough so I didn't have to endure the inevitable 'I told you so,' that would be coming.

"She is quite remarkable," Bran said thoughtfully before his eyes moved to Xanth and Drystan. "I didn't think the mages were going to make it this far."

Corvin snorted out a laugh. But I didn't miss the edge of exhaustion that sounded in the huff that followed. None of the guys had done as well as the Elites would have, but even we'd sucked at the beginning. I missed my girls, and I couldn't wait to be reunited with them soon. I was definitely going to need to bring my A game that day, because frankly, my performance right now sucked.

Aria watched me carefully as we grew closer and I straightened my spine and pushed down the exhaustion that rose. I knew her training routines like the back of my hand and I had no doubt that hand-to-hand or weapons training would be next. I also knew she wouldn't risk me getting more injured by pushing me too soon. Unfortunately, that meant an afternoon of sit-ups and lame stretches if I couldn't convince her I was fine.

"Don't even try it." The smirk on her face clued me in that the brave face I was trying to put on had failed epically. "I remember that red faced, dead eyed look from the early days. You have nothing else left in you. Call it a day, Britt. There's always tomorrow."

I should have just agreed with her and taken my chance to rest. Hell, I should have gone to get something to eat because despite eating earlier before my nap, my stomach felt like it was eating itself already. Instead, for some reason I couldn't figure out, the thought of stopping now felt like the most insulting suggestion Aria had ever made to me.

"I've got more. You don't need to baby me, Aria. I can do this. I need to do this and, frankly, it's not your place to tell me to stand down." The defensiveness that lined my voice had it rising to an unacceptable level, and I immediately felt bad.

Everyone turned to me in wide-eyed shock and if I hadn't already been the colour of a tomato, I was sure I'd be blushing from the embarrassment.

Aria said nothing but her face pinched in concern, because even if I couldn't figure out my behaviour, she'd been in my position and had firsthand experience of it herself. But before she could try to reason with me, a familiar voice boomed through the training hall.

"Is that how we talk to our superiors now, warrior?"

I spun on the spot, my eyes searching her out. The guys had broken the news as gently as they could to me and then I'd cried in relief. The five-mile run we'd just done had been enough to take my mind off it. But now, here she was, standing right in front of me.

I didn't hesitate as I sprinted across the hall and threw myself at her. At first, Geta stumbled back a step, her wings flaring out to the side as she steadied herself from my sudden impact. It was kind of impressive that she hadn't stabbed me from sheer reflex alone, really. Instead, as I clung to her, fat embarrassing tears streamed down my face, she stood there awkwardly. After a beat, her arms gently closed around me and she clung to me just as fiercely. Her face pressed into my hair and she whispered words of apology that only I could hear.

They were words she never should have had to speak and ones she definitely didn't need to say to me.

Geta had made the ultimate sacrifice. Not only that, but she'd shouldered the burden of what was to come entirely on her own. So many people had stood and done the impossible. Taken on the weight of the world, fought the impossible battles in the shadows, and stood against the tyrants that had taken hold of their people. All just to bring us to this point. None of them deserved to drop to their knees and beg for forgiveness. They were heroes, they were warriors, and Geta would take her place beside them as far as I was concerned.

"Don't apologise to me," I told her gently. "I'm so grateful for the sacrifices you made for me, Geta. For everything you went through to get me to this point. I just hope I don't disappoint you."

She leaned back and wiped the tears from my face before doing the same thing that everyone else had done that I'd come across recently. Carefully, she examined the wound on my arm, even though nothing was visible beneath the dressing the doctors had applied. Then she moved each of my fingers, flexed my wrist and tested the strength of my grip. I'd seen her do it so many times before when someone had been injured in training, and watching her do it now finally settled a part of me.

This was familiar.

"I'm glad to see you wearing this," she whispered, her

knuckles knocking against the breastplate. "Remember what I told you?"

I nodded, somehow knowing this wasn't something she wanted to bring up for debate with everyone else. This was part of something Frannie had told her and we all knew the risks with information like that. Despite the hundreds of questions running through my head, I wouldn't ask a single one. The risk was far too great just to assuage my curiosity.

Glancing over my shoulder, I saw Aria setting the guys into pairs and leading them through a series of moves to begin the next step of their training routine. Where they'd looked tired before, they now look excited, paying attention to her every word and movement.

This was how we were going to win. By doing the same thing we'd done before. We'd survived then, and we'd survive now. I couldn't jeopardise our chances.

And just like that, it was like the smoke from that fateful day at the academy finally cleared from my mind. The guilt of surviving was still inside me and I'd feel the loss of my friends until the day I died, but finally I could see the light again.

The hope.

The future.

That was what we were fighting for.

"The others?" I asked, even though I already knew the answer.

"They're coming in small squadrons. Heimdallr is transporting them into the mountain to avoid Odin's notice. They'll all be here in the next day."

The relief was overwhelming. These were the people I'd trained with for months. The men and women who had helped me overcome losing one life by showing me how to live one I'd always craved.

"And the Elites will be here around the same time," Aria told us as she came to join our group.

"Trent!" I suddenly gasped, and Aria cocked her head to the side in question. "We met him and his pack at the base of the world tree. They were trying to follow your trail into Asgard."

Whoops, I probably should have remembered that before now.

Aria snorted out a laugh. "Of course he was. He couldn't stay with the pack if his life depended on it. I suppose they're safe enough in Thyellin without them. I would have still preferred an Elite presence there in case we had to fall back, but we'll just have to trust that the fae will cover our retreat."

I could see her drifting away into her own mind as she went through whatever plans we weren't all party to yet.

"Erm... Trent?"

"Yes! Right! I'll get word out to someone to pick them up. I guess we're having a reunion, then."

Before Aria could step away, I gently grasped her forearm, preparing to ask the one question I'd tried not to think until now. "Aria... my grandmother?"

She pulled me into a brief hug before she moved away, gently shoving my shoulder playfully as she did. "Do you know how much trouble she's given me petitioning to join the Elites? She's safe with the fae. I suspect she's already bossing them around with making preparations for our injured if needed."

I couldn't believe that the girl I'd met at the academy had not only become the Phoenix General of the Valkyrie army, but she'd taken to it so easily. Looking at Aria now, you'd think organising a war was simple. She'd already thought of different eventualities, a safe place for the injured. I'd barely remembered to ask about the only living family member I had left. She truly was made for this.

"You're pretty awesome, you know?" I told her.

She smiled shyly. It was a look I doubted I'd ever seen on

her face before. "Only because I have the right people around me. Now, how shall we torture the boys before we let them go and shower?"

The wicked grin that crossed her lips was far more like the Aria I knew, and it was comforting to see she'd found a way back to it. Hopefully, by the end of this whole thing, she'd be able to show the rest of us, too.

Chapter 36

Bran

The valkyrie was a sadist.

"Why does my ass hurt?" I moaned as I flopped face first down on the bed.

"Awww, poor baby. Do you need me to rub it for you?" Britt taunted.

My head perked up, and I grinned at her. "Well, if you're offering, it would be rude to decline."

She snorted out a laugh and then moved into the bathroom; the mages following closely behind. It made me frown. They were already so close to her. I knew they hadn't spent that much more time with her than us, but how were we ever supposed to catch up?

"Why does your face look like that?" Corvin asked as he stripped off his sweaty shirt and then threw it at my face.

I gagged as I peeled the damp fabric away from my skin. "Ugh, god man. Why do you smell like that?"

"Because I sweat like a real man. Stop avoiding my question. What's wrong?"

I sighed as I flopped back on the bed, making sure that the

disgusting shirt fell to the side and was nowhere near me. "Do you think she likes them more than us?"

I knew exactly how it sounded. The laughter that flowed from Corvin's mouth reinforced that fact. Dick.

Then his face hovered over mine as he looked down at me with a frown on his face. "Are you actually being serious?" he asked.

I didn't answer, but when I tried to roll away, he stopped me with one knee. "Ah man, don't make me be the nice one," he moaned. "I've been nice for like a whole day and it's making me feel weird. I need to find something to push over and kick on the way down or something if I've got any chance of ever being saved from this."

"Can you just pretend for a moment that you're normal?"

"Okay. Listen close because this is going to be painful for me to say and I don't know if I can do it again. Of course, she doesn't like them more than us. She needs help in the shower to keep her arm dry and she doesn't feel like she can ask us to do that for her yet. It's normal. You haven't even kissed her. You're not quite at the naked stage yet."

Corvin shuddered as if what he'd just said had completely disturbed him. But I only heard one thing from his brief attempt at being the nice guy.

"So, what you're saying is that I need to kiss her?"

He inhaled suddenly, like he wanted to argue with me, but then he cocked his head to the side and his mouth snapped shut as he thought for a moment. "Actually, yes. It would be a start and there's no point in delaying for the sake of politeness. We don't really live in that world anymore."

"Right, right... so should I do it now?" I sprung to my feet, only for Corvin to shove me back on the bed.

"No... again, because of the naked thing. I'm worried about you, brother. I don't remember you being this slow on the uptake before."

"Was that an actual joke?" I gasped, knowing it would annoy him.

As expected, Corvin shoved me slightly before pacing away. "See, this is why I'm never nice to you," he complained.

I smiled as he rummaged through the chest in our room, looking for clean clothes. We'd been fortunate that the rebellion could help cater to our needs. They'd been here for longer than they should have been and yet they hadn't run out of supplies in the slightest. I had a feeling that some of the remaining gods were helping more than they wanted anyone to know. Even if the cowards refused to actually stand up and fight themselves.

The shame I'd felt as we walked through these caves was nearly overwhelming. We should have done more to help these people when we realised what Odin was doing. Most of them were ordinary citizens of Asgard. They held little personal magic, but still they stood up and fought. I was a being created by Asgard herself and hadn't done even a fraction of what they had. I didn't deserve their kindness when their suffering was endured because of our lack of action.

And Corvin would be feeling this even more than I was. I watched him carefully as he pulled out clothing for the entire group. He cared more than most people realised. He just hated anyone to know it for some reason, so he covered it up with his gruff exterior and hid behind an uncaring mask, even if he moved all the pieces in the background thinking no one saw.

I'd endured the attention of Hel gladly during our imprisonment in Helheim. I knew he'd tried to draw it to himself as much as he could, but for once in our lives, I got to be the one that stood in front of him for a change. To protect him in any way I could. I knew deep down he would never forgive me for it. It was who he was. He'd always be the first to sacrifice. But even though my suffering pained him too, I hoped it would show him he didn't need to be the strong one all the time.

Drystan emerged from the bathroom early enough for me to realise that he really had only been helping Britt change the dressings on her wound, and a twinge of guilt hit me for the jealousy I'd felt earlier.

Corvin looked up from the chest where he was just delaying for the sake of not wanting to extend our conversation any further. "How's her arm looking?" he asked as Drystan grabbed clean dressings.

When he looked up at us, his eyes glistened with unshed tears that he was trying to hold at bay.

"It looks the same as it did when it was stitched closed. She's healing as slowly as a human. We need to speed it along. She can't go into this fight at a bigger disadvantage than we already are."

I could see his worry for her and I'd be lying if I didn't admit that I'd been thinking exactly the same thing. It was bad enough we didn't know how she would wield the raven's claw. We couldn't let her be at more of a physical disadvantage than she already was. Britt was a warrior, and she had strength in her own right. But it was the strength of a human. She didn't even have the extra graces her wolf had once given her.

"So we need a healer," I reiterated. "There has to be someone on this base that can heal. They can't have gotten to this point and not had one come to their cause."

"It doesn't even need to be a healer," Drystan pointed out. "A witch maybe. What about an angel or a vampire? I've heard their blood has healing properties. Anything would be better than it is now."

He sounded panicked, and I'd bet Drystan was realising how close we were coming to the end of this whole thing. Not only the battle, but also the potential for losing her. The seers of our world might have seen that Britt would be the one to strike down Odin, but that didn't mean she would definitely succeed. It just meant she had the potential if she did everything right. It gave no guarantee of her living, even if she succeeded. We could win and lose her at the same time.

"How much longer will she be?" I asked, looking nervously at the door. I knew she'd hate what I was about to suggest, but that didn't mean I wouldn't put it out there anyway.

"Xanth is helping her wash her hair, so she doesn't get her arm wet. Not much longer, I think," he filled in.

I nodded, trying to figure out how to say what I wanted to. I didn't know why I was nervous. They'd both be thinking exactly the same thing. And Corvin proved exactly that.

"We have to make sure that she survives this," he finally said, letting that uncaring mask fall once again. "Even if it means that we fall in her place. Those that survive will help her through her loss, but we cannot, under any circumstances, let the cost of this war be her life."

I'd heard my brother speak passionately about things before, but it had been a long time since he'd held so much conviction in his voice. It was one thing that Odin had broken in us in the early days. It was hard to believe in something anymore when the one person who had held your ultimate trust betrayed you.

This was a glimpse of the brother I remembered. The one who had hunted down fate herself and demanded she give him a mate. And now he had her. It was only right we would protect her at all costs.

"It goes without saying," Drystan confirmed. "Xanth is nearly back in touch with his magic. As soon as he is, we'll do whatever we can to ensure she's protected."

"Why did he lose it? How strong is he? Does he have a limit like you do?" Corvin rapid fired his questions at Drystan, and thankfully, even though he looked shocked for a moment, he sensed how serious Corvin was.

"Xanth was beaten until he nearly died. It was one of

Britt's friends that saved him from being fed to Odin's portal monster. And he's strong." Drystan laughed at that, shaking his head. "Xanth has never had an issue using his magic in little ways that improved his life and the lives of people around him. And because he used small amounts all the time, it's almost like he's got a bottomless reserve."

Corvin didn't look like he believed him at first. "It can't be that impressive if he could be captured and nearly killed."

It was harsh, but unfortunately, he had a point.

"Don't hate, man. Not everyone can be as awesome as me," Xanth announced as he emerged from the bathroom with a towel wrapped around his waist.

I heard Britt chuckling from behind him and knew this conversation was on pause for now. She wouldn't take kindly to us plotting how we'd sacrifice ourselves in her place if the need arose. But I was definitely curious about whatever magic Xanth could have that had someone like Drystan impressed. After all, he could command the very power of life and death with just a touch of his hand. What could be more impressive than that?

Chapter 37

BRITT

I could see the tension in everyone around the table as soon as we walked into the room. And even though I'd been adamant I wanted to be part of the planning before, I doubted this was an argument I wanted to walk in on. Mainly because Aria was currently standing, her hands braced on the tabletop with her chair lying on its side behind her. She scowled down at her father, who for once didn't have a cheerful look on his face. Who would have guessed it, but the god was absolutely terrifying?

"We have to stick to the path," Thor thundered.

Aria didn't even flinch as he raised his voice and I had a feeling it was because they'd been at it for a while.

Her mates looked varying degrees of pissed off and angry, but there was something about their demeanour that had me thinking it wasn't just how Thor spoke to her, but also whatever she'd suggested in return.

"Well, this seems like entirely the wrong time to have arrived," Xanth said before he pulled out a chair and offered it to me.

I sat down cautiously, my gaze sweeping across those

sitting around the massive table with battle plans haphazardly strewn about it. Geta sat back in her seat, her arms crossed as she scowled at everyone. There were a few people I didn't recognise, and then Aria and her father facing off with each other across the table.

It was silent for a beat as the pair stared each other down and then Aria's eyes flickered in my direction before a look of guilt crossed her face. I sighed as I realised that this was, no doubt, about.

"You can't shield me from this," I told her gently, not wanting her to think I was taking sides. "Don't get me wrong, if you could, I might be selfish enough to let you. But this is the way it has to be. And I deserve the chance to be part of this fight just as much as everyone else."

It was the truth, too. I had four new mates I hadn't spent half as much time with as I wanted. Who was I kidding? A century wasn't enough time. It wasn't fair that we had to risk everything when we'd only just found each other. But everyone else could say exactly the same thing, and some people sitting around this table had already fought longer and lost more than everyone else here.

"What has Frannie said? She must have given us some indication of which direction to travel. I know she's vague, but she's always hinting at something if you listen hard enough."

I loved that batty old Kitsuné. Most people barely tolerated her because she was a handful, to say the least. But Frannie had been there through some of the hardest times in my life. She'd never said a word about what was to come for me. But when she'd wiped away my tears and her gaze had locked with mine, I'd known there was something worth fighting for on the other side of all the sadness and pain.

Aria's face blanched, and she looked down at Kyle in shock.

"What?"

I stood now, but I knew that look. I'd seen it so many times before and I didn't know if I could take it one more time. Why did the losses have to keep on coming? Didn't we deserve a win for once?

"Frannie... she didn't survive the fight with the angels when Odin made his move against the packhouse," Kyle told me gently and I dropped into my seat with a thud at the news.

Frannie. She was our biggest asset, but she was so much more than that. She'd meant so much to everyone she came into contact with. The entire realm would weep for her loss, including me.

I felt the dampness on my cheek as a tear broke free.

"Did she know?" I asked no one in particular. It was the curse of her kind. Seeing everything until they didn't. Until the future was nothing but darkness. And it could mean only one thing. They weren't part of it anymore.

When I didn't hear a response, I looked up, and Aria nodded sadly.

"That means she didn't see the end of this war," a person I didn't recognise said.

Everyone glared in their direction, and they held their hands up in surrender. Couldn't he give us a moment to just feel her loss before trying to get back down to business?

"I'm sorry. I know, I really do. But we've lost so many now, that sometimes you force yourself not to feel it anymore." He shrugged as he explained, absolutely no emotion showing on his face and I wondered what he'd lost to be able to push it all down that far, then decided I definitely didn't want to know.

"There's more than one seer in this realm and the madam Kitsuné wasn't the only one leading the way," Corvin cut in as he took a seat at the table. I realised then that the others were standing behind us in a show of strength despite there being enough seats for them. "The Norns have seen Britt end this once and for all. All we need to do now is decide how to support her so she makes it out of that encounter alive."

Aria and her mates nodded in agreement, and even Geta and Thor seemed on our side. But I could feel the doubt coming from the other side of the room.

"You disagree?" I asked, locking eyes with the Asgardian who had already spoken. The others seemed happy to let him be the voice of discontent.

One hand came under his chin as he looked at me thoughtfully. I'd never felt more like someone was weighing the value of my life than I did at that moment.

"Those of us in Asgard have been fighting and dying for this cause for longer than you've been alive. Why should we tell our people to be little more than cannon fodder if the Norns have already said you can complete the task? With all due respect, perhaps it's time for someone else to make the sacrifices around here."

He didn't even look ashamed to suggest that me staying alive at the end of this was essentially not his problem. Because that was the crux of what he said. As long as the goal was achieved, he didn't care what happened to me afterward.

I tried not to take it to heart. Like he said, they'd been fighting in Asgard for longer than most of us had been alive. I couldn't even imagine the losses they'd sustained.

But that was the thing.

We'd all sustained losses. There wasn't a single person sitting around this table who hadn't lost someone they cared about; who hadn't suffered just as much as the next.

"It also seems to me that this is a problem of Asgard's making," Aria cut in cruelly. "Perhaps we should sit back and let you continue your fight alone. Once Odin has worked his way through the lot of you, perhaps it will be easier for us to step in and deal with the issue once he comes to our realm." It wasn't the first time she'd used the argument to make her point.

I knew Aria well enough to know that she'd never actually do something like that, but she made a good point. This had all started because Asgard hadn't been able to step up and do what needed to be done when Odin started to lose his mind. Now their lack of action was threatening everyone.

The Asgardians scoffed in outrage at the idea and were soon turning to the god at the table. "Thor! You cannot possibly sit there and let them say such a thing."

Thor shook his head and sighed like he was beseeching fate to give him a break. "You were the one to start this inane line of reasoning, Tristan. How can you expect them to agree to fight for you when you told them to their faces that you don't care if they survive?"

Tristan was red in the face and I couldn't decide if it was embarrassment or rage. He'd expected support, not to be chastised for, frankly, being a dick.

"This is the problem with the world we've found ourselves in. Everyone is too concerned with their own pain to care about anyone else's." I saw him open his mouth like he'd argue with me, but I quickly cut him off. "I'm not criticising you for that. At some point, we've all felt the same. But what I'm saying is that we're all in this position because we looked at the problem and thought someone else would solve it for us. We've all hurt. We've all bled. But it's time to look past what happened to us before and decide what kind of future we want for ourselves. Do you want to live beneath Odin's thumb? Or do you want a chance to be free? At the end of the day, no one can do that for you. If you decide to walk away now, yes, you might have a greater chance of surviving. But you're still going to live under the pain of everything that's happened and the guilt of not doing more. The only way you're ever going to be free is if you stand up and fight back. Take back what's yours and show Odin he made a mistake by thinking he could take it from you."

Tristan's mouth closed, and he glared at me. I knew he couldn't argue with my words despite the fact he still wanted to. The others sitting around him looked like they were ready to run out of here right now and do whatever it took to fight back. They were ready for blood, even if we were wholly unprepared for it. I hated that we lived in a world where he had to risk his life and fight, and if he really wanted to turn his back on us and leave, no one would stop him. I just knew that if it was me, it would be something I'd always regret. And if I had to live my life with that hanging over me, then it would be one more thing Odin had taken from me. I was done letting him take what he wanted.

"So," Drystan said, standing at my side, and pointed at the collection of maps in the centre of the table. "Where do we stand and what do you need us to do?"

The meeting got back underway like nothing had happened.

We spent hours looking over lists of resources, troop numbers, and the surrounding terrain. We had intel on Odin's routine, his troop movements—which were significantly reduced thanks to Aria and her mates—and who we could count to stand on our side when it finally came down to it.

It wasn't much. In fact, it was kind of hard to look at and still think we had a chance of winning, but it was more than if we risked it alone. And that was exactly what I'd have to do if all these people suddenly decided they'd had enough of fighting.

The Asgardians filed out of the room once Thor called the meeting to a close. We were all exhausted and there was no point going over the same information repeatedly. We needed time to think and plan. I heard Tristan's mutterings as he passed and knew he was trying to persuade the others to his side.

"He's going to be a problem," Bran murmured to Corvin, and I saw him nod in response before the two of them slipped out of the room to follow.

"Erm, are the ravens going to murder Tristan?" Xanth asked uneasily.

"No!" I immediately objected. "Or at least, I don't think so."

Shit, there was every possibility that they actually were. Did it make me a terrible person that I was okay not wanting to know the truth?

"The brothers won't do anything reckless," Thor told us and then laughed, no doubt remembering something that was as fresh as yesterday to him, but had occurred before any of us existed. Then he frowned. "Actually, I might just catch up with them to... talk." And he rushed out of the room.

"Not my monkeys, not my circus," Aria muttered, rubbing her fists against her eyes as she sank back in her chair with a weary sigh.

We were all tired and we couldn't go into this thing on the brink of exhaustion, but I doubted any of us would rest easy until we'd seen it through.

"You need to tell them," Geta whispered in my ear as she drew level with me.

It didn't take a genius to figure out what she was referring to. It was the thing I tried to keep close to my chest whenever Aria was around. The secret I was worried she wouldn't be able to handle.

Geta was right, though. We needed this out in the open.

"Do you know if the rebellion has anyone that can heal Britt's arm?" Drystan asked. "I've heard vampire blood might have some healing properties. Or a witch with that expertise. We're open to any suggestions, we just need..."

His voice trailed off as he realised everyone in the room stared at him. He paled when he realised what he'd opened the door to, but I reached over and squeezed his hand in reassurance.

It was time.

Geta slipped out of the room, firmly closing the door behind her, and I knew that was my cue to finally speak.

"I don't have my wolf anymore," I blurted out.

Kyle looked confused, but as Aria turned to look at me instead of Drystan, I saw the blood draining from her face.

"That's not possible," Kyle said. "It's a soul bound connection. You can't lose something like that."

I wanted to agree with him. Hell, I wanted to make out like it was some kind of terrible joke, but I was tired of living under this cloud.

"You can if you die," I told him quietly. "And that part of your soul moves on."

Aria was already shaking her head in denial and, as Virion reached out to grab her hand, I wanted to vomit. I hated that this was happening when she'd seemed like she finally felt like herself again.

"I..."

"Did nothing wrong," I interrupted. "This has nothing to do with you, Aria. You gave me a second chance at life. If it wasn't for you, I wouldn't be sitting here right now. I can never thank you enough for that."

Tears came to my eyes as the truth of that statement hit me hard. I wouldn't have my mates if Aria hadn't saved me. I'd never have had the chance to feel what it was like for someone to look at me and love me for who I was rather than what I represented. At the packhouse, I was nothing but an empty womb and a way to steal some pleasure they didn't deserve.

"But you're..."

I was so glad the word broken didn't slip past her lips. I felt it most days. It was hard not to when you could feel that hole inside you that had once been filled with a wolf. Now that my mates were at my side, that ache was lessening. Even with the worry of not knowing how to complete the bond with them. I could feel it growing and at least I knew it was there. But the last steps were lost to me. Hopefully, it would be something we'd figure out with time. If we were lucky enough to get it.

"Whatever we have to do," Kyle said seriously. "We'll find a way to heal your arm."

The others nodded and I could see Drystan sagging in relief. I hadn't realised it was bothering him so much, but I should have. It would kill me to see him hurting if he didn't need to.

"Echo will be here tomorrow. Perhaps one of her mates?" Virion suggested.

I couldn't wait to be reunited with the Elites. They were my first experience of bonding with someone outside of family. They were the sisters I'd trained and fought beside. I'd have given anything to still be one of them, but that wasn't what fate had in store for me. At least I could say I'd trained with the valkyrie army. That was something I never would have experienced if I hadn't... you know, died.

"Then we wait for tomorrow," Braedon said firmly. "In the meantime, perhaps we could take this chance to work with your magic," he offered to Drystan.

My head cocked to the side at his words because this was the first I'd heard of it. Drystan flushed at the mention of his magic, but curiously, he didn't recoil. For him, these were a group of strangers and, for once, he actually looked almost proud of what he could do.

"Let's all break for some food and then we can meet in the training hall," Aria suggested.

Her mates sighed in defeat, and I couldn't help but laugh. I didn't have magic, so this was one I'd be sitting out. I didn't dare admit how much my legs were burning from this morning. A rest was exactly what I needed.

Chapter 38

Xanth

I had a plan. And I was pretty sure it meant I was a genius.

We found Corvin and Bran on the way to the dining hall, the pair looking somewhat disappointed, though none of us dared ask why. We'd eaten in silence while the ravens brooded, but they were free of blood, so I guessed Thor got to them in time.

Drystan was distracted throughout our meal, and I knew he was thinking about his magic. He actually seemed interested in working with Braedon and I couldn't have been happier. If only he'd had someone like him in his life before now. Perhaps everything wouldn't have felt so dark if he'd known he wasn't the only one who could do the things he could. If he'd had someone who called his magic by a different name, one that didn't make people recoil in revulsion.

We escorted Britt to our room after eating. I was practically bouncing with excitement. This was exactly what we needed as a group.

The ravens, despite their sulking, hadn't taken their eyes off her all evening. They wanted to talk, to get to know our mate, and if they were anything like Drystan and me, then trying to resist the bond must have been driving them crazy.

Britt was too in her head about the whole thing. She needed to relax and stop stressing out about whether she was good enough, whether they wanted her. They'd had every opportunity to turn away, and they hadn't. She'd been unconscious and hadn't seen their concern for her at the clinic, but she must have noticed how they stuck close by most of the time. How their gaze trailed her across the room if ever she left their side.

At the moment, they were separated by an ocean of concerns and self doubt.

And I was about to throw them into it head first.

Genius! Someone should start patting me on the back.

"You've got that look on your face again," Drystan told me as we walked behind the other three, who tried not to make it obvious they were all paying close attention to each other.

"What face?"

"The one that means you're up to something," Drystan told me dryly.

"I've been thinking..."

"That never ends well," Drystan quipped.

"Rude!"

Britt glanced over her shoulder to see what was happening and I just smiled the sweet smile of innocence. When she frowned in distrust, Drystan snorted in amusement.

"See. Britt's only been around you for a week and she already knows you thinking is going to end badly."

"I did not think that!" Britt objected as we stopped outside our room.

The ravens looked at me like they were ready to start the interrogation, but it didn't matter. Xanth and I had somewhere to be and step one of the plan was about to be set in motion.

Well, it was really a one step plan, so maybe that didn't count as a step but rather an entire plan... hmmm, could you have a single step in a plan or did I need to come up with a step two?

"You do realise we're all waiting to see what you're up to, right?" Drystan asked, pulling me out of my confusion and back to reality.

"Hmm, what..."

"Is he always like this?" Corvin looked exhausted and I was hoping it was just with me because he was going to need all the energy he had.

Before I even realised what I was doing, I patted his shoulders like I was trying to build up his confidence for the big race.

"I have no idea what's happening right now," Bran whispered as Corvin looked slightly horrified at the prospect of having me in his life for the rest of eternity.

He was such a lucky guy!

Reaching behind him, I shoved the door to the room open and then, thankful that neither of the ravens were armed because I valued my life, I shoved them inside.

"Well, we've got magic practice, so you're going to need to stay here and look after our beautiful mate. Probably best to stay right here, what with that Asgard guy kicking up a fuss earlier. You never know who you can trust, am I right? Sooooo, right here... all night. Did I mention that we're probably going to be gone all night? Yep, yep, yep. Been magicless for like two weeks, probably going to need lots and lots of practice."

I gently steered Britt into the room by the shoulders and then closed the door behind her before any of them could speak. They mostly just watched me like I'd lost my mind, but they'd see the genius of my plan later, no doubt.

Dusting off my hands for a job well done, I whirled

around, ready to leave, and came face to face with Drystan, who gaped at me.

"Smooth," he joked.

"I know right! Foolproof it was. They're going to be all bonded by the morning and I'm thinking we should go with Xanth junior for our firstborn so we can commemorate this moment of genius."

I marched proudly down the corridor as I patted myself on the back, since no one else had the decency to do it for me. After a beat, I heard Drystan's footsteps as he seemed to shake himself out of his awe of my amazingness and follow.

"I worry about you sometimes," he muttered.

Chapter 39

Corvin

"Is anyone else confused right now?" Bran asked as we stared at the door.

We should probably be worried about Britt's other mates. All this time I'd worried about her in the final battle, but now I wondered if Xanth could actually look after himself.

"We need to assess the mages' fighting capabilities before we move forward with any further battle plans," I mumbled, more to myself than anyone else.

Bran gave me that smug look that made me want to punch him, and I knew he was thinking about the fact that I inexplicably seemed to have grown attached to the pair of them. It irked me to no end. I could accept that Xanth was amusing and whenever I looked at him, I might be reminded there were things to enjoy in life. And maybe Drystan's magic, and the protective way he always knew where Britt was, could come in handy at times. Especially given our current situation. So, I could admit that having them around wasn't quite as terrible as I'd assumed it would be.

Britt's soft laugh forced me from my thoughts and I watched as she moved across the room to sit on the end of the bed and remove her boots. "He thinks he's helping," she told us without making eye contact, her cheeks flushing in a way that had my blood running hot.

Just how far did that blush extend? I bet I could make that pretty blush cover her entire body.

I hadn't realised my gaze had been fixed on her until Bran stepped between the two of us.

"He's giving us time together," Bran added, more for my benefit than hers.

Britt nodded, occupying herself by removing her weapons, which she seemed to drag out for fear of having to actually look at us once she was done.

"Look at me." I stepped around Bran so I could move directly in front of her. "You never need to cast your eyes to the ground in embarrassment when you're with us."

It bothered me more than I wanted to admit. She was our mate. She would be our reigning raven and she should never have to look away out of embarrassment, shame or anything else. As far as I was concerned, she stood above all others.

My mate.

My love.

My Queen.

Her head raised, and when she looked up and her gaze locked with mine, there was only one thing on my mind.

My thumb trailed over her pouty lips; I couldn't stop myself from staring at the beautiful woman in front of me I was lucky enough to call my mate. How had I ever doubted she was the mirror to my soul? She was perfection personified, and I found myself falling to my knees at her feet.

She could never know the significance of this moment, and when Bran mirrored my move, she looked confused.

I knew he felt the same as I did. How could he not? We were made from the same ethereal substance, moulded from the very same land into the guardians we'd become. He'd stood by my side for a millennia, and never in all that time had we ever doubted each other.

And never had we knelt at the feet of anyone, not even the All Father himself.

"My heart, I can never show you how deep my loyalty to you will run. There is nothing I wouldn't do for you. If you would consent to being my mate, I promise I will love you for an eternity." It was a plea from the bottom of my heart, and even as the words slipped past my lips, I didn't know if I deserved her acceptance.

I saw the doubt in her eyes then, and I knew I deserved it. I'd doubted her, accused her of trying to bewitch us. It shouldn't be this easy, and she was right to make me work to prove my loyalty to her.

As soon as I tried to stand and move away, she was there. Her hands clinging to my shoulders as she slipped off the bed to kneel in front of me.

It was wrong on so many levels. This woman should never be on her knees, and definitely not for a wretch like me.

"Don't leave," she said softly. Her fingers running down my cheeks in a caress. "Don't misunderstand me. I couldn't bear it if you turned away from me right now."

"I could never." I pulled her in close and felt Bran run a reassuring hand through her hair.

"I don't know how," she whispered. I leaned back in confusion, unsure of what she was talking about. The sadness in her eyes made me wish I didn't, but I needed to understand. "Without my wolf, I don't know how to complete the bond. I might never be able to..." she explained, trailing off when the words became too hard to say.

She'd told us of the loss of her wolf, her confusion at what that meant she was, but it had never occurred to me the ramifications of such a thing. If she was human, she could never hold a mate bond. Fate was playing with us once again, and this time she'd gone too far.

"There will be a way," Bran told us both. "We haven't come this far for it to be impossible. We know that the person to wield the raven's claw will be our mate, our reigning raven. There is no doubt in my mind that person is you, Britt. The Norns have seen you winning this battle. That has to mean there's a way."

Trust Bran to see to the centre of the issue with a clear and logical mind. There was a reason he was considered Odin's thoughts, and I was his memory. Bran could be reasoned and clearheaded while I was the one that never forgot, that always remembered, especially when it came to someone who had wronged us. Bran was peace, and I was vengeance. Together we were balance.

I pulled her back against my chest, needing to feel her there. "We'll find a way," I whispered, reaffirming the truth.

Even if I had to track Fate down once more and force her to fix this, I would. There was nothing I wouldn't do for the woman in my arms.

Picking my mate up from the floor, I placed her back on the bed. Bran and I climbed in on either side of her. Gentle reassuring touches turned into soft exploring kisses and it wasn't long until the passion between us flared hot despite the sad thoughts that had just filled our minds.

Britt's fingers pushed up Bran's shirt, and he quickly pulled it off out of her way while she leaned back and turned her head to kiss me once more.

"Is this what you want?" Bran asked as his fingers ran along the waist of her trousers. "We don't have to do anything now. We can just do this."

Britt looked at us both with a devastating smile on her lips. "I don't want to wait. I don't want to walk out of this room with any regrets. I want everything you're willing to give me."

It was like a starting gun had gone off and the slow exploring kisses turned fiery and passionate as desperate hands tore clothing away, showering it onto the floor. When my hands came to the breastplate she wore, I paused, remembering what the others had said.

"We should leave this on."

Britt rolled her eyes and laughed. "I think we're safe enough here. Take it off. I want to feel all of you."

I hesitated, second guessing whether or not it was a good idea, and her hands covered my own.

"I'll put it back on in the morning. But for tonight, I want it to be just the three of us, forgetting about everything outside that door and being what we were always meant to be, even if just for a little while."

I couldn't deny her when she put it like that. I'd listened to her stories, to the painful journey she'd had to this point. Our own hadn't been much better. I could give her this one thing. No one would hurt her while she was here with us. We'd never allow it, and so Bran helped me to quickly undo the ties as he took the breastplate and carefully placed it on the dresser where it couldn't be accidentally damaged.

When he turned back to the bed, I gave him a wicked grin, and he stopped, his head cocking to the side in question as he no doubt realised I had something in mind.

Sitting up, I plucked Britt off the mattress and she gave an adorable little eep of surprise as I deposited her between my legs. We both sat facing Bran and his pupils flared as he watched me drop a kiss onto her bare shoulder.

My hands came up to tease against the underside of her breasts and she leaned back against me with a sigh.

"I think you should let Bran watch while I make you come for him," I whispered in her ear as she gasped.

Bran, not needing any further encouragement, grabbed a chair from the side of the room and deposited it in front of the bed, sitting himself down. His thumb rubbed along his bottom lip as he settled in to enjoy watching our mate.

Letting my hands trail back down her body, I hooked Britt's thighs, spreading her legs and draping them over my thighs. I ran my fingers up the sensitive skin of the inside of her thighs, enjoying the way she shivered against me.

Bran licked his lips, leaning forward to watch.

As soon as my hands reached the tops of her legs, I let one fingertip tease across her slit as my other hand cupped her breast. She twitched, her hips shifting as she panted, wanting more.

I could sit like this for hours, listening to the noises she made and watching the subtle changes in her body as I built a need to impossible levels inside her. Instead, I plunged one finger inside and pinched her nipple, her back bowing at the sensation.

Bran looked like he was about to leap out of his chair at the sight. Instead, his hands curled into fists and I watched him struggle as he leaned back, making himself wait.

Adding another finger, I slowly pumped them inside her, feeling how wet she already was.

My lips ghosted along her neck as my tongue flicked out to taste her skin. I'd give anything for a taste of her right now, but that wasn't part of the game. This was a show for Bran. We had all the time in the world to do everything we could ever think of in the years to come. I was going to make sure of it.

By the time I worked my way up to her clit, Britt was already begging me for more. "Don't stop, Corvin. Please. Please... oh fuck yes."

She panted as I teased her sensitive nub, sucking her earlobe into my mouth as I did. She groaned as my tongue flicked against her lobe trapped between my lips and I knew she was thinking about what it would feel like against her clit.

As her breathes came faster, I shifted her in my grip.

Pulling her higher into my lap, I slipped two fingers into her channel as I mercilessly worked her clit with her other hand. It didn't take long for her hips to swivel.

"That's it, baby. Ride my fingers. Show Bran how creamy you are."

She cried out at the words and tipped her head forward to stare at the man in front of her.

"I'm going to come," she whimpered.

Bran couldn't take it anymore and leapt from his seat. "Damn fucking straight you are," he growled as he dropped to his knees in front of her. "You're going to come all over my face, like a good girl."

He'd barely touched his tongue to her clit when she exploded. Her pussy gripping onto my fingers as I worked them inside her. Her ass ground against my cock as she rode out the waves of ecstasy, and I gritted my teeth to keep from coming right there and then.

Britt barely had time to catch her breath when Bran stood, picked her up from my lap, and turned her around to kneel on the edge of the bed. He pushed her shoulders forward and plunged inside her at the same time. He cursed as he seated his cock fully inside of her.

"Such a good fucking girl," he praised, dragging his cock out before snapping his hips forward one more time.

"Corvin, I need you in my mouth," she begged, her gaze pinning me from where I lounged back on the bed, watching Bran take her.

The lady didn't need to ask me twice.

I barely made it in front of her before she grabbed my cock and pulled it to her mouth. She swallowed me down, taking my length in one single swallow, burying me deep in her throat.

Bran paused, letting her get used to my size, and then he slowly moved inside her. Britt had no choice but to hold still.

We both surged forward together, spearing her between us before slowly withdrawing.

We set a tandem pace, pulling and pushing as she relaxed between us, letting me fill her body in a show of complete trust.

I pulled her hair into one hand, moving it out of her face so I could watch myself sinking between her lips.

When she peered up at me through her eyelashes, hollowing her cheeks as she sucked down my length, my head tipped back as she pulled a groan from my chest.

She was so fucking perfect for us.

Bran's pace increased, and I knew he was getting close to coming. Looking across at him, I could see him clenching his jaw as he tried to hold it back. His hand slipped beneath her and by the deep groan she gave with my cock in her throat, I knew he was working her clit in time with his thrusts.

Ever the gentleman, there was no way Bran would finish until she'd come at least one more time.

He caught my gaze and gave me a wicked grin and wink, before pinching her clit, and Britt came with a muffled shout of pleasure. His eyes closed as he followed her over the edge, his hips snapping forward a final time as he came deep inside her.

I held onto every drop of willpower I could to stop myself from pouring down her throat. I wanted to feel her pussy clenching around me when she came. So when Bran tipped to the side, falling to the mattress with a happy sigh, I was quick to leave her mouth.

Britt looked up at me in confusion, but with a grin on my face, I picked her up and climbed off the bed. Her legs wrapped around my hips and I moved to the chair Bran had previously occupied.

Settling down in the seat, I pulled her down on my

weeping cock. I wouldn't last long, but at least when I came, it would be in the sweet heaven of her pussy.

"Ride my cock," I ordered, but she was moving before the words had finished coming out of my mouth.

"Holy fuck, yes," she gasped, her head tipping back and her perfect breasts thrusting toward my face.

I wasted no time putting my lips around her rosy nipple, running a tongue around the hardening bud as she set the pace she wanted. Something about her using me for her own pleasure turned me on nearly as much as putting on a show for Bran.

Britt was in complete control. She always would be, no matter what we did. She held us in the palm of her hand, and there was nothing we wouldn't do for her.

My hands came to her hips and I helped her keep pace, assisting her to rock up and down on my length.

I wouldn't last much longer. I'd been too close to the edge too many times to take much more. But like Bran, there was no way I was coming until she did.

My thumb moved to her clit, and she groaned. "I don't think I can," she told me.

"You can."

She looked like she didn't believe me. Well, time to prove the lady wrong.

I slipped my thumb down, feeling where we were joined together and pulling her come back up to her clit to slicken the way. Then I pressed down, making her work her clit against my thumb as she rode my cock.

"Fuck, that feels good," she whimpered.

She picked up the pace, and I knew she was chasing her climax.

Leaning down, she kissed me once and then threw her head back as she screamed out in orgasm, her voice breaking as she did.

My balls drew tight as her pussy locked down around me, and I came harder than I ever had before. It felt like I danced along the edges of consciousness as I pulled her hips tight against me and ground my cock inside her warm wetness, filling her with come.

The thought of a child sprung into my mind, her belly round with our baby as I feasted between her legs. She'd be so fucking beautiful when she was pregnant. And I couldn't wait to see her like that.

I gently held her in my arms as I stood, keeping my softening length fully sheathed inside her as I climbed back onto the bed. I was staying right where I was for as long as I could. My mate was keeping that come inside her for as long as possible.

Bran nestled against her back, pulling a sheet over us all as he softly kissed her neck. Britt sleepily hummed in response, her body finally relenting to exhaustion after being thoroughly overstimulated.

"I'll get something to clean her up with," he whispered, going to climb out of the bed.

My hand snapped out to stop him. "Not yet."

She opened one sleepy eye to peer up at me, and I grinned down at her unashamedly. "I'm okay with that," she said with a yawn and then snuggled in deeper.

And if that wasn't a good enough reason to tear apart Asgard and win this war, I didn't know what was.

Chapter 40

Britt

Stretching lazily, I snuggled against the mate beneath me with a happy sigh. Last night had been unexpected. I'd still half believed there might not be a future for us, but Corvin had surprised me. As soon as his lips touched mine, everything changed.

"You look happy," Bran purred in my ear.

"Mmmm, just thinking about last night."

"Well, if it's a reminder you need." He pressed against my back, his lips nibbling my earlobe as he trailed his fingers down my side.

"You realise we're supposed to be meeting with the others now, right?" Corvin interrupted.

"Boooo," Bran whispered, and I felt the mattress shift as he shoved Corvin away. "They can wait. Our mate has already forgotten all that delicious pleasure we pulled from her last night. I think she needs a reminder."

As Bran's hands moved toward my breasts, I felt a second set slip around my waist as Corvin kissed his way up my throat.

But then his words finally registered, and I snapped

upright so fast that I was pretty sure Corvin almost ended up kissing Bran.

"What the?" Corvin gasped.

"I never knew you cared that much, brother," Bran joked as Corvin shoved him off the side of the bed.

It was nice to see the brothers' carefree attitude. Corvin might even have a small smile on his face, not that I dared to point it out.

"The Elites are coming," I told them as I shuffled off the end of the bed and searched for my clothes. "I haven't seen them since the blood moon."

Finding some trousers, I hopped about the room as I worked them up my legs.

"I've heard a lot about these Elites. I'm curious to see what all the fuss is about." Corvin climbed out of bed and my mouth ran dry as I watched him stretch his arms over his head.

Being distracted mid-trouser, I mistimed my hop and fell flat on my face. And it was the perfect time for the two men in the room to prove how right they were for me, because instead of laughing, they both leaped into action and scooped me up from the floor. As Bran patted me down, searching for injuries, Corvin's hands bracketed my cheeks as he stared into my eyes.

"Are you okay?" And then he ruined the moment as he tilted my head and checked me over.

"Are you actually checking me for a concussion right now?"

"You could have banged your head!" he protested.

Leaning forward, I kissed him on the end of his nose. They were so cute.

"I'm fine, really."

I went to step away from them but found myself caged in by the two ravens who weren't content to let me budge even the slightest.

"Until we find a way to solidify our bond, this is going to keep happening and you need to let us do it," Corvin told me gently.

It was something I didn't want to think about, but I could understand their point of view. The bond between us was definitely there and I could feel it more strongly after last night together. It was nearly the same strength as Xanth and Drystan's bond with me. The problem was I could also tell that neither of them were complete and I had no idea how to go about doing it. I'd always assumed that I'd just know when the time was right. But a part of me worried that was only the case when I'd had my wolf. Rather than the time being right, it was actually that she'd take over and form the bond herself. So now that I didn't have her, what was I supposed to do?

"We'll find a way," Bran reassured me and I felt him lightly kiss the back of my head as he shuffled closer. "Don't worry about it for now. We have enough on our plate without inviting further problems."

"But what if that's what it takes for me to be the reigning raven? What if me wielding the raven's claw depends on us being able to complete our bond?"

Neither of them said anything, and I knew they were worried about exactly the same thing. How were we not supposed to? The raven's claw was the key to ending this whole thing. In any other's hand, it was nothing but a sword. In mine, it was supposed to become some god killing weapon. But no one had told us how that was supposed to work and we had zero ideas and no time to figure it out.

We were officially out of time. The last of the valkyrie and the Elites were arriving now. That meant we were heading into battle in the next few days. They couldn't shield all of us here for long and we couldn't afford for Odin to move his troops, making all our plans useless. The clock was ticking down, and at the moment, all it was counting down to was us losing this fight.

I shook my head, trying to clear the depressing thoughts and instead fix my mind on something happier.

"Come on, I want to introduce you to my friends."

Corvin looked down at his body wryly before meeting my gaze again and cocking one eyebrow. "Like this?"

Erm no. He had zero things to be ashamed of about his body, but it was for my viewing pleasure only. They might be my friends, but this was definitely something I wouldn't share.

"I suppose I can allow you a few minutes to get dressed," I replied cheekily.

Corvin's laugh was one of those things I'd never take for granted because I knew just how rare they actually were. So when he chuckled, kissing the end of my nose and turned to find some clothes, I let myself sink into the feeling of happiness it gave me... and checked out his ass, of course.

We found Xanth and Drystan waiting in the same cave we'd emerged into when we first came to the base. Aria was there with some of her mates, looking concerned about something, and I resisted the urge to ask her what it was.

I just wanted a moment with my friends where we weren't under the pressure of the fight that bore down on us. One innocent moment to be happy and whole again. Then I'd suck it up and step back up to the plate just like everyone else.

As I greeted my two mates who'd been good enough to give me some time alone last night, they pulled us off to the side, away from the others.

"How was the magic practice?" I asked, already seeing that Xanth was brimming with excitement about something.

"I'm back! Not quite at full strength, but getting closer.

Working with Aria and her mates is pretty incredible. I hate training, but somehow..."

"Yeah, it's got something to do with Aria and who she is," I filled him in, already knowing what he meant and also how hard it was to put into words. She not only inspired you to do better, but anything she helped you with became muscle memory more quickly than anything I'd ever tried to do alone.

Xanth looked over his shoulder at where Drystan talked with the ravens and I got the horrible feeling there was something he was worried about telling me.

"Did something happen?" I asked in worry.

"No, no. Nothing like that," Xanth quickly told me. "I just... I've never seen Drystan so in sync with his magic before. It was incredible. It's also the first time I've ever seen him not only interested in it but happy to use it. It was... I wish he'd had this in his life earlier."

I quickly hugged him, knowing how much Xanth cared for his friend and how much he hurt for him, too. The two of them had been through so much, and this was starting to feel like the beginnings of a happily ever after for them. If only there wasn't a storm on the horizon that we had to weather first.

Before we could say anything else, a portal flickered into life on the opposite side of the cave and everyone's whispers fell silent as we waited to see who would emerge.

I didn't realise how nervous I'd feel until that moment. This was the problem with portals. You didn't know who was coming through until they stepped onto your side. This could be the beginning of an invasion for all I knew. My fingers nervously pressed against the breastplate Geta had gifted to me and I shuffled my feet, ready to brace for any incoming attack. It didn't escape my notice that Aria had done the same, and that just built my worry even higher.

But then the first valkyrie stepped through and a sigh of relief gusted through my lips.

Xanth reached for my hand, pulling it away from my breastplate and holding me tight without saying a word. Tears dripped down my cheeks as I watched the last of the valkyries file through, people I didn't recognise mixed in with them. They each saluted Aria and then carried their weapons and belongings through to where Geta directed them.

I realised then why Xanth and Drystan had pulled me off to the side. This was overwhelming, to say the least. I still remembered what some of their faces had looked like in death, and it wasn't something I'd forget soon. These people were my friends and even though there was nothing I could have done about what happened to them, I still felt guilty. There was still a part of me that felt like I'd failed them. And this was the first time I realised I wasn't ready to face them yet either. I had no words for how I felt and I was grateful for the opportunity to figure it out before that conversation confronted me.

"Mages?" Drystan mumbled in confusion.

"They were never going to sit this out," Xanth said with a laugh as some of the newcomers raised a hand in acknowledgement to them before following the valkyrie out of the room.

"I thought the Elites were coming," Bran whispered into my ear.

"They're coming."

I knew those women as well as I knew myself. They would never be the first to step through. Even if it were the valkyrie that they were standing with, they'd still wait for every single one of them to step through the portal before they'd drop their guard enough to enter themselves.

We were the Elite. We protected.

And that was probably why I didn't know how I'd face the valkyrie, because I'd failed to do that, even if it hadn't been up to me at the time.

I didn't know how many valkyrie were supposed to be arriving today, but when there was a break in people, I knew that meant the last of them had arrived. I stepped forward, leaving my mates to stand in support behind me as the first of them arrived.

A squeal ripped through the air as a body collided with mine.

My girls were here.

Mae gripped me in an iron tight hug and Nix joined in on the other side. A flash of white hair caught my eye as another body collided with us and it was more than my legs could take as I tumbled to the ground and took them with me. I didn't even feel Harmony add herself to the pile as we laughed and cried and hugged. Aria waited at the edge of the madness trying to hold on to a modicum of self control, but Echo just swept her legs out from under her and dragged her down with us.

We laughed at the joy of being together.

We cried for the ones that we'd lost. For the hole left behind by our sister who had fallen, and hadn't been able to join me in a second life.

Aeryn would always be missed, but we went on in her honour. We would fight for those like her who'd lost their lives because of the greed of others. Those who were stuck in what felt like impossible situations with no one to stand up for what was right.

And at that moment, I knew what I wanted to do when this whole thing was over. I wanted to fill the world with Elites. With voices that would rise up in the defence of others. I wanted to create a force of good in a world that stood on the precipice of being something great. Someone who would make sure the balance would tip in the right direction this time around.

CHAPTER 41

ARIA

By the time I'd untangled myself from the pile of Elites, everyone—apart from a variety of mates—had left us to the madness.

The guys were standing around, laughing at our antics, but it didn't escape me that they'd taken a protective stance around our huddle, guarding us from all sides.

This was the first time we'd all been together since the battlefield of the blood moon, except we were missing one of our own. It still hurt that we'd lost Aeryn. That she'd been taken from us, not knowing she could have come to me and I would have done anything to help her. She was just like the rest of us, though; and I had no doubt it was her need to save her sister that had stopped her from seeking out help for herself.

Trent and the others were standing awkwardly to the side. They practically radiated worry about having disobeyed not only my orders but their alphas as well.

"Erm, hey," Trent said, his hand rubbing the back of his neck as he stepping forward. He'd always stand in front of his guys, even though he'd stepped aside as their alpha when they petitioned to join Kyle's pack. "I know we were supposed to stay but... we should be allowed to decide for ourselves if we want to join this fight." His voice became firmer as he spoke, and his spine straightened as he stood tall.

The room fell quiet and Kyle looked at me, happy for me to be the one to deal with the issue.

Stepping forward, I watched the unease move through them and hated every second of it. They were right, of course. The fae were more than equipped to look after the rest of the pack, and it had been wrong of us to force them to stay.

"I'm sorry," I finally said. "You're right. We should have given you a choice."

Trent looked surprised, and the relief that swept through Ellis, Harrison, and Ian was obvious. The other Elites gathered around them, jostling and joking about how nervous the guys had been to face us. It was to see that their camaraderie was still so strong. They were all Elites after all, even if Trent and the other guys hadn't been with us since the very beginning.

"We're supposed to be in a meeting to go over the last of the battle plans," I told the Elites, only half serious because I'd needed this moment of freedom with them more than I'd realised.

"Gah, what's there to plan?" Nix scoffed. "We go, we fight, we win. There, I solved it for you. Now, let's figure out where they hide the booze and make this a night to remember."

Harmony laughed that evil giggle which meant she fully supported the idea before looking around at the rest of us. "Don't tell me all the mated women are too grown up to party with us?" she joked.

"What on earth have you been doing with the shifter packs?" They'd been requested to help with the transition to the Council format, but I had a feeling it had been more about the girls impressing the other shifters at the camp before the last battle. I dreaded to think of the mischief they'd been creating.

"We have been the picture of diplomacy!" Nix protested as Harmony broke out into laughter at the sheer idea of it.

"It's probably best that you don't tell me."

At that, we scrambled to our feet, dusting ourselves down as the introductions were made. It took as long as you'd expect, considering Echo and Britt had collected quite the collection of mates between them. By the end of it, Nix's mouth hung open in surprise. "I want one," she muttered.

Harmony shoved her, laughing, "One what?"

"A harem!" she whispered loudly, like it was the answer to the world's problems.

Mae quietly looked over at the men, most of whom pretended they weren't dying from embarrassment at the turn the conversation had taken. The two broody ravens stepped to either side of Britt. One of them kissed her gently on the forehead as she stared into his eyes, completely forgetting the rest of us were here. Her mages clustered closer, hands reaching out just to let her know they were there.

I'd forgotten what it was like in those early days. When the bonds were still forming around you. For the first time in a long time, I let all my internal walls drop, and I reached for my own mates. Virion's eyes snapped to mine, and I didn't miss the emotion in them. I felt all of them reach back for me through the bond and I closed my eyes as I let myself sink into the feeling of completeness.

When arms circled around me and I was pulled against a hard chest, I didn't fight it. I knew it was one of them.

"It's been too long, my love," Virion whispered in my ear. "I've missed you."

I buried my face against the softness of his shirt, forcing the tears to stay down

"I'm sorry," I whispered through the bond. "I shouldn't

have pushed you all away and tried to deal with this on my own."

"You have nothing to apologise for, Aria," Kyle told me. "We knew you were trying to deal with your feelings, and even if we missed you, we knew you would never stay away forever."

"I promise; I'm back now."

And I meant it too. I'd missed too much while I'd looked at nothing but my pain. Instead, I should have been looking to our bond. Finding comfort in the reassurance of the men I'd become soul bound with. Taking lives, lives I didn't know were guilty or not, had been more than I could deal with. But the fact of the matter was if I hadn't done what I'd done, it wouldn't have just been my life or my mates that would've been forfeit; it would have been everyone.

We were remaking not just one world, but every world.

We were standing against the shadows and the darkness they'd brought to so many.

The people who fought at Odin's side might not be there willingly, and it hurt to think that if they weren't, they'd lose their lives because of the evil and greed of someone else. But this was how we made sure the generations that came after us wouldn't fall from the same evil. I had to believe any sacrifices made for that purpose were worth it. If it took my life, the lives of the people around me, we'd all do it without question. We put our lives on the line every single day because we chose to and it was a tragedy that those people hadn't had the same choice. They were just as innocent as the rest of us, and it was unforgivable that they'd been put into this position.

So we weren't just fighting for those who were left behind, sheltering with the resistance or with the pockets of survivors in the magic realm. We were fighting for the ones who had been caught up in the bloodshed, willingly or not. Those who had already lost their lives, no matter what side they'd fought on.

Revenge

We would be the ones to get their revenge.

Chapter 42

Drystan

The smile on Britt's face as she'd reunited with her friends was one that would stay with me forever. I'd never seen that carefree look before, and I vowed she'd have it again in the very near future.

When I'd realised what Xanth was up to last night, I was strangely okay with the idea. The ravens were good guys, and you'd have to be blind to miss how much they loved her. Even if they hadn't realised it themselves yet. I wasn't even troubled by the idea of sharing our mate with them. I guess it helped that Xanth and I had never known that a mate was a possibility for us. We were just making this up as we went along. We were all in the same boat and that felt perfectly natural. We were doing this on our own terms.

Training with Braedon had been incredible. I connected with my magic in a way I'd never felt before. The first thing he'd had me do was let go of the walls I'd built around it. It wasn't easy. I'd been afraid of what I could do for so long that I didn't even know how to let them fall. But he and Xanth had talked me through it. I was glad Britt hadn't been there at that point. I was ashamed to admit I wouldn't have been able to work through my panic if she'd been present. It was foolish and completely unnecessary, but vulnerability didn't come easily for me and I had the scars to show why I'd never put myself in that position again.

Once those walls inside me fell, I felt my magic in ways I never had before. Where I'd always assumed I'd locked down a raging beast, instead I discovered a small, frightened glow, cowering behind the chains I'd wrapped around it.

I'd neglected the power that was a part of me. I could feel how it ran through my entire body now; how it had become so intrinsically linked with my being that it swelled and flowed like an ocean of power. It was something that had only ever tried to protect me and because I'd been punished for what it had done, because I'd seen the horror on the faces of others, I'd pushed it down into a dark hole rather than nurturing it into what it was always supposed to be.

"Your magic gives you power over life and death. It lets you see through to the soul of people and, because of that, it winds through your soul in return. If you're not in harmony with it, you won't be able to use it to your full potential," Braedon had explained.

I'd been meditating for hours by this point. The walls had finally crumbled, and I'd been reunited with a power that seemed as scared of me as I was of it. But once I found that connection and it finally reached out for me in return, the relief that flowed through me was so overwhelming I actually cried.

"Let it flow, let it move around your body," Braedon instructed, and I realised he could see the magic as clearly as I could. "That's right. Don't guide it, just let it do its own thing."

I'd never felt so free; so like the person I was always supposed to be. As the power connected with me, I felt the vibrations of the others around me. I could see the lives each body contained and with it, I could see their pain.

Opening my eyes, I felt my magic rise as I looked around, seeing the world in a way I'd never experienced before.

"Why do some of them shine so bright and others look like they're fading?" I asked, already thinking that I knew the answer.

"Some people live a troubled life, and it chips away at their soul, breaking them down into pieces of what they were supposed to be," Braedon told me sadly. "You're seeing them losing the will to fight. Feeling the pain of their past."

I was almost afraid to look at Xanth then. I didn't know if I could bear to see the pain I knew my friend hid behind the happy mask he wore every day. So when I'd finally worked up the courage to look, I was surprised to see the bright glow.

"You can admit I'm the healthiest person you know. I'm already fully aware," he quipped.

Yep, that was Xanth.

I looked down at my own hands then and caught sight of the subtle glow that lay just beneath my skin.

"If you're trying to see how bright you shine, you won't be able to," Braedon told me, a touch of humour lining his voice. "I learned that one early on. If it makes you feel better, your light is bright now that you're not suppressing your magic."

I nodded slowly, not knowing if that made me feel better or not.

"So, what can I do with this?" That was the important question. It was only from what Hel had insinuated, and from the brief conversation I'd had with Braedon, that I realised I didn't have to just deal in death, or at least I didn't think I did.

"I don't know."

My head snapped in Braedon's direction in surprise.

He shrugged his shoulders. "You have the same type of magic as me, but that doesn't mean it does the same thing. I can direct the flow of energy around a person. I've been able to stop someone pulling a soul where it doesn't belong and I can absorb energy and move it where it's supposed to be."

"What did you do to me then?" I asked carefully, hoping it didn't sound as much like an accusation as it felt like to me.

"I absorbed the soul energy you were holding onto that was interfering with your own life force, and then I allowed it to pass, as it should have done."

I nodded slowly as it sunk in. That made sense. In fact, the thought that I'd had those angels' souls inside me was kind of gross now that I thought about it. It must have shown on my face because Xanth wrapped an arm around my shoulders, completely unafraid of any potential consequences.

"Do you not care that I might suck out your soul right now, or did you just not think it was a possibility?" I asked him, slightly exhausted by how careless Xanth could be with his life when it came to me.

"I keep telling you, you won't hurt me. Besides, even if you lost control, Braedon is here to help." Xanth shrugged, and even though he had a point, it still annoyed me to no end. "You're going to have to trust yourself at some point, Drystan," he whispered.

And there was the truth that I'd never been able to see before. Because Xanth wasn't reckless. He trusted me, and he trusted me so completely, that he'd put his life in my hands to prove it. I'd just never been ready to see it before.

"Thank you," I whispered, finally looking at my friend and realising everything he'd done for me over the years.

He shrugged like it meant nothing, but I felt the way he squeezed me tighter in response. Xanth had always been at my side. Even when people tried to tear him away from me, he'd fought to stay. I'd never be able to thank him enough for that.

"So, we need to figure out what he can do then," Xanth

said, turning back to Braedon, who was trying to make it seem like he wasn't watching us have a personal moment.

He looked worried for a second, and then finally broke the news I definitely didn't want to hear. "I can't help you there, I'm afraid. It's going to be up to you, and I hate to admit, a whole load of luck. Stone always tells me that when you need it the most, it will show you what it can do. I've wanted to use my magic to help more around here and it's been frustrating to not have figured it out yet. So I know exactly how you feel right now."

It wasn't the news I'd wanted and I could tell from the look on his face that it wasn't what he wanted to say, either. There was so much about what was coming in this fight, that it felt like we were leaving it up to chance, and I'd just wanted to figure this one thing out. I knew it would be the best way I could protect Britt. It had to be.

"If it makes you feel any better, you're strong, Drystan. I can see the magic moving through you, and it's brighter than most I've ever seen. You shine nearly as brightly as Thor does, and that's saying a lot. Once you figure this out, I know you'll be a force to be reckoned with."

It didn't make me feel any better, but it set a sense of determination on fire inside me.

The clock was counting down, but I wouldn't fail her.

And that was how I'd ended up watching Britt and everyone around as closely as I could, taking note of the subtle shifts in the light that filled them. Britt, especially, was captivating. After everything she'd been through, her light still glowed, even if there was a noticeable hole where I knew her second soul should have been.

It was because I'd been watching her so closely that I'd seen the subtle ways her light seemed to dim like a flame flickering in the breeze and it scared the shit out of me. I'd not noticed it in anyone else, and after I'd realised it wasn't my imagination, I'd become obsessed with it. So much so that not a single word of the battle meeting had entered my mind.

Something was wrong with my mate and I didn't know if I should tell anyone or try to figure it out for myself.

Throughout the day, I'd stuck by her side. The others had noticed my behaviour, and when they'd put two and two together and realised I was worried about Britt, they'd clustered closer around her as well.

By the time we were getting ready for the feast, she'd had enough of us.

"What?!" Britt snapped. "Why are you all suddenly acting like I'm made of glass?"

Corvin and Bran stepped back, looking at me for an explanation. Xanth shrugged, and I was suddenly the one facing down our irritated mate alone.

"Explain," Britt sighed.

"Your soul is flickering," I told her, and she frowned. I wasn't exactly clear, but Xanth, who'd been there when Braedon had talked through my magic, knew what I meant and immediately looked alarmed.

"Why didn't you say something earlier?" Corvin shouted, grabbing Britt's face so he could tilt her head back and look into her eyes as if he was searching for something.

"Erm, what are you doing?" she asked, her words distorted from the way he had her cheeks smushed together.

Corvin's hand dropped, and he took a step back, shaking his head. He didn't need to say that he had no idea. We could all see the panic setting in. Britt reached for him, a look of sadness on her face, and as she did, I saw the light flicker again.

"There!" I shouted. "It did it again."

At that point, Britt sighed, and from the look she gave me, I knew I'd overreacted.

"My arm hurts," she sighed.

I could already see Bran getting ready to object, and apparently so did Britt, because she suddenly poked one finger at her wound dressing, and lo-and-behold, her light flickered in response.

"Erm... yeah, that appears to be it."

I'd never hear the end of this and I was already bracing for the jokes that were no doubt going to come.

Surprisingly, instead, Bran nodded, a serious look on his face. "We need to follow up on news of a healer," he said resolutely.

And then, in what I was starting to think was typical for them, the ravens turned and walked out of our room without a word.

"I guess they're on that, then," Xanth said dryly and then laughed. "Who'd have thought they'd be so whipped when they finally accepted the truth?"

He was right. There was nothing arrogant about the way they kept walking away. The ravens were struggling with the mate bond and the need to keep Britt safe. This was their way of doing it. If Xanth and I had more knowledge about who could heal Britt, we'd have done exactly the same thing. She would always be our priority and this situation was an example of why she needed all of us. Because where one of us might not be able to help, there were three others waiting to step in. And that felt better than I'd ever have imagined.

"Well, I guess we're going to the feast without them then," Britt said chirpily, like we hadn't just been talking about the fact her arm hurt so much that even her soul recognised her pain.

"Maybe we should rest for a bit," I said, moving to sit on the edge of the bed and patting the mattress beside me.

Britt looked at me like I'd lost my mind. "I can tell you've never been to a valkyrie feast by how you think I'd agree to that."

Xanth jumped onto the bed behind me, lounging across

the mattress as he did. "Maybe we can think of something to take your mind off it," he suggested in that tone of voice that screamed Xanth was full of good ideas.

"Are you trying to distract me with sex?"

"Is it working? Because if it is, then yes I am," Xanth joked.

Britt looked between the two of us, and for a second, I was certain we had her. She took half a step forward and my breath caught in my chest. It had been too long since I'd held her in my arms. Since I'd listened to the way her breath hitched as I trailed my tongue across her skin. Leaning forward in anticipation, I was about to haul her into my lap, when she spun on the spot with a laugh and darted for the door.

As she glanced over her shoulder, I felt the mattress shift and an excited Xanth jostled me to the side. "Oh, the chase is on, little mate. You better hope I don't catch you first."

And then they disappeared through the door.

Of course, I followed them, albeit at a slightly slower pace. Britt wanted to let her hair down and have fun with her friends. There was no way we'd let her miss out on that, even if it was our last night before the final fight. We had plenty of hours to fill and she needed to eat, anyway. Perhaps we could even get someone to heal her before we coaxed her back to our room, and then the fun could really begin. Because now that the idea was in my head, there was no way I was missing my last chance to have a taste of that beautiful woman before we headed into a fight none of us knew if we could win.

Chapter 43

Britt

Xanth caught me three steps away from the large cave that had been set up as a feasting hall. I could already hear the laughter inside when his arms wrapped around my waist and he plucked me up off the floor.

My back hit the stone wall of the corridor at the same time as his lips hungrily met mine. I didn't hesitate as my legs wrapped around his waist and he ground against me. There was a desperation to his kiss that I returned with fervour as he nipped at my bottom lip and swept his tongue over the sting before dipping it inside my mouth.

I whimpered at the sensation of him. The entire world narrowed down to the man between my legs, devouring my lips with a need that seemed like it would never be satisfied. My fingers raked through his hair as I tried to pull him closer to me. Instead, with a sigh, he leaned back, taking in the sight of my no doubt flushed face as he slowly lowered me down.

Once I had my feet on solid ground again, my gaze darted over his shoulder to see Drystan leaning against the opposite wall and watching the show.

"I get it now why you like to boss us around," he joked as heat banked in his eyes. "But it's time to join the party."

Drystan pushed away from the wall, holding his hand out for me, and I readily took it, even if I wasn't as convinced about heading to the feast as I had been before. Now that I'd had a taste, I'd definitely be okay with slipping away. We'd had so little time together it seemed a shame to waste it. He must have seen the look on my face.

"Whatever you're thinking, it can wait. We have all night, and the attack doesn't start until dusk tomorrow. There's plenty of time to spend it with your friends as well. I know you need this. We won't forget about you. Let's make Xanth work for his prize." He winked at me before looking over my shoulder at Xanth who was definitely pouting.

Was it selfish to have everything I wanted? To spend time with my friends and expect my mates to wait for me until the end of the night.

Just as I was about to suggest we leave, Xanth scooped up my other hand and pulled me toward the cave entrance.

"Come on. You haven't eaten since breakfast, and the ravens will come here first as soon as they've torn apart the base looking for a healer."

He was right, but it raised a question I hadn't really considered until now. Because if we were waiting for the ravens to join us, did that mean they were all going to stay with me tonight? How would they all feel about that? They'd made no indication this would be something they'd consider, and I sure as hell wouldn't be the one to bring it up.

There was no door separating off the cave. The corridor opened up into a vast cavernous space. It wasn't like the sleeping quarters, but then there was no need to separate it off for privacy or anything. I was actually surprised that they'd made a space like this. It didn't seem like something which would have been high on the agenda for a rebellion base someone had somehow carved into this mountain.

As soon as we stepped through, we were hit with a wave of sound that hadn't made its way out to the corridor. It was surprising, but at least we could have fun knowing we wouldn't disturb anyone. Not everyone was heading into the fight tomorrow. We had children and elderly here. They'd stay behind and make sure we had somewhere to withdraw to if needed. Someone to care for the wounded should the worst happen.

The valkyrie looked like they were already in full party mode. A massive bonfire had been set up in the centre of the cave and as I craned my head back, I realised I could see stars. Wherever we were, this cave was open to the sky and with it came the sweet, refreshing night air.

Several fire pits were set up around the edges of the cave, each of them with different food being prepared. Not to mention the casks of whatever the valkyrie had already found their way into.

"Let me grab us some food," Drystan said, nodding over to an empty table. "You guys grab some seats for us."

Xanth guided me over to the table and pulled me down into his lap as he sat. Drystan disappeared into the crowd, and I took a chance to watch the people around us as I settled back into my mate, feeling at ease with his arms around me.

"Looks like your friends are getting along," Xanth said over the noise of the room, pointing to the side of the massive bonfire.

Sure enough, there were the Elites looking like they were about to enter some kind of drinking game with some of the valkyrie. That definitely wouldn't end well. I'd partied with both sides and I had serious doubts over who would win. Mae looked small, but she was some kind of bottomless pit when it came to ale. It was honestly mind boggling watching how little it affected her.

Bran and Corvin found us minutes later as Xanth and I watched in awe as the girls slammed down the third mug of ale each and neither looked phased. The laughter was growing, and it was nice to watch everyone sinking into one last night of fun before... tomorrow.

I looked up to find Bran standing in front of me holding a mug of ale and, with a shrug, decided I might as well join them. I'd never been a massive drinker, but if there was one night to let my hair down and feel wild for once, it was definitely now.

Taking a sip, I was surprised by the sweet flavour that met my lips and pulled back the mug to look at the contents inside.

"It's mead," Bran told me as he took the chair beside us. "They make it from honey."

I licked my lips to sweep up the sweet flavour and took another drink, only for Bran to reach over and tip the mug further so I'd finish it in one go. Gulping quickly, I drank it down, laughing as I pulled the now empty mug away.

"Are you trying to get me drunk?"

"No, he's trying to heal you. It's laced with vampire blood," Corvin told me and I stared into the empty mug, slightly horrified.

"I think you're meant to lead with that kind of thing when you give someone a drink," Xanth told him dryly.

Corvin cocked his head to the side like he was trying to figure out what we were saying. I didn't have it in me to complain, though, because I could already feel the throbbing pain in my arm lessening and I doubted I'd have wanted to know beforehand that my drink had someone else's blood in it. Yuck!

A plate heaped with food was set down in front of me and I didn't even hesitate, grabbing one of the ribs and hungrily tearing at the meat. I was getting this inside me before someone ruined it by telling me it was coated in angel blood or something.

"See, now you've traumatised her," Xanth joked as I shoved more food into my mouth.

"I'm starving," I told them, ignoring my cheeky mate, who was trying to stir up trouble.

It was the wrong thing to say because I immediately saw Corvin and Bran sit straight, their gaze moving around the room as they searched for more food for me.

"Oh, will you calm down? I've got more than enough. Not that I don't appreciate the sentiment, but you have to trust me to do stuff like feed myself." This wasn't a conversation I'd ever imagined having, not with the world I'd come from. I didn't even have the luxury of imagining I'd find my fated mate, let alone that they'd cherish and worry about me. A peaceful life had been more than I could hope for; a loving one had seemed impossible.

"What did we say?" Corvin reminded me and I blushed at the memory of last night and all the things we'd done.

I was trying to find the words to assure them I was going to be alright when I realised how quiet the cave had fallen. Looking around, I saw the tables had cleared and all the valkyrie had gathered around the bonfire.

"What's happening?" I asked, looking around and hoping this wasn't the calm before the storm. My first thought was that Odin had found us, or that he'd already struck out at some of the people we'd left behind.

But then the ominous beat of a single drum filled the room, and the valkyrie swayed in time.

"I haven't heard of the valkyrie doing this for centuries," Bran said in wonder, standing from his seat and looking toward the drumming.

The crowd parted and Geta moved toward the bonfire, her

drum keeping beat as she solemnly walked toward the flame. The mages in the room watched in rapt attention and it was my first indication that something magical was about to happen.

Xanth and Drystan looked just as confused as I was. Especially when Corvin stood and drew the raven's claw from its sheath and dropped to his knees before me, holding it out.

"I don't understand," I whispered, looking at the black blade in his hand.

"The valkyrie sing the galdr. It's old magic. They gather before war and bless the fighters with a safe journey, raising the old magic to coat their blades. And should they fall in battle, to guide their souls to a glorious afterlife."

I looked down at the raven's claw, still not understanding why that meant he was giving the blade to me now.

Geta began to sing. It was a language I didn't understand and had never heard before, but the melody was hauntingly sad. As her song echoed around the cave, the valkyrie all drew their weapons and beat them against shields and armour in time with her drum.

"It was always yours," Corvin whispered. "We were only ever keeping it safe for you. It's time to claim it, mate. Embrace who you were always meant to be."

"But I don't know how to wield it." I didn't feel like I was worthy enough to take the sword. They'd held onto it for a specific reason, and even though I knew I was their mate, and this was what we'd been searching for, it didn't feel right.

Corvin pressed the sword handle into my hand as he pulled me to my feet. Wrapping my fingers around the pommel, he gently beat it in time with the drum against my breastplate.

"Feel the magic, mate. Sing our song of war."

I closed my eyes and tipped my head back, feeling the beat reverberate through my body as Geta's soulful words wrapped around me. The bonds inside me rose, answering her call, and I felt the sword in my hand heat.

My eyes opened in surprise, but when I looked down, the sword was just as it had always been.

"I can feel it," I told Corvin in surprise and his smile was blinding.

"I'm sorry I ever doubted you."

I could see his guilt, even though he had nothing to feel guilty about. After decades of captivity in Helheim, I couldn't blame them for being reluctant to trust anyone.

Before I could say anything, Aria and the rest of the Elites were at our table, ushering me over to the fire. Corvin happily watched me go, never trying to hold me back and only encouraging me on. All of my mates stood there, smiles on their faces as they watched my friends pull me closer to the bonfire.

The Valkyrie had started to dance now. They circled the bonfire, dipping closer and whirling away, flaring their wings wide. Every time one of them neared the flames, they'd shove the blade of their sword inside and it would ignite with a blue, glowing flame. Soon enough, it became a daring dance of fire and feathers as Geta's song grew louder and louder, and somehow we knew every step as we moved with them.

And then the song suddenly paused. A wind howled through the cave, extinguishing every fire, pitching the cave into darkness.

My feet stilled as my chest heaved with breath. We'd all been caught up in the dance and the raven's claw in my hand felt like it vibrated with a power I didn't understand. You could feel it rising around the room. The air felt saturated with magic and I could feel every single person gathered ready for this fight.

I didn't know who the valkyrie prayed to or if this was even that. Did magic have to involve a deity? Whatever it was, my heart thudded against my chest in time with Geta's drum and I knew without a doubt that everyone else was keeping the same beat. We were all linked.

I thought that was it. It seemed like we'd reached the pinnacle of whatever magic the Galdr had risen. Then it started again. But it was different this time.

The song sounded violent, dark, and the guttural sounds that Geta sang sent a shiver down my spine. I could feel the anger that resonated through them at the injustice the Valkyrie had experienced. Betrayal rang through the words as the Valkyrie all took up the same song.

The fires caught again, flames surging high in the air as the Valkyrie took up their dance once more, but where it had been dizzying and joyful before, now it was lined with rage. Swords slashed through the air as the Valkyrie leapt and sang. All the Elites, Aria and I included, took up the dance at their side. It was one I didn't know, but my feet moved in time anyway, like I'd moved to this dance for lifetimes before.

Aria's wings appeared from her back as she morphed into her phoenix general appearance, her leathers transforming into the same red set I'd seen on her in the last battle we'd fought. Flames surged down her wings, coating them in the magic only she contained, magic that had been strong enough to raise an entire race of people.

But it didn't stop there.

As the song forged on and the dance continued, every valkyrie that moved to Aria's side shared in her flames. Their wings touched, and the flames leapt, spreading from valkyrie to valkyrie. Even the Elites weren't immune to the effects as the flames coated the weapons they held in their hands.

As they grew closer to me, I felt the raven's claw heat in my hand. In the back of my mind, I felt a growing need, but it wasn't my own. It belonged to something that was trying to push inside, to take root and bond with a part of me that didn't exist.

And then the fire reached me.

The raven's claw caught ablaze, and my heart raced in joy at the sight. The dressings on my arm caught fire next, falling away and revealing fresh, unharmed skin beneath. But again the magic didn't stop there. I felt the sword heat and the magic creep its way up my arm. As it swirled and danced in time with our song, rejoicing at finding the one it was forged for, a dark inked pattern flowed over my skin. It raced up my arm, and I shuddered, my head falling back as I felt it flow down my back.

The raven's claw was mine. I should have never doubted it.

The warriors started to move then, plucking the valkyries from their dance as lips met and limbs tangled. A ragged growl rang through the air and I saw Kyle sweep Aria off her feet before he tossed her over his shoulder and walked from the room, followed by the rest of her mates.

My eyes caught Corvin's then. I saw a need blaze inside them that called to the deepest parts of me. He stalked toward me and my other mates fanned out to his sides. For a moment, a thrill ran through my body, urging me to turn and flee. To let my mates take up the chase and prove that they were worthy of the bond they fought to forge.

But I didn't.

My feet remained rooted to the ground as they approached and Corvin swept me up into his arms.

Why would I ever run from these men when they were everything I'd ever wanted?

Chapter 44

Bran

Doors slammed all around us as everyone sank into the magic of the galdr and took up the opportunity of a last night of passion before the inevitability of tomorrow.

I could feel it beating inside my chest even now as we all strode into our suite of rooms. It was a need for action, to fight, to fuck. The others were clearly feeling it too because as soon as the door was closed, clothes were stripped off while we were still heading for the bed. Even the breastplate dropped to the ground, not needed for the activities of tonight.

This would be the first time we'd all been together in the same room, and even though none of the other men held any attraction for me, I didn't begrudge their presence. We were to be a bonded group and I could feel that bond humming inside me. It vibrated with the call of the galdr and had given us all a single purpose.

Her.

Corvin dropped Britt onto the bed and we all clustered around. Her hands reached, stroking over our flesh as she licked her lips. Her perfect tits bobbed and swayed, her rosy nipples hard, little tips begging for attention.

"These are beautiful," I commented, my fingers tracing the pattern of tattoos that now lined her arms and extended down her back. She hummed in agreement, but I could already see the glaze coming across her eyes just from my touch alone. "They look just like wings."

"Wings?" Britt's voice was breathy and beautiful as spoke.

I knew if I pushed my fingers inside her right now, I'd find her wet and ready. I could see the lust flashing through her eyes and it was there, like a shadow at the back of our bond. If we'd been able to fully complete the bond, I knew it would hit me like a freight train right now. I'd always be able to feel her need and would be ready and willing to fill it.

She pushed to her hands and knees, crawling across the surface of the bed toward me, and my cock twitched in anticipation. How could one person be so fucking perfect?

She grabbed my cock in her hand, slowly dragging her tongue along the length while Xanth climbed onto the bed behind her. His fingers moved through her wetness as she swallowed me down, groaning and sending delicious vibrations straight to my balls.

Corvin and Drystan watched in rapt fascination as she sucked me down. Her hand worked my shaft in time with her lips, her cheeks hollowing out as Xanth started to fuck her with his fingers from behind.

"I need more," she gasped, pulling away from me.

Xanth moved quickly, shifting to the edge of the bed, and guided her over to straddle his lap. He swooped her hair over one shoulder and gathered it in his hand as she leaned forward to take me back into her mouth. Sinking down onto his cock, she groaned in pleasure, swivelling her hips as she bottomed out.

His hands came to her hips to help her keep her pace as she focused on her wicked lips wrapped around my length.

It was impossible to stay still and her hands on my ass

encouraged me to fuck her throat deep and fast. Xanth's hand in her hair held her in place as my thumbs brushed her cheeks, wiping the tears that gathered as she peered up through her lashes at me.

I felt the moment she relaxed into the sensations we were pulling from her body, her throat muscles relaxed, and I slipped deeper still. My head fell back with a groan as she took the entirety of my cock deep in her throat, Xanth's hand moving against her clit.

I could tell she was about to come from the little pants she was giving and went to pull away. I didn't want to suffocate her, but I also didn't want her orgasm to trigger my own. We'd only just started, and I knew we both wanted so much more.

As I pulled away, Britt sagged back against Xanth, riding his cock with her head tipped onto his shoulder. She looked like a true goddess, taking her pleasure from her mate. We all watched as she fell apart, her cries of ecstasy echoing around us.

"Are you ready for Drystan, my love?" Xanth whispered in her ear, and a grin spread across her face as she reached her hands out for him.

"Always," she told him, love flashing in her gaze.

As Drystan stepped forward, Xanth picked her up, spun her around, and set her back in his lap. "I'm not done with you yet," he told her and she laughed, the most joyous sound that it made me want to file it away to replicate as often as possible in the future.

Drystan moved behind her, dropping to his knees as he pushed her forward, Xanth and her both collapsing against the bed.

I shuffled forward a step, fascinated by how easily they could be together.

Xanth kissed her hungrily as Drystan licked across her ass.

"What do you think, sweetheart? You ready to try something new?"

"Fuck yes," she sighed as Drystan's thumb came to her hole pressing inside.

My cock twitched in need. She was so receptive, so willing. The ideas it brought to the surface were things I'd never considered before. But the men in this room didn't intimidate me. I didn't feel ashamed of being with her around them. This was a beautiful thing. That we could all come together with no other intention than to wring as much pleasure as possible from our beautiful mate. She was the centre of our universe, and we worshipped at her altar in every way we could.

Drystan dragged the slick wetness from the pussy up across her ass, working his fingers inside her until she begged for me. Her mumbled words of bliss had my cock dripping in need. I couldn't wait to drive her to the edge and watch her face as she succumbed to the pleasure.

Corvin stood in the same position off to the side of the bed watching the show the others put on in fascination. His hand slowly worked his length as he watched Drystan finally push his cock into our mate's ass.

"Yes... yes... more," she cried as she struggled to stay still while her mate consumed her body.

"We've got you, my love," Xanth told her. His hands brushing over her face and pushing her hair back. He coaxed her lips down to his and kissed her softly. "Let us take care of you. We know what you need," he said gently.

And that was exactly the point of it. I could feel her need vibrating along the partially formed bond. It was more vibrant than it had been before the galdr and I knew it wouldn't be the same once the magic withdrew until we could complete it. For some reason, I knew it wouldn't be now, and even though that saddened a part of me, I also knew it would happen when it was time.

Drystan and Xanth slowly moved in time, one pulling out as the other forged ahead and she became a mewling mess caught between them. Such a beautiful, vibrant mess. She looked wild, like a creature that could only be contained if she willed it so. How could she ever think of herself as nothing but human? We could all see the other-worldly beauty of her. We just needed to help her see it herself.

"Bran," she whispered, locking her pleasure filled eyes with mine. "I need you."

I'd never deny her, and as I walked over, she turned to watch as Corvin took the same chair we'd used before. He winked at her as he sat down, stroking his cock, and her mouth popped open hungrily.

"Don't stop." He stroked his cock again, her eyes tracking his movement. "I want to watch you shatter."

When she turned back to me, she eyed me hungrily, and I moved back to her mouth. "Still want me?" I asked, even though I didn't mean it. I knew she did. I could see it in her eyes that she needed me as much as I needed her.

"More than I need to breathe."

I grinned at her choice of words. Holding the base of my cock in one hand, I cupped her chin with the other. "Let's put that to the test, shall we? I want to see you swallow every drop, sweetheart."

She swirled her tongue around the head of my cock, licking the bead of liquid that had already collected on the head. It hadn't been that long since she'd had me in her mouth, but I was already desperate for her again. I'd never get enough.

Britt opened her mouth wide and waited. The others had fallen still; watching in fascination as I ran the head of my cock across her bottom lip before slowly pushing into her mouth. When I hit the back of her throat, she swallowed and my eyes rolled back in my head at the sensation. Perfection.

We all moved together. Britt looked like she was riding wave after wave of pleasure. Her hands would come to my hips to urge me on, and then she was caressing Xanth's chest. The only reason she didn't reach out to Drystan was no doubt because she couldn't reach him, but he lovingly ran his fingers down her spine, tracing the black inky wings that had appeared there like he could tell what she needed.

His jaw clenched, and he looked like he was holding onto his control by a thread. I'd long given up trying to hold back the inevitable. I could feel the growing pressure in my balls as Britt hungrily swallowed me down.

The magic of the galdr pitched and swelled around us, rejoicing in the way we'd taken up its song. We all moved to the beat that echoed inside us, the one that danced through every fighter preparing for tomorrow.

We were a haze of movement and when her hand came up to cradle my balls, tugging slightly in just the right way, I couldn't hold back any longer. My hips snapped forward, and I came with a yell, filling her throat as she greedily swallowed my come down.

Britt barely had time to swallow before she tore her mouth away from me. Her eyes locked with mine as the wave of her orgasm crashed over her. Drystan and Xanth were helpless but to follow, although I scarcely registered it. All I could see was the haze of pleasure that came over her face, the way her mouth parted and she panted out little cries. How her eyes creased at the corners as she desperately tried to keep them open, to let me see every second as each nerve ending lit up in a fire of passion.

Drystan tenderly pulled away. He moved to her side on the bed as Britt leaned down to kiss Xanth and then Drystan before she pulled away.

When she turned to Corvin, he sat back in his chair, a grin on his face, and holding out one hand to her. She walked over and took it as he helped her into his lap, before sinking down on his waiting cock with a blissful sigh.

"You're so fucking beautiful in everything you do," Corvin told her. "But this? This is where you shine, where the light inside you blazes and captivates every single one of us. I will always be powerless to your pull. Whenever you need me, wherever that may be, I will always be at your side."

She rode him in long, lazy strides, leaning back as he wrapped one hand around her lower back to keep her balance. The other stroked up her front, cupping her breast and pinching the hard nipple that begged for his attention.

"Yes. Just like that," she moaned.

Corvin continued to worship her, capitulating to every one of her cries as she called for harder, faster. He moved with her until she fell forward, pulling his head to her chest and he greedily bit down on her breast. She came with a scream, and his teeth dug deeper as he followed her over the edge, pulling away to lick over the wound and praise her for how perfect she was for him.

By the time Corvin carried her back to the bed, Xanth had already fetched damp cloths from the bathroom and he tenderly cleaned her as she crawled into my arms.

The rest of her mates climbed onto the bed and we all clustered around her, surrounding her with love and finding the reassurance of having each other close by while the thought of tomorrow leeched back into our minds.

I thought Britt had already fallen asleep, but then she whispered, "I'm sorry."

"What could you possibly be sorry for?" I asked, brushing her hair away from her face so she could see how serious I was.

"The bond... we didn't... I didn't..." She shook her head, and I held her tight, the others moving to do the same.

"This wasn't about the bond," Corvin told her gently. His hands stroked up her calf from where he lounged on the bottom of the bed. "There's no pressure to form the bond now. Tonight was about being there for each other. We all feel our mate bond even if it isn't complete, even if it's never complete, that can never be taken away from us."

"But what about tomorrow?" she asked hesitantly. I should have known that as soon as her mind was cleared of lust, her thoughts would turn back to the inevitable fight. "What about the raven's claw?"

"The sword is yours," I told her, hearing the truth that rang in my words. "You will wield it because it is what you were born to do. When the time is right, the magic will show you the way."

I didn't know how I knew it, but I was more certain about this than anything else in my life. My fingertips traced the lines of the tattoos that crawled up her arms again. I'd seen the wings that were now pictured on her back and it was just more proof that she was who we always knew her to be.

Whatever magic we needed for tomorrow was already in motion. It was all just a matter of time now.

Chapter 45

Britt

The reprieve we'd found last night in each other's arms felt like so long ago now that the harsh reality of day had arrived.

It felt strange to have the raven's claw strapped to my back and not the katana I'd carried for so long.

I tipped back my head and breathed deeply of the crisp evening air. The caves had felt homey and I hadn't once felt claustrophobic despite knowing we were deep inside a mountain. But as soon as we stepped outside, I could feel the change.

Out here the world felt free, and for the briefest of moments I could forget what we were about to do, and the blood that was about to be spilled. The only way I could hold on to my sanity was by clinging to the knowledge that this was the end. One way or another, it would all be over after today.

My gaze found my mates who all looked to be doing exactly the same thing that I was—taking a moment to appreciate the world around us.

The bonds blazed unfinished between us. They were strong, but they weren't wholly complete. It should have filled me with panic. But somehow it didn't. I knew in my heart that it was because I'd lost my shifter side, and yet something told me it would be okay. I felt a rightness about the place we were in at the moment. It was where we needed to be and once it was over, we'd find a way. Even if we couldn't, we didn't need a full bond to know we'd always be in each other's lives. It was enough to feel them as much as I did. To know they were always with me.

Standing on the hilltop and looking down at the city was a sobering sight. Even through all the planning and going over all the figures, I hadn't truly appreciated the extent of Odin's forces. But seeing them laid out in front of us, reality set in.

And it felt impossible.

The Elites gathered around me, and even though the mood felt sombre, there was an electric edge to the air. Last night had set something on fire within us, and we were as ready for this as we were ever going to be.

"That's an enormous army," I muttered, not being able to take my eyes off it, knowing my friends would be going down there, and I wouldn't be there to support them. "Maybe we should change the plan. Hit them head on with our full force and fight through to the throne room."

Mae pulled me into a fierce hug, slapping me on the back as she pulled away. "Don't you dare take away my moment of glory. We've got this, you do your bit and we'll do ours. Stop worrying about us. I have a life filled with debauchery planned. I'm not letting some measly demi god army keep me from it."

"Exactly!" Harmony chimed in. I could see the worry in her eyes before I realised it was aimed at me rather than herself. "We've got our end. But if you need more support for..."

"Don't," I told her gently, hugging her just as fiercely as I did my other friends. "We're all worried about each other, but

Mae's right, we've got this. You don't have to worry about me."

I knew it was hypocritical; I'd been the one to start this conversation, after all. I could see now how useless it would be. We were going up against impossible odds. All we could do was have faith in each other and give it everything we had. It was all or nothing. We couldn't leave anything at the door. Now was the time to stand up and show them what we were truly made of.

I turned back to my mates, who were waiting for me off to the side, giving me a moment to say goodbye to my friends. They were speaking with Echo's mates, Corvin and Bran going over the layout of the palace with them again. It was inevitable we'd get split up somewhere along the way. That was the whole point.

Odin's forces were mostly laid out in front of the palace, guarding not just the entrance but also the Bifrost. It left the back suspiciously open, and whilst we still planned on using it, it didn't count as a trap if you were aware you were about to walk into it. At least, I didn't think it did.

Aria and the Asgard rebels would hit Odin with a full frontal assault, engaging his forces out in the open and keeping their attention away from the palace. Echo and I would slip in using the dungeon tunnels Aria had once escaped through. The plan was to head to the throne room through the dungeons and face Odin with as little back up as possible. But we weren't stupid enough to believe he was alone. He knew we were coming after all, thanks to Hel. And he also knew we were in possession of the raven's claw.

Odin might have lost his mind, but I doubted he was arrogant enough to leave himself vulnerable.

No, we had to spring his trap and fight through. Trust that each group would complete their part of the plan. It was the greatest chance we had of succeeding.

Aria approached Echo and me last. Her face was grim, but it didn't take away from how magnificent she looked in her battle leathers, her wings out and her short swords visible on her back.

"If you run into too much trouble, Stone pulls you out," she told us firmly. "If we have to regroup and push through together, we will."

Echo and I nodded, knowing it wasn't an option. From the look on Aria's face, she knew it as well, but she'd always worry about us. It was who she was.

As her arms wrapped around me, she whispered, "I lost you once and I won't survive it again. Don't make me come and drag your ass out of another afterlife."

I laughed at the fierceness in her voice, knowing full well that she'd do it if she could.

"I'd say the same to you, but I don't quite have the same skills."

Aria picked up my hand then, her gaze running along the new tattoos that disappeared under my fighting leathers. She hadn't seen the tattooed wings on my back, even though I'd told her about them. "These are here for a reason," she told me. "When the time comes, trust in the magic."

"It's time," Thor told us, walking over to interrupt us. "We need to move now before we lose our window."

It was painful to watch them walk away. It felt wrong not to be going with them, even if I knew we'd be playing just as important of a role in this fight. But Aria and the others were placing themselves in front of an army which was ten times larger than the forces we had, and it was all to give us a chance to get to Odin. I couldn't help but think we were putting their lives on the line to cover our asses, and I hated every second of it.

I turned back to my mates, knowing it was time for us to leave as well. Xanth fiddled with the sword at his belt and

Drystan batted his hands away from it, rolling his eyes. They weren't as familiar with fighting with weapons. It wasn't their strongest defence, but they couldn't rely on their magic for the entire time.

Corvin and Bran looked the calmest out of the lot of us. They didn't have the connection with the others to be worried about their safety. Their concern boiled down to our own little group. Plus, they knew the layout of the palace like the back of their hands. But what they tried to hide from the rest of us was the guilt that so many could lose their lives today because they hadn't had the strength to stop this before it could reach this point. I just hoped when it was finally over, they'd be able to find some peace.

"Let's do this," I told them as Echo and her mates whispered words of reassurance to each other.

I couldn't do the same. I refused to say goodbye to my mates. This couldn't be the end for us. I wouldn't allow it.

Chapter 46

Aria

My mates and I headed to the front of our force, with Thor and Myra at our side. The Elites came next with the mages and the Asgardian rebels filling out the ranks behind us. It hadn't been an easy sell for the plan to go this way, especially with Tristan whispering into the ears of anyone who would listen that we were using them as nothing but shields.

Picking up my pace, I broke into a slow jog, pulling the swords from my back as I did. My hands tightened and released against the pommels as I adjusted my grip, paying attention to the sound of footfalls behind me and the pace of our troops.

I could feel the bond between my mates and me vibrating with magic, and I knew they were getting ready to hit the first of Odin's ranks with as much as they had. It would burn through their reserves quicker, but once we were fully engaged in battle, it would be too close quarters to throw large scale magic attacks, anyway. We couldn't risk hitting our own soldiers, and we'd have to rely on our physical weapons at that point.

As we rounded the corner and the first of the Asgardian army came into sight, Kyle sent a massive blast of Earth magic into the centre of their ranks. The ground split open as it rumbled beneath them, making them stumble into the crevices Kyle created and Virion filled with flames. It was brutal and part of me felt it was unnecessary, but the only way we'd get through was to take out as many of our enemies as we could with each attack.

Sykes pulled on his magic and a cyclone dropped into the centre of the army, pushing more of the enemy soldiers into the fiery pits. Those that were lucky enough to have escaped the pits were hammered with swells from the river as it swept along the Bifrost, raining boiling water down upon them.

It felt so wrong charging into a battle and witnessing the horrors we'd brought down on these people, but there was no moment to feel, no time for regret, because our weapons clashed and we engaged the first of their scattered fighters before they could form organised ranks.

My mates had dealt significant losses to the other side, but even then, it wasn't enough. We were still vastly outnumbered and as we met the first of their ranks head on; it became more and more apparent how impossible their numbers truly were.

The angels flew forward, touching down at the head of the army as they formed a single unit headed by the two remaining archangels. They created a shield for the clambering Asgardians as they rearranged their ranks, drawing weapons and preparing for a counteroffensive.

This was a seasoned army, and we were a ragtag group of rebels. Most of the Asgardians at our back had been normal people. They might have spent years conducting ambushes and raids of the enemy's camp, but they'd never been in a war like this.

The archangels snickered at the sight of our force. We must have looked pathetic to them given how small our numbers were. They probably wondered why we were even bothering.

I drew to a stop, Thor, Myra and my mates doing the same as we headed the fighters at our back. I heard movement behind me and hoped it was the mages getting in position. They weren't the most seasoned of fighters but we needed them to help deal with the archangels.

"So this is the day you've chosen to die," one archangel sneered at us.

Instead of rising to the bait like he wanted, I merely raised my arm. My fingertips slipped beneath the tattooed image of the Gjallarhorn that curled up my arm and pulled the enchanted object free from my skin.

The angels laughed. It was like a repeat of the last time we'd faced them at the packhouse after they'd arrived from their slaughter of the valkyrie. Strangely, none of them even suspected that anything was amiss.

"Legion!" the archangel yelled. "We advance at the sound of the horn. Cut swiftly, hit true, and leave none alive!"

His cruel eyes locked with mine while he shouted and I resisted the urge to send a throwing knife in his direction. We couldn't afford for the charge to begin before we were ready. But it was like he dared me to do it. When I raised the horn to my lips, a flare of excitement rushed through his gaze. He'd have enjoyed watching his soldiers mercilessly cut us down.

There was no space in the world we were building for people like him.

And so I blew.

The single note of the Gjallarhorn vibrated across what would become our battlefield, and as the angels advanced toward us, we broke into a run of our own.

A cry of victory rang out from the archangel, but our screams of rage drowned it out. Metal clashed against metal and blood flew in vicious arches. It would have felt like the beginning of the end, but then the sky turned black as the last of the setting sun's rays were blocked from the sky.

The Valkyrie were here.

And we would have our revenge.

Chapter 47

Echo

The sound of the Gjallarhorn reverberated through the tunnel as we pulled ourselves up through the trapdoor. My heart tripped a beat and my hands fisted at my side in frustration. I should have been out there with my sisters. I should have been fighting that battle, too. It felt wrong to be crawling through the darkness when I knew they were fighting for their lives out there.

Britt and her mates were behind us, as we'd already agreed. I had one role in this battle—to get as far as I could into the palace until we sprung whatever trap Odin had laid for us. Then we were to hold the line at all costs so Britt and her mates could do what needed to be done.

We weren't fools. We knew this was the worst possible role in this whole thing. Odin wouldn't have left himself vulnerable, and whatever we were about to face, it would be in close quarters and in unfamiliar territory. The likelihood of my mates and me making it out alive was slim. But everyone faced the same terrible odds in their parts of the plan, too. Aria was up against two entire armies. And Britt... well, she had to kill the most powerful god that had ever lived.

Maybe we didn't have the worst role when you thought about it that way.

As we gathered in the dank dungeons, a shudder rushed down my spine at what the people held here must have gone through. There had been a great debate whether we should have scoured the dungeons first and freed anyone who was alive inside. From the smell of things, nothing but death lingered in this place. In the end, the decision had been made to return for them once everything was over, if there was anyone left alive to do so. Freeing them into the middle of a battle would only end one way, and this was the best chance we could give them of survival. Even if turning away from the dungeon doors was one of the hardest things I'd ever done.

"The level above this is the first open area in the dungeon before we enter the palace," Corvin told us grimly.

We all knew what that meant. It was the one place we couldn't avoid no matter which tunnel we used to gain entrance to the palace, and it was also the most likely place that we'd trigger whatever trap Odin had for us.

It was time then.

I looked around at my mates, fingertips brushed against my hands, and I stopped myself from reaching out to embrace them. Falling into their arms now wouldn't strengthen me for what was to come next, it would only cause me to find any excuse I could to have them turn back.

I drew the swords from my back, feeling my magic rush through the blades in greeting. The leather of the pommels creaked beneath my hands as I gripped them hard.

My eyes locked with Britt's and so much went unspoken between us. She knew what we were risking by doing this and she hated every second of it. She'd argued that we should join the others outside and let them risk the dungeons alone. Not a single person had agreed with her. Not even her mates. This was the best chance they had of making it through to the throne room. After that, it would all be down to her. And Aria and I hated that just as much as she hated this fate for me. No one was going into this happy.

War wasn't made for happiness though, and even if this wasn't a war of our own making, it was one we had no choice in fighting.

Without a word, we moved as one, rounding the corner into the open area that would determine our fate. When my eyes took in the sight before us, my breath hitched and I knew we were in trouble.

"Oh, of fucking course," Stone scoffed.

There was no point in being quiet now. The thing in front of us had seen us and there would be no sneaking past. It filled nearly the entire space, and I didn't see how Britt and her mates would find a way past.

"Malice," Bran sneered, recognising the monster before us.

The creature was so vast that it filled the cavernous space before us. The numerous black tentacles snaked across the ground as it hooked its eyes on us. A whisper of awareness seemed to cross its gaze, like it had been waiting for us.

Before any of us could react, a portal flickered to life next to Damon and a smokey tendril snapped out. Diving forward, I slashed in an upward arc, severing the shadow from the portal and spinning to take the second tendril that had followed.

Damon dived to the side, his arm wrapping around my waist as he did, dragging me down with him and away from the portal.

"What the fuck just happened?" Xanth asked, looking shocked.

But no one had time to answer him as two more portals opened in the middle of our group, four tendrils snapping out of them this time.

I rolled to cover Damon, slicing one of the celestial blades through the shadow that tried to claim us. Samuel dealt with one of the other tendrils, the Michael sword cutting through it, making the smoke disappear into nothing. But the others weren't so lucky. Bran tried to stake the tendril that moved toward him, but his sword passed through it, causing no damage at all. It wrapped around Drystan before he had time to move.

Samuel and I moved at the same time, trying to reach him before Drystan ended up sharing the same fate as the mage elders we'd seen drained and turned to dust. It seemed Xanth already knew the consequences of what was about to happen as well because even though he didn't have a weapon that would apparently hurt the creature, he still reached for his friend.

I was only a step away when it pulled Drystan up into the air, a shriek of victory echoing around the room. Britt cried out in distress, but Drystan just flashed her a reassuring smile. The dagger in his hand flashed with a blue energy I didn't recognise, and he plunged it into the tendril that had snatched him away.

The creature screamed. It sounded like nails drawing across granite, and a shudder rippled down my spine in response. Drystan crashed through the air as the creature recoiled, and a flash of a doorway beyond caught my eye as Drystan was unceremoniously dumped on the ground at our feet.

Aubron immediately pulled him up, pushing him back into the group as we backed away a few steps in retreat.

"Did you see the door?" I asked quickly, already seeing the creature's tentacles recoiling like it was preparing for another attack.

"We need to hurt it again. Get it to move so you can make

a run for the door," Tas ordered. "Make your way as far around the edge of the room as you can and we'll draw its attention to us. Echo, Samuel, you have the weapons that can hurt it. Damon, Aubron and I will draw the tentacles while you two deal with them."

"We can't leave you to deal with this," Britt said in horror, but I was already at her side, pushing her in the direction she needed to go.

"We've dealt with this thing before. And we should have finished it then. We've got a score to settle and you've got a job of your own." I shoved her again, knowing we didn't have time to debate this.

One of the creature's giant tentacles slammed down on the floor and it let out a roar of displeasure before it surged up to its full height. The door on the other side came into view beneath its massive body as it pushed itself high onto its tentacle.

"*You've* got a score to settle," Xanth yelled in outrage. "I was nearly chow for that damn thing and I, for one, want to see it in pieces. Do you know how many of my family died, with that being the last thing they saw?"

The pain on his face was the same pain that Stone had whenever he spoke of what had happened at the mage library. Especially on the nights when he let himself feel the guilt of not having acted sooner. I understood that for Xanth it was more personal, but none of us had the luxury of holding on to personal grudges in this fight.

"You have a job to do," Samuel told him, herding him in the direction he needed to go. "Lingering here is exactly what Odin wants you to do. If we're going to end this, then you can't play into his games. Don't let it all be for nothing. End it, if not for yourself, then for the ones who weren't lucky enough to still be alive to fight today."

Xanth nodded, but I could see the determination setting

into his face. His gaze flicked to Britt and then he was moving, following them across the room, getting as close to the creature as they dared.

"Time to kick some... tentacle," Stone said, drawing a groan from the group.

But there wasn't any time to mock him mercilessly for his sense of humour because I could already see the creature turning in the direction Britt and the others had gone, and we needed to draw its attention back to us.

With a yell, Aubron sprinted forward two steps and javelin threw one of his swords. It sailed through the air, embedding just below the creature's eye, and another shriek filled the room. As two more portals flared into existence on either side of us, one of the creature's massive tentacles slammed down, aiming right for us. There was no chance of diving to the side unless we wanted to jump into the portal. Instead, all we could do was cluster together, raise our weapons and brace for the inevitable hit.

Aubron, Tas, and Damon all took a knee, moving as one as if this was some kind of practised move I'd missed out on. Samuel flattened me to the ground between them and their swords pierced deep into the tentacle that tried to crush us.

The smell of rotten flesh rolled over us and I gagged as a thick black liquid oozed from the wounds. Shadow tendrils blasted through the portals heading toward our group at the same time as the creature screamed in pain. Samuel and I were quick to deal with them as the others strained to hold the tentacle aloft.

When it wrenched back the injured limb, they were lucky enough to keep hold of their swords, and I looked in desperation to see if the others had made it.

I couldn't find any sign of Britt or her mates, so all I could do was hope they'd made it through.

There was no time to think about it because instead of

retreating away from us like last time, the monster shifted, and with a sweep we hadn't expected, a tentacle slammed into our side, catapulting us into the stone wall.

And then there was nothing but darkness.

Chapter 48

Aria

Even with the Valkyrie entering the fight and attacking the Asgardian army from the rear, we were still vastly outnumbered.

This wasn't the same as fighting the demon army. These were seasoned fighters and some of them matched the Valkyrie in experience and skill.

There had been a moment when it felt like we could actually win. The sight of the Valkyries had stunned the angels enough that we'd gotten the upper hand over their forces as we clashed. The Asgardian army had fallen out of rank in their panic, and the Valkyrie had mercilessly cut through them.

But it didn't take them much time to regroup.

They had seasoned captains in their ranks who, with a shouted order, had them all rushing back into position and then pressing forward as one fighting force.

My blade clashed with the angel in front of me, and his glare cut me deep. There was no doubt on his face over what he was doing. All he was concerned about was cutting through me and those around me. Surviving was all that mattered to him and we were what stood in the way of that.

So why wasn't I thinking the same?

I could feel the bloodlust at the back of my mind, but I held onto my awareness with an iron will. I fought hard; cutting down those who turned to fight me and the flames on my wings did as much damage as my sword as we danced the dance of death.

But I wasn't fighting with everything I had. I was holding back. I gritted my teeth to duck under the swipe of a battleaxe, my short sword slashing in close under my attacker's swing, and I knew I was making reckless mistakes.

I'd left my side wide open, and it was only Virion fighting mercilessly at my side that saved me from the angel who saw the opening and tried to run me through.

I felt a grip on my leathers and Kyle pulled me in close, yelling, "Get your head in the fight," he screamed. "I refuse to lose you today, Aria."

Even though I knew what he was asking for, and what I needed to do, I couldn't make myself let go of the control. I didn't want to be that person who cut through the Asgardian army last time, unseeing of the damage I had done. I didn't want to become that weapon, seeking blood to quench an unending appetite. There was no way I could survive the fallout again.

But what was the alternative? Fighting while my mind struggled to hold back my nature, and making one mistake after another until I got myself, or even worse, one of my mates, killed?

I knew there wasn't really any decision at all. If it was me or them, I'd choose to save them every time. I'd sacrifice anything for them, even my sanity. So why couldn't I let go?

A flash of magic caught my attention in the corner of my eye and I saw the mages ensnare one of the archangels in the trap they'd been practicing. It felt unreal that it was actually working. He thrashed and screamed but then Thor brought down a bolt of lightning and there was one less archangel to worry about.

A call rang out behind me and I spun on the spot, knowing it wasn't part of the plan. I assumed it meant we were about to be flanked, or someone was in trouble, so I couldn't quite understand what my eyes were seeing at first.

Throughout the course of the fight, our fighters had spread across the field, holding the line but also pushing forward. The only chance we had was to keep up the pressure for as long as we could. The Valkyries had advanced from the rear, attempting to pin the larger army in closer fighting quarters. It was what we'd gone over time and time again and every time we went over the battle tactics, everyone had agreed it was our best chance.

But now the Asgardian rebels were pulling back and forming a secondary line behind us, leaving the rest of us isolated in the middle of the angel ranks.

It was a death sentence when we were so far out from the Valkyries and their warriors.

Thor stepped to my side, his hammer slamming into an angel that had seen his opportunity to strike in my distraction.

"Tristan!" he boomed across the battleground.

I saw him then, the man from our tactical meetings who had questioned why the Asgardians had to fight. The one who thought we owed it to them to fight in their place, that they'd paid in enough blood already.

He locked eyes with my father, simply shook his head and then every Asgardian rebel fighter who stood at his side turned and left. Abandoning us to our fate.

"Cowards!" I screamed, my rage building and lashing out in the only way it could as I darted back into the fray, hacking through the wing joint of one angel as I kicked another in the small of his back. I'd run him through with a sword before he even touched the ground.

My mates, the Elites, and my parents moved closer, and we did the only thing we could, moving back to back and creating a circle to fight the angels that were now closing in around us. The mages huddled in our centre as we protected them as much as we could. They could send out weak attacks from their position, but they weren't close combat fighters. They should have withdrawn with the rebels. It would have been their only chance of surviving this madness.

Our odds had gone from bad to impossible, and now that I knew how perilously close we were to losing this fight, to me losing the people I loved, I desperately tried to find that sense of bloodlust I'd held at bay. Only, it wasn't there anymore. I'd pushed it so far down that I couldn't reach it.

My hands tightened on my swords as I defended my position as best I could, but the numbers we faced meant it was only a matter of time before I failed. Before we'd all fail.

We were already showing signs of tiring. The Elites were holding up well, but they weren't without injury. It was only a matter of time for us.

"Heimdallr," Thor shouted up into the sky. "The time for impartiality is over, old friend. Choose a side. You're with us, or you're with Odin. The sidelines are home to only cowards and the dead. I need you. *Please.*"

My father desperately looked around him as he fought back the soldiers that pressed in closer to our position. But no one came. There was no portal, no new fighting force to swoop in at the last minute and save the day.

It was over.

All we could do was hold our ground for as long as we could and pray we'd bought Britt and the others the time they needed.

Chapter 49

Britt

We stumbled through the doorway gasping for breath after sprinting for our lives beneath the shifting creature. I could already see in Xanth and Drystan's face that they weren't happy about leaving. This was the thing that had torn through the mage library and consumed their friends, family... what was left of their people. They wanted blood, and it was denied them.

"What was it?" I asked, shuddering at the memory of the impossible creature with its strange powers.

"It is Malice. It's a monster that feeds from darkness and hopelessness. Odin must have either summoned it, believing that it was a solution to Asgard's problems or it was his own madness that called to it. Whichever it was, it's clearly been feeding from the madness seeping from Odin and the pain he has brought this land for longer than I dare to think. It should only be the size of a horse, if that. I've never seen one exhibit powers like that before." Bran looked back at the door we'd just escaped through in concern and I knew what he wasn't saying. He didn't see how Echo and her mates could stand against it.

We'd just left them behind to die, and that didn't sit well with me at all.

"If we attack from the rear while it's distracted by them, we might do some actual damage before it retaliates," I said, turning to go back the way we'd come.

Surprisingly, it was Xanth's hand on my shoulder that stopped me. "We have to continue on," he said grimly.

I shook my head, not ready to accept we were about to leave them behind. I knew this was the original plan and that they'd argued for it themselves. But now, faced with the reality of turning our backs on them, I didn't know if I could do it.

"We press on and we end this. It will perish with Odin. For it to have fed to this extent they have to be linked," Corvin told me.

I knew he was right, but that didn't make it any easier leaving them behind.

Why were we always having to make decisions like this? When was it going to end?

And that thought was the only reason I could walk away. Because it was going to end now, and we were going to be the ones to do it. I had to trust my friends to do what needed to be done, just as much as they were trusting me.

As we quietly moved through the palace, I winced at every one of our soft footsteps that echoed around the empty halls. It seemed deserted. What should have been a bustling centre of this opulent city felt dead and forgotten.

We also should have passed guards by now. Odin couldn't be that confident that the Malice would keep us occupied to have left himself completely unprotected?

"Why aren't there more guards?" I whispered to no one in particular.

I'd already seen the suspicious looks the others were casting about and knew they were thinking the same thing. It was feeling too easy, and that could mean only one thing.

Odin wasn't done with whatever he had in store for us.

"It isn't much further. The antechamber is on the other side of those doors and then we're only a doorway away from the throne room," Bran told us, nodding to the unguarded doorway ahead.

"So what we're saying is that whatever's next is behind that door," I answered dryly, and he nodded.

We all still held our weapons at the ready. None of us had sheathed them, expecting to encounter more security measures than we did. That we hadn't had us all on edge and I was starting to think I kept catching sight of something stalking us through the shadows. I was either paranoid or the Malice had freaked me out more than I'd realised.

"Something feels off," Drystan said, his head cocking to the side like he was trying to listen. "My magic is sensing someone, but it's not in a single spot. It's all around us."

Our group clustered closer together, but we kept moving. There was no sense in stopping. If we were going to face another fight, then we couldn't let it push us to lose ground. We were actually doing the impossible. We'd made it this far. Close enough that the end was in sight. Whether we had it in us to push across the finish line was something we still had to prove.

We paused at the doorway. Corvin's hands settled on the ornate wood as he pressed his forehead against it. Something was making him hesitate, and when he glanced over his shoulder at me, I could see the pain in his eyes.

"This is... stay close," and then he pushed open the doors, falling back a step toward Bran and letting Xanth, Drystan, and I step through in front of them.

I didn't question it. There wasn't a single part of me that thought it was suspicious for them to want to guard the rear, not after what Drystan had just said.

But as we stepped across the threshold, the light in the

antechamber flickered. The room appeared empty as we walked inside. Not a single person or creature stood in front of us in the silent room. Xanth and Drystan stayed on either side of me as we cautiously approached the centre. We knew what it was like to have enemies leap out of the shadows when you least expected it. The problem was expecting them didn't make it any easier.

My heart raced in my chest and I could feel a cold sweat gathering at my throat, slipping down my chest into my breastplate. There was the sound of creaking leather as Drystan adjusted his grip on his daggers, twirling them around his hands to hold them in a throwing position.

The sound of the doors closing startled me in surprise and when I turned expecting an attack, all I saw were Bran and Corvin standing on each side of the closed doorway, hanging back at the edge of the room.

My mouth opened in question to ask what they were doing but there was no time to speak as the light in the room failed, pitching us into a sudden momentary darkness, before it surged bright enough to blind my vision for a fraction of a second.

It was only because I already had the raven's claw in my hand that I could deflect the blow that came for me. Meeting the oncoming sword in a clash of steel, I stepped forward into my attacker's space, sliding the swords against each other before spinning to the side and running the edge of my blade against his lower back. It glided across the armour, causing no damage, but the move had surprised him enough to dart away out of my reach as he laughed.

I followed through on sure footsteps as I went back to back with Xanth and Drystan, facing the people who had somehow hidden in the shadows from us.

"Nicely played, little human," the man cried cheerfully as he shrugged in his armour as if trying to test its strength.

"There have been few who have been able to get past my guard so easily. It's a shame you won't live past this day."

I quickly glanced around the room, seeing that there were five of them, three men and two women, all armed and ready to attack. Curiously, one man had a blindfold tied over his eyes.

"Who are you?" I asked, and the man before actually looked offended by the question.

He scoffed in outrage. But then, seeing how serious I was, he sighed. "My name is Tyr. I suppose it isn't surprising that you mortals have forgotten..."

"Ah right, offended god. Yeah, we don't need to hear any more. I'm guessing the same goes for the rest of you. Relying on swords because Odin has already sapped you dry? Kind of surprising that you're standing out here, so willing to die for him when he's the one to have got you in this mess. I'm guessing you're not the god of knowledge or wisdom," I taunted.

I had no idea what I was doing apart from buying time and hoping to spur them into doing something stupid.

One woman hissed at my words, but Tyr had the good graces to laugh like we were two old friends catching up rather than two people about to kill each other.

"There's no need to be a poor loser," he told me. The glimmer of annoyance in his gaze was the only sign that my words had got to him. "Just because you thought the ravens would stand with you doesn't mean you have to be mean. They were always Odin's..."

His words cut off suddenly, and a gurgle omitted instead as the sword pierced through his throat from behind. One of the other gods fell to the ground as Bran pulled his sword from his back and, as the blade was torn from Tyr's throat, he fell, revealing Corvin standing behind him.

"Fucking hell, man. I really thought you'd swapped sides

on us there," Xanth said, bending at the knees as he sighed dramatically.

The other three gods in the room shouted in outrage as they suddenly found themselves outnumbered. One of them flickered, his form fading to shadow as the two women leapt forward to attack.

"Stop!" Xanth calmly said, his voice echoing in a way I'd never heard before.

The surprising part was that they actually did. Swords raised over their heads, their mouths still open as if they were mid-shout, the two women froze on the spot. Their shadowy friend seemed stuck with half his body still solid and the other having partially faded away.

The normal playful Xanth disappeared as he straightened his back, malice shining in his eyes as he stepped closer to the frozen gods.

"Just stop," he growled. "Stop moving, stop breathing. Everything about you stops."

He stood staring down at the nearest god, frozen to the spot as her eyes seemed to glaze with panic.

None of us said anything, whether it was because we didn't want to interfere or we were just too shocked to form the words, I wasn't sure.

This was a side of Xanth none of us had ever seen, and I appreciated how strong his magic had to be. He held three gods in his thrall and none of them even moved a fraction of an inch.

One of the women was the first to succumb as her eyes rolled back in her head and she crumbled to the ground, the frozen muscles of her body no longer able to hold her up. I heard the blindfolded god fall, but I couldn't take my eyes away from my mate and the woman he passively stared down while she slowly suffocated.

This wasn't the Xanth I knew. This wasn't the man I'd travelled with, spent my nights with, and shared a mate bond.

And if there was one thing that I knew about Xanth, it was that in the years to come, when he looked back at this moment, he'd never be able to forgive himself if he killed these people this way.

This wasn't the same as killing someone in a fight when it was them or you. There was something cold and detached about this act. It was too personal, too close, too filled with a hate I knew Xanth could never possess.

And Drystan clearly thought the same thing.

"Enough," he whispered softly as the last god fell unconscious and collapsed to the ground. "They can't hurt us anymore."

Xanth slowly shook his head in denial and I could tell from the way he still stood tensely over their bodies that he hadn't released his magic yet.

"This isn't you, Xanth. Not like this. You will never forgive yourself for this. Leave them here, Thor and the others can deal with them however they see fit when we finally finish this," Drystan told him.

Xanth tore his gaze away from the fallen forms and looked at his friend. I saw the tension slowly leak out of his muscles as Drystan patted his shoulder in solidarity. Xanth reached out and brought us both into a fierce hug, his breath shuddering as he slowly exhaled. Then we turned to the ravens, waiting for an explanation.

"It seemed suspiciously like you were about to betray us back there," Drystan pointed out. A flicker of his magic touched his fingertips before he pulled it away, and I knew he was angrier than he was trying to show.

Corvin stepped closer and I could see the hesitation as he did. "It was supposed to seem that way," he told us carefully.

Drystan's magic flickered again and this time either he

found it harder to pull under control, or he wanted the ravens to see it and remember what he could do.

"This has always been the plan should Asgard find itself under siege," Bran told us, moving to his brother's side in a show of support. "We did not know how many we would face, and it was the best way for us to attack from the rear and even our odds. We would have told you back at the mountain base, but we genuinely did not think Odin would stick to the old plans when he knew he would be fighting against us. It was only when we realised Hod was trailing us through the corridor outside that we thought it was a possibility."

Bran nodded over to the blindfolded god and I resisted the urge to ask anything else about him. He wasn't my problem anymore.

I couldn't help but wonder though if the ravens found it difficult to face people they'd lived alongside for so long. It couldn't be easy to raise your sword against someone you once thought of as a friend.

We didn't have time to discuss this though, not that there was anything to discuss. There was no doubt in my mind that Corvin and Bran were on our side. I could feel the bond between us and I could feel their true feelings for me.

But here we were, standing outside the doors to Odin's throne room with no further obstacles in our way.

As if the others all realised the same thing, they fell quiet, looking between themselves before moving to form a line.

"Any chance you'd be able to pull that on Odin?" Bran asked, half hopeful, half joking.

Xanth grinned, looking at the raven like he hadn't just been questioning his loyalty. "Probably not, but that doesn't mean I won't try. Any chance you're going to go all killer-raven again."

"Probably," Bran joked back. "But I can't hold it for long so we have to wait for the right time."

That was basically our entire plan. No one knew what strength Odin retained. It had been so long since anyone had laid eyes on him that we didn't even know how much of his sanity remained. All we had left was the hope that we could draw his attention enough for me to land a blow with the raven's claw, and even then we had no idea if it would work. Ever since the galdr, I could get a sense of something from the sword, but nothing clear. I was the raven's mate, but I hadn't completed a bond with them, and we had no idea if that counted as me becoming the reigning raven or not.

Deep down, I knew it wasn't enough. But there was also something that I couldn't dismiss. We'd done everything that Frannie had set us on the path to do. We had to trust that it was enough, that whatever step came next was one we hadn't reached yet. Unfortunately, that meant whatever needed to happen was going to happen behind those doors and we couldn't delay facing it any further. Our friends were putting their lives on the line to buy us time. This was our final move, and it was time to find out if it had all been enough.

Chapter 50

Echo

The ringing in my ears was the first thing I noticed. Then it was the fact that someone shook me by my shoulders and begged me to wake up. As my eyelids fluttered open, I focused in on Stone's concerned face.

"Fucking hell, sweetheart. Don't do that," he said as he hauled me toward him and hugged me fiercely.

I could have just stayed there. Pain flashed down my back, but I didn't care because I was in his arms and it felt like the safest place to be.

"Okay, I need you to hold your breath. I'm taking you through this wall, which should lead outside. Find cover and wait for us," Stone said as he helped me to my feet.

I was quick to shake him off, even if I did stagger forward a step once he lost his grip.

"I'm not running," I told him sternly. "I'm not leaving you all behind to fight this thing alone."

I saw my celestial blades on the ground where I'd laid and stooped to pick them up. It was only when I stood up again that I caught sight of my other mates fighting the creature who'd slammed me into the wall and knocked me unconscious.

And they didn't look like they were winning.

I was pretty sure Tas had dislocated his arm from the way it hung limply at his side, and blood already covered one side of Aubron's face.

Damon darted into the nearest tentacle, moving faster than any of the rest of us could as he slashed a deep wound across the black, tough skin. He leapt back, narrowly missing the portal opening to his left in response. It was only his speed that kept the shadowy tendrils from being able to reach out and seize hold of him.

I staggered again, my head swimming slightly from the blow, tightening my grip on my swords. The blue magic pulsed down the blades as it struggled to take, but with a deep breath I pushed, and soon they blazed to life.

"Where do you need me?" I asked.

"Outside," Stone grumbled before he took position at my side.

I was about to argue with him, but then a plan formed in my mind.

"You once told us that if we lost contact with you, we'd become stuck in the wall," I told him, stepping back and running my hands across the stone he'd been about to send me through. "How thick do you think this is?"

A slow grin spread across Stone's face. "Thick enough to do more damage than a sword could," he pointed out.

Had we just figured out a way to survive this? The tricky part would be getting Stone in contact with a tentacle and the wall at the same time.

"Whatever we're doing, we need to do it now," Aubron shouted back to us, and Tas leapt out of the way of another shadowy tendril. Samuel severed it just before it could reach Aubron, who was at his side.

"We're slowing down and this thing isn't even tired yet," Aubron pointed out.

"Samuel, can you get Stone in contact with one of the tentacles if we can coax it to hit us again?" I asked, knowing the plan was a risky one, mainly because it would involve us avoiding the blow and I hadn't exactly succeeded at that last time.

Samuel looked hesitant, but then reluctantly he nodded. "If we time it right, and I dive at the last second."

The thought alone made my stomach heave. It was a terrible plan, strangely though Stone looked almost excited to try it.

"There is something very wrong with you that you like the idea of this," I pointed out.

But there wasn't any time to debate it further because the creature wouldn't sit around and wait for us to have a discussion.

"Damon, draw its attention. You're the fastest of us. I'll handle the portals. Tas, Aubron, you need to do as much damage as you can. We need to piss this thing off," I instructed.

Tas pulled off his sword sheath and used the leather strap to bind his wounded arm to his chest as Aubron quickly helped him. I didn't even see Samuel pluck Stone off the ground, leaving nothing but his whoop of joy in his wake.

Damon's hand on my shoulder drew my attention away from my injured fae mates.

"So far, we've been centring our efforts on one spot. I think if we hit hard enough in the same area, it's definitely going to notice," he told me.

I nodded distractedly. I could see where most of the wounds were focused, but I didn't see how doing the same thing over and over again would warrant a different result. We needed to really piss this thing off, and the only weapons we had that packed enough of a punch were my celestial blades and Samuel's Michael sword. I couldn't cover the portals and attack the creature at the same time and Samuel was currently busy evading a flailing tentacle so he and Stone could trigger the second part of the plan.

We needed something else. Something big.

"Go, now," Aubron shouted as the creature shifted and we suddenly had an opening.

Damon sprinted away before I could say anything more and I watched as he darted in and out, raining down blow after blow on the spot he'd pointed out. Tas and Aubron were at his side, hacking away at the creature with the last of their strength. It was less than a second later that the first portal opened and two of the shadowy tendrils came into sight.

It was easy enough to sever the dangerous power the creature somehow wielded, and I wasn't caught off guard by the second portal opening behind me. Spinning on the spot, I wielded my dual blades with the skill Aria had instilled in me, my celestial magic cutting through the attack as the creature shrieked in annoyance.

Portal after portal opened, and I carried on the dance, ducking and weaving through the onslaught of tendrils, not allowing a single one to pass me and gain access to my mates.

The creature shifted behind me. Glancing back, I saw it raising up on its tentacles again as it reached for Samuel.

I'd been wrong before. We didn't need to hurt it more to piss it off. We just needed to taunt it with what it couldn't have.

The creature reached for Samuel, but he darted away. Its black, eerie eye tracked his movements around the room while the others continued to deal as much damage as they could to its vulnerable underbelly.

The portals slowed, and for a moment I thought we were wearing it down. I should have known better.

Suddenly, a portal four times the size of what we'd seen before opened in front of me and more tendrils than I could count whipped out toward me at once.

It was impossible to avoid them all, and all I could do was slash through the first of them before tucking and rolling to the side. Three slipped past me, but I came out of my roll, swinging both swords in an upward arc and severed the closest two. I was moments away from severing the last one when it wrapped around Damon's ankle and tugged him from his feet, yanking him back toward the portal nearly faster than I could move.

If I hadn't already been about to cut through, I never would have made it in time. As it was, Damon had nearly drawn level with me before I completed the downward swing of my blade and severed the tendril before it could steal my mate.

"Fuck, that was close," Damon muttered, springing to his feet and wincing when he put weight on his ankle.

I nearly didn't hear him because the creature screamed out in frustration at being denied its prize again and the portal beside us flickered out of existence.

But then it moved faster than I'd have thought possible as it twisted, slamming back down to the ground at the same time as it tried to strike out at us with the tentacle we'd been focusing our attacks on.

"Look out," Damon called out, colliding with me as he pushed me to the ground and the tentacle swept through the air above us.

Everything happened so fast then that I couldn't see how they did. But as the tentacle missed us, its momentum slammed it into the wall and suddenly Stone was standing on top of it, his hand pressed to the wall as the tentacle slipped through.

Damon grabbed my arm, pulling me to my feet and across

to the other side of the room as fast as we could move. Aubron and Tas were quick to follow us and Stone disappeared from view as the creature's screaming began.

My eyes frantically searched through the chaos, looking for my two other mates as the creature before us flailed and shrieked. Arcs of black blood flew from its severed limb in the first sign that our idea had actually worked.

Stone had apparated the tentacle through the wall, and then severed his connection with it, essentially trapping it inside. The stone wall remained intact, but the tentacle had a clean cut, as if a giant blade had amputated it.

A sigh of relief heaved out of me as Samuel dropped to the ground beside us. Stone staggering out of his grip, looking a little green around the edges.

"That was..." He heaved a little and then shook his head instead of continuing.

All the while, the creature screamed and flailed. Tentacles slammed into the walls and ceiling, knocking a section of stone free where it had fled to the other side of the room. For a moment, it looked like it was actually scared of us. But then it reared back up, its black eyes fixed on our spot, and I could have sworn it had a look of revenge in its gaze.

We'd definitely succeeded in pissing this thing off.

As another portal opened a few feet away from us, I sighed in exhaustion. Was this the plan? Keep hacking away at this thing until it lost enough blood that it succumbed to its injuries? It didn't seem possible to inflict that much damage before we were too exhausted to continue on and we couldn't keep throwing Stone at it, hoping to sever another tentacle. I doubted it would fall for the same trick twice.

I was already stepping forward, ready with my blades for the next onslaught of tendrils, and then staggered back a step when a man stepped through the portal instead. He ducked to the side as a huge portion of the stone roof was flung in his direction and looked at the creature in disbelief.

"Well, at least we didn't miss all the fun," he deadpanned.

I had no idea what was going on, but I recognised him from the battle of the blood moon. I swear to all that is magical. If Hel stepped through that portal after him like she did last time, the next thing Heimdallr would see was my boot in his face.

When Chasan stepped through the portal next, sporting silver armour and a massive broadsword instead, my legs nearly failed me. Herschel followed, carrying a double-headed axe and a grin that definitely didn't match our current situation.

Samuel cried out in relief as the last of the angel rebel fighters stepped through and formed a wall in front of us.

"So, we're just slicing this thing up until it gives up?" Chasan asked cheerfully.

"We take the eyes and the tentacles," Heimdallr called out. "Once it's blind and immobilised, it won't pose an immediate threat. Then we move outside to help the others. Move quickly, they don't have much time left."

Those words lit a fire inside me that I didn't realise had gone out. Aria was in trouble. We'd lingered here for long enough. We needed to get out there.

"Those with wings, aim for the eyes," I instructed. "The rest of us will keep the tentacles busy."

There was a yell of agreement, and then everyone moved.

Heimdallr moved with brutal efficiency and it didn't take long to realise he knew the creature's moves before they even happened. He'd severed a tentacle alone in just three strikes of the massive sword he wielded, leaving the rest of us feeling more than a little inadequate.

Samuel and I dealt with as many of the portals as we could, but it was almost as if the creature realised this was its last chance to inflict damage and they opened and closed faster than we could keep track of.

I felt a burning sting down one shoulder before Samuel could take the tendril that had slipped from the small portal at our rear.

The floor had grown slippery with the amount of black blood we'd drawn from the creature and Heimdallr worked on claiming his next tentacle when the creature screamed and jolted, slamming itself into the back wall.

The entire palace shuddered and a massive section of the ceiling dislodged, falling to the ground and pinning a tentacle as it did.

I waited for the next portal to open and when it didn't come, I cautiously glanced behind us. The angels were landing, weapons dripping with blood as they faced down the now blinded creature.

"Echo, Samuel, take the pinned tentacle," Heimdallr shouted, pointing his sword in the direction he wanted us. "The rest of you, with me. It won't be able to summon its portal defence while it's blinded."

Samuel and I glanced at each other before moving to do as instructed. As I raised the celestial blades above my head, I had a moment of doubt that this was the right thing to do. It was the strangest thing. Glancing over my shoulder, I watched as the others advanced toward the cowering creature.

It had done so much damage to so many people and yet moving against it now while it was injured and vulnerable felt cruel. I knew it wouldn't hesitate to kill any of us if it had a chance, but that didn't mean I enjoyed cutting through the pinned tentacle in front of me.

If it wasn't for the fact that I needed to reach Aria outside, I wasn't sure I'd have had the stomach to do it. But the fight still raged on and this was the only way we could join with our friends anytime soon.

The thought of Britt flashed through my mind and the urge to go after her surged strong.

"Only she can fight the battle that lies in the throne room," Heimdallr said behind me.

I turned to look at the god I'd never been able to work out. I knew he saw more than any of us could ever understand, and I also knew he'd spoken with Frannie and the other seers to help us reach this point. If he said this was what needed to be done, I knew there was no choice, really.

But that didn't mean I had to like it.

Chapter 51

Corvin

I never thought I'd walk through these doors again. The once decadent throne room sat dark and empty. The air held a dank edge that spoke of how long it had been since this room had seen daylight.

I had so many memories of this place, all of them blackened by the last time we'd been here. The day that Odin had betrayed us.

We crept into the centre of the chamber, waiting for the attack.

He was here, I knew he was. I could feel the madness clawing at the edge of my mind like an infection wanting to invade me. I'd thought the link we shared with Odin had been severed centuries ago, but I could still feel a hazy awareness at the edge of my consciousness that proved it held on by a thread. Looking over at my brother, he nodded when I caught his gaze, and I knew he felt it, too.

There was no point in issuing a warning to the others. We all knew he was here, it was the reason we'd come. Unfortunately, the connection wasn't strong enough for me to get an idea of his exact location or his intentions. But I was pretty sure we were all certain of those at this point.

A crack of stone rang through the air that had us spinning toward the sound. We weren't fast enough as an enormous stone statue flew through the air, impacting with the mages and sending them careening into the wall.

An ominous laugh followed. It was one I recognised, even if it had an edge to it I'd never heard before.

My first thought was to pull Britt behind us and strike with as much force as we could. Overwhelming him seemed like the best plan, but without knowing how far his power had degraded, it could also be the swiftest one that ended in our deaths.

No. We had to play this carefully.

My gaze flicked to the mages who lay unmoving at the edge of the room. I saw the rise and fall of their chests and knew they weren't down for good. Xanth's leg stuck out at an unnatural angle, but it was an injury he could survive. At least with them out of the way, they were out of danger for now. Odin was never so reckless that he'd concentrate his attention on an enemy that had already fallen when he still had three standing and waiting for his blood.

The laugh echoed on the other side of the room, and this time we turned slowly. He was playing with us. Trying to disorientate us and make us panic. The god of war and death was nothing if not an excellent tactician.

"Welcome home, old friends," he mocked. "I trust you had a pleasant reunion with the friends I arranged for you."

I didn't respond, and neither did Bran.

Odin laughed again, no doubt thinking he was getting to us. His voice croaked from lack of use and he sounded nothing like the man I'd once admired so much that I'd pledged my eternal life to him.

"Oh no, don't pout. You know it's nothing personal. I

couldn't have my subjects thinking your behaviour would be tolerated. It would have done nothing but encourage rebellion." For some reason, he seemed to find that statement particularly funny as he wheezed out his laughter.

Had Odin really degraded to the point of barely being able to keep his breath as he taunted us from the shadows?

Of course he hadn't.

The attack came swifter and with nearly as much force as I remembered from the days when we'd sparred. With a double-headed axe in one hand and a broadsword in the other, he moved in a way that no one else could have done. It was as if the weapons weighed nothing as he swung both toward us in tandem, in a way that should have been impossible.

Bran's sword countered his axe, and I could barely take the force of the blow of his sword. Britt darted forward, seeing what would have been an opening for most people, but Odin moved faster than any other. His blade edge ran along mine as he shoulder checked Bran away, twisting to the side as he did, so Britt found herself between both our blades.

She dropped to her knees, sliding along the tiled floor with her own momentum and avoided the blow in a way that had even Odin impressed.

"A fine mate you've picked," he quipped as he swung his axe over his head and slammed it into the blade of my sword with enough force that it pushed me to one knee.

"Stop!" Xanth called out as Drystan dived for the god, his magic coating his hands in blue flames.

My heart tripped over a beat as Odin froze. Drystan was able to wrap one hand around his bicep, and I knew he'd be syphoning some of his power. But then Odin pushed forward like he was wading through mud as he fought the magic. Finally, he shook and whatever hold Xanth had on him shattered. Odin dealt a vicious kick into Drystan's stomach, causing him to stagger back, and Bran took his chance.

Darting forward, then quickly throwing his weight back, anticipating another swing of the axe to head his way. We'd sparred with Odin enough times that we at least knew some of his moves.

But apparently not all of them.

Because Odin released his grip on the axe, letting it fall to the ground, and having the sword in both hands, he easily reversed his grip, shoving it quickly behind him under his arm so that the tip of the blade pierced Bran's shoulder.

Before Odin could complete his move and angle the blade down to pierce Bran's chest, my brother let his knees fold beneath him, rolling to the side and sacrificing his shoulder to save his heart. It was a move that would put one of his arms out of action as the deadly blade ripped through muscle and ligament, but it was one that would at least leave him alive for now.

Britt cried out in horror at the sight of Bran's injury, leaping back to her feet as she kicked the axe toward Bran. He wouldn't have the strength to wield it with one hand, but at least it was out of Odin's reach.

"Clever girl," Odin taunted, dancing back a step and letting his sword fall as the three of us circled.

I could see him cataloguing the way we moved, looking for vulnerabilities. We could dart in to attack because he might have lost a lot of his magic, but he was a skilled warrior in his own right. One that greatly outmatched us still. But we also couldn't afford to keep up this dance forever because it wouldn't take him long to discover our weaknesses and exploit them.

Odin's gaze darted to the raven's claw before it returned to me. He dismissed Britt as the bigger threat despite her holding the godkiller. Did he know we were unsure if she could wield it? Or was it our history of sparring and my knowledge of his fighting style that made him see me as a bigger threat?

Xanth was out of the fight, Drystan at his side, trying to help with his broken leg. Hopefully, he'd been able to syphon enough from Odin to fix it, or at least enough to get him out of here. Even Bran struggled to get his bleeding under control and I knew for now he was safest where he was.

There was a time when I knew Odin's mind as well as my own, but it was long gone. Not knowing what he thought was throwing me off more than I'd considered.

Britt and I moved as one, but as we did, I realised where the flaw in my logic had been. Because Odin didn't see me as the biggest threat, he saw me as the weak link and he knew exactly how to exploit that.

Quickly shifting the sword into his opposite hand, he pulled a dagger from behind his back and, while he made a move as if to strike out at me, he sent the dagger sailing through the air toward my mate.

She'd already twisted seeing the sword coming toward me and moved to counter attack. But she hadn't seen the dagger in his other hand.

It was a momentary decision that I'd never forgive myself for because, rather than defending myself for the attack that was coming, I dived to place myself in the dagger's path.

Everything happened in the blink of an eye and I realised too late that I should have trusted my mate to look after herself.

Britt dodged to the side, the dagger just drawing the edge of its blade across her cheek as Odin reached out and plucked me from the air, quickly pulling me back into his chest. His sword moved behind my back and I watched in horror as he mirrored Britt's twist and his sword cut through the air in front of her.

The tip touched the breastplate and my heart skipped a beat as I thought this was the reason Geta had been so adamant she wear the armour. That one of the seers had seen this moment, and she knew this would be the only thing that could save her life.

But then the armour parted like butter, and Odin drove his sword deep into her chest as his other hand wrapped around my neck, holding me close to watch the shock register in my mate's eyes.

The scream of rage ripped through my body as I watched Britt's mouth open and then close as she tried to draw in a breath that would never come.

"Watch the light fade from her eyes," Odin whispered into my ear. "All these years you begged for her and now that you have her, you lost her so easily."

Pulling the sword from her chest, I watched as she fell, already knowing that the light inside her had been extinguished before she hit the ground.

It was over.

We'd lost.

There was no point in living anymore.

Chapter 52

Aria

I had lost count of the number of injuries I currently had. I didn't even feel them anymore. There was no time to feel pain, no time to let our screaming muscles have time to rest. We fought, or we died. There was no other choice.

Virion sent a blast of fire into the circling angels. They'd pulled back, realising my mates still held their elemental magic after we'd thinned their ranks. It was the only advantage the cowardly rebels had given us. They'd cleared part of the battlefield of our fighters, putting magical attacks back on the table again as long as we were careful.

Kyle's magic was too volatile to let loose when the Valkyrie were fighting close by and I could already see Liam and Sykes were running out of energy. It wouldn't be long before the angels realised it, too.

I had just about given up all hope when I saw the doors of the palace thrown open and the angels poured out. At first, I thought we'd been wrong, and they'd pulled a force inside without our spies being aware. The only reason they'd be turning to fight our forces outside would be if those on the inside had already failed.

But then I saw a face I recognised, and I realised we hadn't been as abandoned as we'd first assumed.

"About fucking time," my father yelled.

A shout rang out across the battlefield and I knew it was some kind of response from Heimdallr that I was probably best not to hear. But the sight of reinforcements was the boon our side needed and I could see the way it energised those around me.

Myra appeared at my side, darting forward as she cut through the angels creeping closer, with a skill I'd never witnessed. When she returned, I saw something in her eyes that I'd never seen before. They shone with an energy that I felt inside, the one I'd tried to squash until I couldn't reach it anymore. Yet she hadn't lost herself to it, she still retained control. It was almost like she was releasing it in small measured amounts as a boost for when she fought.

It was a level of control I'd not had the chance to learn yet.

"You have a gift inside you that carries a weight few could bear," she told me quickly. "But it is a gift that comes to us in times of war. It is a gift that keeps those we love safe and helps restore the balance in our world. Don't shackle yourself in trivial things like guilt when your actions have the purpose of saving those who need your aid. We fight for those who cannot."

"But how do you live with taking so many lives? How do you look at yourself in the mirror when you know the cost of being there?"

"Because I don't look at the lives I've taken. I look at the lives I saved and I know I fought on the side of good. The cost of war does not sit on your shoulders. It sits with those who sent soldiers to their deaths because they were not brave enough to stand in their place and settle these matters themselves."

Look at the lives that I'd saved.

Revenge

The bloodlust flared to life inside of me again as the words registered in my mind. Because she was right. Failing to do all that we could now would mean the end of all things. All the people who had fought and lost their lives until now would have died for nothing. All the people waiting in the mountains for someone to tell them this nightmare was finally over would perish, even after everything they'd been through.

It would all have been for nothing.

And I couldn't accept it.

So many faces flowed through my mind. The pupils who perished at the academy. The pack members slaughtered at the packhouse. The fae betrayed and trapped on a farm where they were abused and tortured. All the mages and the now empty library.

My friends.

So many lives lost and now we finally had a chance to end it all.

I felt the magic catch inside me. My resolve hardened as my gaze focused down to just the ground before me and the first angel who was unlucky enough to step forward first.

Finally, I sank into it. I felt my mates move to my back; the bloodlust hooking into our bond and flowing out to reach for each of them. It strengthened them where they had been tiring. It showed them the path to finally end this thing, once and for all.

We moved as one. Metal clashed with metal, and the smell of iron hung in the air. We were brutal as we let the need for revenge flow through the bond uniting us in one cohesive fighting force. The Elites moved to our backs, sweeping up the chaos we left in our wake with vicious efficiency.

We would do this to save the people we loved.

And we'd save each other once we finally reached the end.

Chapter 53

Britt

Nothingness was all that greeted me, and it took a while for my mind to catch up with what had happened.

My hand flew to my chest where I remembered the sword cutting through me and a pain unlike any I'd felt before flashed deep in my chest. It brought me to my knees with a gasp and I choked back a sob.

I'd failed.

Odin had won so easily, we'd been fools to believe we stood a chance.

And now my mates were back there with him and I knew it wouldn't be long until he sent them after me. That thought hurt nearly more than the memory of being stabbed through the chest and the echo of pain that lingered with me still.

All this time, I'd thought the breastplate would save me. Geta had told me not to take it off because I'd need it, but then when it came down to it, what use had it been?

This was the second time I'd died, but I didn't remember this place. In fact, I had a hazy memory of dying in Aria's arms, and then she pulled me from the pyre as I passed through the gates to Valhalla. There was no memory of a place in between.

I struggled back to my feet, looking around at the nothingness that spread in either direction.

"You lasted longer than I expected," Hel's voice laughed from behind me where there had been nothing moments before.

I turned slowly. There was no point in fighting the inevitable, and I wouldn't give her the satisfaction of begging.

"And the others?" I asked, knowing the bargain we'd struck, and that she was here to collect her prize.

Hel cocked her head to the side like she was listening and a slow grin stretched across her lips. It was lined with a malice I'd come to expect from her.

"They're going to be some time, yet. Father wishes to play with his toys for a while."

I wanted to stab her so much. I wanted her to feel a fraction of the pain I did right now. But I didn't have any weapons in whatever this place was, and as satisfying as it would be to feel her nose crumble beneath my knuckles, I knew it wouldn't end well for me.

"Why did you warn him we were coming? You could have had everything."

"Everything? You took away the things I cherished the most and even if we did bargain for me to have them back, I knew they would always be yours," she snapped.

My eyes widened in alarm as I realised she was talking about my mates. Hel actually had feelings for the ravens.

"Besides, you were never going to win anyway," she added quietly. "No one ever does."

It was the first time she'd looked like a normal person to me as a moment of sadness took over her expression before she pushed it down, and that malicious sneer took back its usual place. Was this the real Hel I was looking at, or was this the mask she chose to wear?

Flashing her teeth, she stepped closer. "There's no point in delaying. Odin may want his time with your mates, but your tricky mage struck a bargain with me and I'll be claiming what's mine. We're going to have so much fun together while we wait for the boys to join us."

I stood proudly as she approached, not wanting to give her the satisfaction of seeing me cower. I knew in the days to come Hel would do her best to break me, but I wouldn't make it easy for her. I'd fight every single step of the way.

Her palm slammed into the chest as she laughed at my bravery and the agony of the wound that killed me flared through my entire body. But I kept my feet this time, no matter how much I wanted to fall beneath the weight of my pain. I felt a tug deep inside me, a tearing sensation that made me want to beg for mercy... and then nothing.

Hel screeched at me, grabbing my face with her other hand as she viciously dug her nails into my cheeks. She pushed against my chest again and whilst that same sensation flared hot inside me again; it was weaker this time.

"What have you done?" she hissed, pushing me back, so I fell to the ground at her feet.

The blinding pain in my chest was enough to have me panting for breath as I tried to hold myself together. The hope of what this could all mean gave birth to a light inside me. Was this what Geta had been talking about when she said the breastplate would guide my spirit?

"How is your soul still bound to your body?" Hel shouted, lashing out and kicking me in the side. "You died. You belong to me!"

A growl ripped through the air, echoing around us as Hel went to lash out again, except this time, the blow didn't land.

I didn't realise I'd closed my eyes to prepare for what was

to come until the silence dared me to seek out what was happening.

I couldn't quite understand it at first. Hel had retreated several steps as she stared down at the snarling wolf standing in front of her. Its teeth gnashed in the air as it faced down the goddess.

This was... my wolf. I'd recognise her anywhere.

"What's happening?" I whispered.

Hel took several steps back, frowning at the animal in front of her. She looked as confused as I was, but she didn't seem to want to risk getting too close to the wolf.

Tears stung my eyes as the wolf turned and approached me. She brushed against my side, all traces of her aggression gone, and I tangled my fingers in her fur. The gaping hole inside of me ached at her mere presence, almost as if the other half of my soul were crying out for her.

"I've missed you," I whispered, the tears finally flowing.

"This isn't right," I heard Hel mutter, but I couldn't take my eyes away from the wolf I'd missed for so long, for the part of me that had never made it into the second life I'd been given.

A warm sensation filled me as a sense of peace flowed from the wolf. I could feel her reassurance, even if she couldn't utter the words I needed to hear.

We were together again.

When I finally raised my eyes and saw Hel watching us curiously, I caught the panic cross her gaze before she quickly pushed it away.

"Stay with me and you can be with her," she purred in complete contrast to how she'd seemed earlier. "Take my hand, and I'll guide you to an afterlife at my side, where you can be reunited with the wolf."

It was tempting. I knew a deal had been forged with Hel and she was going to claim me either way. But if I could do this and keep my wolf half, maybe I'd find the strength to survive until I was reunited with my mates once again. Maybe I could endure if she was with me again.

I hadn't even raised my hand a fraction of an inch before my wolf butted her head against my chest in warning. I looked down at her in confusion, not understanding why she'd try to keep us apart. The look on my wolf's face screamed disappointment, and it was all I needed for my brain to kick into gear.

Why was Hel trying to bargain with me if she could seize my soul, anyway? Except she couldn't because she'd just tried and hadn't been able to tear it from me. So if she was trying to persuade me to willingly leave with her now, did that mean there was another choice to be had?

My gaze snapped to Hel as soon as the thought came to me, and she snarled in response.

Before she could move, the wolf leapt, but before she reached the enraged goddess, a shimmer of darkness crossed her form and she shifted into a beautiful raven. With claws extended, she attacked. Slicing vicious cuts across Hel's face as she staggered back, trying to escape the onslaught. Cursing and flailing, Hel tried to bat the giant bird away, but it was no use. Eventually, she took a staggering leap backward and disappeared.

A sound of relief passed through my lips, but before I could do anything else, the bird wheeled through the air, diving straight for me. I didn't fight the inevitable. This was a part of me I'd missed for so long. Why would I want to keep it away?

As the raven slammed into my chest, the white hot pain flared through my body and I felt myself being thrown backward.

And then I began to fall.

Chapter 54

Britt

I gasped for breath as agony flashed through my entire body. My hands grappled against the ground as I tried to make sense of what was happening.

The noises of the room slowly registered in my mind. The sound of clashing metal had me groaning as I rolled to the side. I knew I had to move. I couldn't lay here and give Odin a second chance at killing me.

As my hand touched my chest, I felt the blood that had pooled on the surface there. It dripped to the floor as I rolled. The bright red colour against the marble had my eyes focusing on the here and now.

I wasn't healed. Not physically, at least.

Corvin stood facing Odin down. Bran, Xanth and Drystan were all down on the ground behind Corvin as he tried to shield them. The raven's claw gleamed in his hand as he met the mad god's attack blow for blow. I could see that he was tiring, and it was clear that Odin was only playing with him now.

The flare of Corvin's eyes was the first sign he'd seen me

move. It had Odin dancing back a step and glancing behind him to see what was happening before he laughed.

"Well, well, little girl. Back with the living," Odin taunted. "You might as well lay down and die. Take the easy way out. Did you really think you could stand against the god of war and death and come out the other side?"

I could see the complete conviction on his face. There was nothing about this situation that Odin saw as wrong. In fact, he was enjoying himself and the misery he wrought.

I staggered forward a step, riding the wave of pain that came with it. I wasn't out of this fight. I wouldn't give up while I still had a single breath left in my body.

"I'm. Not. Done. Yet," I gritted out, steeling my spine as I took another step forward.

I could feel the tattoos that crawled up my arm heating with power, and I knew the magic was rising to the surface.

"Oh, you don't even know what pain is yet," Odin warned as he stooped down and picked up the double-headed axe again.

My gaze quickly moved across my broken and injured mates. Drystan was crouched over Xanth, his hands pressed against his leg with a determined look on his face. Bran was trying to struggle to his feet, his hand gripping the injury to his shoulder as he reached for his sword once more.

It was only when I met Corvin's gaze that I saw the same determination there that I felt.

An energy I didn't know I possessed moved through me and I darted forward at the same time as Corvin threw me the raven's claw. It sailed through the air and I caught the handle, spinning the blade and meeting Odin's sword in a brutal clash of metal.

The weapon in my hand sparked and flared with power, making Odin stagger back a step in surprise.

This was what I'd been made for. Now that every piece of

me had returned, I could feel my place in this whole thing. I knew my purpose.

Pain seared through my back as the energy rose, and in his panic, Odin started collecting a power of his own. His hands glowed as he gathered his magic to the surface, but it was too late to stop what had already begun.

Black raven wings tore from my skin, shredding the back of my fighting leathers as they announced my presence to the world. Corvin and Bran gasped at the sight, but I didn't have time to meet their wonder with my own because Odin made his move.

In a blast of light, he threw everything he had at me. The pulse of magic careened into me and I raised the raven's claw in defence. The force of his magic slid me across the floor as I braced with everything I had. I heard my mates shout out in distress at the sight.

The pain in my chest from the unhealed wound flared hot, threatening to steal my consciousness. If I was going to make it through this, if I was to finally do what no one before had been able to, then I'd have to push past every limit I'd ever encountered and fight harder than ever before.

The wings at my back flared out, keeping me on my feet. The blade heated, absorbing the magic Odin had thrown at me, and I used it to my advantage.

I let the blade swing, moving with the momentum of the blow as I turned. I followed through the swing in a blinding arc of power infused steel, using Odin's magic against him.

There wasn't time for any more miracles. I had to make this blow count.

We moved as one as the raven's claw slashed through the air toward the man who stood between us and a future.

Drystan's hands filled with magic as he dived from Odin, Xanth at his side as he drove his dagger into the god who was too busy preparing to counter the blow from the raven's claw charged with his own magic.

We struck at the same time, and as we clashed, the magic coating my blade turned Odin's sword black as it bounced away.

Odin cried out, barely keeping his feet as he shook off Drystan, his sword going wide as he tried to strike out at the mages. I knew Drystan had drained some of his power, and I just hoped that it, coupled with the drain of magic Odin had summoned, would be enough to slow him down.

Odin staggered back a step, one hand going to the wound at his side and coming away in a flash of red blood. It was the first sign we'd managed to injure him, that he wasn't as invincible as he seemed.

"This is nothing but the thrashing of dying creatures," he sneered at me. "Fight all you want, but the end is already upon you. There's nothing you can do to stop it now."

Odin retreated; his stumbling steps the first sign his strength had started to leave him.

I stalked his every step, my own wounds completely forgotten as I catalogued every sign of weakness he had.

"You're wrong," Xanth told him as he and Drystan moved to his side. "There's always a chance, but not while you're still in the world. If killing you is what it takes, then none of us will stop until you're lying dead on the ground."

It was the first time I'd seen fear in the god's eyes. Was he finally realising this wouldn't be as easy as he'd first assumed?

Something about the look strengthened me. I wanted him to be afraid. I wanted him to look at us and see the price of all the mistakes he'd made. The cost of the malice he'd spread out across the realms. We'd trusted him. He'd stood at the head of everything as an example of good and then he'd turned on us. Capitalising on the trust of those around him, to commit atrocity after atrocity.

Revenge

"Did you think you could sit on your throne and never face judgement?" I asked as Corvin helped Bran from the ground and they moved to join us. Their wings sprung from their backs and I saw the need for violence in their eyes.

"Did you think we wouldn't seek our revenge?" I added viciously.

Power flowed through my body, flooding into my limbs and lending me a strength I'd never experienced before. The fear in Odin's eyes only fuelled me—the way he staggered further away, his gaze darting around the empty throne room like he was looking for someone to help him. Only there wasn't anybody. He'd seen to that himself.

Finally, a sneer crossed his lips. "You think you can kill me, little girl? You think death is an end for a god like me?"

"Oh, I know it is."

And then we moved as one, all of us working toward one single goal.

Odin's death.

The two ravens moved in tandem, darting in close as they struck out with their weapons with a strength I'd only seen them exhibit once before as they tore through the angels that threatened us.

Odin rallied, his axe and sword meeting every blow and striking back in desperation. He ducked beneath Corvin's strike, narrowly missing his wing when he followed through with a swing of his axe.

I jumped into the melee, knowing it was only a matter of time before Odin would tire and we'd gain the upper hand. He barely held his own as it was already.

"Stop," Xanth called out, his voice lining with the last remnants of magic that filled him.

Odin staggered and this time he wasn't able to raise his sword quite as quickly as the last time, and my blade caught his side before I had to spring back to avoid the swing of his axe in retaliation.

Drystan dived into the fray, one arm wrapping around the waning god's neck as he drew on what magic he had, to pull as much of the life from Odin as he could. In a last attempt to save himself, Odin dropped his weapons. Leaning back, he grappled at Drystan's arm to pull him loose as he dodged to the side to avoid Bran's sword, getting close under the raven's guard as he did.

I saw my opening as I shifted my grip on the raven's claw to go for an underhanded strike into the centre of his chest, but before I could complete the move Odin's hand had wrapped around the back of Bran's neck, and his foot moved between Bran's and he threw him off balance.

Corvin was already moving in a brutal strike that he had no way of stopping, and Odin gleefully pulled Bran into the path, laughing as Corvin's blade impaled his brother through his stomach.

Odin grasped Drystan's arm with both hands at that point, no doubt thinking he'd finally turned the fight in his favour. He even cried out in victory as Drystan loosened his grip, shoving the god forward away from him.

But he'd taken his eyes off me, and Drystan had already seen what was about to happen, pushing Odin onto the blade of the raven's claw as I plunged it into his chest.

The sword cooled suddenly, dropping to a temperature where it almost hurt to keep my grip. It burned against my palms as I refused to give up my hold, not wanting to give Odin even the briefest of chances to gain an upper hand.

I needn't have worried though because the blade had hit true. It was a mortal hit from a god killer and there would be no surviving the blade that pierced him through his heart.

"You... can never win," Odin gasped as he dropped to his

knees, his hands clawing at the blade and drawing more blood to the surface.

Drystan moved again, pulling what life was left in the god away with his magic as his eyes desperately moved around our fallen.

Bran wasn't moving and I couldn't see what was happening past Corvin, who huddled over the body of his brother. Xanth's hands moved over Bran as he tried to deal with the wound, and I forced myself to believe he had to be alive if he was still trying to save him. Tears threatened to spill from my eyes at the thought of losing him, but I refused to let them fall in front of this monster.

"We already have," I told him coldly, twisting the raven's claw, and watched the light fade from his eyes

I wrenched the sword free, and Odin's body fell dead to the ground.

For a moment, no one moved. Drystan and I stared down at Odin's prone form in disbelief. He was dead. We'd actually done it.

"Move," Drystan shouted, diving for Bran and quickly placing his hands on his chest as Corvin scrambled out of the way. "I couldn't get much, but I should have absorbed enough of his life force to pull him from the brink."

I watched with silent tears streaming down my face as I held my breath and waited. It didn't take long for Bran to gasp in a ragged breath and push Drystan out of the way.

I felt it all then. The relief of seeing him alive, of seeing them all alive, and the pain of the wound that had never healed. It had killed me once, and I fell to my knees, believing that it might actually do the same again.

It didn't matter, though. We'd won. And my mates would make it out of this in one piece. I could deal with dying again if that was the outcome.

Xanth caught me as my body pitched forward, the adrenaline finally leaving me and numbness took its place.

"No," Bran whispered, pushing Drystan away. "Brit needs it more. I can survive this."

Drystan's head snapped in my direction and his eyes widened in surprise as he saw me in Xanth's arms. He scrambled to my side, and a sense of relief flowed through me. Maybe today wouldn't be the day I died for a third time.

"Is Bran okay?" I whispered as Xanth and Drystan pulled the breastplate away from me, hissing at the sight of the wound on my chest.

"Fuck, I thought this was healed when you stood back up," Drystan swore, his hands moving to either side of the wound as they warmed against my skin. "How did you fight with this?"

"I think it's because I'm a badass," I quietly quipped as Xanth snorted in amusement, even with the tears flowing down his cheeks.

"You don't get to joke about shit like this, sweetheart," he chided softly, his grip on me tightening, as Drystan frowned down at my chest.

"I've got nothing left." His eyes moved to the doorway, and I realised he was considering finding someone to drain just so he could heal me more.

My hand wrapped around his wrist when he looked like he was about to stand up and leave.

"Is Bran okay?" I asked him again.

For a moment he looked confused, but then my question registered, and he nodded. "His wound is healed enough that he should be fine as long as he gets medical attention soon."

I smiled gratefully, catching sight of Corvin helping Bran to his feet as he slung one of his arms over his shoulders and helped take his weight. My chest ached, but I breathed a little easier. When I finally worked up the courage to look down, the wound was little more than a deep gash now. Odin had his uses after all, it would seem.

"Let's get out of here," I suggested. "I think I've had enough of Asgard for a lifetime."

Xanth and Drystan carefully helped me to my feet, the wound of my chest pulling tightly as I gasped in pain. At least I didn't feel like I'd pass out, and I took that as a good sign.

It took longer than I'd expected for our group to limp its way out of the throne room and to the palace's main door.

"Anyone considered what we're going to do if they're still fighting out here?" Xanth asked as we shuffled our way forward.

"I vote for telling them we're done for the day and heading home," Bran wheezed and I nodded vehemently in agreement.

"We'd have heard it before now if the battle was still being fought," Corvin told us seriously, fussing with his brother who was trying to bat his hand away.

It genuinely hadn't occurred to me to be concerned about the outside. Maybe it should have, but my mind wasn't ready to move past the current moment and toward whatever came next.

The doors swung open as we approached and several figures stood as dark shadows against the fires burning outside. I knew it was Aria without even needing to see the wings. The Elites stood on either side of her, weapons in their hands, and as they came into focus, I could see how hurt they all were. Even then, I knew they were still getting ready to come to our aid.

"Cool wings," Aria quipped, and I smiled at the way she was trying to cover up her panic as she took in the blood covering us all. "You look suspiciously like you were going against orders and trying to die again," she added with a frown.

"You've no idea," Corvin told her grimly as we all made our way outside.

I wasn't joking when I said I was done with Asgard. I needed out of this palace and out of this realm. I wanted a break from gods and their machinations. If one more person told me about how we needed to save the world, I was going to lose it.

Every single part of my body ached and the weight of the wings on my back was making it even more difficult to walk.

We stopped at the top of the palace steps, looking out over the battlefield that spread before us. The smell of charred flesh lingered in the air and I tried not to think about what it meant.

A group of Asgardian soldiers were kneeling on the ground while the Valkyrie watched over them.

The extent of the dead was unlike anything I'd ever seen and it was only then I realised how many massacres I'd witnessed in my short life.

"How bad are our losses?" Corvin asked, turning away from the devastation in front of us.

"Bad enough," Aria told him grimly. "But enough to rebuild."

The soldiers looked confused when the valkyrie stepped away from them, leaving them weaponless but unbound. We weren't in the position to take prisoners of war, besides the war was over. We didn't come into this fight with any intention of punishing anyone at the end.

We had a single goal, and it had been fulfilled. Without Odin's madness feeding on the world, the realms were safe for now. What was the point of more death when we had so much to rebuild?

"We all need healing," Corvin told Aria. The rest of us were too in shock about our current situation to be that organised.

Aria and the Elites showed Corvin over to where an aid station had been set up, and he set Bran down as he went to find something to finish healing him with. Xanth and Drystan seemed to sense I needed another moment before I was ready to do much of anything. The shock of everything we'd been through had worn off, and I didn't know how I felt about it now that it was over.

"What do we do now?" I asked, looking between the two of them and hoping they had the answer I was looking for.

They both wrapped their arms around me, letting me take a moment to soak up the reassurance that we'd made it through.

"It's time to figure out how to live for a change," Xanth whispered into my hair as he held me tight.

Now that was a plan I could get on board with.

Epilogue

Britt

Two weeks later

My back ached as I slipped the raven's claw from its sheath and laid it across the desk. It had been a week of backbreaking work, and even though we were learning how to live in a world after the battle, I couldn't quite bring myself not to have the sword with me at all times. At least I'd figured out how to shift my wings away and didn't need to deal with those all the time.

After the battle, we'd returned with Aria to Thyellin. The fae were already waiting to portal us and our wounded there. Thor had found out that the Asgardian rebels had returned to the mountain base. The few injuries they'd sustained were being dealt with by the medical facilities there, but we didn't want to join them. I'd never been more grateful that Aria had the forethought to make alternative arrangements in the event we needed to fall back to a secondary position.

We hadn't been on the battlefield when the Asgardian rebels had fled. I didn't really know them all that well, but I could see how upset Thor was by their betrayal. When he returned from their meeting, it was pretty obvious they didn't regret their actions.We'd sustained numerous losses on our side, and some of the injured might not make it. The rebels believed it proved their point they weren't needed for the fight. We'd been victorious without them, so in their minds, the 'retreat' had saved Asgardian lives. They didn't care that the valkyrie and warriors had fallen in their place, or that their presence could have prevented it. If anything, they seemed to believe that was what the valkyrie were made for.

It was an attitude that had allowed the evil that swept across the realms to take such a deep root. And knowing we hadn't completely eradicated it was a bitter pill to swallow.

"The library is salvageable, but we've lost a lot of the books from the smoke damage. We were able to clear the rubble through to the next corridor and the mages think they can have those classrooms restored in the next few weeks," Corvin told me as he walked into the office that had once been the headmasters.

I looked around at the virtually untouched room and marvelled at how far we'd come.

My mates and I had stayed in Thyellin for two days, regrouping and meeting with Aria and the others to discuss my plans. As soon as I'd mentioned them, she'd been a whirlwind of planning. Everyone had pitched in as soon as word spread.

Now, here we were three days into the restoration project of the old academy. It wouldn't be all that different from the dream Dominic had when he first opened the doors to every race that wished to attend. Our mission was to train fighters here. But not just any fighters. We were training Elites. And we were going to spread them across the realms in a show of hope. They would be the force that stood for those who couldn't fight for themselves. They would be the diplomats that prevented disputes from turning into wars.

This was a new world in its infancy and it stood on a precipice. It felt vulnerable to the strong rising up to subjugate the weak again. We couldn't let that happen. We'd lost so many lives, spilled so much blood to reach this place, and this time, we had to do better.

We would do better.

And the Elite Academy was the first step.

"Hey, are you okay?" Corvin asked, moving to my side when I didn't answer him.

He pulled me into his arms and I leaned against his chest as I tried to put my thoughts into order.

"It's strange being back here," I admitted. My mates had watched me like hawks for the first day, worried about what returning to the academy would be like. "I have so much hope for this place, and then, every so often, I have to remind myself I don't have a single clue about what I'm doing."

"None of us do, but I think that's a good thing." I looked up at him like he was crazy and he just grinned down at me in response. "The old ways didn't work, Britt. We need something new, someone not bogged down by how everyone thought it had to be. Are we going to have problems in the beginning? Of course, we will. But we'll work out the kinks and everything will be stronger for it."

I knew he was right. It was exactly what everyone kept saying, but that didn't make the nerves go away.

I reached for the paperwork on the desk. We needed extensive supplies; the packs and the mage library had sent us details of anything they could donate to our cause. Corvin's tight hold on me didn't relent and I found myself fixed in place, unable to reach them.

I looked up at him in question, and I could already see he was up to something just from the look in his eyes. "We've got a surprise for you," he told me.

It was then that I looked around the room and realised

none of my other mates had found their way in here yet, which was strange in and of itself. They were never far from my side, and I found I didn't want them to be either.

"Come on." Corvin grabbed my hand and tugged me toward the door. I tried to reach out for the raven's claw, but he waved me off. "You don't need that where we're going."

My feet ground to a stop and he must have been able to tell from the look on my face that it wasn't an option because he dropped my hand with a sigh, "Fine!"

Skipping back into the office, I grabbed the sword from the desk and then yelped as I was suddenly thrown over Corvin's shoulder. A slap landed firmly on my ass cheek as he strode out of the office, and I yelped again.

"What was that for?!"

"Delaying our carefully thought out plan."

"I literally took two seconds," I huffed in outrage, even though a part of me kind of liked it.

Corvin wound his way around the remains of debris yet to be cleared and into the part of the academy that hadn't been widely used when I was a student here. We'd found a suite of rooms that weren't too badly damaged and had set them up for ourselves so we could be here while the work was underway. They were basic for now because we didn't know if we'd be staying in them for long, but they were more than enough for our needs.

When he stepped inside, quickly closing the door behind him, I was met with an unfamiliar dimness. Corvin finally let me off his shoulder and slid me down his front as he set me on my feet. I was about to ask a question when his lips tenderly met mine, kissing me softly before stepping backward.

Looking around at the candles sitting on every surface of the room, I was confused about what was going on. Had we lost power again? This was supposed to be the side of the building with the least damage.

Then my eyes fell on them as Corvin dipped down to one knee at the centre of their row. All of my mates knelt before me and my heart surged as I took a step closer, apprehensive about what was about to happen for some reason.

"I love you," Xanth simply stated. "I didn't know there was a possibility for me to have someone like you in my life, but now that I have you, I don't think I'll ever be able to let you go."

"When you leapt into my life, sword raised and a battle cry on your lips, I knew exactly who you were. It shouldn't have been possible. But you lit up the darkness I'd let consume me and showed me so many reasons to stand in the light. I've never loved anyone until you. Not even my own parents. And this feeling is so unlike any other that I've experienced that sometimes I don't know what to do with it. But I can't wait to find out." Drystan's voice hitched. "I can't wait to find out with you."

"I searched the ether and demanded that fate give you to me and it was the single best decision I've ever made, because it gave me you. I'd endured lifetimes of emptiness until my eyes finally landed on you. At first you seemed too impossible to be real. I love you, Britt. And I will spend an eternity loving you like no other has before," Corvin told me, as my hands came up to press on my chest, certain my heart was about to explode out of it with how hard it beat.

And then I looked at Bran, and his smile was blinding before he spoke. "You have given me nearly everything I could have ever hoped for in my life. You gave me a reason to live, a heart so filled with love that I don't know what to do with it. You gave me back the brother I thought I was going to lose beneath the weight of the pain that smothered him. But there is one final thing I want to ask you, because I'm a greedy fucking man and I want to have it all." He paused as his gaze searched mine, and then he finally added. "Will you be our mate? Will you bond with us?"

Tears filled my eyes as he asked the question I didn't know I needed to hear and I exploded forward out of the spot Corvin had left me standing in. I fell into his arms. "Yes! Of course it's a yes!"

We had been so busy since the end of the battle that all we'd had were stolen kisses and lingering touches until we fell into bed, exhausted at the end of every day. I hadn't even considered the fact that now the wolf turned raven had returned to me, I was finally whole once more.

Bran kissed me fiercely, his mouth colliding with mine as his tongue surged forward and stroked against mine. I wrapped myself around him as he stood from the ground, carrying us to the bed. Hands tore at clothes, dropping them to the floor as we went.

Xanth and Drystan backed away and as I was about to object, Drystan told me, "Don't worry, sweetheart. You're not leaving this room until we're all bonded to you."

A flash of lust rushed through my body in anticipation of everything that was to come. I couldn't believe we'd been so distracted by rebuilding that we hadn't found time to be together like this. It was something I'd make a conscious effort to prevent in the months to come. This was what we'd been fighting for, after all.

Bran climbed over me, a wicked grin on his face as he dipped down and dropped delicate kisses along my stomach. "I've been thinking about this for days," he murmured, and then his head disappeared between my thighs and he swiped his tongue across my pussy.

My head fell back to the mattress with a sigh as he pulled one of my thighs over his shoulder, teasing my opening with one finger while he circled my clit with his tongue.

Corvin's kiss almost took me by surprise because I'd closed

my eyes in bliss, sinking into the feeling of my body slowly waking up for what was to come.

His hands came up to tease my nipples as he nibbled my lips, the bond between us waking up with every touch. I could feel the raven awakening inside me for the first time since I'd fought Odin.

Bran sucked on my clit, and my back bowed. I felt him drag his fingers through my wetness, moving it down to my ass, and I squirmed in delight. I'd never considered anal play to be something I'd be interested in, but after last time, I was definitely a convert. I wanted them both. I wanted to feel them moving inside of me together; something about bonding with my ravens at the same time felt so right.

My nipples tingled from Corvin's attention and I pulled him back to my lips as Bran worked the first finger inside my tight hole. The pain mixed with pleasure as he slowly dragged his tongue across my clit and I sighed against Corvin's lips, my hips swivelling as I felt that telltale sensation building at the bottom on my spine.

"You look so beautiful when you come," Corvin whispered in my ear. His fingers traced across the apples of my cheeks as he told me, "Your blush starts here, and then it slowly spreads." He kissed my cheek, heading down across my neck. "To here." His lips travelled across my breasts as he sucked and nibbled his way. "Then here. Your nipples harden, begging for attention, just like this." And he sucked one into his mouth, grazing his teeth across the tip, as he did. "Then your breath quickens." I could feel myself panting now as the orgasm built inside me. "And then finally, when you can't hold back anymore, your mouth falls open with a little gasp and you cry out, making the most delicious sounds."

The orgasm hit me hard then and Corvin's lips crashed down on my own as he swallowed down my cries, his talented fingers working my nipples as Bran stretched me ready for taking them both.

The bond was practically vibrating in a frenzy now. I could feel something clawing at the back of my mind, needing to be released. And as Bran climbed onto the bed, lying down and rolling to pull me on top of him, I kissed him deeply, tasting the flavour of my release on his tongue.

"I love you," he whispered, sheathing himself inside me in one move.

My back bowed at the sudden sensation of being filled, and Corvin's hand caught my chin, turning my head to steal another kiss as he straddled Bran's legs and moved behind me.

I rode Bran's cock in slow, delicious movements, revelling in the sensation of having my mate inside me.

Corvin's fingers traced the image of my wings on my back and they flared into existence, spreading out behind me. It threw me off balance at first, but he helped me spread them out to the side so they wouldn't get in the way, and then his fingers made their way to the bottom of my wing joints and my toes curled in delight. Bran chuckled that deep masculine laugh as my eyes rolled, knowing what his brother was doing.

"We learned that one pretty early on," he told me. "There's so much we're going to teach you."

Before I could say anything, Corvin's hands came to my shoulders, and he helped me bend forward. Bran caught my lips in a kiss and I felt the head of Corvin's cock thrust through my ass cheeks, accompanied by a cold, wet, slippery liquid.

I was surprised when I glanced over my shoulder and saw him with the bottle of lube. These guys really had been making plans.

But then Corvin pushed inside, and my breath caught in my chest at the sensation.

"Relax," Bran told me, his hand moving between us as his fingers danced across my clit. "We've got you."

I closed my eyes and sank into the feeling of being so impossibly filled. Every nerve felt so much more sensitised, and every movement so much keener. I needed them to move. I needed something, anything, but I couldn't express it because all that came out of my mouth were garbled words of pleasure.

And then Corvin stopped when he was fully sheathed inside me and the raven inside me rose, dragging the bond up with her. I could feel them both everywhere, inside me, around me, slipping into my mind as easily as they slipped into my body. But instead of feeling impossibly full, stretched to my almost limit, I felt a sense of peace I'd never had before.

I opened my eyes and stared down at Bran in wonder, seeing a mirror of my expression on his own face. "I can feel you."

Corvin gently kissed my shoulder, whispering. "This is everything I've ever wanted and more. I love you so much, Britt."

They both moved then, and the waves of pleasure that they'd built inside my body spread to every piece of me.

My hands pressed against Bran's chest and I watched in fascination as my nails grew to talons. Curved, black, and wickedly sharp, I tried to yank them away, afraid I'd hurt him. Bran quickly snatched my hands, plastering them to his chest with a grin as he miraculously kept up the pace of his cock hammering inside me.

Corvin pressed against my back, one of his hands coming to my shoulder and showing me the talons on his own hand. It was only then that I looked down to see them decorating the tips of Bran's fingers as well.

That was when I knew, and if it wasn't for the ecstasy they were pulling from my body right now, I could have cried. Because my raven was finally showing me the way.

Bran slowly drew one talon along the crest of my shoulder, Corvin taking the opposite side as they carved their marks into my skin. There wasn't an ounce of pain, just an electrified pleasure that vibrated through our bond. My toes curled at the knowledge of what was happening and that slow build up inside me was now a cresting wave threatening to break.

Corvin eased up the pressure behind me as he reached around and presented me with his wrist. "I want your mark where I can always see it. Make it deep," he purred.

Quick as a flash, my hand darted out and my talon stroked across his skin, leaving a crimson line as evidence of my devotion. I felt my raven cry out in victory inside my head and that bond we shared wrapped tighter around my soul.

Bran locked eyes with me, his love shining brightly through them. "Over my heart, my love. Right where you belong."

I watched in fascination as I drew the talon across his skin, watching his face as his soft smile turned into a gasp of pleasure.

That was it then. The bond flared to life, and both ravens lost their grip on whatever control they had. They hammered into me and I cried out in satisfaction, knowing my mates were buried as deeply into my soul as they were in my body.

I came first. My body locking down on the men inside me. Bran swore loudly as his hips thrust up into my cunt and he gripped my hips hard as he emptied himself inside me. Corvin only lasted for two more thrusts before he followed us over the edge, grinding himself deep as he filled me with come.

I should have been exhausted. I should have been sensitised to the point of not being able to take any more. But the ravens' bond was so bright and vivid inside me that it had pulled another bond to the surface, and my raven was ready to claim the rest of what was hers.

Corvin and Bran covered me with soft kisses as they gently

withdrew from my body, moving to the side as I trailed my hands across their bodies. My wings shivered and shifted away as they each kissed me over their mating marks. I didn't want to just cast them aside. We should have taken time to luxuriate in the bond that we'd forged, but there were two more men in this room I needed to make mine before I'd be able to rest.

In the end, Bran picked me up and placed me on my feet, turning me around to watch the two mages. Xanth held Drystan's chin firmly in his hand as he kissed him, dominating the kiss as his tongue surged into the other man's mouth. His hard cock twitched against Drystan's hand as he gently stroked him and my mouth ran dry at the perfect sight of the two of them together, finally being able to explore the feelings they had for each other.

Xanth nipped at Drystan's lips before he turned Drystan's head toward me, showing him my naked body standing before them. "Look at how perfect she is," he purred in Drystan's ear. "Are you ready to make her ours forever?"

Drystan nodded dreamily, stepping away from Xanth and reaching for me with eager hands. "I feel like I've waited for you all my life, even though I didn't know you were out there."

He pulled me close and his lips found mine. Drystan picked me up, and I wrapped my legs around his waist. He didn't pull his lips from mine as he shifted my hips and sheathed himself inside me in one smooth glide. "Perfection," he sighed, leaning his head against mine.

I glanced over my shoulder at Xanth who watched us with fascination, his thumb coming up to swipe against his bottom lip. "The things I want to do to the two of you," he said as he strode forward, his hands coming to my hips as he kissed my shoulder, nibbling at my neck as if he was trying to decide.

"This is not the time to fuck about Xanth. I can't hold back. I can already feel the bond growing. If you want to do this together, we need to do it now." Drystan sounded pained as he talked and I swivelled my hips, urging on his madness because it grated up against my own.

He was right. I wouldn't last much longer, either. I could already feel the bond reaching for the two of them as it begged to be satisfied.

Xanth grinned. Pushing his body against my back as he backed Drystan up to the wall. "Think you can stay on your feet?" he asked.

Drystan stared deep into my eyes, a smirk coming to his lips that made me want to roll my eyes. Men! Talk about fragile masculinity. I didn't have time to say anything though because I felt the head of Xanth's cock pushing between my legs, seeking entrance where Drystan already had my pussy filled.

Fuck yes. This was exactly what I wanted.

"Do it," Drystan cried out desperately, his hips swivelling like he couldn't stop himself. "Now, Xanth. We need you."

The bond shivered with every word he spoke and even though my talons had withdrawn; I knew the raven was at the surface, reaching out for them.

Xanth slowly pushed his way inside, sliding into my pussy, stretching me to the limit with Drystan already fully sheathed. My head had tipped forward so my forehead leaned on Drystan's shoulder and he kissed my neck, telling me how good I was doing.

It didn't hurt. I didn't need the reassurance. It was everything. Feeling the both of them moving inside me made my body sing, and I thanked the universe for giving me these men as mates.

"Holy fuck," Xanth gasped. "I... can you feel that?"

Drystan hummed, and I was confused at first. They both moved in tandem, fucking me together, their hands on my hips, helping me ride the wave they created. And then I felt it, too. The bond was pulling not only them, but their magic as well. It felt like electricity flooding into every cell of my body before it collected inside my chest, a glistening ball waiting to explode.

"I think... oh shit," I gasped.

We moved like we wouldn't survive if we stopped. This thing was building between us that had to be forged and there was no stopping it, not that I even considered it for a second.

I knew the orgasm was going to devastate me. It felt like it would remake me completely and my body surged toward it with reckless abandon.

There wasn't even a build up this time. The waves of lust exploded inside me like nothing I'd ever felt. I heard Xanth and Drystan shout as they both came simultaneously.

And that electrified ball inside of me shattered. It flowed through the tattoos that spread across my body and I felt them morphing, changing shape, and moving toward my mates. They left my body, spreading onto the two of them, creating swirls of magic that decorated the cap of their shoulders, leaving behind the image of a raven, its wings spread wide in flight.

Drystan leaned back heavily against the wall, his chest heaving from exertion as Xanth carefully withdrew from my body. I could feel the joy that radiated from them both as if it was my own. It lingered inside me alongside Corvin and Bran.

We were finally joined as one. An unbreakable bond tying us soul to soul.

Xanth helped me down to the ground and over to the bed. My legs felt like jelly as I climbed onto the soft covers. Bran was there waiting, a peaceful look of wonder on his face as he pulled me against him.

"Did we mention how fucking beautiful you are yet?" he murmured as I sagged against his chest.

I didn't think I'd be able to move in the morning. A wave

of exhaustion washed over me, but it came with a sense of peace like I'd never felt before.

I was vaguely aware of the others collecting around me, their bare skin brushing against mine. It was a level of closeness that I needed, even though I could have felt each of them if they stood on the other side of the building.

The bond was satisfied. It had recreated each and every one of us. Where we had a single soul before, there was now a collective. Lives that had been bound together in love.

We had fought through the worst the realms had ever created to make it to this time and place. To build a new world. One we could finally be proud to be a part of.

It was only right that as we set out in this new world, that we were a completed version of ourselves.

These men were as much a part of me as I was them now, and it was time to forge a future together that we chose for ourselves.

Fuck fate. It was our time now, and what a beautiful life we were going to lead.

Epilogue

Echo

Two months later

Sitting in the garden of our house, surrounded by the trees and plants Tas had agonised over for the last month, was something I never imagined would happen in my life.

I could feel the happiness of my Kitsuné as she sank into the tranquillity of nature, knowing we were entering an era of peace. It had been hard fought for and there was a time when it felt impossible to achieve. Yet, here we were.

Climbing to my feet, I headed inside as I heard my mates coming in through the front door. There was something I needed to talk to them about, and I'd been waiting all day to do it.

Stone was the first to run into the kitchen, sweeping me up into a hug and spinning me around. I let my head tip back as I laughed and enjoyed the moment.

This was what we'd been fighting for, the small moments, the joy to be found in the everyday when there wasn't a shadow hanging over it.

Thyellin was bustling with life now. So many people had

joined the fae to settle here. There was a thriving mage community and even some of the pack had stayed on, having found fated mates in the chaos that followed our withdrawal from Asgard with our injured.

The betrayal of the Asgardian rebels had been all the harder once news of the fated unions had reached them. They'd wanted to meet to see if there was a possibility of mates for them as well. Some had been adamantly against it at first, but in the end, it was a bridge we needed to build, a step toward a union we'd need if we were going to prevent the future from falling at the same hurdles.

The angels from the rebellion had returned here, too, but those who had fought against us had fallen in the last fight. It was a loss we didn't see the angels recovering from, but there was a small ray of hope on the horizon because there wasn't a single rebel angel in Thyellin who hadn't found a fated mate. Their children wouldn't be pureblood angels, but who was nowadays? The next generation would be a vibrant mix of everything the realm had to hold, and I couldn't wait to see how it turned out.

"I've got something I want to show you," I told the guys, darting out of Stone's arms and running up the stairs.

They followed, though they were confused, and I stopped outside the empty room next to our bedroom. The door was closed, and I held onto the handle, waiting for them before swinging it open.

We'd spent the last month cleaning the whole place and working on the repairs. There was a way to go, but the house finally felt like a home.

I stepped into the clean, empty room and the guys followed, their confusion deepening from the fact there was nothing in there.

"It's... lovely," Damon said, his frown deepening.

I couldn't keep the smile from my face, and Stone squinted in suspicion. "What's going on?" he asked slowly.

Standing in the corner, I spread my arms wide, miming a small shape. "I figured we could put it in this corner. It's visible if you peek in through the door, but it's far enough away to be out of any drafts."

Tas was the first one who appeared to understand as he stepped forward, hope lining his face as he glanced down at my stomach.

"Are you?"

I grinned again but was interrupted by Aubron before I could say anything.

"I don't get it. What are we putting in here?" he asked.

"A crib," I added quietly.

My feet left the ground as Stone swooped me back up with a whoop and then gently placed me down as he softly kissed me, his hand pressing against my abdomen.

Arms wrapped around us, and we became a laughing, crying huddle of joy.

"We're having a baby!" Damon cried.

"I bet it's going to be a mage, ruggedly handsome and wonderfully mischievous," Stone decided.

"If you think about it, it's more likely to have fae blood," Aubron declared. "Probability is on our side." And then he and Tas high-fived at the idea.

Men.

"Actually," I clarified. "She's going to be a Kitsuné."

This was the only part of the news I was nervous about giving. And all of them froze as they turned to look at me with fear in their eyes.

"It's not over," Damon whispered, his gaze darting to the window as if he'd find the answer outside.

That wasn't exactly what I'd thought they'd be worried about, but I could see why he'd brought it up. Frannie had told us Kitsunés were gifted after a period of terrible bloodshed. It was the price the world paid when a new celestial was born.

"No, no. It's over, it's definitely over. Trust me, the price has more than been paid for our little girl already," I told him, hugging him gently as I did.

"You can't know that." Aubron shook his head and I could see him already making plans. He might not rule as king here, but the Council consulted him for his input on most decisions.

"I can," I said softly, getting to the part I knew they'd worry about.

Stone was the only one who seemed to understand. "No." His voice cracked as he said. "No. We did everything they wanted. They can't do that to you. It's not fair. It's..."

The others looked confused, not understanding what upset him.

"It won't be like that." I told him gently. Damon kept me tucked under his arm like he was getting ready to protect me from whatever was coming our way. "Frannie didn't have any links in this time to ground her here. I have you. *I have all of you.* No matter what I see, no matter what the visions show me, I will always find my way back to you."

I'd been so terrified when the first vision had come to me. It had been something as mundane as knowing someone in the palace renovation project would knock over a can of paint. Before I knew what I was doing, I moved it to the side, out of the way. Then the realisation had struck me.

At first, I didn't want to tell them. I didn't want to be the one to admit I'd slowly lose my mind how Frannie had. I knew it would break them to see it happening to me, and I didn't think I'd survive putting them through it.

But then the visions showed me other things. They showed me our child. Aubron accepting a role as governor for the fae. Thyellin prospering, children running in the streets, and the people celebrating the anniversary of the end of the war. And I realised what the purpose of those visions were. Because we'd been in all of them, and not only were we happy, but I was whole, safe and... sane. My mates clustered around me and together we had a strength that could weather anything.

It would always be them when it came down to it.

The family we'd made and the bonds that tied us together would always be my grounding force.

"Are you sure?" Aubron asked.

"Absolutely."

A sigh of relief moved around the room, and tender touches brushed against my stomach. We whispered our words of devotion and sank into the reassurance and happiness we always found in each other.

"So... the future?" Stone asked, eventually. Of course, it would be him that would be too curious not to ask.

I smiled the same smile that Frannie had always given us, and he sighed in disappointment. I wanted to tell him. I wanted them to know about how beautiful our future would be, but I wouldn't risk it. We were already on the right path and I wouldn't endanger it for anything.

Epilogue

Aria

SIX MONTHS LATER

"That was suspiciously too easy," Kyle said, pulling off his coat as he dropped it on the sofa, collapsing down on it.

I couldn't help but laugh as I climbed onto his lap and he wrapped his arms around me. He wasn't wrong. Everyone had been suspiciously too easy to deal with considering we'd just left the first ever council meeting for the realms. It probably helped that all we had on the agenda was the opening of the Elite Academy, and everyone was excited to see the project finally coming to fruition.

The Council had been a dream of Kyle's for so long. He'd always wanted it for his people and we'd been so close to starting it before we left for Asgard. And then something incredible had happened. The dream of a Council to govern the shifters had morphed into what it was now.

Every race had a representative on the Council. It had started slowly at first. But as we'd all banded together in the vast rebuilding projects around the realms, bonds and relationships were forged. Fated mates were back. More and more bonds were being discovered every day now all the races mixed once more. It just made sense that the mixing of communities would come with a mixed representation on the Council.

"What time do your parents get here?" Kyle asked, shifting beneath me and then pressing me down onto the couch as his lips met mine.

I smiled into his kiss because I knew he wouldn't be happy about what I was about to say.

"They're already here," I whispered through our bond.

Predictably, he sighed, his forehead pressing against mine as he did. "Any chance we can make the others entertain them for like an hour?" he asked hopefully.

"Sure," I answered aloud. "I'm sure my father, the god, will have absolutely no idea about what we're doing up here."

For a minute Kyle looked like he was considering if he cared about that and I was starting to think we were about to have a really awkward dinner with my parents in a few hours. In the end he sighed, having come to the same conclusion as I had.

"I suppose it would be rude to make the King of Asgard wait."

"Not as rude as making him wait while you fuck his daughter senseless." I laughed, as Kyle shrugged like it wouldn't make a difference.

Asgard was going through changes, just like everywhere else. They'd moved to a governing system where they elected their ruler for a ten-year reign. It hadn't been a surprise to anyone when they'd voted for Thor. My father had been the one who stood by them for all this time. Of course, they trusted him with the future they'd all fought so hard for. He hadn't wanted it at first. I was pretty sure he had dreams of running away somewhere quiet with my mother now the weight of the world didn't sit on their shoulders. In the end, there was no one else *he* trusted to take the role, so it hadn't really been a choice.

I'd felt sad for them when he broke the news to me, but apparently one of the plus sides of living for an eternity was a decade didn't really mean all that much. After fighting for so long, he and my mother had flourished while rebuilding the world they'd risked so much for.

Surprisingly, Hel hadn't tried to take the throne for herself. She'd stayed in Helheim, weakened and without allies. The flow of souls had returned to her realm, and it wouldn't take long for her strength to return, but she was busy rebuilding herself. For now, she was contained, and if she ever wasn't, well, Asgard was all the stronger now, and she'd have a hell of a fight on her hands.

"Come on." I slipped out from under him, pulling him off the couch as I did. "Virion should be back now and I want to hear what they found."

Kyle only half-reluctantly followed me downstairs after he heard that. I knew he was as curious as I was. This was a project we'd all been watching closely for the past six months. It felt like proof we'd actually won. We might have taken down Odin, but it didn't mean we hadn't already passed the point of no return with the damage he'd done.

We headed outside, bypassing the library we were still trying to figure out a different use for. That room held too many memories, and most of them were bad. These days we always met outside. The hard work I'd put into the garden while trying to recover had surprisingly paid off, and Liam and Sykes had spent weeks building a covered area big enough for the entire pack to sit.

The pack was smaller than it had once been, but it was slowly growing. Some members had moved away with their mates, but most had stayed. It felt like we grew every day as more and more bonds formed. We were more than a shifter pack now, and it felt so right.

There was no sign of the magic my mates had in any of the other shifters, but we weren't worried too much about it. Echo had already let a secret slip that I was holding close to my chest. She'd made me promise on my favourite sword to keep it. Even though I was dying to scream it from the rooftops, somehow I'd held it in that the next generation born into the pack would be the first to return the old magic.

As we rounded the corner, we heard their voices before we saw them. My father's booming laugh filled the air and my other mates soon joined in. Braedon had the grill set up and Liam and Sykes ran dishes from the kitchen, setting up the outside tables.

I hugged my mother, relieved to see the smile on her face that had been there for months now. We'd slipped into life as a family as easily as if we'd always been together. We'd missed so many years, but there wasn't any resentment. Neither of us had a choice in what had happened, and all that mattered now was that we were reunited again.

"Finally!" My father cheered. "Now we can hear the results."

Everyone turned to Virion, who lounged on a seat, sipping his drink. I laughed as I realised he'd made them wait until we got there. It was a good job I didn't let Kyle distract me upstairs. I doubt we'd have been as easily forgiven.

Virion stood dusting off his hands against his shirt as he did, drawing it out and making Sykes throw a bread roll at his head. He ducked out of the way with a laugh.

"Okay, okay, I get it. So, as you know, we've been monitoring the world tree for the past six months and mapping the rot that was spreading. Whilst it appeared to get worse for the first month, I can officially confirm the rot is now receding and we're confident to say that the world tree is recovering. At the rate the rot is subsiding, it should be completely gone in the next few months."

Thor sagged back in his seat, grabbed his drink, and gulped it down.

"Damn, for a second there, I figured you were making us wait because it was bad news." He shook his head as my mother wrapped her arms around him.

We'd all been nervous about the world tree. It was the only way we could gauge if we were actually going to survive the whole thing. Echo kept telling me it would be fine, but when the rot had spread that first month, I'd actually doubted her. Hearing we had evidence it was over was the reprieve we'd all been waiting for.

"So, that's it then," Braedon said, interrupting my thoughts. "We actually won."

No one said anything. It was like we were afraid to jinx the fact something was actually going right. Sykes was the one to break first.

"Time to celebrate then," he cheered. "Because I don't know about everyone else, but I'm sitting out of the next war. Consider this my retirement."

Retirement.

That sounded pretty good.

Epilogue

Lyra

Eight months later

I stood at the windows of the penthouse, staring out across the cityscape in front of me. The human realm was definitely a lot different from what I was used to. Unfortunately, with my wings, I was trapped in the penthouse until we returned home, which shouldn't be much longer now.

There was more magic here than the humans were aware of, and I watched the flares across the city with interest.

Dom came up behind me, one of the twins cradled in his arms.

"Did she wake up? I didn't hear her." I grazed my fingertips across her perfect cheek and she stared up at me with her big blue eyes.

"I heard her fussing when I passed their door. Dylan is still fast asleep," Dom told me quietly. "What's got you out of bed at this hour?"

He wrapped an arm around me, cradling Nyla against his chest with his other.

Twins had been unexpected, and the birth had been difficult since we were sheltering in the human realm with no real support. It wouldn't be for much longer, though. Things in the realms had been settled for a while now. We could have returned for the birth if we'd wanted to. But something about being here had seemed right. We were comfortable in the bubble we'd created inside this penthouse, away from the outside world.

"I was just thinking about our return to the magic realm and how I'd feel leaving this place," I admitted.

"I would have thought you'd be excited to leave given you haven't been able to step a foot outside."

I shrugged. I should have been happy to leave.

"I am. I'm looking forward to seeing everyone again. This place was just starting to feel like home. That's all."

Wyatt emerged from the bedrooms, Dylan cradled against his chest. "This one wasn't happy to suddenly find himself alone," he grumbled.

The twins never did like being apart.

Wyatt kissed me gently, tugging the blanket I had around my shoulders tighter until he was satisfied I wasn't cold. I wasn't. It was pretty impossible given how warm they kept the apartment.

"I spoke with Kyle yesterday. He offered us a house at the pack if we want it."

"Is that where you want to go?" I asked carefully.

This was what bothered me the most. We all came from so many different places. How were we supposed to decide where we wanted to settle?

Caleb and Kieran moved out to the lounge next. Both of them dropped sweet kisses on the twins before coming to stand by the window, too.

"I don't have any strong feelings about moving to the

pack," Wyatt admitted, looking to Caleb, who shrugged. "Where do you want to live?"

"Angelus is definitely out," I told them. "There's nothing about that place that calls to me."

"We could find a way to stay here," Kieran said slowly and then scrunched up his face when he no doubt saw the flaw in that plan. My wings.

Dom herded us all over to the couches and we carefully sat down, the twins already fast asleep. "Let's talk this out. We have options. We don't have to settle down in only one place. Perhaps we could move around, see where we land that feels like home."

Home. It was such a small, yet important word. Home was something you fought for. But when it came down to it, we'd missed the fight where the others had laid everything on the line.

"I think I feel guilty we weren't there for them in Asgard," I admitted. "I don't feel like I deserve a place in the magic realm."

It wasn't an easy thing to admit, but when I worked up the courage to see the look on my mates' faces, I saw more understanding than I'd expected. Had they been feeling the same way, too?

"I think we should go to the academy," Caleb finally said.

It was an option I hadn't considered. Could we even do that? He must have seen the confusion on my face when he forged on.

"We have skills that can help the students develop. Plus, it's a safe place for the twins. I bet we could build a house on the grounds so we wouldn't have to be in the academy itself. I just... I never felt like I had a place in the world until I was at the academy. And it gave me so much more than a home. I feel like... maybe I'd like to keep giving something back, like we did then."

The others were considering it. I could already tell. The way Caleb described it did sound pretty perfect. I had rare magic, and I knew I could help the students there, especially angelic students. There were so many mixed mate bonds now, just like our own, that there would be an influx of students across the years with unusual magic.

"It's an interesting idea," Kieran admitted.

Dom shuffled in his seat and I recognised it as his guilty tell. We'd been together long enough that I'd picked up a lot of their mannerisms. "What aren't you telling us?" I asked, and he looked at me in surprise.

He didn't answer at first, instead buying himself time by shifting Nyla to a slightly different position and fussing over her even though she was asleep. When he looked up to see we were still waiting, he rolled his eyes like we were the ones being ridiculous.

"I may have been approached... with a job offer," he admitted.

I resisted the urge to throw something at him, only because he was holding our daughter in his arms.

"I knew it," Caleb cheered before shushing himself and looking around anxiously at the babies.

"So you don't want to move to the academy?" This whole thing was getting confusing now. Hence, why we were still here and hadn't returned to the realm most of us were from.

"No, I mean yes, I do actually think it's a good idea. Not to mention it's close to the pack and Thyellin isn't that far away. It puts us near everyone we'd want to be," Caleb pointed out. "But I'll admit I didn't think about it until I heard someone on the phone being all suspicious and cagey about something."

"Why didn't you tell us?" I asked, knowing Dominic would have a reason to keep it from us. Whether it was a good one, we'd have to wait and see.

"I thought if I suggested it, you'd go along with it because it's what I wanted rather than it being something we all agreed on," he admitted.

"You realise that's stupid, right?" Wyatt laughed, shoving him gently so not to jostle Nyla.

It never failed to surprise me how these men had formed such tight bonds with each other as well as with me. There'd been no question about how this relationship would work. None of them had worried about how Kieran would fit in. We'd just become this family without even trying, and then Nyla and Dylan came along, cementing all of those bonds into place.

My pregnancy had taken us out of the final battle, but that didn't mean we couldn't help mould the new world into something that prevented the same thing from happening again. An Elite Academy was the thing that Dominic had dreamed about, and now that the fight was over, it was becoming a reality and he wasn't there to see it. But more than that, it was something we'd all dreamed about at one time or another. Trapped in our own personal prisons, we'd all looked for a saviour to come for us, and now we had a chance to give that to the world.

I'd never been happier and the thought of returning to the magic realm didn't feel as daunting anymore. Dreams of building a home together should have been natural, and they were really. We'd just been so hung up on the 'where' that we hadn't seen to the centre of the whole thing.

Because it didn't really matter where. All we really needed was each other. The place was irrelevant.

"I think we should do it," I decided. "I want to do it."

Happiness swept through our bond, and I could see the excitement in my mates. This was something we'd all be able to be a part of. A way to show our children there was good in the world.

It was coming full circle for some of us in our group, and a whole new beginning for the rest. But one thing was for sure. It was a future filled with hope, love, and happiness; not just for ourselves but for everyone we'd fought for along the way.

Note from the Author

After four years, the Destiny Series is finally finished. I can't describe how that feels. Destiny Awakened was the first book I ever wrote and published and it has seen so much love from so many people.

I want to say thank you to everyone who has been with me since the beginning. Thank you to everyone who took a chance and read the series, which turned out to be pretty massive compared to the three books I originally thought it would be.

This was a story that was so hard to put down. These characters had so much to give and I hope I did them justice. I wanted the series to end on a message of hope and I think I did that. Could there have been more? Probably, but I had to stop writing at some point and this felt right to me.

I know there will inevitably be the question of will there be anymore. Originally there were some spin offs planned and I'm sure those who have read the series recently will see where they were. At the moment, I don't know if I plan to write anything else for this world. I'm trying out this new thing where I just write what I want and let the muse run away from me. So, maybe there'll be more in the future, maybe there won't. But either way, I've got some more amazing ideas for stories for you and I hope you love them just as much as this one.

There are so many people who have helped in a variety of ways to make this series a reality that it would take pages to go through them all. But it would be criminal for me not to take a moment to thank Kris and Em. The Destiny Series brought us together and they've helped me through every single word. We were still editing this book right up until the finish line and it was stressful, to say the least. I wouldn't have been able to do it without you ladies supporting me and encouraging me on. Thank you, from the bottom of my heart.

If you want to stay up to date on my releases and other books, all the information is available on my website www.catejcooke.com.

About the Author

Thank you for reading my book! If you'd like to stay up to date with the news about upcoming releases and other events, check out my website. www.catejcooke.com

Newsletter exclusive content is also available to subscribers featuring extra scenes for some of the books.

Printed in Great Britain
by Amazon